The Demon

and

The Witch

The Demon and the Witch

Book One of the Saga of the Witch

Rohan Davies

First Published in Great Britain in 2024

Copyright © 2024 Rohan Davies. All rights reserved.

Rohan Davies has asserted his moral right to be identified as the author of this work in accordance with the Copyright, Designs and Patents Act 1988.

The characters and events portrayed in this book are fictitious. Any similarity to real persons, living or dead, is coincidental and not intended by the author.

All rights reserved. No part of this book may be reproduced, or stored in a retrieval system, or transmitted in any form or by any means, electronic, mechanical, photocopying, recording, or otherwise, without express written permission of the publisher.

A CIP catalogue record for this book is available from the British Library.

ISBN: 978-1-7385416-0-7

Cover design by: Rohan Davies
Published by: Witchlore Publishing
www.rohandaviesbooks.com

TO DEVON

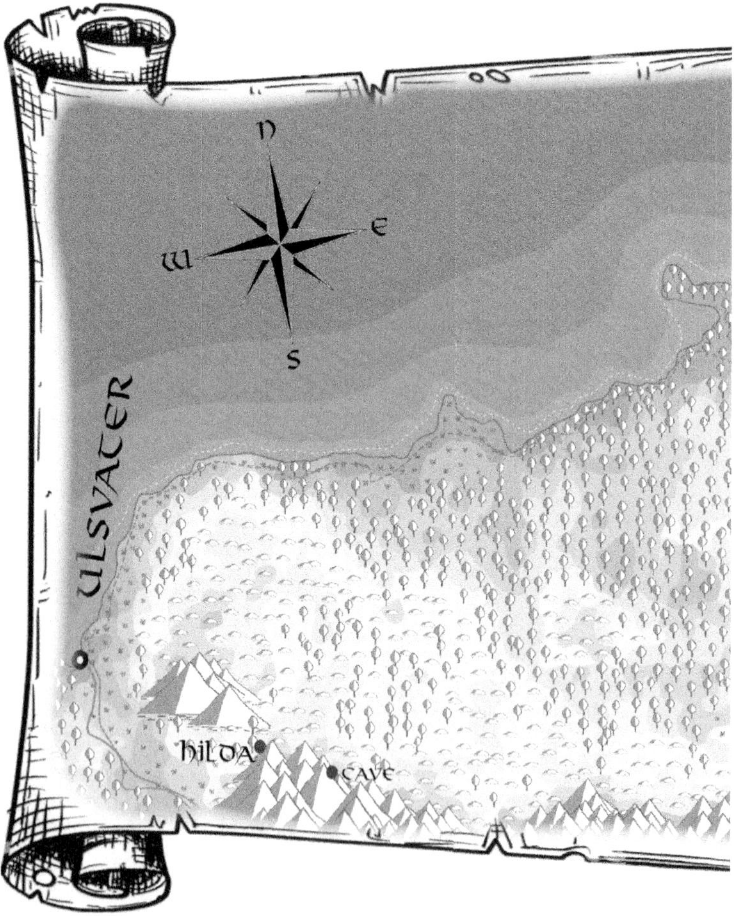
N
E
W
S
ULSVATER
HILDA
CAVE

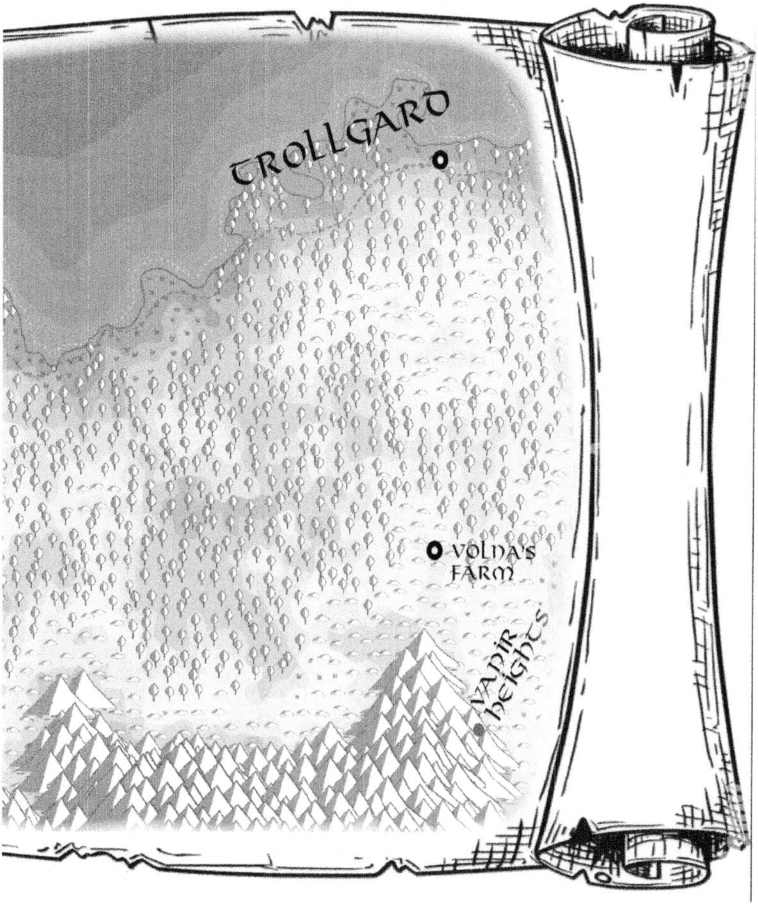
TROLLGARD
VOLNA'S FARM
VANIR HEIGHTS

CHAPTERS

1.	Frost in Summer	1
2.	Daughter and Apprentice	10
3.	The Trial	27
4.	Wounds	42
5.	Witch Weather	55
6.	Veil of Fire	68
7.	Healing	75
8.	Telling Tales	88
9.	Flight	98
10.	Stranger	109
11.	The Seer	124
12.	Runes	136
13.	The Taming of the Wind	153
14.	A Meeting of Old Friends	165
15.	The Demon	175
16.	The Prison of Ice	183
17.	Hunt and Quarry	192
18.	Buried Secrets	202
19.	The Siege	217
20.	Gathering Clouds	226
21.	Storm and Fury	241
22.	Trust	254
23.	Smoke and Stone	263
24.	The Ashes of Childhood	275
25.	The Eye of the Storm	284
26.	The Journey	291

Glossary	I
Acknowledgements	V
About the Author	VII

- 1 -

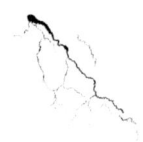

FROST IN SUMMER

Anike froze in the act of picking a berry as the hairs on the back of her neck rose. She very slowly turned her head while her hand inched towards her dagger. A wolf nearly the size of a pony was standing in the centre of the sunlit clearing not ten paces away, its yellow eyes fixed on her and teeth bared.

She had not realised that any dire wolves still lived in the forest. She saw at once that her knife would be of little use against the beast and released her grip on it. Steadying her breathing, she weighed her options. If she ran, it would be on her in seconds, and picking up and hurling the bag containing the herbs she had gathered that morning would not be more than a slight distraction. Her best hope was that the creature was not really hungry, not hunting but had come upon her by accident. Even larger predators and the smaller monsters tended to avoid humans unless they were desperate, or if they sensed a threat or easy prey. Appearing to be either would get her killed.

Beads of sweat formed on the young woman's brow. Standing as still as she could, trying not to betray fear in her breathing or stance, she sought the balance between fear and aggression. She kept her eyes on the dire wolf, trying not to imagine how the teeth would feel closing on her flesh.

The creature regarded her from the centre of the clearing, sunlight glinting from its silver-grey fur. Behind it, another dire wolf, then a third, emerged silently from the dark green trees. Anike's heart skipped a beat as they came to stand beside the first and largest wolf, which stared at her before turning its head to look back the way it had come.

It gave a low growl, then its head came forward and it bounded across the clearing. Anike tensed but it was not attacking. The great beast loped past her and disappeared amongst the dark trees. The other two pack members followed their leader, also casting glances over their shoulders. Anike realised they were not hunting but fleeing. She shivered as she wondered what could have frightened three dire wolves.

She took the incident as a sign to abandon her herb gathering for the day and retrieved her satchel from the ground. As she looped it over her shoulder, she heard cries of alarm from the direction the dire wolves had run. Shouts but not screams, and no howls from the wolves themselves. The sounds were a couple of hundred paces away, much closer than the town, and in the face of an unknown threat that had scared such dangerous creatures, she very much wanted to be amongst people. There were often hunters or woodsmen in the forest so Anike headed towards where she thought the sounds had come from, forcing her way through the undergrowth.

As she pushed through the bushes trying to find the best path, she heard cracking behind her. Branches were snapping as something made its way through the trees, and it was coming in her direction. Her imagination painted a picture of a large creature with fangs and talons, even more dangerous than a pack of dire wolves. She broke into a run, battling her way through the thick undergrowth with branches lashing at her feet. She glanced back, hoping and fearing to catch a glimpse of what was following her but as she looked over her shoulder, her foot caught in a bramble and she fell straight into a thorny bush.

She panicked, started to thrash wildly and managed to pull herself onto her side, but the thorns tangled in her long dark hair and her tunic and she was unable to stand. The needle-sharp points held and her struggling only caught more. She forced herself to relax and hold still, then start the agonisingly slow process of removing one branch at a time. All the while, she could hear the sounds of snapping undergrowth coming closer.

The air around her abruptly became bitterly cold and she saw the green leaves beside her turn white with frost. The chill pierced through her clothes to the bone. A branch cracked with a sharp report only a few paces away, and she raised her head to see what had been following her.

A man stepped forward from between the trees, his clothes, hair and beard silver with frost. Her eyes were drawn first to a large woodsman's axe held loosely in his right hand then Anike saw his face and, to her surprise, recognised him. Gern Haffordsson was a woodsman, always ready with a smile when he visited her master Olaf to buy elixirs, but now he stared down at her with eyes that belonged to a dead man, devoid of life or feeling as if the soul had frozen behind them. "Gern..." Anike started but was cut off before she had a chance to say more. Without emotion and without moving anything except his lips, the frost-covered man spoke a word she did not recognise in a voice as clear and dead as ice. At that word, Anike felt as if the life was being pulled from her body, her heart held without beating and her blood frozen in her veins. The sensation lasted only for an instant but it left her feeling weak and faded. Anike had never seen witchcraft before, but this could be nothing else.

Gern took a step closer. The cold surrounding him was so intense that it almost burned. He unhurriedly raised his axe to strike and fighting the numbing chill, she instinctively tried to raise an arm to ward off the impending blow. The brambles that had previously held her snapped as she moved. The lithe green tendrils, caught in Gern's unnatural attack on her, had turned grey and brittle and offered almost no resistance as her arm came up.

Feeling this, without time to think but only to act and hope, Anike rolled and the dead bramble shattered around her as she flung herself out of the way of the descending axe. She felt it strike the ground a hair's breadth behind her back as she completed her roll, leaving the patch of dead bush in her wake. Before Gern could raise the axe for another strike, she was up and running, strength from fear and desperation sustaining her as she tried to put some distance between her and the man who had drained life out of her. A few strides and she was out of the aura of deathly cold surrounding him. Her head was reeling – he had just tried to kill her with witchcraft. It was little wonder that the dire wolves had run from this man, a witch with the power to control the elements.

She dared not risk another look behind her as she crashed through the thicket, seeking the source of the shouting she had heard earlier. The snapping of frozen branches told her that Gern was following her, unhurried and inexorable. Her only chance was to reach help before he caught her again and gasping for breath through the unnatural exhaustion, she fled.

After perhaps a hundred paces of this headlong plunge, she crashed out of the undergrowth into another clearing. Four young men stood there, all with drawn weapons. They had been peering into the trees on the far side of the clearing but turned towards Anike as she emerged into the sunlight.

"Bjord!" she gasped.

"Anike, what are you doing here?" the man asked in surprise. The Arl's son was tall, his neatly-trimmed blonde hair falling to his broad shoulders and he held a sword ready in his hand. At the sight of Anike, he lowered it, and his companions relaxed as well.

"You should be careful today," he continued as Anike came to a halt in front of him. "There are dire wolves in the forest and they might easily make a meal of a tasty morsel like you."

Bjord's companions chuckled as Anike caught her breath and tried to summon the energy to speak. "There is worse coming!" she gasped out. "Its Gern Haffordsson. He is a witch, and he is chasing me." She had to pause for breath – whatever Gern had done to her had left her too weak to speak for long.

"Gern? A witch?" said Bjord scornfully. "A woman's fancy! But never fear, lovely Anike, I will protect you." He flourished his sword in mock bravado. Anike stared at him disbelief, but before she could say anything in response the air in the bright clearing went bitterly cold. Bjord's mocking expression vanished and Loga, one of his companions, shivered.

Looking back in the direction she had come, Anike pointed at the figure emerging from between the trees. "There he is," she gasped.

Gern came forward, the grass freezing around him, each footfall crushing icy stems beneath his boots. With his dark beard turned silver in the frost and his clothes stiff with ice, he looked like a man caught in a winter storm, save for his blank eyes which unhurriedly took in the people in the clearing.

"Gern, hold!" cried Bjord, levelling his sword and pulling Anike behind him.

Gern's expression did not change, but he stopped. Anike could read nothing in his gaze as he stared at them all. He spoke a single word, different from the last one but another that she had never heard before.

Before the sound of his voice had died away, the earth around Anike's feet had surged upwards and gripped her ankles. Loga screamed in fear and Anike saw that the ground had entangled the men's legs as well. The soil held Loga fast as he tried to flee, and he overbalanced and fell. Slad and Tavic, Bjord's other companions, seemed frozen in fear of the living earth. Bjord alone stood firm, but Anike saw the colour drain from his cheeks. She drew her knife, wondering if it would be of any use against a witch.

In one smooth movement, Bjord swapped his sword to his left hand and scooped up a boar spear from the ground. He readied the missile, steel-tipped and nearly as long as Anike was tall, and cast it at Gern with all his strength. The spear arced over the ten paces separating the two men, striking a glancing blow to the witch's right shoulder and cutting a deep furrow in the flesh. Gern staggered under the force of the strike and his axe tumbled onto the cold ground, but he showed no sign of pain and his face betrayed no recognition of the blow. He recovered his balance even as blood started to seep out from beneath his tunic.

Gern spoke a third unknown word. Ice formed around his body, encasing it in a translucent barrier like a suit of armour, leaving only his face uncovered.

"By Odin's single eye!" Bjord cursed and snatched an axe from the trembling Tavic. He hurled it at Gern but it bounced off, leaving a white line in the ice where the blade had struck. Anike had been considering throwing her knife but if the axe had not penetrated the ice, her knife never would and Gern was too far away for her to be sure to hit his face.

Without even a glance at the axe, Gern advanced. A few paces closer, he raised his left arm and pointed it at Bjord who was looking around for another weapon to throw. Gern spoke the third word again and ice dust formed in a path in the air between his hand and Bjord's chest. Bjord's torso went white, and he fell with a cry. His sword dropped from his hand and he lay gasping on the ground, his breath forming mist in the cold air. Gern came forward, as inevitable as a glacier. Anike changed her grip on the knife, preparing to throw. She had never killed a man but looking into Gern's eyes she doubted he was truly a man any more.

Gern came up to Bjord, but instead of speaking another strange word, he reached down and picked up the fallen sword in his left hand. Anike drew back her arm, knowing that she had only one chance and focusing on the target of Gern's face, but before she could release the blade she saw the light come back into Gern's eyes and he stopped, wincing in pain. He looked down at Bjord, his face a mask of anguish and grief. "My lord!" he said, his voice thick with emotion.

Anike halted her throw in surprise but Bjord was not so reticent. He reached up to grasp Gern's left arm and pulled him to the ground. As the man fell, Bjord somehow wrested the sword from him, despite his feet being locked in earth. Before Gern could start to rise, the young warrior slammed the hilt into his face, and he slumped, out like a light.

Shivering, partly in relief and partly in the intense cold that still radiated from the unconscious form, Anike looked down at Gern. For the moment, he was not a threat so she bent down and tried to scrape at the earth gripping her feet with her knife.

Bjord was also digging at his own earthen manacles, and he had more success. He freed one foot and looked at her. Their eyes met and Anike saw his jaw unclench. She realised that he had actually been frightened but had fought despite his fears and saved all their lives.

She had never doubted his bravery in the past but was still impressed by his actions in the face of real terror.

"Are you hurt?" she asked, breaking his gaze and looking away.

"I will live," he replied.

Anike looked in her bag and pulled out some herbs. "Jarl's narrowleaf. It will restore a little of your strength." She handed a leaf to Bjord. "I wish I had time to make a potion from it, but the raw herb will have to do for now." She put another leaf in her own mouth and bit into it. The sour taste seemed to flow through her body, restoring her energy. Bjord did the same, and the colour came back into his skin as he chewed. Suddenly, the earth sank back into the ground, freeing them all and the bitter cold faded, leaving only a memory of frost in the warmth of a summer day.

"This witch shall stand trial before my father," Bjord said as he got to his feet, prodding the unconscious man with a booted foot.

"I knew Gern, at least I thought I did," said Anike. "He has been coming to buy potions from Olaf for years. He was always friendly, and ordinary. Tough, like most woodsmen, but nothing odd or sinister about him." She shivered, despite the heat of the day returning. "If I had not seen him using witchcraft myself, I would not have believed it."

"He must have been concealing his dark nature, biding his time, waiting for the right moment to strike."

"It was so unlike him. He seemed a good man. I wonder what made him choose today to reveal it?"

"A witch is like an earthquake, Anike. The ground can seem stable for many years, but you never know when one will strike. Perhaps he saw you alone and took his chance, or maybe men are just not supposed to understand the warped motivations of a witch. If Odin thought it suitable for humans, he would have given its power to the jarls." Bjord saw power as the divine right of the jarl caste, the warriors and rulers.

"My father will hang this witch, after a fair trial," he continued, "probably on the morrow. The people of Trollgard will see that we can protect them from unnatural threats as well as raiders."

Witches were so rare that Anike had not really thought about how the laws applied to them before. As she understood matters, it was not unlawful to be a witch but if they did anything wrong the Arl would impose the severest of penalties. Gern had attempted to kill the Arl's son with witchcraft for no reason, so there was no doubt that his fate would be execution after the trial and Anike could see the need for harsh measures against witches, rare as they were. She could not forget his eyes, completely blank while he attacked.

The last moments before he fell troubled her in a different way though, for he had seemed to come back to his old self. Perhaps it made no difference. A man could be judged by his actions and they condemned Gern.

Anike looked at the unconscious man on the ground, trying to see something in his features to explain what he had done. As she did so, the ice armour around him melted away leaving no trace on the grass. Bjord turned to his companions. "Tie the witch up!" he ordered. Loga brought over a heavy boar spear, and Tavic and Slad bound Gern to it. "Bind his mouth as well – witches are supposed to be gagged." Loga wrapped some cloth around Gern's mouth, and Slad and Tavic hoisted him on the spear between them then started off towards the town.

Bjord turned to Anike. "Odin must have guided me into the forest today. I am glad I was here when you needed me. I would have been greatly saddened if any harm had befallen you, Anike Dareksdottir." Anike coloured slightly and looked at her feet. "I was relieved to find you and your companions in the forest," Anike told him, then suddenly uncomfortable with the personal tone in his words added, "I am glad your hunt brought you this way, my lord." She emphasised the honorific.

"You should come back to town with me, Anike," Bjord continued. "We have captured the witch, but the dire wolves may return."

"I saw them. You are right, my lord. I will come with you." She suspected that the wolves had kept running but she had most of the herbs Olaf had wanted her to gather, and the experiences of the morning had left her deeply unsettled.

She fell into step beside Bjord as the enormity of the past hour began to dawn on her. She had survived a battle with a witch. Realisation and relief flooded through her, then she thought of what her father was going to say and her heart sank once more.

− 2 −

DAUGHTER
AND
APPRENTICE

Anike and Bjord walked down towards Trollgard from the forest, with Bjord's companions carrying Gern behind them. The town of nine hundred people lay on the north coast of Gotlund and the sea beyond it danced in the light of the summer sun. They walked into the town through the south gate, disrupting the rhythm of the afternoon as the townsfolk stopped to watch them pass. As they approached with Gern suspended on the spear, the flow of farmers, foresters and the occasional trader parted before them while those more distant stared and pointed. Once they had reached the marketplace, Anike touched Bjord's arm. "I must go to my father," she told him.

"I understand, Anike. I would see you home, but I must deliver the witch to my own father. I will come to see you later." He put a hand on her shoulder, then turned away.

Anike watched him go in the direction of the arlberg, the walled compound containing the Arl's hall and the surrounding buildings. He walked ahead of his companions who were taking it in turns to carry Gern between them. She had known him since they were children, but Bjord had recently been more open in his admiration of her, and she felt uncomfortable with the attention. He was handsome and strong but as they had grown up the difference in their status had become more apparent. The three castes had been ordained by the god Heimdall in the distant past and created boundaries that were not lightly crossed, and Bjord was a jarl, the highest caste of warriors. Even though her father had been a close friend to the Arl, Anike was a karl, the middle caste of free craftsmen but at least she was not of the lowest caste of thralls, made up of servants and slaves. She sighed and headed towards the house she shared with her father, Darek Voludsson.

A light breeze carried the smells of the market to Anike as she walked through it. The scents of fish and game mixed with the sharp odour of metal from the forge. Now Bjord was no longer at her side, she allowed herself to relax and took a moment to enjoy still being alive. The marketplace in the town centre was busy with traders, smiths, dyers and other craftsmen going about their day or packing up empty stalls. As she crossed it, she nodded at Drakna, a hunter who had recently married her closest friend, Inge Gudrunsdottir. Her greeting was returned with a wave coupled with a curious stare and she realised her torn clothes and tangled hair were drawing attention. She pulled her hood up and walked a little faster.

Most of the buildings inside Trollgard had stone walls, a legacy from the time the dwarves had ruled Gotlund. They had been driven back underground some four centuries before but the stone buildings they had constructed for themselves and the humans they had enslaved still stood as witness to their extraordinary skills. Over the years, the town had expanded beyond the walls and buildings made of wood from the forest to the south had sprung up. The wood town was now nearly as large as the stone town within the walls.

She passed through the market and then between the buildings of the northern part of the town until she reached a small house close by the north wall. On the other side lay the sea shore, though Anike knew that by this hour her father's fishing boat would be pulled up on the sand along with a dozen others. She lifted the latch, pushed open the door and called out, "Father, I am home."

The inside of the house was dimly lit with only one of the shutters open to let in the daylight, and the low fire cast a red glow throughout the single large room. As Anike's eyes adjusted, the shapes within resolved themselves into familiar objects. A shelf held earthenware plates and cups, and cooking pots hung beneath it. A large wooden table was set against one wall with two chairs next to it and a neatly folded fishing net occupied half of the tabletop. Against the other wall was a smaller workbench with boxes of herbs, small earthenware bottles for potions and salves, and three cauldrons of various sizes. A stool was tucked under the bench. The fire was in the centre of the room, straddled by an iron tripod to hang cauldrons and pots. A little over halfway up the walls and reached by short ladders, the two wooden sleeping platforms held numerous thick furs. Two barrels stood against one wall, one containing water and the other the strong ale that Darek favoured.

On a low bench in the middle of this tidy home, her father sat like a heap of hair and furs. His left sleeve hung empty from the elbow down. Ten years before he had been injured on a raid. Across the sea to the north lay another large island of the Archipelago, Lartenland. It was too far to see even on a clear day, but boats crossed and the people of both islands raided each other frequently. Darek had been a skilled warrior and high in Arl Svafnir's regard before a Larten axe had slipped past his shield. By the time they had returned to Trollgard, a rot had started in the wound which would have carried away his life if Olaf had not removed his arm. While he no longer took part in raids, Darek was still a powerful man who could cast fishing nets with one hand nearly as well as his mate Joran could do with both. But his injury ran deeper than his arm, and after the day's work was done he would come home and stare into the fire, nursing his ale until Anike returned to cook for him. He looked up at her now from between his unkempt beard and hair, the same raven-black as her own, and took in her torn clothing. "Thor's hammer, child! What happened to you?"

"Father, I am fine. Bjord saved me." Anike spoke soothingly, trying to reassure him before going on to explain. Rather quickly she added, "He captured the witch who was chasing me."

He blinked. "A witch? What are you talking about, child?"

"It was Gern Haffordsson, Father. You remember him? He came upon me in the forest. He had dead eyes." Anike shuddered and wondered why that was the first detail she thought of. She told her father about the chase and battle. "Bjord was hurt, but he knocked Gern out. He says there will be a trial tomorrow," she concluded.

"I told you that the forest was dangerous, Anike. Olaf should not send you out there alone for his herbs."

"Be reasonable, Father. I do not go far and only a few of the herbs I need are on the shore or the cliffs. This is the first time I have been hurt." Anike did recall a time when she had climbed a tree to evade an angry boar, but she did not mention that. "It is not as if fishing is always safe either. Remember old Hulag going overboard in the spring?"

"That was his own fault, going out alone in that storm. Fishing is safe enough." Darek stood, flexing his arm, winced, and started pacing. "You know I promised your mother's shade that I would keep you safe. You are all that I have left of her."

He paused, and when he spoke again, his voice was hoarse and choked. "Isolde gave her life for you. She knew that the witch weather that night was a terrible omen, and she offered herself to Frigga so that you would be born alive. It would be a dishonour to her memory to let that sacrifice be in vain."

Anike had heard the story of her birth many times before. Witch weather, sudden violent storms from clear skies that usually only lasted minutes, were omens of death and destruction. According to her father and the midwife who had been present at the birth, her mother had cried out to Frigga, goddess of birth and motherhood, offering her own life when she had seen the storm gathering and Frigga had intervened, her answer marked by a flash of lightning. Anike had lived but Isolde died in childbirth in place of her daughter. Her father had brought her up alone.

Anike honoured her mother's sacrifice but she had never known Isolde and it was a shadow of what her father felt. He never had a bad word for her, always making her sound kind, brave and loving. She had been one of the fisher folk but she had also been a shield maiden, and her father said she could throw a spear as well as any man. Anike felt that if her mother was alive she would want her daughter to be strong, courageous and caring and to look after her father in her place.

She knew he would not be able to fish forever so at some point she would need to be the one that kept them. For that, she would need her own skills and profession, and the respect and acceptance of the townsfolk. She hoped it would be many years yet but she intended to be ready and that meant taking a few sensible risks to establish herself, including going to the forest to gather herbs. However, she suspected that her dishevelled appearance was reminding her father of the danger she had faced and upsetting him, so she changed clothes, brushed the dirt out of her hair and washed her face before turning to him again.

"Father, how many witches have we ever had in Trollgard?"

"Three in my lifetime, before today. Arl Svafnir hanged them whenever they appeared."

Anike had some recollection of the previous witch who had burned down the market in broad daylight, killing half a dozen people, but she did not remember the ones before at all. She thought of Gern's dead eyes suddenly animating again and wondered what had been going on in his mind. Perhaps the sight of Bjord lying there had brought him to his senses, aware that killing the Arl's son might be going even further than he had intended. If so, the change of heart had come too late to save his own life.

Her father's voice cut through her reverie. "It's not just witches. There are monsters in the forest too."

"Dangerous creatures hardly ever come close to the town, Father, and I am careful. I do not go too far." She did sometimes, but not too often.

Darek took a long swallow from his ale. "See that you don't, child. I worry about you, and more so every time you go out of town." He settled himself down having said his piece and winced as the stump of his left arm brushed his side, but in a moment the expression of pain had gone. "It's time you were married so that you don't have to go wandering off into the forest and putting yourself at risk. You are nineteen and comely, and you can cook. You would make someone a good wife."

Anike wondered how her father would manage without her but saying that aloud would hurt his pride. "It would be strange living somewhere else," she responded.

"I have heard it said that Bjord himself admires you."

Bjord would be a good husband for any woman, but Anike was troubled by the difference in their status. "Whatever Bjord might say, or even want, his father will marry him to a woman of the jarl caste, probably the daughter of another Arl," Anike told her father.

"Don't be too sure. Sometimes men will look beyond caste, and you would not be the first to rise to jarl by marriage."

"I have my herbs and potions, Father. I don't need a husband. Olaf says I will be ready for my masterwork soon and after that I will no longer be an apprentice and I can set up my own stall."

"It will not be easy to compete with Olaf, Anike."

"Trollgard is big enough for two herbalists. Even with my help, Olaf can barely keep up with the need for elixirs. Unfortunately, people get injured quite a lot."

"I don't want you getting hurt too, girl. You need to be careful when you are out of town."

"I have my herb lore even if that should happen. Speaking of which, I need to get these herbs to Olaf. I will be back as soon as I can, then I will cook and later I ought to take a look at your arm. I have not examined it in weeks."

"Don't trouble yourself, girl," Darek said. "I am fine." He scowled at her. "Don't fuss."

Anike smiled at him and picked up her bag. She left the house and closed the door behind her. Her father might have been right about marriage. Olaf had said she was skilled, but could she really make a living as a herbalist? Despite what she had told her father, she was worried that she would be unable to support them by herself once his strength waned. A husband could help look after them once her father's fishing days were over, she conceded to herself. Anike had spent little time considering men except as patients. She had never felt much attraction to any and had little interest in talking about weapons or raids. Now she was no longer a child she preferred the company of her master or women her own age.

She smiled to herself, recalling running and swimming with the other children, Bjord amongst them. The encounter in the forest had shown her that things could change rapidly at any age. Gern had been full of good cheer when he had last come to see Olaf but today he was revealed as a witch, and tomorrow he would be dead. Nothing was certain in the long term and extra stability from a marriage was at least worth consideration. If she did need to marry, she hoped that she could find a man who respected her wits rather than merely admired her looks, though she doubted she would have that much luck. Olaf seemed to be the only person who had noticed that she had a mind.

Anike started to walk towards the market but after only a few paces she saw her friend Inge, a woman a year younger than herself, coming towards her. At the sight of Anike, Inge's pretty face broke into a smile and she ran up to hug her. Anike held her golden-haired friend close. She had been her playmate and companion since they were children, though Anike had seen less of her since she had married the previous year. Inge now worked on the animal pelts her husband Drakna brought home from the hunt.

Inge released Anike but kept her hands on her elbows, looking at her appraisingly. "You look terrible," she said.

"Thank you so much," Anike replied drily.

"Actually, you seem a lot better than I had expected," Inge told her. "Imagine, a real witch attacking you!"

Anike smiled ruefully. "I don't have to imagine it."

"Was it terribly frightening?"

"At some moments, yes," Anike told her, "and not just the witchcraft. I have never had someone try to kill me before. He tried really hard, Inge."

Inge took Anike's hands in hers. "Come back home with me and we can talk more."

Anike felt warm at her friend's concern for her and was tempted but she knew that if she went with Inge she would find it hard to leave again. She found Inge's company very pleasant but she did not want to let Olaf down. Her master would also be worried about her. "Thank you, but I have to get these herbs to Olaf's. He has been waiting all day for this bloodmoss."

Inge looked disappointed, and Anike nearly changed her mind. After a moment's indecision, she shook her head. "Come over later, Inge. We can talk after I have cooked for my father, and then I can put the day behind me."

Inge hugged her again. "I will," she said.

They walked together to the market before parting, Inge heading back to the house she shared with Drakna, leaving Anike to cross between the stalls. It was good of her friend to have come so soon, though it surprised her how fast the news of her involvement with the witch had travelled. She had thought that Bjord would attract all the attention and she would have been more than happy with that.

Lost in thought over the events of the day, she nearly walked into Bjord as he came towards her across the market. He put out his hands to steady her. She recovered her balance and looked up into his blue eyes. "Thank you," she said.

"I was coming to see how you were, Anike."

"Inge says I look terrible," Anike replied, "but I feel a lot better now." While the witchcraft Gern had used had left her drained as if after an illness, the sunlight and seeing Inge had restored her somewhat.

"You could never look terrible, Anike," Bjord told her.

Anike shifted from foot to foot under his gaze. "And you, are you recovered, my lord?"

"Yes, Anike." Bjord smiled at her. "My father made me drink one of Olaf's invigorating potions, or it might have been one that you made." He paused. "You do not need to address me as 'my lord', you know."

Anike looked around at the market, where the stall holders were all now packing up their wares. "We are not children anymore, and there are eyes upon us," she said. "I do not think it is my place to call you by your name so openly."

"That need not always be true, Anike," he replied softly.

Anike's eyes widened, her mind running over the conclusions she might draw from that comment, ranging from Bjord wanting time in private with her, all the way to a hint of marriage. She had no idea which he had in mind, so opted for a general response. "I am honoured," she managed.

"Do you have a kiss for the man who saved your life today, Anike?" Bjord asked, leaning towards her.

Instinctively, Anike pulled back and away before she had time to consider whether that was a sensible thing to do. While she had been half expecting something of the sort for months, Bjord had taken her by surprise by trying it in so public a place. Unfortunately, the suddenness of his advances meant that she had reacted with panic rather than offering him her cheek.

Bjord's eyes flashed and his handsome face flushed. Her public refusal had wounded his pride.

She tried to recover. "Bjord, I am sorry. It is only that you caught me by surprise. And I have duties to my master." She spoke rapidly.

"Go to him then!" Bjord snapped.

Anike took a pace back, heart racing. "Thank you for thinking of me," she managed. "I have to see Olaf now." She walked past him, glancing back to see his eyes following her.

"Take care, Anike," he called after her. "I will be seeing you again soon." His voice was hard.

Anike swallowed, nearly missing a step. She hoped his temper would pass and that the next meeting he promised would go better. She relaxed a little as she walked away, but chided herself. She certainly did not want Bjord angry with her, and if only she had caught herself in time the encounter would have gone much better. She didn't particularly like the idea of kissing Bjord but if she had to have a man there was much to be said for the match provided he was looking for marriage rather than dalliance. True, he was opinionated, arrogant, and quick to anger, but he was fiercely loyal, brave, handsome and strong. He could make a good husband but his marriage would probably be politically motivated, regardless of either of their desires. Nonetheless, she resolved not to panic like a startled fawn at their next meeting.

Olaf Karnaksson's home and store faced the southern edge of the market. At the front of the building, a large wooden hatch could be lowered and Olaf used it as a stall to sell cooking herbs. Inside, he prepared elixirs – salves, oils, and potions for the people of Trollgard – and customers had to come in to buy or barter for these more valuable items. Olaf was also of the karl caste, but skilled herbalists were rare and Olaf enjoyed status close to that of a jarl.

She pushed open the door to the familiar blend of smells. Steam from brewing potions mixed with a scent of crushed herbs filled the inside. The building was larger than the house Anike shared with her father. A wooden wall divided the shop at the front from Olaf's home at the back.

Anike had been apprenticed to her father's friend some five years before. She had learned to make potions and poultices from the herbs and roots of the plants that grew in the area. The skills for preparation and brewing had come to her easily but Olaf, whose legs were not what they were, tended to send her out into the countryside to gather herbs while he concentrated on brewing the potions and selling his wares.

There was a good market for elixirs. A herbalist could prepare salves that would close wounds in seconds or pull a man back from the brink of death, and potions that could make an exhausted man strong or bring sleep. Heroic warriors might be held in the highest regard but master herbalists were greatly valued for their skills, and Anike was glad to have had the chance to learn from one of the best.

Fenris, Olaf's dog, bounded through the doorway with an excited bark when he heard the front door open. Olaf lived alone save for his dog. His wife and son had been killed in a Larten raid fifteen years ago, a raid that had also claimed Bjord's mother. He had not remarried but some years later had adopted an abandoned puppy. Fenris was now a black wolfhound as tall as Anike's waist, but unlike his legendary namesake would wag his tail rather than bare his teeth.

Anike braced herself against his weight and stroked his head as he rubbed against her.

"Anike, it's good to see you safe," Olaf greeted her. A tall man, now running slightly to fat, Olaf had long limbs and fingers. His red hair and beard were cut short, and he wore a heavy leather smock stained with years of spills from the cauldrons. "How do you fare after your ordeal?"

"I am fine, Olaf. I was lucky Bjord was nearby hunting boar." She laid her bag on one of the wooden tables that occupied much of the room and started to unpack and sort the herbs. "I had time to get a good selection before the dire wolves and Gern interrupted me."

"But how are you feeling? It must have been a terrifying experience."

This was the third time in less than an hour that someone had asked her how she was. Anike felt a flash of exasperation at being pressed but immediately regretted her reaction. Olaf genuinely cared, and it was natural he would probe a bit more deeply.

She unpacked the last of the plants. "I was frightened, yes, and Gern's witchcraft left me a little weak, but nothing a good night's sleep will not fix." She turned to him. "I am troubled, though. Olaf, did you ever suspect Gern was a witch? Did you ever see anything in his face that gave you a hint?" Anike had tried to banish the memory of Gern's cold eyes, but it kept returning. "How could he have been coming in here for years and we not know?"

Olaf frowned. "It is a strange and terrible thing to find out that someone had such a dark secret for so long. He practised a deception on us all."

"I saw his eyes, Olaf. They were like a dead man's, and he did not seem to feel any pain, at least not until the last moment." She told him about the battle, and how Gern had ignored his wound until just before Bjord struck him down.

"He might have used witchcraft to make himself immune to pain. That could be the sort of thing a witch could do easily," Olaf suggested. "There is even a potion for that, you remember?"

Anike nodded. "Gern was no herbalist, but you may be right about his witchcraft. Maybe it went wrong somehow and that made him want to kill us."

"Or he could have been hunting for a sacrifice to whatever fell power he served. Odin gave up his eye in exchange for knowledge and if even the gods have to pay their dues, perhaps Gern had to sacrifice something for his black craft." He stirred a potion thoughtfully. "I have heard tell of witches who live in the wilds without killing every traveller they meet, but that might be just myth. The few I have seen have just brought death."

"Gern could have been like those hermit witches but something happened to him to push him over the edge," Anike mused as she started to trim the roots she had brought.

"It's possible, but equally he might have just been biding his time and took advantage of finding you alone. We will probably never know."

Anike thought of the fleeing dire wolves and shook her head. "I doubt that he was after me particularly. But we shall hear him at his trial, and he may tell us what drove him to attempt murder."

"You would have been too young to hear the last witch trial, I think," Olaf said. "Gern may not even get the chance to speak, particularly since Bjord will be giving evidence against him."

"What do you mean?"

"Arl Svafnir will not want any confusion or doubt. He will ensure that the evidence is clear, so he will give Gern little chance to contradict his son – or you, for that matter."

Anike froze, her knife paused over a root, and her hand trembled. She had realised, deep down, that she might have to speak at the trial and she dreaded the idea of a crowd of gathered townsfolk looking at her.

Seeing her reaction, Olaf continued, "I doubt you will have to say much. I am sure that Bjord will do most of the talking and you will just have to agree with what he says. You can manage that, can't you?"

"I suppose so. That does not sound too hard," Anike said hesitantly.

"It would be a good idea to agree publicly with Bjord at the moment."

She told Olaf of her meeting with the Arl's son in the market, and how she regretted her reaction.

"You do need to plan for your future. Bjord admires you. He will get past his anger, and you are right that a public show of agreement will soothe his pride."

"And after that?"

"Obviously he is the Arl's son, but consider. People value what they have to work for but they become frustrated if they make no progress. You are beautiful and clever, learn quickly and have a respected trade. I know you are not a jarl but you could still make a good wife for him. You just need to be more confident in the woman you are becoming and show him someone who will support and stand with him. Give him some signs to show him his efforts are appreciated and keep his hopes up."

"But -" started Anike.

"You could think of it as giving your father security as he gets older."

"I know that my father will not be able to haul nets with Joran forever," said Anike.

"No, and that will sadden him as he wants to be useful. However, you must realise what really drives him?"

Anike hesitated. "Me," she said.

"Yes. After Isolde died, you are all he has left. He wants you to be secure and safe, and if that happens he will be content even if he can no longer work on a boat."

"I do not think Bjord sees me as a future wife and he is not someone who changes his mind about anything."

"He may not have decided yet, and you should find out. I have cautioned you about making assumptions before. It is lazy. You have a theory and then you test it. I know you understand this as you have devised several new elixir recipes. You predicted what the combination of herbs would do and you tested it. This is the same. If you consider something might be possible, then try it. And an Arl's son can marry a karl."

Anike smiled tentatively.

"It's not as if you are a thrall. The jarl caste is small, with few women of Bjord's age. Arl Oster of Ulsvater married the captain of a trading vessel."

"I did not know that," Anike admitted.

"Think on it. You and Bjord are going to be the centre of attention for a few days. You may well find yourselves thrust together. If you are open to it, perhaps you will see an opportunity to nudge things in the right direction."

"You are right. Thank you," Anike said. Olaf meant well and his advice made sense, but she was not sure that she could work up the courage to ask Bjord about his intentions. However, if he was as forward as he had been earlier, she might only need to steer things and she felt she could manage that.

Anike finished preparing the herbs and sorted them carefully into boxes for drying. "I told Granny Caryn I would look in on her today and try to get her back on her feet."

"She just enjoys the attention she gets from being injured. Are you sure you feel up to a long visit today?"

"I promised her, Olaf, and it will make her happy."

Olaf sighed. "She will stir herself when she needs something, but don't let me stop you if you think it will do some good."

Anike smiled. "Thank you."

Granny Caryn, who was nearly sixty, had hurt her knee in a fall while trying to replace a roof shingle the previous week. The potion that Olaf had given her should have healed the injury but she still seemed unable to walk, despite all outward signs vanishing. 'Granny' was a term of respect rather than kinship. She was not related to Anike at all but was a great aunt of Tavic the Swift, one of Bjord's companions. Anike packed some dried nettles into a small bag. They were of little medicinal value by themselves but made excellent tea, and were part of her plan to get Granny Caryn walking again.

She bade goodnight to Olaf and made her way through the town until she reached a large house by the south wall. She knocked on the door and called out "Granny Caryn, it is Anike. I have come to check on your knee." It was opened by Tavic's mother, Edi, who ushered her in. Granny Caryn was propped up by furs in a large chair by the fire, a position which commanded a view of the entire room.

"You are looking well today, Granny." Anike smiled at the old woman.

"It's sweet of you to say so, Anike, but I'm afraid my knee is still weak."

"It is not painful though, is it?"

"No, no, just no strength in it. See here." Granny Caryn leaned forward and tried to rise. Her right leg buckled but Anike, who had been watching closely, saw it bend before it had even taken any real weight.

"Oh, that is a shame," Anike said. "No matter. I have brought some nettle tea for us. I can have a look at the knee while it brews."

"Nettle tea? That sounds good. Edi, can you boil some water?"

Edi raised her eyes to the roof and gave a long sigh as she went to the fire. Anike passed the dried nettles to her and she put them in a small pot to boil. As the fresh smell filled the room, Anike knelt to examine the old woman's knee. "Let me know if this hurts," she said, probing with practised fingers.

"No, just weak."

Anike found no sign of injury, and the muscles were no weaker on the right leg than the left. The potion had worked and whatever was stopping Granny Caryn from standing, it was not physical. The question was whether she was choosing not to. If she was pretending, as Olaf suspected, there was nothing Anike could do but she thought it might be more that Granny Caryn had lost confidence in herself. She believed the woman's fall had made her think of herself as old and fragile. Anike hoped that if Granny Caryn realised that she could stand then she would be able to.

She stood and poured the older woman a cup of tea. "Invigorating, is it not?"

Granny Caryn sipped it. "Very nice," she said.

"Can you taste any unusual flavours?" Anike asked her.

Granny Caryn lowered the cup. "Have you put anything else in? You said it was nettle."

"Now, Granny, would I do that?" Anike said in a tone of mock injury, smiling. She reached out, put Granny Caryn's cup down beside her and took her right hand. "I am going to support you and we will try a few steps. Put your weight on me."

Granny Caryn looked doubtful, but Anike's pull was insistent and she draped the old woman's arm over her shoulders. "Now let us try a step."

It was more of a hop, but Granny Caryn did manage a step forward. "Well done, Granny. How about another?" Anike braced herself as Granny Caryn tried another pace, favouring her left leg but putting some weight on her right.

The door opened to admit Tavic. Hoping she was right, Anike took a chance and allowed herself to stumble, taking care not to drag Granny Caryn down with her. She hit the floor and was rewarded by seeing Granny Caryn standing unsupported, the surprised look on her face giving way to a wide grin.

Smiling herself, Anike came back to her feet. "I am sorry I tripped, Granny."

"Never mind," the old woman said happily. "No harm done. I can stand again." She took a cautious step forward. "I can walk. It must have been that tea."

"It must have been," Anike agreed, glad that she had trusted her judgment and relieved that she had been right that Granny Caryn's residual affliction had only been a lack of confidence. "I am glad to see you standing tall again, Granny." She leaned forward to give the old woman a gentle kiss on the cheek. "I have to be going now but I will see you soon. Do take care next time you are on the roof."

"I will try to," Granny Caryn said happily. "Visit soon, Anike."

Anike walked to the door but just as she got there Tavic gripped her arm, halting her. "If you had been wrong and you let her fall she would have been hurt," he whispered harshly in her ear. "You were reckless. I would have held you accountable if you had made her injury worse."

Anike removed his hand. Tavic was not Bjord and she had no trouble standing up to him. "It was worth it," she told him. "Look how happy she is, and your mother too." Tavic followed her gaze to Edi, who was also smiling, relief radiating from her. "I know what I am doing," she told him.

He dropped his gaze. "Your little trick did work, I must give you that, I suppose," he said. Anike looked at him carefully. He still seemed a little jumpy. "Do you want to talk about Gern?" she asked. Tavic still seemed unsettled and she doubted that her unorthodox treatment of Granny Caryn entirely accounted for it. He had been terrified by Gern's witchcraft and it could take time to recover from such fear.

"No," he said sharply, then "Thank you, I have talked about what happened enough for one day," he added more gently and somewhat to Anike's relief.

"I know what you mean," she said. "Goodnight, then."

A few minutes later she was at her own house. Darek looked up from his chair as she came in, not seeming to have moved since she left him. She went to the fire, sorted through the food and started to make a stew with fish, vegetables and some of the cooking herbs she had gathered that day. "The herring were plentiful this morning," she commented as she dropped the fish into the pot.

Any reply Darek might have made was interrupted by a loud knock. Expecting Inge, Anike hung the pot over the fire, wiped her hands and turned towards the door.

"Anike Dareksdottir, are you within? I would speak with you," came the deep resonant voice of Arl Svafnir Sigurdsson.

- 3 -

The Trial

Anike opened the door to Arl Svafnir. Around the same age as her father, the Arl was a powerfully built man with blonde hair like his son and a thick blonde beard. Despite the late hour, he still wore his ringmail and a sword hung at his side. The light from the doorway revealed Bjord standing a little way behind his father.

"I apologise for calling so late," the Arl said in his rich voice. "May we come in?"

Anike's mouth seemed to have fallen open of its own accord, so she shut it and re-focused. She had not expected to see the Arl, though thinking about it now she realised he would want to talk to her before the trial. Not yet trusting herself to speak, she opened the door wide and gestured for him to come in. Darek had stood. Svafnir acknowledged him with a nod then turned to Anike. Recalling her manners, she indicated chairs by the large table. "Will you sit, my lords?"

Svafnir took the indicated seat at the table, and Bjord, after testing the other chair to ensure it would hold his weight, joined him. "Please sit too," the Arl said to Anike, so she collected the stool from beneath the herb table and drew it over to opposite the Arl. Darek retreated to the bench beyond the fire.

When Anike was seated, Arl Svafnir started to speak. "At midday tomorrow I will be trying Gern Haffordsson for witchcraft and attempted murder. It will be in the market before the people of Trollgard as this is too important a matter to be heard in my hall. I will be judging Gern on what is said then, but I would like to hear your account now." He lowered his voice a fraction. "I do not wish to be surprised when you speak tomorrow."

Anike swallowed. "My lord, the first I knew something was wrong was when the dire wolves ran past me, fleeing Gern." She went on to describe what had happened, hesitantly at first, then more confidently as the Arl nodded at her to continue.

She came to the point where Gern had raised Bjord's sword. "He was about to strike Bjord but then he suddenly hesitated. It was almost as if he woke up and recognised Bjord. He called him 'my lord' and seemed to change his mind. Then Bjord pulled him down and knocked him out."

She looked at the Arl, gauging his reaction. While the Arl considered her words, so did she. She had not framed Gern's change in terms of waking up before but that did seem to fit. It was as if he had been acting in a dream, or a nightmare.

Svafnir looked at his son. "You didn't tell me that Gern hesitated."

"He didn't, Father," Bjord said. "It happened so quickly that it is not surprising Anike is mistaken. It was Tavic that called out. Gern was trying to kill me with my own sword when I brought him down." Unconsciously perhaps, Bjord twisted a gold ring around one finger.

Anike stared at Bjord, wondering if he really remembered events that way, or if he just wanted the story to emphasise his own bravery. Striking down a man who was no longer attacking might not seem heroic, even if that man was a witch. She was sure Bjord was wrong, though. The light had come back into Gern's eyes, and she had seen how he had suddenly registered the pain of his wound.

"Well?" the Arl asked her. She turned back to see him regarding her silently, and she trembled under the steady gaze. Svafnir obviously didn't want her to undermine his son, but something in his tone when he had spoken to Bjord made her wonder if he had recognised something important in her account. Gern was going to be executed regardless of what she said. If she contradicted Bjord, the Arl would ignore it or perhaps even publicly dismiss her words, leaving her looking weak and scared. Worse, she would be insulting Bjord again. In contrast, supporting him could go some way to undo the damage she had done with her rejection in the market. Anike did not really know the significance of Gern's hesitation. She felt it could be important, but it did not alter the fact that he had tried to kill her.

"I must have been mistaken, my lord," Anike said, dropping her eyes. "Bjord is right."

"Thank you, Anike. I knew I could rely on you." A slight smile graced the Arl's face. Bjord was less restrained. He released the breath Anike had not realised he was holding and let his hand fall away from the ring. His smile was much broader than his father's.

"I will require you to repeat this account at the trial tomorrow," the Arl told her.

Anike shifted on her stool. "There will be a lot of people listening," she said.

"Do not concern yourself with them. Concentrate on me. I am the audience that matters." The Arl rose and turned to Anike's father, who hastily pushed himself to his feet, wincing slightly. "Thank you for allowing me into your home, Darek."

"Of course, my lord. You are always welcome," Darek replied.

"Come up and join me when I call on you tomorrow, Anike. If you hold to that tale, all will be well. I bid you both goodnight." The Arl went to the door and Anike hastened to open it for him. Bjord nodded to Darek and smiled at Anike before following his father out.

She closed the door behind him and felt some of the tension leave. The Arl's visit had unnerved her and she was glad to be out of his presence. She felt that she had managed to undo the harm caused by her rejection of Bjord in the afternoon, and that gave her a sense of relief. She was still unsure if she wanted to develop a relationship with Bjord but now she was on firmer ground.

She felt some disquiet about the implied instruction not to tell everything she had seen. Stories were enjoyable, but could also make points in a way that people could remember. History was recorded in tales passed from skald to skald but she knew that the world was a more complex place than the stories suggested. Anike did not know if Gern's change of mind was real, or might mean anything even if it was, but she was uneasy that it would be left out of the lore of witches.

Darek put his arm around her shoulders. "Don't worry, Anike. Everyone will be supporting you tomorrow and they will applaud your bravery." He gave her a squeeze.

Anike doubted that anyone would admire her bravery if they knew how she had given in to the Arl, though they might applaud her good sense. She had agreed to an expedient course of action, perhaps even a wise one, but the braver path would have been to insist on telling the complete truth.

Anike had just moved the stool back to its normal place when there was another knock on the door, this one much lighter. She opened it to admit Inge.

"I can't stay too long," she said. "Drakna wants to be up early. I think he is planning to hunt down a dire wolf for its pelt before the trial."

"Tell him to be careful," Anike held her hand at chest level. "They really do stand this high at the shoulder."

Inge looked a little taken aback. "Truly? I will warn him not to face one alone."

"That would be wise. I think the dire wolves have gone though," Anike added. "They actually seemed frightened of Gern."

"Bjord wasn't frightened, though? When he saw the witch?"

"I think he was a bit but that did not stop him. There is no doubt about his bravery. Sit, Inge, and have some ale."

They settled by the fire, and Darek retreated to his bed, leaving them alone. Orange light played across Anike's face. "I was lucky Bjord was hunting in the forest," she told Inge.

"Bjord," said Inge in a slightly dreamy voice. Anike raised an eyebrow at her married friend and Inge continued in a more normal tone. "If he could have saved anyone, I am sure he was glad it was you."

"Maybe, though I am not sure he is looking at me as a wife. I am not highly enough regarded for that and being on show tomorrow will not help. Standing in front of the whole town is not a prospect I am looking forward to. I do not enjoy people staring at me."

"People stare at you all the time, especially men. Men like Bjord," Inge added wistfully.

"That is not the sort of attention I want from men. I want to be respected and have people see something worthwhile in me."

"With your looks, it may be asking too much of a man to see much beyond the outside! Men can be pretty single-minded."

"Little wonder I prefer the company of women then. Except for Olaf, men are not interested in what I think."

"If you were married to Bjord, that would change. They would have to listen to the wife of the future Arl," said Inge.

"That's true, I suppose, but there is little chance of that happening." Anike paused, considering. "Though Bjord did seem better disposed towards me when he and the Arl came here just now."

"The Arl was here? Lucky you keep the place tidy."

"Yes, he was. He wanted me to tell him what I was going to say at the trial tomorrow."

"That shouldn't have been difficult."

"No, except for one part which seemed to trouble him." Anike told Inge about Gern's last-minute wavering, and how Bjord had portrayed those moments. "Perhaps Bjord really did not see it, but I know what happened. I am just not sure what it means. It was as if a cloud had lifted from Gern. He seemed to realise what he had done and was mortified by it."

"It must have been a trick."

"No. It was only Gern's hesitation that gave Bjord his chance." Anike thought of Gern's eyes again. "But before that, he really did try to kill us."

"You can't forgive that, Anike."

"It's not about forgiving but understanding. What made him reveal that he was a witch, and then why did he stop when he was winning? I like to understand, Inge, and the unknown troubles me. If Gern is executed, no one will be able to ask him."

"Of course he will be hanged. He tried to kill Bjord."

"I know. If he had just attacked me, Arl Svafnir might have allowed him to pay a bloodprice to me instead of execution."

"You wouldn't want a witch to serve you, surely?"

"Perhaps not, but the bloodprice could have been paid in silver."

"Even so, attacking anyone with witchcraft is really serious so I doubt the Arl would allow it," Inge said. "And why would you want to learn more? We were not meant to understand witches and witchcraft. Fortunately, it will all be over once the trial is done."

"I hope so," said Anike, though the idea of more witches hidden in the town or countryside nearby nagged at her. While she could not be sure of the significance of Gern's apparent return to normality, his ability to hide his witchcraft for long years meant that more witches could be concealed amongst ordinary people, perhaps waiting for a sign before revealing themselves. A star had fallen a few nights before, she recalled. While this was often considered a good omen, Gern might have taken it as a harbinger of a different sort. She wondered again whether the Arl knew more than he was saying. It was not her place to question him, but she had a sense that there was more to his reluctance to have her relate Gern's apparent change of heart than a wish for his son to be seen as heroic.

Inge finished the ale and left for her own house, and Anike suddenly realised how tired she was. She kissed her father's forehead and went to her own bed. Despite her exhaustion, sleep eluded her and she lay on her back, looking at the roof. Instinctively, she felt that people should have the chance to hear everything for themselves so that they could be alert to the possibility of witches among them and that meant her duty to the town was to put the whole story before the people. The Arl clearly believed otherwise and if she told the whole truth he, and no doubt Bjord, would be angry with her at first though deep down Bjord would surely admire her for her bravery. Ultimately, her duty was to the town rather than to the Arl, and she was entitled to make her own choice as to how to fulfil it. She hoped that the townsfolk would understand her decision too, and dreaming of a town where she was respected and honoured for her bravery and confidence, she drifted off to sleep.

The first rays of the dawn sun crept in through the shutters. The night's sleep had restored her and Anike felt strong for the first time since Gern had worked his witchcraft on her. The rest had also shored up her resolve to give her full account at the trial, despite what Arl Svafnir had told her.

She rose and started to prepare a meal of grain and vegetables for her father and herself. While the water boiled, she tidied the house and cleaned everything that had been used the night before. The events of the previous day had been too taxing for her to keep to her practice of doing the housework before she went to bed.

Her father had slept fitfully, and Anike recalled that she had intended to examine his arm the night before. Now it would have to wait until later as he would be out on the boat as soon as he had eaten. She watched him climb down from his sleeping platform, moving a little stiffly, and she frowned.

Darek caught her looking at him and smiled. "Don't worry, child. The Arl will not have you speaking long. Keep it simple, just as he said, and you will be fine."

Anike just nodded as she filled a bowl and handed it to him. Darek started on his meal, and Anike took some for herself. They ate in silence and once they had finished Anike spoke. "You will come to watch me, Father?" she asked.

"Of course I will. I doubt many of the town will miss it, and I won't let my little one stand before a crowd alone. I will make sure I am back home well before the sun is high." Anike smiled her relief as she cleaned the bowls.

"Get yourself off to Olaf's now, girl, and work hard. The morning will pass in no time," Darek told her. He laid a strong hand on her shoulder before leaving to catch the morning tide.

Anike walked to Olaf's house. As always, there were elixirs to prepare, and she focused on her work to distract herself from the coming trial. She could not forget it entirely as she could see a group of men constructing the platform and the scaffold in the centre of the market through Olaf's front window. Hanging was the least honourable form of execution, giving the criminal no chance of an afterlife in Valhalla and doomed to spend eternity in Niflheim as a powerless ghost in a grey land.

As far as Anike could tell from fragments of conversation drifting in on the breeze, no one seemed in any doubt about the outcome of the trial. More people than usual came into the shop to make small purchases from Olaf. They kept glancing at her as they bartered with him, which did little to settle her nerves. She concentrated on her work as best she could, trying to ignore the stares.

The morning wore on and the business of the market slowed as more people drew near the scaffold. It seemed that most of Trollgard had come to see Gern hang. When the sun was high enough, Anike and Olaf left the shop and the crowd parted to allow them through. A few called out praises to Thor and Freya that Anike had been saved but most just watched. She found the attention oppressive but, as with the dire wolves, she forced herself to be calm. With Olaf's reassuring presence beside her, she walked forward steadily until she reached the front of the crowd.

Darek pushed through the throng to join her, coming to stand on the other side. Anike could smell the ale on his breath. It was early in the day for him, but his work would have been finished and she could forgive him this indulgence as she could have used some ale herself. It occurred to her that he had been drinking more in the last couple of weeks and she decided to talk to him about it later. At that moment she was just glad to have him with her.

Clouds were gathering, drifting in from the sea to stand like sombre guards. Horns sounded, and the crowd looked to the east side of the marketplace to watch Arl Svafnir striding out from the gates of the arlberg towards the platform where the gallows had been raised. The townsfolk scattered out of his way like a flock of sparrows before a hawk.

Gern was dragged along in his wake. Bjord held one arm, and the other was held by a tall woman whom Anike knew slightly. Siv Blatandsdottir was a lean woman, as tall as Bjord. She had short hair, so pale as to be almost white, and she held herself like a drawn bow. Siv had fought alongside Arl Svafnir for many years and was his right arm in the governing of Trollgard. A small group of men including Loga, Slad and Tavic followed closely behind, and with them was a white-haired but vigorous man with the bearing of a warrior whom Anike did not recognise at all.

Gern was gagged, his hands tied behind his back and as he looked around Anike saw fear, resignation and regret passed like clouds over his face. Shouts of anger and hatred from the crowd buffeted him like a raging sea.

Anike looked at the man who had tried to kill her hanging limply between Bjord and Siv and could not share the crowd's enthusiasm for his death. There was no fight left in him and what she mostly felt was pity. Gern surely now regretted meddling with powers that men should leave alone. Was death the only suitable punishment? It seemed that the people of Trollgard thought so, but Anike wondered if there was some alternative.

Gern climbed onto the platform unaided and stood there with his eyes lowered, flanked by Bjord and Siv. The roar of the crowd swelled. Cries of 'Witch!' and 'Death!' stood out from the general noise, and he seemed to shrink in on himself.

Arl Svafnir raised his hands. The crowd fell silent as his gaze swept over them.

"Good people of Trollgard," the Arl began. "Today we hold the trial of Gern Haffordsson, accused of using witchcraft to try and kill my son, Bjord Svafnirsson, and Anike Dareksdottir. He is further accused of using its dark power to bring harm to Loga Beodaksson, Slad Vursson, and Tavic the Swift."

"Death to the witch!" and similar angry cries rose from the crowd again, but under the Arl's steely gaze, dropped away quickly. Svafnir was not playing to the crowd, but controlling it.

"I will now hear from Anike Dareksdottir," Svafnir stated, and looked down at Anike. Heads turned towards her, and she quailed inside. She had assumed that Bjord would speak before her, but realised it made sense that she would be called on first as she was Gern's first victim. Olaf's hand on her arm steadied her and she squared her shoulders, stepped forward out of the crowd and climbed onto the platform. She looked out over the sea of faces, many of whom she knew and all waiting for her to speak. She let them blur together and become anonymous then turned to the Arl.

"Tell me what happened yesterday, Anike," he told her gently but firmly enough that his voice carried to the far edge of the now silent throng.

Anike took a deep breath and looked at his chest, not daring to meet his gaze. "I was in the woods gathering herbs -" she began.

"Speak up!" a woman called from the crowd.

Anike stopped, blushing. She took a deep breath, fixed her attention on the Arl and continued, keeping her voice as steady as she could and trying not to babble. "It went cold, and something came through the woods. I ran, but it caught up with me, and I saw it was Gern. He used some sort of witchcraft to take my strength away and tried to hit me with his axe, but I got away, and found Bjord and -"

"Thank you, Anike," Arl Svafnir cut off her gabbling.

"But -" said Anike, blinking.

"You can go back to your father now."

"I wanted to tell the rest," Anike stammered, but her uncertain words went unheard as the Arl raised his voice to address the crowd again.

"I thank Anike for her evidence and commend her for her good sense in seeking out my son, who will take up the tale. Bjord Svafnirsson, step forward."

Dismissed, Anike stood for a moment in shock. The Arl had ruthlessly denied her any opportunity to contradict his son and the crowd had already turned its attention from her to Bjord, who was striding forward to stand by his father.

Olaf was beckoning her to come back down. Darek managed a slight smile but quickly resumed a worried expression. Anike stepped down from the platform and she saw him relax. She joined him back in the anonymous crowd and took a deep breath. Darek put his hand on her shoulder and gave it a squeeze.

On the platform, Bjord was starting on his tale. The audience's attention was now entirely fixed on him, and Anike felt some of the tension leave her. She had not managed to say what she wanted, but at least she had avoided upsetting anyone or seriously embarrassing herself.

Bjord was enjoying himself, relishing the chance to tell a heroic story in which he played a leading role. He could not resist some embellishment, describing protecting Anike and Loga by deflecting shards of ice with his sword. It jarred when compared with the cold truth that Anike remembered, but so naturally did the words seem to come to him that she wondered if Bjord really had perceived everything the way he was telling it. She doubted it. This was his moment and he was not going to let accuracy get in his way.

Bjord reached the climax. "As Gern's blow descended towards my head, I caught his wrist. His strength was no match for mine so I wrenched my blade from him and pulled him to the ground. He started to mouth words of some yet darker witchcraft but I struck him with the hilt of my sword, and he fell senseless. And so I vanquished the witch." He nodded to his father and held one hand aloft to acknowledge the cheers of the crowd.

There were no shades of grey here, just a story of good triumphing over evil, and on hearing it Anike realised what had troubled her so much about leaving out Gern's last-minute reversal. It was not the concern that there might be other witches hidden but that the remorse and regret Gern had shown was ignored. At the last, he had turned from his dark path rather than finish off his victims and witnesses to his deeds. The trial paid no heed to that. A sense of injustice grew within her as the Arl perfunctorily called Loga, Tavic and Slad to confirm what Bjord had said. They did so readily, adding praises for his action.

Finally, Svafnir turned to Siv. "Ungag the prisoner," he commanded, and Siv took the gag from Gern's mouth.

"Gern Haffordsson, you have heard what has been said against you. Do you deny using witchcraft on my son and these others, and trying to commit murder?"

The crowd waited.

Gern straightened up and met Svafnir's gaze. His words when they came were calm. "My lord, I regret what I did and I wish I had never done it. I acted during a moment of madness when I doubted the value of life, but it passed. I mean no harm to your son nor to any of the others. None were killed, so I offer to pay whatever bloodprice you set for them."

The old man Anike had not recognised stirred at that, but Arl Svafnir gave no indication that he had even heard Gern's offer. Gern looked at him a moment longer, then sighed. "If you will not let me pay the bloodprice, I ask that my death be swift."

There was no leniency in the Arl's expression. Gern nodded in resignation, but suddenly his eyes snapped shut and his face tensed in concentration. "No! I will not!" he shouted, then the set of his shoulders relaxed and he opened his eyes again. Anike saw tears in them and was struck by the contrast between his outburst and the manner in which he had put his plea for a quick death. Fear could show itself in many forms, she supposed.

Svafnir gestured to Siv who replaced the gag. He spoke, his voice carrying through the market, cold anger in each word. "There is no place in the world for one who harms another with witchcraft and no afterlife in Valhalla for a witch. Witchcraft does not earn a man a quick death. Gern, you will hang until you die." Tears ran freely down Gern's face now and his body crumpled.

"A coward as well as a witch," Bjord sneered, dragging the condemned man upright.

At a nod from Svafnir, Siv fixed a rope around Gern's neck and looped it over the scaffold. Anike heard his muffled screams as Siv and Bjord hauled him up by the neck. She turned away and buried her face in her father's chest, feeling his arm holding her close. The roaring of the crowd, the cheers, and prayers to Odin seemed to be accompanied by a smell of death and decay. Gern's cries were drowned out by the noise of the crowd, and she could bear no more. She pulled free of her father and ran from the execution of the man who had tried to kill her.

Anike walked slowly west along the sandy beach until she came to the rocks beneath the cliff to the west of the town. She could not share the crowd's vilification – the knowledge of Gern's remorse set her apart. Unwilling to return until she was sure they had dispersed, she sat and listened to the gulls until a shower driven by a harsh north wind encouraged her to climb the cliff and go a short distance inland so she could sit beneath the trees next to the coast road.

She had been there about an hour, lost in her thoughts, when she noticed someone coming along the road from Trollgard. It was the old man who had been on the platform with Arl Svafnir. His white hair was long and his face lined but he walked swiftly. At his side hung a sword and on his back was a bow, both very expensive weapons and together they marked him as a person of some importance. She assumed he was a visiting jarl and bowed her head as he came past but to her surprise, he stopped and beckoned to her. Puzzled, she got up and approached him.

"Anike, is it not?" he asked, and when she nodded, he continued. "I am Masig Valisson."

She did recognise that name. He was a hero, a renowned warrior, hunter and archer with a long history of deeds told by skalds, now in service to the Arl of Ulsvater. Up close, she could see that he was very old indeed with perhaps a few years more than Granny Caryn, remarkable when most warriors were killed in battle in their youth.

"My lord," she said. "Forgive me for not recognising you. How may I serve you?"

He smiled at her. "Do not trouble yourself, Anike. I only desired to tell you that I recognised your bravery today, and to wish you well."

"Bravery?" Anike asked.

"You were not comfortable before a crowd, and yet you spoke anyway and you even tried to contradict Svafnir."

"I apologise if I gave offence."

"Not at all. I admire spirit, but Svafnir was never going to be turned from his course. That may prove to be unfortunate, but it is the way of things."

"I do not understand, my lord."

The old man shrugged. "I ramble. Sometimes it is better to serve the future than the present, but that is a hard thing to do. But do not let me detain you further. I wish you well, Anike. I hope you can nurture that courage." He turned back to the road to Ulsvater.

"A wish you a fair journey, my lord," Anike called after him. Unexpectedly, the conversation had cheered her and it was time to return to Trollgard.

Olaf looked up from his work as she came in. "It's over, Anike," he told her.

Anike wiped her eyes. "I know," she said. "I saw that the body has been taken down. I should be happy that justice has been done and that the town is safe but I feel there could have been another way. This is not as simple as the Arl thinks. It was Gern's moment of hesitation that troubled me. Arl Svafnir did not want me to mention it today, and I thought it might be because witches could hide among us."

Olaf frowned. "Do you think it would be a good thing if everyone suspected their neighbour or accused them of witchcraft whenever there was a quarrel or there was an unusual run of luck?"

Anike thought about it. "No, I had not considered that, and perhaps you are right. Paranoia could take over, and I can see that the Arl would want to prevent that. But I realised I was actually more concerned that Gern stopped attacking even though he had the advantage, and that he regretted his actions. He did not take a life and he chose not to, in the end. That ought to mean something."

"Even though he would have killed you had you not kept your wits about you?"

"Yes, I think so. Maybe not enough to spare his life, but his repentance should be worth something, don't you think? By chance, I met Masig Valisson on the road just now, and he hinted that he disagreed with Svafnir's judgment."

"What do you mean?"

"I think he thought Gern might still be able to serve somehow. If it had been him giving judgment he might have set a bloodprice."

"I would place less weight on his words than I would on Svafnir's judgment. Masig is a great hero, but not a ruler. You want to save everyone, Anike. For a herbalist, that is not a bad thing, but sometimes sacrifices have to be made. Witchcraft is like a festering wound and it needs to be cut out for the good of everyone else."

"Wounds do not regret what they have done." She frowned. Olaf's words had struck a chord, not about witches but something else. She tried to grasp the memory, but Olaf was speaking again.

"If they were remorseful, would it matter? The flesh will still need to be cut out."

"That analogy only works so far," Anike replied. "Wounds cannot make choices."

She stopped and cursed softly. "Wounds. By Freya, I am a poor herbalist and a worse daughter. I am sorry, Olaf, I have to go home. Thank you for everything today, but I have to check on my father's old wound."

- 4 -

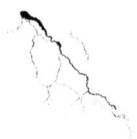

Wounds

When she got home, her father was waiting by the fire, ale in his hand. Bleary eyes peered at her as she came through the door. "Inge came over to talk to you, Anike, but she went away again. I couldn't tell her where you were."

Anike flushed, chiding herself for neglecting to consider how he would worry after she fled the scene of the execution. "I am very sorry, Father. I needed to clear my head so I went for a walk. No harm done. I am back now." She crossed over to him and kissed his forehead. "I will have a look at that arm of yours, then I will start on dinner."

"Let's eat first," he said. "You will feel better after a good meal."

Anike decided not to upset him further by insisting. "Very well, but the arm straight afterwards." Her father grunted. Anike prepared some of the fish he had caught that morning, efficiently gutting, filleting and adding cooking herbs before frying them. Darek continued to quietly drink while she worked, staring into the fire. Anike had used to ask him what he saw in the flames but he had always replied that he just liked the colours. She no longer asked, but suspected that his mind was wandering through memories of Isolde, her mother.

She hurried through the meal, chafing at the delay. Her father ate slowly, playing with his food until Anike lost patience and pulled the plate away. "Now let me have a look at that arm."

"It's fine, girl. Let it be," Darek told her, trying to pull back. He winced.

"Is it?" Anike pulled up her father's sleeve and gasped at what she saw. She was used to the stump, a little above where the elbow should have been, but not to it looking as it did now. The skin was a livid red instead of its usual smooth pink, save for the centre which had turned a sickly grey. Dark lines ran up the arm all the way to the chest and the smell of decay rolled over her. As she had feared, it was the same smell that she had noticed earlier in the marketplace.

She stood aghast at the ruin of her father's arm. "Father! You should have told me!"

"I didn't want to worry you. When I drink enough, it doesn't hurt much and I am sure it will get better if I leave it alone."

"What happened?" Anike pushed aside her anger at Darek's stubbornness and ran practised fingers over the skin, making him wince again.

"It got caught in a net, about ten days back. We snagged a giant crab and my arm was crushed against the gunwale during the struggle. It hurt a bit at the time, but these things happen on a boat. It will pass."

"Pass? Do you not realise that the wound rot has set in again?" she nearly shouted. "Olaf had to cut your arm off to stop it spreading last time."

Anike yanked a torch from the bracket in the wall and held it so she could examine the infected arm. "I will need to look at you again in the daylight, but I think I have caught it in time. Just. Do you not remember what I do all day, Father? What are my skills good for if I cannot look after you? You have to tell me when something hurts." She thrust the torch back into the bracket above her work table.

"Stay there!" She looked through her elixirs. Olaf allowed her to keep some of those she made in the shop, and she had prepared others at home. She found a small bottle and went back to her father. "Drink this!" she snapped at him. Darek drank and grimaced at the taste then an expression of relief came over him.

"That feels good," he said. "It doesn't hurt now."

"It's only temporary. It just numbs the pain." She went back to the table, found the salve she needed then put a cauldron of water on the fire to boil some bandages. She heated the tip of a small, sharp knife in the fire and when it was glowing red she made two deep cuts into her father's arm. There was a brief sizzling sound then the blood, dark with poison from the infection, started to drain out. Darek whitened, but the numbing potion had done its work and he did not cry out. When the sluggish black blood gave way to a more normal red, Anike cleaned the wounds and applied the elixir. The cuts she had made closed up and the livid flesh faded towards a more natural colour. Anike drew a deep breath and wrapped her father's arm in bandages soaked in the remains of the salve.

"I will look at it again tomorrow to check that the salve has done its work," she said, but her father had already closed his eyes as sleep took him. Anike watched him, noting his breathing becoming deeper and steadier. It was little wonder that his drinking had increased in the last couple of weeks. The pain must have been agonising at times and she could only admire his strength of will to keep going out on his fishing boat day after day.

Guilt that she had not examined his arm the previous night washed over her and she was angry at herself for failing him. Her own troubles were no excuse. While it looked as if she had caught the infection in time, she would know for sure in the morning. She cleaned her knife and ran it over a whetstone, then started preparing a replacement for the healing salve she had just applied, crushing herbs with her pestle and mortar and then letting them simmer in her smallest cauldron. As she worked, she kept looking at her stubborn father, who had trusted in his own strength rather than her skill and risked his life to avoid worrying her. She would have to keep a closer eye on him in future. Eventually, the salve was ready. She poured it into a jar and went to bed.

When she woke the next morning, Anike threw the shutters wide, allowing sunlight to illuminate the house. Darek was beginning to stir. Relieved that he had slept more soundly than he had for the last few nights and not wishing to interrupt his rest, Anike busied herself preparing food and allowed him to wake in his own time. The aroma of cooking soon roused him but he swayed as he got to his feet.

"Sit down, Father," she told him, and to her surprise, he did so without argument. Lifting his sleeve, she removed the bandage so she could examine the arm in the light of day. The skin was less red than the night before but the rotting centre was still a sickly greyish colour, almost white in places. Some of the dark marks had receded from the stump but Anike could now see they ran right into the side of his chest. In the daylight, she could also make out grey tracks running alongside them.

Anike bit her lip. She was too young to have seen her father's wound when he had first sustained it but she had treated a few others like it while working for Olaf. The pale tendrils showed that the old wound rot had recurred, no doubt triggered by the accident in the boat, and it had advanced further than she could cure with the salves she had to hand.

"Am I fit to go back to sea?" Darek asked, starting to rise. Anike put a hand on his chest and pushed him down.

"The only place you are going is to your bed, Father. You should have told me about this much sooner. I am going to see Olaf to get something stronger for you." She went to the table and found the potion to relieve pain. "Drink," she told him, handing him the flask. "This will give you some relief till I get back."

Darek swallowed the potion and grimaced. "Ale tastes better."

"Stay here, Father. You will be of little use on the boat until you are cured." She put a bowl of porridge in front of him. "Eat this," she told him firmly and watched him take a mouthful. "I will be back soon," she added and left the house.

Anger at her father gave way to apprehension as she crossed the town. While she had slowed the secondary infection and made her father more comfortable, the underlying rot had not responded to her treatment. Surgery would not work now that the decay had reached Darek's body. Fortunately, Olaf did have a potent recipe for wound rot and there was still time to use it.

It took a few minutes to reach Olaf's shop and Anike went in without knocking, calling her master's name. There was no answering call, just a thump and a happy bark as Fenris came out from the back of the shop. Anike scratched his head as she looked around. Olaf was not in the shop. She called again and crossed to the doorway leading into the living room. He was nowhere to be seen.

"Where is your master?" she asked Fenris, but the dog only licked her hand. She shrugged – no doubt he would return later and she could not wait. Olaf kept his most potent remedies in a chest, amongst them the particular elixir she needed, which he called the bloodseal potion. She opened the chest, which had been pulled out from its usual place tucked under a work table. There were fewer elixirs in it than she remembered and the potion she was looking for was not there at all. She looked through the jars and bottles again, taking them out one by one, then stood up and looked about her, puzzled. There were half a dozen cupboards, so she worked quickly and methodically through them, but the potion had not been misplaced. It had gone, as had many of Olaf's elixirs for treating wounds.

Anike had never brewed the bloodseal potion herself. It was rarely needed as most wounds could be healed in good time to prevent rot from setting in. She half-remembered that the recipe included some unusual ingredients. It seemed she did need to find her master.

Closing the door on a disappointed Fenris, Anike went to the neighbouring shop of Bledvan the potter. "Have you seen Olaf this morning?" she asked, as soon as the owner's face appeared in response to her urgent knocking.

"He went out earlier," Bledvan replied. "Quite a noise, there was. Siv came to see him. The ships that went to raid Lartenland have come back, and there were injured."

"So he went to the arlberg then? Or to the boats?"

"The hall. The wounded were being taken there when Siv came. There were a great many of them," he added grimly.

Anike thanked Bledvan and headed for the arlberg. She remembered the two boats that had set out for the south coast of Lartenland the week before. Raids, both ways across the narrow sea, were a fact of life for coastal towns. It was often easier to raid for stores and livestock than build them up at home, and raids gave opportunities to capture treasure, hostages and slaves. Injuries and death were common and returning raiders often received Olaf's attention, but many being taken straight to the arlberg suggested that the expedition had gone particularly badly. The timing of the raiders' return could not have been worse for her father.

Anike walked briskly through the open gates into the arlberg. The compound had been built by the dwarves for their governor before they had been driven back underground. It was the largest structure in the town and supposedly had remained essentially unchanged for over five hundred years. On one side were the stables, and on the other a wooden lean-to where most of the Arl's thralls lived. Ahead of her, the doors to the Arl's hall itself lay open and moans from injured raiders drifted out.

She followed the sounds down the short corridor and through a second doorway. The main chamber was over twenty feet wide and stretched ahead of her for about three times that distance. A cooking fire burned beneath a chimney at the far end. Stone arches supported the building's high roof and along one side was a raised recess upon which the Arl's throne stood. The walls were decorated with tapestries interspersed with trophies. The largest, a dire bear skull over three feet long, hung behind the throne and the pelt of the creature covered most of the floor of the recess. A large map of northern Gotlund dominated one wall.

Long tables normally took up most of the main floor but they had been pushed to the side and the seriously injured raiders were lying in the space created. There were nearly a dozen of them. Others from the boats stood around the large room, comforting friends, resting or just talking quietly. Olaf was next to one of the men lying on the ground, dressing a wound. Arl Svafnir was moving among the injured, speaking to each as he did so. The raid leader, Rogar Bjornsson, stood with Bjord and Siv in one corner. Anike could see from the number of wounded and the sombre mood in the room that the raid had gone very badly indeed.

Olaf finished with the warrior he had been tending and looked around. He saw Anike standing by the door and beckoned her over. She hurried up to him.

"Good," Olaf said. "I was about to send a thrall to fetch you. Start at that end and see what you can do." He pointed up the hall, then directed his attention to the next wounded raider.

Anike shifted nervously from foot to foot. Her father's condition was serious but men and women here could be in even more urgent need, and she could not let them die either. She looked through the potions and salves Olaf had brought, tallying them quickly and realised that the one she needed for her father was not amongst them, but the elixirs that did remain would help treat the raiders' wounds. Hoping that Olaf was carrying the bloodseal potion on him, she hurried down the hall to the last injured man.

The raider had a blood-soaked dressing on his leg. Whispering reassurances to him, Anike removed it. The cut was not deep and did not seem to be infected but it had bled profusely. She selected the right poultice from those that Olaf had brought and applied it. The flesh sealed before her eyes.

The next raider, a lean and muscled woman, was worse, with blood seeping from a deep spear wound in her side. Simple curing salves were of limited use on the most serious wounds, so she gave the warrior a potion to stabilise her. The woman would still need time to heal but the potion would ensure she would recover rather than die.

She worked her way down the line, dispensing remedies until she came to Olaf who was treating the last of the severely wounded. Anike joined him and held a dressing in place while he tied off a bandage. "Olaf," she began, "My father is ill. He had an accident and his old wound started to rot, but he hid it from me and the decay has advanced a long way. I need, I mean he needs, some of the bloodseal potion."

Olaf looked at her, his brow creased in a frown, "Anike, I am so sorry. I gave the last of it to one of the injured men earlier. I have none left."

"You must have another at home?"

"No, I don't think so." Olaf closed his eyes in concentration. "No, that was the only one I had made up."

Anike felt the blood drain from her face. She had been counting on Olaf and he had let her down. No, that was unfair. It was not Olaf's fault, but her own. It was she who had let her father down, who had failed to notice the signs until it was too late. If she had checked her father's arm earlier or even if she had been more cautious and gone to Olaf the previous night, the potion would still have been there.

She pushed away the clenching feeling that gripped her. "We can make some more," she said.

"Most of the ingredients are common enough and you probably have them in your bag, but this recipe needs the flowers of a particular plant, Freja's blossom. That I do not have, and it does not grow in the forest or by the shore. Freja's blossom is only found next to pools where the water has been churned under a waterfall."

Anike thought quickly, "The closest large waterfall would be at Vanir Heights. Does it grow there?"

"Yes, I have harvested Freja's blossom there before."

"If I leave now, I can be back before nightfall. How is the potion made? I want to start on it as soon as I get back."

Olaf gave Anike instructions. It was not a complex recipe to brew, once she had the missing ingredient.

"I have the rest of what I need. Olaf, I must go. I would stay longer to help here but my father will die if I do not get this potion to him, and these people have you."

"Darek is my friend, Anike. I can manage here. I wish you a safe and speedy journey."

It would be a hard walk, Anike knew. South of Trollgard the land rose sharply, and the waterfall at Vanir Heights was at the head of a ravine beyond the forest, where a mountain stream fell in a cascade from the steep cliffs above. It was further than she usually ventured and she would have to set a fast pace to get there and still be back before it became too dark to travel safely.

She had not planned on a hard journey when she left her house and was not prepared for it. She needed supplies and some equipment, and she had to tell her father what had happened so she headed home. Despite Olaf's assurance that he could cope, she still felt a pang of guilt on leaving the injured raiders but it paled in comparison with that caused by failing to check her father's arm earlier. She hoped that the extra day it would take to find Freja's blossom and brew the potion would not prove fatal.

Darek was huddled by the fire beneath layers of furs when she came in. He looked up at her, ale in his hand and an empty bowl of porridge at his feet. "Is that all the food I get today, Anike?" Despite his apparent need for warmth, Anike felt encouraged. A healthy appetite rarely went with the final stages of a fatal illness. She smiled and went to heat more porridge for him. There was time to save him.

"Father, there is a potion that will cure you but there is none in Trollgard right now. Rogar's boat came back last night and Olaf is still with the maimed and injured. There is no need to worry, though. He has told me how to make the elixir. I just need to gather some herbs."

"I am feeling much better now," her father protested.

"What I have given you so far is not a cure. It has only hidden the pain. You still need a proper remedy, and soon."

"Can't Olaf give me something himself?"

"I am sorry, there is nothing else he can do. I asked him." Anike sighed. "Olaf cannot travel so far, and the wounded men at the arlberg need him. This is the only way."

Darek looked at the floor. "How long will you be gone?" he asked.

Anike frowned, thinking about what to say. Worrying about her would not help his condition, and she would be gone for the whole day. "This recipe has quite a few ingredients, Father. It will take time to gather everything I need. I will be back by nightfall, I think."

"So late? How far do you have to go? I won't have you risking yourself doing something stupid for me. There could be another witch out there, or the dire wolves might find you."

"Witches are rare, and I am sure the wolves are far away by now. There is no real danger and I will be careful. I often go into the forest to gather herbs and I do know my way around." There could be some risk in the trek to Vanir Heights but if she didn't make it back it would not matter what she had told her father.

"Just make sure you stay safe," he said.

Anike was relieved. She had expected him to put up more of a fight. She hoped it was a side effect of the potion she had given him rather than a sign of the illness draining his strength.

"Let me see your arm again before I go." Anike pulled down his sleeve and removed the dressing. The darker lines of infection did not seem to have advanced since first light, but the grey rot was still expanding and Anike judged she had two days, three at the most, before her father's condition became irreversible. The sooner it was treated, the better.

She redressed the arm and kissed him on the forehead, then quickly packed her bag with supplies. The healing salve she had made the previous night went into it, together with some of her dry herbs, her pestle and mortar and her smallest cauldron, not much bigger than a cup. She tested the edge of her dagger, then fastened the sheath to her belt. "I will be back as soon as I can," she told her father and stepped outside, drawing her dark green cloak about her.

She headed for the south gate. The summer breeze had been replaced by much cooler air, threatening rain. As she passed through the market, she noticed that the wind had picked up and grey clouds were flowing in from the sea. Stall covers flapped and strained against their ropes as gusts caught them.

A firm hand fell on her shoulder, pulling her up short, and she turned to look into Bjord's face. "Where have you been, Anike? There are injured men and women who need your attention in the arlberg."

"Is that why you are following me? By the gods, Bjord, my father is dying. I need to go." She pulled out of his grasp and glared at him.

Bjord did not step back but raised his arms placatingly. "Dying? What do you mean?" he asked in a puzzled tone.

"His old wound has flared up. He had an accident working his nets and it has set off the rot again. He needs a particular potion, but Olaf has used the last of it on the raiders. I can make more but I need to find one rare herb for the recipe. Please do not try to stop me."

Bjord looked concerned. "Where does this herb grow?"

"Vanir Heights."

"But that's miles away, Anike. It's not a safe journey. The country is wild so far from the town. Don't you remember the dire wolves? They are still out there somewhere, and there could be other monsters."

"He is my father, Bjord. I have to go." Anike considered the threat of monsters to be an exaggeration. She threw back her hood and stared at him defiantly.

"I see that. I would do the same for my father." He paused. "I will come with you."

Anike stared at him. Her first reaction was one of astonishment but it quickly gave way to relief, mixed with both excitement and a warm feeling she could not quite identify. They had been much closer when they were younger, but coming into adulthood had brought distance and complication. Still, she was pleased and a little flattered that he wanted to be with her after the previous day's difficulty with the attempted kiss. She certainly did not want to insult him any further by refusing and it could be very useful to have Bjord with her to protect her if they did meet a monster. It would also be a chance for Bjord to appreciate her skill and determination. She wanted him to see her in a better light, not just as someone pretty who ran from witches. She was still unsure how, or even if, she wanted to develop the relationship but it made sense to spend some time with him and earn his respect.

She felt a little guilty to be thinking of herself. "All right," she said, "but I need to speak to Inge first. I want her to look in on my father while I am away."

Bjord nodded and they walked along the northern edge of the market until they reached the house Inge shared with her husband. They found her sewing cured rabbit pelts together outside it, a pile of finished clothes lying ready for sale on a table next to her. She looked up as Anike and Bjord came towards her and her eyes widened in surprise. A small smile touched her lips before vanishing at Anike's next words.

"My father is ill, Inge," Anike told her before explaining the situation. "Can you look in on him later, please? Make sure he eats and is not doing anything stupid, like going to his boat."

"Of course I will look after him, Anike, don't worry. Good luck." Inge glanced at Bjord, "With everything."

"Thank you," Anike said, taking her friend's hands in hers. "I will be back as soon as I can." She started to turn away.

"Anike, wait. Drakna found some dire wolf tracks in the forest, heading west. Please take care."

"Thank you, but I am not going that way. Don't worry, I will be coming back." She gave Inge a reassuring smile.

Anike and Bjord crossed the market heading for the south gate. As they reached it, Anike heard the sound of pounding feet behind them. Both she and Bjord turned to see Tavic approaching them at a run.

"Bjord, hold up!" he called. "Your father is asking for you."

Bjord scowled. "What does he want?"

"He didn't say," replied Tavic, coming to a halt in front of them, "but he was talking to Rogar. My guess is that it is something about the raid."

Bjord looked uncertainly between Tavic and Anike.

"Your father said to bring you quickly," Tavic added.

Bjord cursed under his breath. "Wait for me here, Anike," he decided.

Anike's cheeks coloured at Bjord's peremptory tone, but he and Tavic had already started back to the arlberg. She waited for a few minutes, quietly fuming. The delay chaffed at her, and Bjord's unthinking assumption that she would obey his order without question stung. Arl Svafnir would not be concerned about her father with so many of his raiders lying injured in his hall and might well be displeased when Bjord told him he planned to go with her. He could even forbid him to do so.

The wind was gusting more strongly now and only small patches of blue sky were showing between the clouds. Rain would make the steep walk even harder. She reached her own decision. Her father's life was at stake and she could not wait for hours until Arl Svafnir let Bjord go. Such a delay might mean she would not get back to town before it was too dark to travel. She doubted she would be in any real danger and at first she had intended to go alone anyway. Bjord could follow if he wanted.

Anike looked up at the darkening clouds gathered over the sea. In the distance, a flash of lightning lit them from within. Hoping to make progress before the weather worsened, she started out of the town gate and towards the forest.

- 5 -

Witch Weather

The first raindrops landed on Anike as she was crossing over the farmland near the town and she hurried onwards, drawing her cloak tightly around her and covering her head with the hood. By the time she reached the forest, it was raining in earnest.

She followed a small trail formed by the passage of animals and man over the years, but it was overgrown in these early summer months. Pushing past branches was tiring, and while a childhood of running and swimming had kept her fit, she still had to take a measured pace.

Her eyes were drawn to some bright yellow flowers growing in the centre of a clearing she was passing. She recognised them as jarl's roses, useful for sleeping draughts and potent to numb pain, and thinking of her father's discomfort, she stopped to pick them.

She allowed herself a short rest on a log. After a moment, large drops of water landed on her head as a gust of wind shook the branches above her, reminding her to move on. A sudden crack of thunder warned her that the storm had grown in strength. The trees gave some shelter, and she hoped the gale would blow itself out before she had to cross the open moor.

Eventually, she reached the ragged border between the trees and the rolling folds of harsh barren land rising in green and grey waves towards the mountain cliffs. Her hope for a break in the weather had been in vain. The storm had blown the thunderheads inland in a dark surge and lightning flashed within them where they lay covering the peaks. The rain fell in sheets, propelled by the cold north wind. Anike looked back over the forest towards the coast and saw no break in the clouds. It could be hours before the storm died away and she did not want to wait. She wrapped her cloak as tightly about her as she could, and started up the next rise.

Once she had left the shelter of the trees, the wind whipped past her, driving the rain into her back and a chill into her body. She crested a rise and lightning split the sky above her. A moment later, the crash of thunder struck her with almost physical force.

From the top of the next rise, she could see some buildings ahead of her and some way to the right of her course. A farm, she supposed, though she did not know who lived there. There was a large wooden longhouse, with several barns and some smaller dwellings clustered around it.

Anike considered changing direction to seek cover there until the storm eased. Both tradition and law required shelter to be given to travellers who came in peace, but she decided not to delay despite the lure of a warm hearth. The storm had already slowed her, making it doubtful that she would be back before dark, and she could accept some discomfort for the sake of not losing more time.

The force of the wind lessened as she descended into the lee of the rise, but the rain fell unabated. She picked her way down to the edge of a small stream which she jumped, but her foot slipped as she landed on wet stone. She fell to her right, landed hard and all the air rushed from her lungs. Her legs slid into the stream, and the cold water soaked her trousers.

Gasping, she pulled herself clear of the water. Her whole right side felt bruised and a sharp stab lanced through her chest as she clambered to her feet. Tentatively, she probed the tender area. There was some pain, but nothing seemed to be broken and she could still move.

She had the healing salve she had made the previous night but while the bruises were painful, they were not serious so she decided against using it. She did, however, need to rest and warm up. The storm showed no sign of abating so reluctantly she headed for the nearby farm. Safety now took precedence over speed. She had intended to be back by sunset, but if she pressed on and collapsed or fell it could be days before someone found her and by then it would be too late for her father.

The stream led up to the farmstead and walking next to it kept her at the bottom of a fold of land, out of the worst of the wind. She approached the outer buildings and stopped when she noticed a runestone near a path running between two large barns. Standing around three feet tall, it was typical of those used to mark a burial and though she could not read the runes, she knew they petitioned the gods to guide and protect a departed soul. The stone was weathered but had been kept clean, so she guessed it had been raised some years ago for a well-loved family member.

She walked through a gap between two of the outer buildings, hearing the familiar sounds of pigs, chickens and at least one cow coming from within. She could not see anyone outside, so it was likely the people were all sheltering from the storm.

Seeing the glow of a fire through gaps in the wooden walls of the largest building, she went to knock at the main entrance. There was a pause, then the door opened to reveal a grey-haired woman somewhat older than Olaf, shielding her face against the rain.

"I am seeking shelter from the storm. May I enter, Mistress?" Anike asked.

"Come in," said the woman, opening the door a little wider. "We would be honoured to offer you shelter."

"Thank you. My name is Anike Dareksdottir. I am a herbalist from Trollgard." She stepped over the threshold and the woman closed the door behind her.

"I am Volna Griseldasdottir, and this is my farm. Come in and warm yourself by the fire – you are soaked." She took Anike's cloak and hung it on a peg by the door.

Half a dozen people were gathered around a large fire at one end of the room. The inside of the building reminded Anike a little of the Arl's hall but on a smaller scale. A long table that could seat a dozen or so occupied the centre of the room and a hearty smell rose from a cauldron large enough to cook for a similar number.

The fire burned brightly, making a pleasant contrast to the storm outside.

"Welcome to my community," Volna said, walking up to the gathering and making shooing gestures. "Give our guest a little room." There was a quick shuffling and a space appeared next to the fire.

Anike approached gratefully, put up her hands to warm them and felt the heat slowly return to her body. Volna came to stand beside her.

"I will not trouble you long, Mistress Volna," Anike told her, turning to face her host and letting the fire warm her side. Beyond Volna, a boy of about seven was looking at her curiously and a man in his twenties standing next to him, probably the boy's father, was staring at her admiringly. He looked away in embarrassment when he realised Anike had noticed his gaze. The woman on his other side poked him hard on the shoulder. Anike returned her attention to Volna. "I will stay only while the storm is at its worst," she said.

"You should remain until it passes completely," Volna told her. "Rain can make these hills treacherous. People have been lost in weather like this."

Anike thought of the runestone at the edge of the farmstead. "Wise advice, Mistress, but I must press on as soon as I can. My errand is urgent." She turned again, allowing the fire to warm her back.

"It must be important to take you out in such weather."

Anike looked into Volna's kindly eyes, feeling touched by the older woman's concern. "It is," she said. "I have a pressing need to find some herbs." She steered away from mentioning her father, fearful of being overcome with emotion.

The fire had made her feel a little warmer and the pain in her side had eased slightly. She went to a window and peered out through the gap between the closed shutters. The lightning seemed to have stopped but rain was still falling and the wind tore at the roof. Volna came to stand beside her. "You are welcome to stay here as long as you need." The words were spoken with depth and feeling beyond mere courtesy and Anike turned away from the storm. "Perhaps a little longer. Thank you."

Custom required a guest to offer a host a gift in return for their hospitality, so Anike looked through her bag. "Mistress Volna, it is poor compensation for your kindness, but I would be honoured if you would accept this potion. It is made with maidensreed and will give you strength even if you are exhausted." Anike held out a small earthenware flask.

"Thank you, Anike." Volna accepted it and smiled at her. "Bruna, some stew for our guest, please."

A girl, a few years younger than Anike, took a bowl from a nearby table and filled it from the cauldron with a large spoon. Keeping her eyes down, she handed it to Anike and backed away.

Anike took the bowl gratefully, thanked the girl, and tried the stew. It tasted as good as it had smelled. Fish was the staple of her normal diet, so lamb was something of a treat and skilled use of herbs had given the stew a deep and subtle flavour. She ate it with relish and felt herself warming from the inside, strength spreading through her body.

"This is wonderful," said Anike. "I rarely use mint in my own cooking, but it goes very well with lamb." She took another mouthful. "Allow me to offer you some news from Trollgard." Anike told Volna about Gern and the trial. The other members of the community pressed in to hear, and Anike was pleased to have brought something interesting to them. She had misgivings about Arl Svafnir's treatment of her evidence and the abrupt punishment, but she wanted to put that behind her and presenting the tale to people who did not know her seemed a good way to start. Uncomfortable with her own role, she left that out.

"That is news indeed," said Volna, when Anike had finished. "May Thor protect us, and keep all witches away from our farm."

Anike finished the stew and the girl took the empty bowl. While she had been talking, the sound of rain had dropped to a light patter and she turned to Volna. "Thank you for your kindness and hospitality, Mistress, but I must be leaving now."

"Rain still falls. Will you not stay longer?"

"I will take my chances now, I think." Anike went to the door and looked out. The wind was still strong enough to sway bushes, but the rain was light. "I cannot wait for fine weather."

"It would be safer to stay a little longer," Volna urged her.

Anike shook her head. She thought of her father and how he would worry if she was not back by dark, but it would be much worse if he did not see her until the next day. "No, Mistress, I must press on. The storm has already delayed me, but I can still reach Vanir Heights and get back to Trollgard tonight."

"You might break your neck coming down the mountains in the dark, Anike, but if you must go, be careful. Remember that you are welcome to stop here on the way back to Trollgard if you need to." Volna laid a hand on Anike's shoulder. "Take some bread and stew with you anyway."

"Thank you, Volna. That is kind. I will take a little food but I hope to be well into the forest before dark, and I know that area well. My father is waiting for my return."

The little boy Anike had seen earlier came over with a closed jar, warmed by the stew inside it, together with a large hunk of bread. Anike put them both in her bag. "Freja's blessings on you, Mistress Volna," she said, taking her cloak from the peg and throwing it over her shoulders before stepping outside.

She had a moment's misgiving as she left the comfort of the farmhouse, but the weather had eased during her time in the farm and the falling rain no longer threatened to wash the ground from under her feet. Out over the sea, the clouds were starting to break up and small patches of sunlight sparkled on the waves.

Anike started up the hill again, setting a fast pace for the last leg of her trek and hoped the Freya's blossom would not take too long to find. She was confident she would not get seriously lost following the slope down to the sea on the way back but it would be easy to miss the best trail in the dark.

The rain had stopped completely by the time she reached Vanir Heights. From the crest of the small rise, she could see the waterfall tumbling down the cliffs over a hundred feet into the churning pool at its base, reflecting a multitude of lights in the sun that struggled through small gaps in the clouds. Anike paused to take in the beauty and grandeur of the scene. The water had carved out a steep-sided basin, and the stream flowed out from a pool at the bottom of it through a narrow cleft in the rise. Looking back towards the coast she could see the sea, now reflecting the blue of the sky as the clouds chased each other towards the mountains, though Trollgard itself was hidden by the folds of the land. High above her, an eagle circled, its harsh cry cutting through the sound of the tumbling water.

She tried to make out if there was any Freja's blossom by the cliff at the far side of the pool, but saw to her dismay that a black bear had claimed the area. It stood motionless in the stream, one paw raised as it waited for a fish to come within its reach. The beast was large, with a thick coat, but it looked a little thin.

Anike drew back out of sight, then moved cautiously forward until she reached the side of the ravine near the pool. She crawled the last few feet and peered over the edge. The floor of the basin was around thirty feet below her and, though not sheer, the sides of the ravine were wet from the rain and steep enough to make a climb difficult.

The bear's paw suddenly struck down into the water. It moved with surprising speed but still came up empty. Bears did not usually attack humans but she could not risk searching for flowers with such a large and hungry predator in the enclosed area. The animal growled, a deep rumbling sound, and moved around to a different part of the pool. As it did so, it sniffed the air and its head came round towards her. Anike froze, trying to steady her breathing, but the bear made no move to approach. She saw that it was limping, keeping its weight off its right hind leg. This would probably slow it down, but she knew that a wounded animal could become hungry and desperate. A large predator hampered by injury sometimes found people easier prey. Fighting it was out of the question, particularly as she was only armed with a knife. It was far too big and strong for her and while Bjord might have battled it successfully alone, even he would have been at some risk. Anike knew that predators did sometimes retreat from aggressive prey to avoid sustaining injury – she had once seen Fenris back off from a cornered cat – but she doubted that that would work in this case. The bear was already hurt and likely to take any chance for a meal.

It was no good wishing she had waited for Bjord. She was on her own, and she needed to find a way to get past the creature. Looking up, Anike could see the sun amongst the remnants of the storm clouds and realised it was mid-afternoon. Unless she devised a plan quickly, she would still be trying to avoid the bear in the dark.

She could not match such a beast physically but she might be able to outwit it. She observed it pacing the edge of the pool from the safety of the top of the cliff. It was clear the wound did hamper it. The sides of the basin were steep but they were rough with ample foot and hand holds. Anike could scale them, and bears were usually as capable climbers as humans. While the rains earlier in the day had made an ascent more difficult, it had been dry for days before and the bear had not left the pool. Anike felt certain that its injury was preventing it from getting back onto the moor, so luring it away was not going to be an option. She would have to use trickery.

Anike took the jarl's rose she had picked earlier out from her bag. The bear was bigger than a man but she had enough to make a sleeping potion that could bring it down. It took her a while to find some moss on the bluff near the ravine that had been sufficiently sheltered from the rain to remain dry but eventually she gathered enough for a fire. She ground down the yellow flowers with her pestle and mortar and added a few dried herbs for catalysts to make a paste. The mixture went into her tiny cauldron and she struck sparks until the moss caught alight. She watched as the yellow colour deepened to rich gold, then scraped the finished pulp out of the cauldron with a wooden spoon before it burned.

While she would have liked to trap a rabbit for bait, it was still too light for them to leave their burrows and she needed an alternative. She took out the bread Volna had given her and poked a hole in it so she could press the golden paste inside, then crushed the sides of the loaf together again, trapping the sleeping draught within. The whole hunk of bread went into the lamb stew and she turned it over and over until the bread smelt as good as the stew itself.

Going back to the edge of the basin, Anike judged the distance to the bear. It was too far away for her to throw the bread to it so she needed to get closer. Hoping that the creature would continue to pay her little attention, Anike started to descend the small cliff, intending to approach quietly until she was close enough to make the throw.

She kept a close watch on the bear as she made her way downward, ready to climb back up if it approached. When she was halfway down, it looked around and growled. Startled, she felt her foot slip on a wet stone and she tumbled the rest of the way down the slope, dropping the bread as she did so.

Pain shot through her chest from her second fall of the day but she fought it back and rolled to her feet. The bear had started towards her. A surge of panic rose inside as she looked for a way out. There was little room to run and she dismissed diving into the pool. Bears were excellent swimmers. Her back was to the cliff and while she could climb it, the animal would be on her before she was out of its reach. Even hampered by its injured leg, the creature was approaching fast.

She could see only one chance. She grasped the edges of her cloak with both hands and raised it high above her head, spreading her arms as wide as she could and yelled at the bear, venting her fear and frustration in incoherent words which boiled out towards the approaching animal.

The bear slowed and responded to Anike's display as a threat. Roaring, it reared up onto its hind legs with its claws bared. It towered over her and she realised just how large it was. She held her pose, fighting against the instinct to cower, terrified that she had misjudged its strength and resilience.

The bear opened its jaws wide, then toppled sideways, its injured leg unable to support its weight. Anike had turned before it struck the ground and by the time she heard the crash of its body landing, she was already scrambling up the side of the cliff. Below her, the beast struggled to its feet, looked up and roared at its departing meal, unable to follow with its injured leg.

Anike reached the top of the cliff and pulled herself over the edge, panting. The bear had put its front paws on the lower rocks, ready in case she slipped and fell within its reach. Seeing that she had reached safety, it gave a final roar and dropped its head. It sniffed and turned towards the savoury smell of the fallen bread. Anike watched as it nuzzled cautiously at the food and then opened its mouth to gulp it down. She sighed in relief as with a final growl the creature ambled back to the pool. The bear reached the edge of the water, and then gently folded its legs beneath it, its head dropping to rest between its paws. She watched it until its breathing slowed.

More carefully this time, she climbed down and started circling the pool to search for the white bloom of Freja's blossom, keeping a cautious distance from the snoring black animal. A few small silver-scaled fish darted away as her shadow fell on the water, meagre fare for a bear even if it did catch them. The bear shifted. Anike froze, but it was only settling itself in a different position and her herbcraft kept the beast slumbering.

After five anxious minutes, she found a patch of Freja's blossom almost under the waterfall, partly hidden by the spray. She quickly picked most of the plants, leaving a few to grow and re-seed. She had enough for the potion her father needed, with plenty to spare for Olaf's remedies for some time to come.

The bear was still snoring peacefully and Anike was struck again by how thin it was. The wound must have trapped it in the ravine for some time. The fish in the pond would not satisfy it for much longer and she did not like to think of such a magnificent animal dying slowly of starvation.

Anike laid a hand on the hilt of her knife. Most people she knew would kill the bear now, to put it out of its misery or to forestall any possible future threat, but Anike could not hurt a helpless animal. Carefully, she approached it and looked at the wound. It was a deep set of several cuts close to the body, and judging by the close spacing they had been made by a single claw. Anike supposed that it had been attacked by another bear, an even larger one, and it had been worrying at the wound, slowing its healing.

Anike tentatively touched a leg. The animal stirred but did not wake, so she took the healing salve she had made the night before from her bag. The bear was not a man-eater yet, and if it was able to get to open ground, it would be able to forage once again.

As she spread the salve, the flesh and torn muscle started to knit before her eyes. There was not enough to close such a large wound entirely, but she was confident that the healing had started and the bear would be able to clamber free before it starved to death. Satisfied, she climbed the wall of the ravine and started back down the slope towards the forest.

The sun had just dropped behind the shoulder of the mountain range. She could reach the forest before it was fully dark but would have to pass through most of it in the night, which was not an appealing prospect. Dealing with the bear had delayed her and she began to reconsider Volna's offer of overnight hospitality.

She had not gone far when she saw Bjord coming across the moor towards her. "Anike!" he called out, and his pace quickened. He was still damp from the rain but seemed untroubled by it. He was a welcome sight after the bear and she changed direction to walk towards him. She was surprised, and also relieved as she had not been looking forward to making the journey home in the dark alone. A flash of pleasure that he had followed her despite her precipitous departure from Trollgard ran through her too.

"Are you safe?" Bjord asked when they were close enough to hear each other. "When I couldn't find you at the gate, I thought you might have gone home to wait for me." His face flushed in anger. "I didn't believe you had just left after I told you to wait. You were stupid to come out here alone."

Anike's good mood evaporated at Bjord's words. "I had no idea how long you would be gone, and my father's life was in the balance. I had to go, with you or without you," she snapped. "I did not need you, Bjord! I found the herbs I was after and I defeated a bear in the process, all without you!"

If anything, Bjord's expression became darker. "You fought a bear?" he asked, his face showing disbelief and anger. "You?"

"Of course not. I am not an idiot. I tricked it." Anike forced herself back to some sort of calm before she said something she would regret later. "I found it in the ravine by the waterfall. I put it to sleep with a potion and sneaked past it."

"Anike, are you mad?" Bjord clearly did not feel the same urge to curb his temper. "You could have been killed."

A slight tremor in his voice betrayed the fear that drove his angry words. She was flattered that he was so concerned for her safety but considering that she was standing before him with her task completed, she had hoped for some sign of respect. Pride in her success overcame her instinctive reaction to apologise.

"I may not have your sword arm, but I do have my wits," she said in firm measured tones. "I saw that it had a weakness, and I used that against it."

"What weakness?"

"It was trapped in the ravine for one thing, and it had a deep cut on one of its legs from a fight with another bear. The injury hampered it, so I was able to outmanoeuvre it and put it to sleep with my herbs."

"You finished it off, I trust?"

"Of course not."

"So it is injured and asleep? You fool! You should have killed it while you had the chance. Injured predators are a threat to my people. We have to hunt them down before they attack foresters and farmers."

"I know that, but I cured it so when it wakes up it will be able to hunt wild prey again."

"You did what?" Bjord looked at her in astonishment. "What in Odin's name got into you? Wait here while I go to deal with the mess you have created. Don't go anywhere this time. I mean it."

He turned away, loosening his sword in its sheath and unhooking his shield from his back. As he turned towards the waterfall, Anike heard him mutter "Why did I have to fall for someone so soft-hearted?"

Anike was sure that it was only Bjord's anger that had let those words escape him but before she could consider the implications or even try to stop him, the whole world grew dark. She looked up and saw clouds forming out of nowhere with terrifying speed directly over their heads, like black dye dropping into water. There was a rushing noise and then the sky seemed to boil as the clouds were lit from inside with a red glow. Lightning flashed. This was witch weather, omen of disaster. As the thunder crashed all around, her heart leapt to her mouth. She was sure that this foretold the death of her father, just as her mother had died after another such storm at the time of her birth.

Lightning flared again, no longer far above them in the sky, but striking the cliffs and the moor all around. Anike covered her ears against the thunder as bolts ignited the grass nearby, and she saw Bjord draw his sword in an act of defiance. Between crashes, she heard an eagle cry out in agony mingled with the bear's roars of pain and fury.

Bjord's sword was trembling in his hand as he stared fixedly at the sky. She followed his gaze up to the chaos above them. Dropping through the pulsating clouds was a ball of lightning – or was it fire? Around the size of a shield, it burned with searing colours, changing between white, electric blue, crimson, and blazing orange so fast that the eye could not follow. It plunged like a diving hawk, but instead of striking the ground, it came to a sudden halt and hovered a few feet above the earth some twenty paces from them. It hung there like a piece of the sun, brilliant and terrible, then as if sensing a target, flew straight at Bjord.

Bjord's sword fell from his hand as he stared at the oncoming ball of energy, his mouth dropping open. Anike flung herself at him and he staggered two paces but she found herself in his place, directly in the path of the scintillating sphere of energy. She barely had time to cover her face with her hands before the world exploded.

- 6 -

VEIL OF FIRE

Anike was surrounded in all directions by fire and lightning. There were no mountains, no sun, not even a sky. She stood on billowing clouds of smoke shot through with flashes of light. A savage wind tore at her bare skin and whipped her long hair into her face. Heat from the flames beat at her naked body and her nerves seemed to dance in response to the play of the lightning. She thought she could see faces forming in the fire and smoke and then dissolving instants later, and the wind lashing at her carried echoes of voices. Wherever she looked, flames, lightning and smoke cascaded, the patterns in constant flux.

This could not be Midgard, the realm of men, but neither did it seem to be Hel's domain of Niflheim. Stories painted the afterlife for those who did not die in battle in shades of grey, a dark and dismal realm of stone, silent save for the whisper of ghosts pining for their lost lives, but this place was fury given form. It was how she had imagined Muspelheim, the kingdom of Surtur, the fire giant who had covered the northern islands of the Archipelago in flames during the battle of Ragnarok.

The blaze rose in a roaring wave and crashed over her, blistering her face and flesh and an arc of lightning transfixed her, sending her body into a spasm. The wind whirled around her faster and faster, drawing the fire and smoke into a vortex of destruction focused on her.

Anike opened her mouth to cry out and the energy rushed into her, stifling her voice, burning her lungs, searing her heart and spreading throughout her being to leave her charred to the very core. At last, she was able to scream.

The agony passed and she was left naked and cold, floating in a black void with nothing to see, hear, or touch. She waited for Hel, goddess of death, to appear. Her life had ended, and she would spend forever in this cold, dark place with nothing to look forward to and nothing to worry about. She would never find out whether Bjord had actually loved her or what that meant. She would not hear Olaf's instructions again, or the silver sound of Inge's laughter. She would never save her father.

After an indefinite period, it might have been minutes or days, she perceived a change in the void around her. The blackness faded to an ash-grey hue, like smoke without heat or substance, but with an impression of movement. She had a sense that there was something hidden from her, as if behind a veil. Fear of the unknown, primal and sharp, flared in her but with it came renewed will. There was something there, something she could try to touch and if she could reach it she might be able to find a way home. Perhaps all was not lost, either for her or for her father.

A spark, fuelled by anger, despair and hope, lit inside her and started to grow. Her father did not deserve to die. It was wrong, unfair. She would not accept that her choice to save Bjord from the ball lightning had doomed him. Rage at the injustice of that fate blossomed inside her, crystalising into determination and driving back the despair. She had will and now she had purpose, even in this void. Light radiated from her heart. It cut through the grey haze which wavered and faded, then blew away like smoke before a storm. The shapes it had concealed solidified and then snapped into focus revealing a scene of ashes and destruction.

She was standing in a burning building. Flames licked at the wooden walls and wrapped around the beams like serpents. The roof above her was ablaze. Anike could taste the smoke, and the heat of the flames beat at her but she seemed strangely detached from the sensations. Through the haze she could just make out a large room, somehow familiar, and a figure struggling towards a door to escape the fire. She had no idea how she had come to be there and even before she perceived the room clearly, she was already feeling waves of rage course through her at the thought of being confined.

The roof near the door collapsed, and the figure she could dimly see fell with a scream as a blazing beam landed on top of him. Her way out was blocked, and her sense of being enclosed by the structure around her intensified. She turned, seeking another exit.

A man came charging at her out of the smoke with an axe raised to strike at her. She recalled when she had last seen him, staring at her over his son's head as they stood by Volna's hearth. She felt no fear or surprise, only frustration that he was trying to stop her and contempt for his stupidity in attacking her. "Wind!" she said and gestured at him, conjuring a blast of air which lifted him off his feet and sent him flying across the room. She heard the crack as he struck the wall, and he crumpled to the ground, his head hanging at an unnatural angle.

Satisfied, Anike disregarded the body. The heat around her intensified as the flames ran together to cover the walls and roof. While painful, it was somehow distant and unworthy of any concern. She felt alive, every nerve tingling with power.

The building around her aggrieved her by its very presence, so she turned to face the closest wall. "Fire!" she commanded, and a door-sized area burst into white-hot flames and turned to ash. She stepped through the gap into the cold night air.

The burning longhouse lit the entire area and Anike could see it was the farmstead where she had met Volna. Figures, illuminated by the beautiful, flickering orange light, were running about gathering buckets to fight the flames, while others stood wailing, calling out the names of friends and family. They were insignificant to her as individuals, but watching their frantic movements in panic and confusion pleased her.

Behind the people, the high and solid structures of the other buildings of the farmstead loomed against the stars. They had been constructed to organise and compartmentalise the humans who lived here. Without understanding why she now felt that way, the constraints and order they represented repulsed her and Anike raised her arms and swept them in a wide arc. "Fire!" she said again, sending

THE DEMON AND THE WITCH

a swarm of tiny flames from her hands to the other buildings. Where they struck, roof and walls burst into flame and she laughed as the blaze spread through the structures. People shouted and ran, some trying to escape the fire, some filling buckets from the stream. The scene had a dream-like quality with flickering light, frightened and frantic calling by the animals, the panic of the humans and the crash of buildings collapsing as they succumbed to the flames. Anike felt that she had never seen anything more beautiful.

A figure approached from out of the flickering shadows, sword and shield raised and she turned to face it, and part of her recognised it as Bjord. His eyes were wide, and his face was set in an expression of determination as he cautiously advanced. Behind him a barn collapsed with a roar of flame, illuminating the area with a sudden orange glow which lit up her face.

"Anike?" Bjord said, hesitating as he recognised her. "You are doing this? How?"

Anike regarded him with disdain. How dare he challenge her? He had no right even to ask her questions. Memories of him flitted through her mind, and in each one she saw how flawed he was and how he had mistreated her by trying to force unwelcome attentions on her or giving her orders expecting unthinking obedience, just because of the rules of the castes. He did not respect her and it was time for him to see how wrong he had been.

"Lightning!" she cried, and a bolt leapt from her raised hand to strike Bjord full in the chest. He was engulfed in a ball of dazzling blue electricity, arcs dancing between his body and the ground. He screamed, and fell hard, twitching for a moment and then lay still. Anike smiled and stepped past his body.

When she reached a clear space she slowly turned to survey her handiwork, exulting in the power flowing through her and in the destruction she had wrought. The fire was spreading, and while it did not look as if there were enough men with buckets to get it under control, she preferred not to let them try. She picked a man running from the stream carrying water as her next target but before she could act, a voice came from beside her. "We have done nothing to hurt you, we sheltered you. Please stop, Anike, before anyone else suffers."

Her attention distracted, she turned to see Volna, cradling a young child against her chest. She was looking at Anike with dazed incomprehension.

Anike started to shape her power to burn the woman but part of her resisted, unsure of why she needed to destroy Volna, who was only concerned about her home. This woman had been nothing but kind to her and even now, as Anike stood before her, reducing to ashes what she and her family had spent years building, there was no anger in her voice, just baffled puzzlement. Anike remembered Volna's smiling face, her kind tone, her welcome from the fury of the storm and her generosity in insisting that Anike leave with food. There was nothing about her to hate or for Anike to direct her anger against.

As this realisation struck her, it was as if a blaze within was doused. The power that had coursed through her retreated to deep inside and she felt as if a veil of fire and smoke had lifted from her eyes. The scene was unchanged, but instead of seeing beauty in the flames and feeling a sense of achievement as buildings fell, she saw pain, fear, and loss. Guilt overwhelmed her as she looked round in horror from Bjord's body on the ground to the collapsing homes and Volna's distressed face. It was she who had done all this, though she could no longer understand how, nor could she even remember why she had wished it.

"I... I am so... forgive me!" she cried, knowing how empty the words must sound. Tears streamed down her face as she turned and ran into the night, trying to escape what she had done. She ran until she could run no more, then threw herself on the ground, sobbing. She had not only killed Bjord and the man with the axe, who surely had a wife and child, but probably others in the burning buildings too. She had destroyed Volna's home. Sorrow and pain welled up inside her, but beneath everything she could still feel a centre of power pulsing like a second heart, something that had not been there before but now threatened to erupt and bring more destruction.

She knew she had enjoyed what she had done while she was doing it, but now she could not imagine how she had felt that way. She was horrified by her acts, but it was as if that core of power inside her had cast a light that made her see the destruction differently. As her thoughts touched that energy, it seemed to glow, illuminating some of her memories and shading others, and once more she started to find beauty in the chaos she had wrought. Her body started to tingle with power.

Unsettled and alarmed by this shifting in her perceptions, Anike focused her will on the glow, trying to quench it. As she concentrated, the fire within her dimmed, the feeling of power subsided and the sense of exaltation that had come with it faded away, giving way to dismayed horror.

She embraced the pain. She did not want to view what she had done through the haze of the power glowing within her, to feel happy about the devastation she had caused. The core of energy pulsed but for the moment the barricade of her will kept it in check. She still could feel the faint tingle in her nerves but staring into the cold clear night sky she found more strength to keep it dormant.

The change within her was stark and the obvious cause was the ball of lightning striking her. As her thoughts touched the memory of the blazing sphere, the throb of energy inside her grew stronger and more insistent, supporting her belief that there was a connection, a link between it and the power. She calmed herself and smiled grimly into the darkness. Whether the fireball had brought power or merely awakened something that had always been buried deep within her, there was little doubt it had wrought a profound and disturbing transformation, the rise of a new dark force.

With a chill, Anike understood that she was now a witch. Worse, her witchcraft had killed at least two men. She had caused more harm than Gern, though like him she had ultimately come to her senses. The irony that she had tried to understand Gern's motives and now found herself in his place was not lost on her, even in the despair of her realisation.

Bjord must have carried her all the way to Volna's farm, not realising that he had been bringing its doom. Her instinct was to return to help

Volna and her family but it would do no good to go back there now. They would kill her, or at the very least capture her and take her to Trollgard to face the Arl's justice.

Her return to sanity had been too late to save Bjord. She was still numb, appalled by all she had done but while she could not change any of that, she still could cure her father. She had time to get home and make the potion he needed and shouldering her bag again, she set off downhill towards the forest.

- 7 -

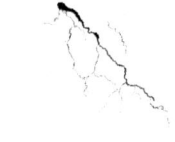

healing

By the position of the stars, Anike could see that it was after midnight. She must have been unconscious for hours while Bjord carried her to seek help, before waking in the midst of the conflagration. She had no recollection of starting the fire but she did not doubt that the energy simmering within her was the cause. She sought something to help her remain in control and looking into the cold depths of the night sky seemed to help. She felt the sea of fire inside subside a little though it still ebbed and flowed, barely contained by her body and mind.

The parallel between her behaviour and Gern's was obvious so she presumed a similar encounter had turned him into a witch too. He had lived deep in the woods, and witch weather far from the town might have gone unnoticed, particularly if it had been overcast. She supposed he really had been as normal as he had seemed until this power from the sky had intruded, unlooked for and unwelcome.

Gern had been executed for less than she had done. That would likely be her fate too, once news of what happened reached Trollgard, but right now she still had the chance save her father. She quickened her pace.

Once within the forest, the moon was hidden by the leaves. The trees pressed in all around her, looming and solid, making her feel enclosed and surrounded. On edge, she proceeded more cautiously, alert for the slightest noise. A hoot came from above her head and she looked up, startled. For an instant, the pale plumage of an owl glinted like ice in the moonlight and she was suddenly overwhelmed by an elemental hatred. "Fire!" she said, and the owl became a torch. It screeched and tumbled to the ground, feathers burning and turning black as it fell. Anike felt alive at the act, her body almost aglow.

As the flames subsided, the forest seemed to close in on her, oppressive and confining. "Fire!" she said again, and the nearest tree lit up like a giant brand. She watched the tongues of flame run up the trunk and into the branches, smiling as the tree charred and crumbled to ash, but her delight at the destruction of the owl and the tree confused her. She had always lived in harmony with the forest and her work was dedicated to saving life. Her emotions were now in utter contradiction with her thoughts and morality. Unable to reconcile how she was feeling with the person she believed herself to be, she concentrated, remembering her joy at the beauty of white blossom on the trees in spring. As the memory came into focus, the haze over her perceptions cleared. The energy receded into her core, and once again she felt disgust at what she had done.

Anger, hatred and fear seemed to be connected to the awakening of power within her, making her see things in a different light, a light coloured by fire and fury. She needed to keep these emotions in check before they took over and let the destructive energy out but it was hard because the power that coursed through her seemed to have burned new channels for her feelings. Things that had never troubled her in the past now seemed hostile and threatening.

A couple of years before, she had eaten a bluecap mushroom and for hours afterwards the world had been a place of fragmented light where the only thing that seemed important had been the sensation of the moment. Olaf had caught her tasting herbs at random and trying to feed them to Fenris, without caring that they both might die, and he had had to watch her for hours until she came back to her senses. In many ways, this felt similar. Her will seemed to have been weakened and her first instinct now seemed to be to destroy what she did not like. She sought an anchor from her past to fortify her old personality but the image of Bjord falling back as the lightning bolt hit him intruded, disrupting her search for a positive memory. For all his faults, Bjord had tried to do what was right when it mattered. She had killed her childhood friend, who would not now grow into the

THE DEMON AND THE WITCH

Arl he had been born to be. Anike cried for the man who was lost and for what she had done. Remorse and sorrow filled her and she sobbed freely. The tears quenched the fire inside her, reducing it to a glowing ember.

After she had cried herself out, she stood up, wiped her eyes and started through the forest again. She made her way downhill, but as she walked she thought about whether she really ought to stay in Trollgard. While she had to get the Freya's blossom back, remaining afterwards did not seem like a good idea. She had given her name to Volna, who would surely soon be coming to demand justice from Svafnir for all the deaths at her hands, including that of Bjord. Of course, she could solve this by going back to kill Volna and her family with witchcraft and so keep her secret. Even as this idea came into her mind, tempting in its simplicity and possibility of more destruction, she felt the heady rush of power. With the awareness of this sensation, she recognised the gulf between her old self and someone who needed the merest excuse to kill, and she faced the warped desire directly. It faded, but this thought process had highlighted the real problem. She was a danger to those around her. The power seemed ready to burst out at any moment and as she had no idea how she had shaped it into fire and lightning, she did not know how to stop it.

If she were to live in Trollgard again, she would have to do something to stop herself from unleashing it, ideally to rid herself of it entirely. She doubted that would be an easy or quick process, and she would have to find a way to suppress or control it in the meantime. What she had done was really an accident, she told herself. She wanted to believe that it was not truly her fault, but the townsfolk would never trust her if they knew what she was and what she had done. While she might, just possibly, be able to bluff convincingly enough to save her life in the face of Volna's accusations, suspicion would remain and her first slip would be enough to hang her. Anike shuddered at the thought of a rope around her neck but at the same time felt a surge of rage at the idea that ordinary people might dare to judge her.

She pushed that anger away, realising it was tainted with arrogance born of the power inside her. She was relieved that she had recognised the dark influence before she had hurt anyone else. She could stay in command of her thoughts and emotions while she remained alert and focused. Keeping her attention on the cold night sky above her seemed to help, but it was difficult to stop her mind's eye from sliding back to the burned farm. She felt waves of flame surge inside her, rekindled by the memory of invoking her power. Stopping and breathing deeply, she realised how easily the strange desire to destroy could creep up on her. She calmed herself and the flames within her dimmed. Anike felt she had taken the first steps towards controlling the force, giving her some confidence. She would have to adjust to her potential to perform acts of wanton destruction but hoped that, with time and practice, she would be able to suppress the dark urges entirely.

Allowing the cold of the night to slow the pulse within her, she walked through the forest back to the town. She wondered again if the fire from the sky had given her this power, or whether it had always been there, hidden in her soul behind barriers which had been burned away, taking her inhibitions with them. However it had come about, quite how she had channelled the energy was a mystery to her now. It seemed that some instinct was triggered when the power surged, enabling her to shape it into destructive forms. In her current calmer state, she had no idea at all how she had tapped into or directed it and she had no wish to experiment.

In the distance behind her, branches snapped as some large night creature made its way through the trees, but the noises grew ever fainter as she walked on.

Dawn was breaking when she emerged from the forest. She was cold, but she almost relished the feeling as it quelled the fire inside her. Looking at Trollgard starting to awaken as the first fingers of colour lit the sky, she patted the bag to check that the herbs were safe and set off over the farmland separating the town from the trees.

The gates were being unbarred for the morning as she reached them, and Anike pushed through a small scatter of people and made her way into the stone town. She became acutely aware of the houses surrounding her, so rigid and so similar, and felt a vague unease. She wondered how she had managed to live within such confinement, both from solid stone pressing in from all sides and by the bonds of law and tradition. She did not notice how novel this line of thought was until she became conscious of a growing desire to shatter the town walls. Only then did she recognise it as coming from the change in viewpoint insinuated into her mind by the power inside. She fought down the disquiet while she headed back to her house.

Entirely oblivious to the monumental events that she had been through, the early risers were preparing the market for the day. Anger flashed at their ignorance and indifference but she caught the feeling and calmed herself. She had never been so much on edge as she was now, but even hot-tempered Bjord had found ways to reign in his anger. She could learn to do the same.

Her house seemed reassuringly ordinary when she reached it. Opening the door, she found Inge inside cooking breakfast. "Anike!" the young woman exclaimed. "What happened to you? Your hair... Where have you been?" Inge put down the bowl of porridge she was holding and came towards her friend, her face full of concern. Anike had forgotten her own singed hair and smoke-stained clothes and had not even considered how she appeared. She closed the door behind her and turned to Inge to answer but her eyes were drawn to the cooking fire which was dancing in a beautiful interplay of flames. She stood transfixed with delight until a loud snore from above brought her back to reality, informing her that her father was both alive and asleep. She shook her head to clear it.

"Never mind that now, Inge. I am back."

"We were worried when you didn't return last night. What happened to you?"

"I had some bad luck." She wanted to stop there, but Inge's expression remained shocked and curious, so she swallowed and continued. "I had to shelter in a farm up in the hills, and there was a fire. I barely got out." She felt guilty for being evasive, but this was not the time to go into the cause of the fire and she could decide what to say about that when her father was better. "The important thing is that I have the herbs I need and I can prepare the potion now."

Anike could hear the steady sound of her father breathing so knew that he was still asleep. She climbed onto his platform and laid a hand on his forehead. It was far too hot for her peace of mind. She pushed back the bedding and lifted his sleeve. His arm looked worse, with dark lines re-establishing themselves and the grey skin even paler. She had returned in time, but not by much. Returning to the floor she went to the barrel and emptied the last of its water into a small cauldron which she hung over the fire to heat.

"Can I help?" asked Inge.

"Just watch this and take it off when it boils," Anike told her.

The mesmerising dance of the flames still tugged at her but while her father may have spent hours staring into them, it had not been her habit to do so. She sensed that this delight in fire was not a feeling to be trusted, particularly when it distracted her at such a crucial time. She pulled her gaze away and moved to her work table, taking out the Freya's blossom from her bag.

"Is that it?" asked Inge. "Is that what you went to find?"

Anike turned on her sharply at the stupid question. Inge took a step backwards at Anike's expression, and tripped. Her arm caught the poles that supported the cauldron and they collapsed with her to the ground, spilling water onto the floor. Anike felt a sudden urge to destroy the clumsy girl, to obliterate her so that she could not interfere any more.

She raised her arm to direct the power surging through her but horror at what she was about to do made her deny the impulse and she thrust the temptation away. Her vision seemed to clear. "I am so sorry, Inge," she went on more gently, bending over her friend with her arm still extended, but opening her hand to help her up.

Inge looked at her and hesitantly took the proffered hand. Anike pulled her to her feet. "Forgive me, please. I have hardly slept, and I am so worried. Are you hurt?"

"No, I am fine," replied Inge. She dusted herself down. "I do understand how hard this is for you," she said reassuringly.

Anike fought down a surge of resentment at the presumption that this girl could understand what she was going through. Inge was not safe yet, she realised. "Thank you." She fought to keep any trace of hostility out of her voice. "You are a better friend than I deserve at the moment."

The apology rang hollow against the growing sense of frustration and anger at the delay Inge was causing her. Unsure that she could contain the power if something else went wrong, she decided to get Inge out of the house. "There is only a tiny bit of water left. I will use that, but can you get some more from the well, please?"

Inge nodded. "Of course." She picked up the bucket and went out, smiling sympathetically back at Anike as she did so.

Anike watched her go and set the cauldron up again. A little water had remained in the base and she judged there was still enough for the potion. Once again her attention was caught by the tongues of flame dancing over the wood, slowly consuming it. She wished it could burn hotter and brighter, boil the water faster and make up for lost time. More flames were always a good thing.

"Fire!" she commanded, and the hearth exploded. The cauldron was flung into the air and burning wood shot in all directions. The brands struck the stone walls, leaving black soot marks. One fell onto her father's sleeping platform, still alight. Appalled at what she had done, the attraction of fire evaporated and she rushed to his bed to grab it.

Her father blinked sleepily at her as she hurled the brand onto the floor. "Sorry, I scattered the fire when I tripped," Anike muttered.

"You are back," Darek said groggily. "I was worried about you."

Anike laid a hand on his good arm. "I am sorry I took so long. There were some delays, but I have the herbs I need now and I can brew your potion," Darek tried to rise and she moved her hand to his chest to stop him. "Rest, Father, it is not ready yet."

Darek nodded and clasped Anike's hand. "It is good to have you back but please try to avoid getting either of us burnt again." He sank back into the furs.

Anike smiled weakly and went back down to the floor. She collected the wood and rebuilt the fire, deliberately concentrating on it as a mere tool rather than allowing herself to reflect on its beauty again. She had just hung the cauldron over it when Inge returned with a large bucket of water.

Inge looked at the scorch marks and Anike suppressed the irritation she felt at the scrutiny. "There is no need to worry. I just tripped," Anike told her crisply. "It is harder to concentrate when the work is for someone you love. Could you heat the water, please?"

As Inge filled the cauldron, Anike turned to her work table. While the water boiled, she cut the flowers of the Freya's blossom away from the stems then mixed them with other herbs, measuring each one precisely. Focusing on the task helped quiet her emotions. She added the mixture to the steaming water and counted silently, then poured a ladle-full into a small jar and stirred it twice one way, then once in reverse, and repeated the sequence twice more. A fresh smell rose from the finished elixir.

Darek had sat up to watch while Anike worked and when she was done she carried the potion up to him. "Drink it all down," she said. He put the cup to his lips, took a sip, and made a face. Anike stared at him levelly and he finished it, grimacing. She pulled down his tunic and watched as the white lines faded from his chest, followed more slowly by the black ones. She sighed in relief as a normal colour suffused his whole skin. Darek collapsed back onto his bed.

"You will feel tired, Father," Anike told him. "Your body has been drained by fighting the infection over the past few days." Behind her, Inge let out the breath she had been holding. She handed up a bowl of porridge to Anike, who fed Darek a few mouthfuls. He swallowed eagerly, then his eyes closed and his breath slowed and deepened as sleep took him.

"He will live, Inge," Anike told her friend, her voice weak.

"And you saved him, Anike. He will be proud of you even if all he does is berate you for taking risks."

Anike felt a chill pass through her and shuddered. Inge did not realise the cost of saving her father's life. Two deaths, maybe more, was a heavy price to pay even before considering the destruction of Volna's farm and the displacement of her family. She looked at her father sleeping peacefully for the first time in days, but then remembered the girl who had brought her the stew when she had sheltered at Volna's, and hoped she had survived. If she had known in advance what would happen, would she still have gone to find the herb, or would she have let her father die?

She shook her head to clear it. She could torture herself with those thoughts, so all she could do now was try to do her best in the future. Her lack of control had nearly hurt both Inge and her father but if she could somehow rid herself of this power she would still have a life to live. In the meantime, she needed to keep away from those she loved. Inge had come far too close to suffering Bjord's fate, closer even than Volna. Anike felt a shiver of fear pass through her as she thought of what she had done to the good woman and her farm. In her relief at her father's cure, she had forgotten the penalty hanging over her and she needed guidance. "I must talk to Olaf," she told Inge.

Olaf was chopping roots, surrounded by three boiling cauldrons, when Anike entered his shop. "Did you find the Freya's blossom, Anike? I went to see Darek late yesterday and did what I could for him but without that flower..." His voice trailed off.

"I did find it, Olaf, yes. I made the potion and my father is recovering now. Thank you for keeping him safe until I got back."

Hearing Anike's voice, Fenris came bounding out from the back but he stopped as soon as he caught sight of her, well out of arm's reach. She looked down at him in surprise. Her first thought was that his sensitive nose had picked up the scent of burning even though she had changed clothes, but when she held out her hand to him, he backed away baring his teeth and growling, his ears laid back.

Suddenly Anike found this more irritating than puzzling. This ungrateful creature, whom she had petted for years, had forfeited every right to be in her presence. It did not even deserve to live.

Even as she caught that appalling thought and pushed it away, Olaf's hand descended on Fenris' neck and he pulled the dog back, then shoved him towards the back of the house with a curse. Fenris yelped and ran.

Olaf turned back to Anike. "I'm sorry. I don't know what came over him. This is the last thing you need after such a hard journey. Was there a fire? Your hair looks singed."

"Yes," said Anike vaguely, thinking about the departed Fenris. The dire wolves had reacted in a similar way to Gern. She recalled that in some stories a witch would make animals nervous. They could sense something unnatural and it frightened them. This could be a problem, but it was minor in comparison to others. She turned to Olaf and brought her attention back to the conversation. "The farm I took shelter in burned down."

She considered how to broach the subject of witchcraft with Olaf. He was the most learned man in the town, and if anyone could help it would be him. On the way over from her house she had decided to tell him everything, but Fenris' reaction had shaken her, reminding her of how others would see her. She did not feel like a killer, at least when she was not looking at the world through the firelight cast by the power within her, and she did not want Olaf to think of her as one and reject her, so she retreated from her plan of full honesty and settled on telling him the bare essentials.

"I need to talk to you about something." Anike looked down at her hands then up at Olaf, finding him regarding her with a quizzical expression. "Something that happened in the mountains yesterday."

"Go on," he said.

"It was when I was up at Vanir Heights." She took a deep breath and pressed on. "The gods made a storm – witch weather – and in the middle of it, they sent down a ball of fire, or lightning, or something between the two. It struck me and its energy seemed to pass into me." Anike spoke more confidently once she had committed herself to telling the tale. "From then on, a power has burned inside me, and when I was at a farm in the hills it burst out and set the building alight. It was that fire I was caught in."

Anike closed her mouth. She found herself feeling proud of the destruction, carried away by the memory of her power and she realised she was about to tell Olaf about throwing lightning at Bjord.

As she became aware of this shift in her perspective, she deliberately reminded herself of the harm she had caused and felt the hubris drain away, leaving her feeling frightened and ashamed again.

"Witchcraft..." breathed Olaf, taking a step back.

"I fear so, though it might be some other power from the gods. I thought witches were born witches. This is completely new to me."

Olaf kept his eyes on Anike, but his right hand was feeling for something on the bench behind him. "It sounds exactly like witchcraft to me and nothing good comes from that." His hand closed on a knife and he thrust it in front of him so that the blade separated him from Anike. "If witch weather enhances a dormant capacity for witchcraft, it would explain how witches like Gern emerge so suddenly. There is an external catalyst."

Despite the tension, Anike was glad that her master was still thinking clearly. "Please put down the knife, Olaf. I did not have to tell you. I just want help. I need to know how to get rid of this." She looked at him beseechingly. "I do not want to be a witch. Give me a chance, Olaf."

Olaf looked at her for a long time, and then the knife wavered. "I should tell the Arl," he said uncertainly.

Anike allowed herself to relax a fraction. If Olaf was thinking of telling the Arl, it was less likely he would use the knife. "Arl Svafnir does not understand me like you do, Olaf."

Olaf shook his head. "Svafnir would want to know." He started to edge towards the door. An image of Olaf burning and screaming crossed her mind. He would not be able to tell the Arl if he was dead.

"No!" cried Anike to Olaf, but also against that image, focusing on the good man in front of her who was struggling with the situation she had thrust upon him. The desire to destroy receded and she continued in a more normal voice. "You cannot tell him. He would condemn me without thinking, and it would not matter to him that I want to be cured." She thought of Bjord, writhing in agony as the lightning played over him. Svafnir would put the rope around her neck himself when he found out. She pushed that picture away too.

Olaf looked at her for a long time. "How can I trust you now? You ask much of me. I have always thought a witch was devoid of redeeming features and that they only lived to hurt others."

"I do not want to hurt people. I do not want to be evil," she told him, her eyes pleading.

The blade wavered a fraction.

"Surely telling you all this unforced counts for something?"

Fear, anger, sympathy and puzzlement warred in Olaf's expression. After a long moment, he lowered the knife and placed it on the table. "Anike, I have thought of you as the daughter I never had. You are intelligent and loyal, and if you want to expel this blight from your soul, a darkness you never sought, then what more can anyone ask of you? While some infections do need to be cut out, it is better to cure a malady if that is possible. I had to amputate your father's arm but I would rather find you a cure."

Anike sank onto the closest stool. "Thank you. I hoped you would have some advice for me, or perhaps there is even an elixir that can cure me?"

"I do not know of anything like that." Olaf frowned. "I cannot advise you myself, but that does not mean that no one can. You need someone who knows more about the gods and unnatural forces than I do."

Olaf paced around the table as he considered. "I wonder... there is a seer, Hilda is her name, who lives near Ulsvater. I met her once when my own master took me there. I found her to be cunning and more than a little intimidating. She would be very old now, but she did not seem to be the type to surrender to death easily, so she probably still lives. I have not heard much of her in recent years, though."

"A runecaster? I did not realise there were any in these parts." Anike had heard tell of wise women and cunning men who could read the runes and tell the future, but she had never met one.

"She lost the favour of the Arl of Ulsvater, I believe, so she moved to somewhere outside the town a few years back." Olaf sat down. "Rulers are not always comfortable with those who answer first to the gods."

Anike weighed that thought. Arl Svafnir clearly did not like dissenting voices and she could imagine that Oster, the Arl of Ulsvater, was the same. Ulsvater was twenty miles along the coast to the west. She had never travelled so far, so it was not surprising that she had never heard of the seer.

"There is a herbalist in Ulsvater, is there not? I am sure you have mentioned her. Ungrid, you said her name was. She would know where this Hilda lives, I suppose?"

"Yes, Ungrid," agreed Olaf. "I imagine many people in Ulsvater would be able to direct you, though."

"Why did you find Hilda intimidating?"

"She has been touched by the gods, and that sets her apart but if you too have been so touched, then someone who understands what that is like may be best placed to help you. If she cannot tell you a way to cure you of witchcraft, she may well be able to direct you to someone who can. You will need guidance before someone is killed."

Anike smiled at him, but she was blinking back tears. Olaf would be horrified and disappointed in her when he found out everything that she had done but she did not want to leave the truth of what had happened unsaid. She opened her mouth to tell him the whole story but before she could say anything more, Tavic burst in through the door.

"Olaf! Anike! Come quickly! A cart has just brought Bjord into town. He is badly injured."

- 9 -

TELLING TALES

Anike went white and spun around, her mouth dropping open. The news that Bjord had survived cascaded through her consciousness – she had not killed him. Perhaps she had not killed the other man either. Yet even as relief filled her, a darker impulse rose unbidden in her mind. Bjord's survival threatened to expose her. The obvious response would be to kill him, and as soon as possible. Desperately, she shook her head and the destructive desire evaporated, but she had been right to fear discovery. As soon as Bjord woke, he would mark her as a witch.

Olaf interrupted her thoughts. "Injured? How?" he asked Tavic, rising to his feet.

Tavic looked from one to the other. "He was lying in the back of a cart, out cold but still breathing."

Anike fumbled for something to say. "What do you mean, lying in a cart? What did the driver say?" she asked.

"The horse cantered in, terrified. It was dragging the cart behind it, but there was no driver. It took three of the stable hands to calm it."

The cart could only have come from Volna's farm. She must have seen that Bjord still lived and decided to have him brought to his father, or to Olaf for treatment. A weaker man than Bjord would have been killed but even he must have been badly injured by the lightning. The horse and cart would have had to use one of the few wide trails through the forest, a less direct route than she had taken, so it must have left the farm shortly after she had. The mystery to her was what had happened on the cart's journey to Trollgard, but with no driver to tell the Arl about what had happened at the farm even

THE DEMON AND THE WITCH

the brief respite before Bjord regained consciousness would allow her to get out of the town.

As she considered what to do next, Olaf took the initiative. "We will come at once. What are his injuries?"

"Burns mainly, I think," replied Tavic impatiently.

"An unusual injury," Olaf said, frowning. He looked at Anike and she froze, wondering how much he suspected. His gaze rested on her for a moment, but all he said was "Get the elixir," and pointed to a cupboard. Anike could not see a way to refuse him and flee without giving herself away, so she went to collect the remedy. Olaf selected some other jars from a shelf.

"Quickly!" urged Tavic, and led them out from Olaf's shop.

Olaf took Anike's arm. "Do you know anything about this?" he whispered harshly.

She pulled free, trying not to think of Olaf as a threat that had to be destroyed. If he pressed her further she was not sure she could hold herself back, so she reluctantly decided she had to lie. "No, nothing," she told him. "I did not see him after I left town."

She hated herself, but Olaf did not challenge her further. Instead he said, "Try not to worry, Anike. Bjord is strong."

"I cannot think clearly, Olaf. I just hope he is not too badly hurt." To forestall further questioning, she wondered aloud, "How could there be no driver on the cart?"

"An accident?" Olaf suggested. "Or perhaps someone attacked the driver and the horse panicked? I imagine the Arl will send people to find out once Bjord is out of danger."

"It must have happened quite close to the town or the horse would never have made its way here, no matter how frightened it was," she commented.

"I think we should concentrate on Bjord, Anike. He is fit and healthy, and now he is here he will receive the best of care." He lowered his voice. "Right now it would be a good thing if you can be involved in saving him."

He was right, Anike realised. If Bjord and his father felt, or better yet acknowledged, a debt to her, that would surely do no harm when

Svafnir came to consider her punishment. Once she was free of witchcraft, she wanted to come back and spend the rest of her life here and that meant accepting his verdict. Unfortunately, Olaf did not realise how difficult her position was. No one but her knew how Bjord had come to be injured yet.

Anike did wonder about what had befallen the cart, though, and hoped that no harm had come to the driver. She wanted to know that she was not responsible for any more deaths. She carried enough guilt over what had happened at the farm.

They reached the arlberg and Anike felt a shiver of fear pass through her. It was almost as if she was handing herself over to Svafnir for trial. She would be entering a stone cage but she reassured herself that she could always burn the place down, kill some people, maim a few more and escape in the confusion. She caught that thought, labelled it as distorted and pushed it away. It seemed that she was finding it easier to recognise the influence of her power on her impulses. Gathering her courage to face both the Arl and her own treacherous desires, she walked into the arlberg beside Olaf.

Bjord was lying unconscious on a pile of thick furs on the floor near the door. His face was covered in small scorch marks. His chest rose and fell, but his breathing seemed slightly ragged. Someone had removed his armour, and Anike could see charred holes in his tunic and the burned flesh beneath. She remembered the lightning playing over him before he fell and shuddered, the consequences of her misuse of power laid out before her.

Arl Svafnir was kneeling next to Bjord, one hand clasped around his son's. He looked up as Olaf and Anike came into the room. Olaf went over to Bjord and Anike followed, feeling the Arl's eyes on her. She glanced at him and found his penetrating stare directed at her rather than Olaf. She quickly looked back down as Olaf bent to examine Bjord and put his ear to the young man's chest. "His heart is still beating strongly, but it sounds irregular."

Anike had been expecting this, as irregular heartbeat and breathing were consequences of natural lightning strikes. Bjord had followed her from town and she felt she had to say something too, before someone read too much into her silence. "Thank Thor he is alive," she exclaimed, then added, "These do not look like the effects of a fire, even if someone were caught in a burning building."

"I agree. It does not look as if he was injured by flames. I would say he had been struck by lightning." Olaf looked up at Anike and she saw genuine relief in his face as when their eyes met. Anike let out her breath slowly.

Arl Svafnir was looking straight at her. "He told me he was going into the mountains after you," he said in a voice tinged with menace.

Anike told herself not to panic. If she lost control someone would get hurt, most likely not just her. "He did? He did not find me," she lied, keeping her gaze fixed on Bjord so that she did not have to look the Arl in the eyes. "I thought he had stayed in town after I left without him." Guilt clutched at her guts again and she had the disturbing feeling that if she tried to suppress the emotion entirely, it would build and literally explode out of her so she sobbed, voice catching, "I am responsible for this. If I had not gone out alone, he would not have had to follow me. There was a storm, and lightning everywhere. He must have been caught in it, so it is my fault he was hurt. I never wanted that." The confession was disingenuous, but the tears glistening in her eyes were genuine and the tension inside her eased a little.

"You are not responsible, Anike," said Olaf firmly.

"Quiet, Olaf! Men take risks to impress women who lead them on," Arl Svafnir snapped.

Anike looked up indignantly. "But I did nothing of the sort!" she objected, then realised she was contradicting her lord to his face and let her eyes drop.

Svafnir pressed on. "You knew how he felt about you, and you kept yourself just out of reach, even after he saved your life." His harsh expression matched his tone.

In response to this hostility and disapproval, Anike's desire to strike down this bitter man rose like a poised serpent. Her eyes blazed with fury and she started to raise her head again but as she did so her gaze passed over the Arl's tight clasp on Bjord's hand and suddenly she understood. He was lashing out in fear at the most convenient target. He loved his son but could not tell him when it mattered most, so his frustration came out another way. The coil of fire inside her sank back down. Her expression softened and she met the Arl's eyes. "Let me make this right, my lord. Please? I will treat Bjord and bring him back to you. I swear."

The Arl held her gaze. "Yes, you will," he said.

Anike looked away, the consequences of her impulsive promise starting to sink in. Herbalism had limits, and Olaf had often told her never to promise success when treating someone but, trapped by her guilt, she had failed to heed that advice. She wished that she had found some excuse not to come into the arlberg. As she felt herself starting to panic, the feeling of being contained pushed in on her again and the storm within her gathered in response. Fighting against it, she closed her eyes to suppress the expanding desire to tear down everything around her. She pictured the wind fading to a breeze and thunderheads paling to white. The urgent pulse of energy within her slowed as her image diffused the storm within.

She opened her eyes to look at Bjord again and took a deep breath to steady herself. "I will treat the burns first," she said and glanced at Olaf, conscious that she could not afford a mistake. She was relieved to see Olaf nod slightly. She took a salve, applied it, and watched the skin heal. "Now we can stabilise him," she went on. Trying to make an unconscious man drink a potion could choke him so she found another poultice and spread it over Bjord's neck and chest, confident that Olaf would have stopped her had she used the wrong remedy. When she was done, she put her ear over Bjord's chest and listened. His heart was beating strongly and evenly, and his breathing had steadied.

"He is out of danger," she said, lifting her head, "but it will be a while before he wakes."

Olaf's hand on her shoulder guided her back and he took her place, listening and observing Bjord's colour and breathing. He looked up at the Arl. "I agree with Anike. Your son is through the worst now, Svafnir."

Svafnir's expression was still grim but less hostile. "How long before he awakens, Olaf? I need to know what happened."

"Perhaps this evening, perhaps tomorrow. The effort of remaining alive has drained him, and he needs to rest."

"Can you not speed up the process?" the Arl asked. "Safely?"

"I exhausted my stock of those kinds of elixirs on the raiders yesterday, I'm afraid. But I can make more."

"I can do that!" Anike put in, seizing her chance to get out of the Arl's presence. "I want to help." Olaf looked at her and nodded. Anike turned to the Arl. "Have I your leave to go and prepare that elixir, my lord?"

"You have. But when Bjord wakes, we will talk." The Arl turned to Olaf. "You will stay here and watch over my son."

Anike fled.

Once clear of the arlberg and through the gates into the town, she slowed to a normal walk. She was glad that Bjord was going to recover but her relief was tainted by the knowledge of the problems it would bring, and she would need to be clear of Trollgard by the time he named her as a witch. It had been rash of her to agree to make up the remedy that would hasten his recovery time but she had been so desperate to escape from Arl Svafnir, and the risk of losing control with so many people around her, that she had snatched at the first opportunity that presented itself.

Reaching Olaf's shop, she pushed open the door. She watched Fenris slink away as soon as he realised it was her and felt a sting of rejection. An impulse to tear the creature apart for its lack of respect poured into her but vanished as her mind caught up with her emotions. Fenris was right to be frightened of her.

When the dog was safely out of sight, she started to assemble the equipment needed for the elixir, then paused. Bjord would recover in any event given a little time. Her remedy would speed up the process but he was not in any real danger without it, particularly with Olaf there. She could just leave. It would be a long while before she was missed, and even longer before anyone discovered she had left town. Olaf would realise where she had gone, of course, but he could not tell anyone without giving away his part in the decision and having to explain why he had let a witch so close to Bjord.

The difficulty with this plan was that it closed the gates of Trollgard against her in the future. Aside from the importance of being true to her word, even one given in haste, abandoning Bjord would seal her fate as far as the Arl was concerned.

Another thought insinuated itself into her mind. She could prevent Bjord from waking at all. She could mix a poison in with the salve and his heart would stop without him ever having the chance to denounce her.

Appalled at herself, she threw down the cauldron. She was shocked that such an idea had even entered her mind. It seemed that the energy churning inside had eroded her sense of right and wrong so much that she had briefly contemplated murder as a solution to her problems. This idea had not been accompanied by a rush of anger, fear, or even hatred, and she realised she needed to be even more on her guard against dangerous impulses than she had assumed.

She made herself sit, and think through everything carefully. The only sensible thing she could do was weaken the revival salve slightly so it would take a little longer for Bjord to wake, giving her time to get away.

Alert for the now familiar destructive influence, she considered the idea but found nothing wrong with it so she set up the cauldrons again and started work.

An hour later she left the workshop and headed back to the arlberg. After she had finished the poultice which would revive Bjord gradually, she had taken another elixir from the store to dull pain in case some of his burns still troubled him.

A group of townsfolk had gathered outside the arlberg gates. Slad was barring their way, spear held horizontally across the threshold. Anike heard him call out, "There is nothing more to tell you yet. As soon as we know what happened, the Arl will decide what to do."

The crowd muttered and milled about restlessly, apparently unsatisfied. Anike started to push through, between comments of "Are we safe?" and "I heard the wounds were terrible." She faltered, doubting the wisdom of re-entering the arlberg and coming into the Arl's presence again, and was jostled by the ebb and flow of the crowd before regaining her determination to complete her promise. Squaring her shoulders, she pressed forward.

Knowing she would be expected back, she nodded to Slad who frowned but raised the spear to give her room to duck under it. She went into the hall and halted abruptly at what she saw.

The Arl was now on his throne, but her eyes were drawn to Volna who was slumped before him. There were rents in her tunic, and even from across the hall Anike could see the blood soaking the cloth on her back. Olaf was leaving her side, an empty pot in his hand. For an instant, Anike considered turning and running but Olaf had seen her and beckoned her over as he walked back to where Bjord still lay.

Keeping her eyes on Volna, she reluctantly made her way to his side. No one had seized her as she came in so it was safe to assume that she had not yet been denounced. Volna had not been seriously wounded during the burning of the farm and whatever misfortune had befallen her must have happened since then. The deep gashes spoke of something dangerous in the area and her arrival so soon after Bjord had to be connected to the driverless cart. Anike decided that it was worth risking a few minutes' delay to find out what lurked outside the town.

She could see the map of northern Gotlund hanging on the wall behind the throne. Anike did not know exactly how big Gotlund was but had the impression that it was several hundred miles across, much further than she expected ever to travel. She had never really paid much attention to the map before but could see a clearly marked road running along the coast from Trollgard to Ulsvater. Her course planned, she put the jar containing the revival salve on the table. Olaf gave her an approving nod.

"What is going on?" Anike whispered to him.

Olaf indicated Volna. "That woman has just come in. She had to be virtually carried from the town gate, and she collapsed in front of the Arl. I have just applied a salve to her wounds. Svafnir wants to know how she came to be hurt. There are claw marks on her back — something large and strong attacked her."

"Has she said anything?"

"Nothing coherent yet but it should only be a few moments. Her wounds have already closed." He looked grave and lowered his voice. "I am going to struggle to replenish my stocks if you don't come back cured, and soon. My supplies have been badly depleted these last few days." Anike glanced about her but no one else seemed to have heard Olaf's words. All the attention was on Volna, who was getting to her feet to address the Arl.

Anike slowly inched back towards the entrance as the Arl leant forward on his throne to address Volna, his voice carrying throughout the hall. "Now, good woman, who are you and how did you come by these wounds?"

"My lord," Volna replied weakly, "I am Volna Griseldasdottir from a farmstead above the forest. I was attacked by a monster as I was coming to Trollgard."

A murmur ran through the crowd. Volna continued, "I have never seen its like, a huge beast with wings and great claws. It slashed me and tossed me aside then seized the thrall who was driving and started to eat him. I hid in the undergrowth until it left. The horse bolted with your son still in the cart." She bit her lip, trying to hold in the horror of it.

"This is grim news indeed, good Volna. Now tell me, where did this happen?"

"Just before we reached the farmland, my lord. We were almost through the trees when the creature attacked." At her words, Anike recalled the crashing she had heard as she was coming back to the town and counted herself lucky that it had not been she who had stumbled onto the monster.

"So close?" The Arl sounded shocked.

"There is more, my lord," continued Volna falteringly.

While everyone else had been listening intently, Anike had got halfway towards the door. She could not imagine that Volna was about to say anything good, so she turned and walked out as quickly as she could without running. The next words followed her. "I was bringing your son..."

Anike broke into a run as soon as she had cleared the hall, knowing that she could be pursued in moments. She doubted she had time to go home and did not want to be caught inside the town. Beyond what capture would mean for her, she knew that if she was cornered she would not be able to hold herself back and more people could die.

For a moment she wished she had gone to her father on the way back to the arlberg but she realised that had she done so, the Arl would have been told she was a witch before she returned with the salve. This was better, even though she had lost the chance to say farewell.

Slad glanced at her as she tore past but made no move to stop her, probably assuming she urgently needed something from Olaf's shop. She decided to take the west gate, which opened onto the road to Ulsvater. She had to slow her pace because of the number of people outside the arlberg and before she could make her way through the crowd three short bursts from a horn sounded, followed by a longer blast, not from behind her but from the south gate – the warning signal for a monster attack on the town. There were shouts from the crowd and some screams. As Anike pushed her way through the now-panicking throng, she could hear commands and shouts coming from the arlberg behind her.

- 9 -

Flight

Each town gate was under constant watch. The warning horn was a rare sound but all who lived in Trollgard knew what it meant. Everywhere men and women were disappearing indoors, some hurrying children in front of them, and a few re-emerging with weapons in their hands. This horn had sounded from the south so whatever was coming was probably approaching from the forest.

Anike recalled a dire bear that had moved into the area the previous winter, a beast that made the bear at Vanir Heights look small. It had stood well over the height of a tall man at the shoulder while on all-fours and weighed more than five horses. The Arl had led thirty men to bring it down and it was said that the Arl himself had struck the fatal blow. Its skull now hung in the arlberg but the cost had been high, with good people killed or maimed in the fight. Anike hoped that whatever threatened the town now was less dangerous.

She had been ready to leave Trollgard without seeing her father or collecting supplies but as she watched the townspeople running here and there, she decided she could risk a visit to her house first. She owed her father some explanation and there was some equipment she wanted to collect. The tumult and disorder in the town had lightened her mood unexpectedly, and she felt more confident as she dodged between the anxiously scurrying people.

She reached her house and darted inside. Her father had got up and was unwrapping his war axe. She could see at a glance that he was moving with more energy and purpose than he had in days. His face broke into a broad smile when he saw her and Anike's heart filled with relief. She hugged him hard. "Father, I am so glad to see you up."

Releasing him, she looked up at his face, serious again. "I have to go. I have to leave town, right now."

"I heard the horn." He hefted his axe. "You are going to the battle as well?"

"No, I have to go somewhere else," said Anike, then his final words registered. "What do you mean, 'as well'? You were at the borders of Niflheim two hours ago. You are not going anywhere."

"Your potion worked wonders, child, and it's better to go to Valhalla than to Hel's realm."

"Father, I am going to be away some days at least." She was not sure that she would be able to return at all but to say that out loud made the prospect seem too real. She continued, "Please do not get yourself hurt when I am not here. I could not bear it if I came home to find that something had happened to you."

"There's plenty of life left in this old warrior yet!"

"Of course there is, but it will be a few days before you return to full strength. You were very ill. Think about what would happen if you became fatigued during the battle," she told him. "You would not want anyone risking themselves to save you if that happened, would you?"

Darek spun the axe around. "I feel fine, girl."

"Of course you do now, but your stamina was drained by your illness. At least stay back with the reserves? That is an important role in any battle." She crossed to her work table. "I do not have time to argue. Just promise me you will be careful and not take chances."

"Where are you going?"

Anike swept her herbs, suturing kit and smallest cauldron into her bag. "Away. Trust me, it is better that you do not know where. I will be gone for a week, perhaps longer. Now, swear to me that you will not take any risks, and go to see Olaf if you feel in the least ill." She grasped his arm and looked into his eyes.

"Anike, what has happened? I don't understand this rush. Why can't you tell me where you are going?"

"Father, you have to trust me. The Arl might command you to tell him where I am, and I cannot ask you to lie for me."

"The Arl?" Darek stared at her, his mouth open. "What is going on? What has happened, Anike?" He rarely used her name unless he was really concerned.

Anike began to feel frustrated, and the power inside her drummed a little more insistently. She took a deep breath. "It is complicated, and it would take far too long to explain. I need to be gone. I really do not want to see the Arl just now. I promise that I will tell you everything when I get back."

Her father looked into her face, read her resolve and nodded. "Very well," he agreed reluctantly.

Anike felt the pulse of energy inside her quiet as her tension drained away. "Good," she said. "Thank you."

Darek watched as she lifted a stone near the fire to reveal the store of silver she had saved over the years. She quickly counted half of it into a pouch and put the remainder back under the stone.

"I hope I will not need to spend much of it," she said as she rose. She looked around to make sure that she had everything she would need and went over to her father. She gave him a kiss on the cheek. "I will be back when I can. Remember, Father, whatever you hear, I never set out to cause any harm." She released him and headed for the door.

"Anike? What did you do?"

She paused as she stepped over the threshold, the desire to cry and feel her father's arm around her tearing at her, but she gathered her resolve and shut the door behind her.

"Be safe," she whispered and headed for the west gate before she lost the courage to go. There was nothing her father could do to help her now and it would take too long to explain everything. It was better not to start. All she could do was plant a seed of belief in her innocence before Bjord arrived with his accusations.

Anike could not imagine leaving Trollgard for good but at that moment she had no idea how she could return. Even if she did manage to rid herself of the witchcraft, she would still have to convince Bjord and the Arl that she had done so, and somehow atone for what she had done. She hoped that curing Bjord might count for something, especially if the man she had flung against Volna's wall had also survived.

Although she desperately wanted to believe that no one had died, part of her still felt pride and pleasure at the moment when her enemies fell before her, and that disturbed her. She could only hope that she was strong enough to resist the corrupting influence of witchcraft.

She could hear the shouts from the south gate, punctuated by a deafening cry somewhere between a screech and a roar. It was clear that the creature, whatever it was, had not been killed or driven off.

The west gates of Trollgard were closed when Anike got to them. She was not surprised. They would be secured until the monster was no longer a threat or unless the Arl decided to send more men out to surround it. They were held closed by a long wooden bar, raised by a pulley from the platform on top of the wall. She looked up to see a warrior standing there, staring towards the southern side of the town. She needed to persuade him to open the gate so she climbed the ladder to the platform. The wall was a little too high for her to feel comfortable with the idea of simply dropping from the top of it.

Stepping off the ladder, she was relieved to find that the guard was Bjord's companion Loga, whom she had always got on better with than either Tavic or Slad. He nodded in acknowledgement to her before turning his attention southwards again. Anike followed his gaze and for a moment she could not work out what he was watching. She could not see any movement, any monster, nor even a hastily assembled war band but then she noticed that several buildings at the southern edge of the wood town had collapsed. As she watched, the shattered wooden limbs of one seemed to shrug and shift. The broken roof fell away as the monster clawed its way out.

Anike's first impression was that of a huge bird with feathered wings so large that they could serve as a roof but she soon realised that this was only part of the monster. Walls tumbled around it as it shook itself like a dog drying its wet coat, and she saw silver flanks glistening in the sunlight, highlighting its large and muscled body. It was as if several creatures had been combined to make the stuff of nightmares, the head and wings of a giant bird of prey set on top of the round body of a bear. The front pair of powerful legs ended in enormous raptor talons and the rear feet were clawed paws. The feathers were mottled brown and white and around the chest and shoulders, these merged into the silver scales that covered the rest of the body. The monster was almost the size of the house. It started forward, crashed through a fence, and a scatter of terrified chickens surged through the gap. A claw slashed, impaling one and lifting it. The great beak snapped once.

Shouts sounded from near the south gate, and a group of armed men came into view. Arl Svafnir, Siv and Rogar were mounted on horses at the head of a dozen or so warriors on foot. Raising their weapons, they formed a loose wedge pointing towards the monster, which turned towards them, letting out a scream of defiance.

Anike saw her chance. "Let me out quickly, I can help them. There are going to be casualties very soon," she said urgently.

"I am not supposed to open the gates until the Arl orders it," said Loga uncertainly. "The safety of this side of the town is my responsibility."

"You only need to open them for a moment," she pleaded.

"Would you have me go against the Arl's orders?" said Loga sternly.

Anike knew that Loga could not have received any specific word from Svafnir since the monster had been sighted and was just repeating his normal instructions. She also knew he was not one to follow orders blindly so she pressed on. "Look at that creature," she told him. "Some of those fighters are going to get hurt. If you don't let me out to help them, the injured could die." She felt a pang of guilt saying this as she had no intention of helping, but she had to escape and Olaf was on hand to help those wounded. It felt strange to be so focused on herself, to be putting her own needs ahead of the safety of others.

Perhaps some of her conflict entered her voice. Loga was still not convinced, so she pressed on. "The monster is not by this gate – that is why I picked it. Nothing is going to get in if you just lift the bar for a moment. Please?" She paused, watching Loga's expression and wondered if she could invoke Bjord's name in support, but before she had a chance to say anything else, Loga nodded. "That does make sense," he said.

"Thank you," she said, laying a hand briefly on his arm.

"I don't question your spirit, Anike, just your sense. You are no warrior. May the gods protect you if that creature sees you."

Anike looked to the south again. The men were approaching the monster now, flanking it on either side. Most carried war darts – short spears with flights, tipped with iron and about the length of a man's arm. They would cast a volley, hoping to wound and slow the creature before charging with axes and long spears.

As she started to climb down the ladder, she heard the Arl call for the spears to be thrown. The monster screeched again and the sounds of battle being joined filled her ears as she descended. Loga had lifted the bar by the time she reached the ground, and she opened one gate just enough to squeeze through. Once outside, she pulled the stout barrier closed and was relieved to hear the bar drop back into place. She did not want to leave the town vulnerable.

She had no intention of approaching the battle but she did not want Loga to realise that and sound the alarm so instead of following the road she skirted the town wall southwards. As soon as she was hidden from Loga's view among the wooden buildings huddled untidily near the outer wall, she changed direction and headed directly away from the town, running in short bursts and trying to stay in cover as much as she could. After a few moments, she reached a more open area and looked back, peering from around the corner of a barn to see what was happening in the battle.

The monster was surrounded by the town's defenders. War darts lay scattered on the ground all about it and a couple were lodged in its wings. Shield on his left arm, Svafnir hurled another as he rode by, but it bounced off the creature's scales. Siv charged it, steering her horse with her knees, great axe in both hands drawn back ready to strike. Rogar was advancing on foot with sword and shield, his fallen horse struggling to rise behind him.

The creature screeched and surged forward to meet Siv's charge, raising one claw to strike. Trained for battle between riders, Siv's horse reared back in the face of this greater threat. She leapt clear as it fell and rolled away. The monster pivoted with unexpected agility and slashed sideways at Rogar. His shield shattered under the force of the blow and he staggered back with his left arm hanging uselessly at his side.

Anike turned and headed away from the melee as rapidly as she could, making her way between buildings towards the road that ran along the edge of the beach. She felt another rush of guilt at leaving but she could not see how she could help, and her presence might even be a distraction. As she cleared the wood town, she glanced back. Warriors had surrounded the monster again, trying to trap it against the high stone walls and jabbing with their spears, but the scales were turning their thrusts aside. Siv charged again, now on foot, and her great axe struck high on the creature's neck where scales had given way to feathers. This time the monster cried out in pain. It reared back, allowing Svafnir to dart in, his sword striking sparks as the blow to the exposed chest was deflected by the beast's scales.

Under the coordinated assault, the monster backed up a few paces then turned swiftly and broke through the ring of men, leaving several lying on the ground. By ill luck, it headed west towards Anike, alone and now exposed on the road. As it left the buildings of the wood town and saw her clearly, it let out another screech and changed direction towards her. It was some distance away but the creature had reached a surprising speed, its gait something between a lumber and a lope.

Anike looked about her for a way to evade it. She doubted it would be able to catch her in the forest but it was coming fast and she would never reach the trees in time. The west end of the bay was closer to her and there the rocky headland rose steeply from the beach. She could climb the cliff but the creature had not left the ground despite having wings, and looked too heavy to follow. Anike left the road and fled towards the cliff face.

Sand shifted beneath her feet as she sprinted across the strand. Risking a glance over her shoulder, she saw that the creature was closer than she had hoped. Its stride was a sort of lopsided canter she had never seen before, but it was fast. Despite its great size, it was easily outrunning her. Measuring the distance to the cliff with her eyes, Anike realised that she would only be able to reach the large rocks at the base of the cliff and would have to try to hide from the monster between them. She redoubled her efforts, her boots now clattering on pebbles as she approached the cliff, but the sound of the creature's pursuit came ever closer. Fear gripped her, spurring her on. Reaching the rocks, she looked back again to see how much distance she had to spare and saw the monster no more than twenty paces behind her. There was no time to hide.

Terror overwhelmed her, then abruptly vanished to be replaced by mere irritation and a sense of irony that it was this particular creature that was inconveniencing her. It leapt at her, claws stretched wide, but she now knew what to do about this annoyance.

"Movement," she cried and lifted straight up, soaring above the monster's lunge. It screamed in frustration as it passed beneath her and Anike looked down on it with a sense of detached admiration. It was a magnificent fusion of animals, much greater than the sum of its parts but its behaviour was now irritating her and she had to direct it elsewhere.

The monster made a sound like a rumbling growl as it landed. Its claws clattered on the rocks, which shifted beneath its weight. Beating its wings to steady itself, it glared up at her. Anike glided smoothly onto the top of the cliff, her body feeling as if it was being carried upward by a river. Looking down, she met the piercing gaze of the mighty animal. It seemed confident in its fluid strength and did not yet realise it was beaten. Its powerful wings spread for balance, it examined the cliff, apparently looking for a way up.

"Movement," commanded Anike again, concentrating on the cliff edge. A net of energy seemed to surround her for an instant and a crack appeared in the rock, running around her in a jagged semi-circle about a dozen feet across. The top of the cliff fell away from beneath her boots, crashing down towards the creature in an avalanche of boulders, leaving her suspended in mid-air.

The monster gave a squawk of surprise and reared sharply backwards to avoid the landslide, twisting with grace and agility to land on all four legs facing away from the cliff. From this angle, Anike could see that the jump had reopened a deep wound in the right hind leg from which now dark blood oozed, a splendid discontinuity in the creature's elegant form. It twisted its head to screech at her again then started back across the beach, sensibly abandoning its misguided attempt to catch her. Drifting through the air back to the new edge of the cliff, she watched the creature head towards Trollgard. She hoped it would return to town, destroy more buildings and bring panic to the townsfolk, reducing order to chaos.

A fierce gust of wind blew her hair into her eyes interrupting her concentration. She paused, feeling that something was very wrong, and became aware of the veil of fire filling her mind again. Gathering her will, she pushed against it and the firelight infusing her thoughts receded, leaving her horrified that she had again allowed the power within her to corrupt and warp her perceptions. She took a step back from the edge of the cliff. Any idea of how she had flown or broken the rock had vanished when the fire within her mind receded.

She watched the bizarre monster heading back towards the town. Strangely, she had admired it, seeing it neither as odd nor as an enemy. It was far more dangerous than the previous winter's dire bear or the dire wolves but for a moment she had regarded it as a mere distraction. The energy inside her had made her arrogant, but not without some cause given what she had just done.

The spectre of losing control within Trollgard as she had at Volna's farm frightened her. For a moment she had wished the monster would tear it down. Witchcraft brought with it desires she had never known she possessed and she desperately needed to rid herself of this curse before she brought down disaster on everyone she loved.

Power had been there when she needed it, even though now she had no idea how she had controlled it, and who could withstand her if she could fly and throw lightning down at opponents? Her witchcraft could manifest to strike out at both real and perceived threats. It seemingly was summoned by raw emotion rather than thought, and she could not understand what had led her to utter the words 'movement' and 'fire'.

She wondered what she could achieve if she could learn to direct her powers constructively and not just in the heat of threat or battle. She imagined flying up cliffs to reach plants she had never gathered before, rescuing boats by calling winds to aid them when they were becalmed – things that might be possible if she could just understand the energy inside her and bend it to her will.

She could even become a warrior with the elements as her weapons. The pictures formed in her mind of setting fire to Larten boats before they landed and watching the enemy sailors tumbling into the sea, of herself in the sky hurling lightning down on Trollgard's enemies, and if the Arl did not care to use her as a weapon, she could oust him and take his place.

"No!" she cried aloud, stamping a foot to ground herself and dismiss the insidious temptation. She needed to be rid of this power. It was too easy for it to lead her from good intentions to doors that were better left shut. It was time to seek real help.

She took a last look at Trollgard. The monster seemed to have thought better of attacking the town again and was heading back towards the forest. There was little she could do. Even if she could somehow let her witchcraft loose, she was more likely to attack the town than the monster. She uttered a short prayer to Freya to protect her home and another to Odin that Hilda the Seer would be able to help her find a way to be safe around people again. She wanted to return to the life she knew. There might even be a way to get Bjord to forgive her.

Anike looked at the bay in the sunlight. Surrounded by such life and beauty, she felt that the world could still be a wonderful place, despite everything that had happened. Her heart lifted with hope as she made her way along the cliffs to join the coast road to Ulsvater.

She walked for the rest of the day and into the evening, with the sea to her right. The cliffs dipped away in places before rising again to dizzying heights above the waves crashing far below. The forest lay mostly to her left, though in parts the road twisted inland to pass between the tree trunks. As she travelled, she kept an eye on the road both ahead and behind her, slipping into the trees to avoid the few travellers she saw, and gathering herbs when she found them. When it was nearly dark she walked a little way into the forest and after brewing potions and some root broth on a small fire, she found a hollow beneath a fallen log and eventually she slept, wrapped in her cloak.

On waking, she was relieved to find herself in an unburnt clearing. She had been concerned that without her conscious resistance, the power might have burst out of her as it had at the farm. Away from battle and people, she felt more relaxed and in control and she began to hope that she could resist any further use of witchcraft.

In the early morning, she passed through a small fishing village where a shallow river had carved out a valley but by midday she had reached a point where the road again ran atop a high cliff. A brisk breeze blew from behind, whipping the waves into white horses. She saw a sail in the east, a small ship running before the wind. Shading her eyes against the sun, she recognised the lines of one of Svafnir's small warships. She could just make out there were about a dozen men on board though the ship was too far out for her to recognise any of them. She watched it sail past and disappear around the headland into the bay ahead of her and wondered who was on board.

- 10 -

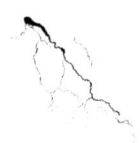

STRANGER

The afternoon sun was warm on Anike's face as she stood on the coast road. Around her, the trees had given way to a scrubby grassland dotted with sheep and she could look down on Ulsvater, which lay beside a wide river. Like Trollgard, strong walls divided the stone town from the farms and cabins of the wood town. Fishing boats bobbed on the water. The roof of the Arl's hall was clearly visible above the smaller stone buildings clustered around it but unlike in Trollgard, the arlberg lay in the middle of the town.

South of her, on the east bank of the river, Anike could see that the land rose until it became the mountain range that lay to the south of Trollgard but on the far side the ground was flatter and the forest extended almost to the sea. A large road ran south along the nearer bank of the river.

The coast road led down to a gate on the eastern side of the town walls. Anike followed it, aware of the curious, perhaps slightly suspicious, stares she received as she passed through the wood town and hoped that she would find a more hospitable attitude within the stone town – she needed to get someone to tell her how to find Hilda.

Passing through the gates, she was struck by subtle differences between Ulsvater and Trollgard. The gates here were topped with a walkway, and there was more space between the stone houses. The market lay against the south wall rather than in the centre of the town but on walking through it, the bustle of craftsmen and traders felt similar. The smell of cooking blended with the earthier odour of livestock. Fish, meat, and furs were being sold alongside goods brought in by wagon or boat and the ringing of hammer blows from the northern edge indicated a smithy. It felt like a community that would look after its own, and she was the stranger here.

She decided to ask a trader about Hilda. Out of the variety of stalls, she selected one selling cooked fish surrounded by an enticing smell of spices. She had eaten little on the walk from Trollgard and her mouth watered at the thought of a proper meal. She beamed at the middle-aged man at the stall and he smiled back, blushing slightly.

"How much for a cooked herring, good sir?" she asked.

"To you, young lady, two coppers."

Anike laughed in genuine amusement. "My father is a fisherman so I can recognise a good herring when I see one, but I also know its value. One copper is plenty for a single fish and I am happy to pay that." She held up a coin. "I have just come from Trollgard and I would like some directions to the house of someone I have to visit."

The man took the coin. "Done!" he said, chuckling. He skewered a fish on a stick and flung it onto the hot coals. "A fair walk from Trollgard. Who are you looking for?"

"An old woman called Hilda. Some call her a seer."

The man froze in the act of turning the fish on the brazier. "Hilda? I wouldn't go near her if I were you. She has the evil eye."

This was not the most encouraging response but at least Hilda was still alive and known here. "Evil eye?" Anike asked cautiously.

"People who go to see her are cursed," replied the man harshly. "Bad luck falls on them and those they know." He shook his head and glared at her. "If I had not already taken your coin, I would have turned you away to avoid her curse spreading to me but it would bring down ill favour from the gods if I broke my bargain with you." He looked away and ignored her pointedly while the fish sizzled on its impaling twig.

The calm which had gradually come over Anike on the journey from Trollgard deserted her and irritation at the obstacle the man was placing in her way struck sparks of embryonic fury. People were vexing, limited by their rules and fears and the best way to overcome these restrictions was to destroy those, like the vendor, who were trapped by them. Again, the absurdity of that line of thought brought her up short. She took a deep breath and let the irritation flow out of her as she watched the fish fry. She grabbed the stick as soon as it was done and left the vendor to his own devices.

Reflecting more rationally on his reaction to Hilda's name, she suspected that his fear and warning of the evil eye were born of ignorance. Olaf had assured her that there was a herbalist in Ulsvater and she decided to seek a more measured response from someone whose trade required thought.

There was a faint scent of brewing potions on the wind so she headed off between the buildings to track it down. She found the herbalist's shop a little way down a wide alley. A broad window ledge displayed pottery jars with a variety of plants growing in them. On a roof on the opposite side of the road, two men paused their work to watch as she approached the shop.

She knocked at the heavy door, pushed it open and saw a woman chopping roots on a table within. Ungrid was younger than Olaf, but not by much. She was lean, with greying hair and the weathered face of one who spent a great deal of time outdoors. She looked up when Anike stepped inside, and her eyebrows rose in surprise upon seeing a stranger.

Ungrid's shop was organised into discrete areas. Herbs had been planted in separate pots, an idea that instantly appealed to Anike and one she decided to use herself if she ever set up a shop in a stone town. The far wall had shelves stacked with potions and next to them were boxes of dried herbs. A series of cauldrons hung above a black fire tray which stood on iron legs at the centre of the single large table. Two sizeable sleeping platforms looked down onto a hearth at the back of the large room.

Anike guessed that Ungrid lived with several members of her family and the way the fish seller had reacted to Hilda's name made Anike glad that no one else was present. Ungrid ought to be more forthcoming if she was not distracted by anyone else's worries.

"Good afternoon, Mistress Ungrid," she said.

Ungrid put down the small knife she was using and wiped her hands on her apron. She looked Anike up and down. "Can I help you?"

"I hope so, Mistress. I am Anike Dareksdottir, apprenticed to Olaf Karnaksson in Trollgard."

Ungrid straightened and her mouth cracked into a small smile. "It has been too long since I heard from Olaf. Does he still have that oversized hearthrug on legs?"

Anike laughed. "Fenris and Olaf are both well." Improvising, she added, "Olaf sends his greetings and good wishes and hopes that you are in good health. Fenris would no doubt like me to bark a greeting to you but I will forego an attempt to mimic him."

Ungrid's smile broadened at that. "So what brings you to me, Anike, did you say?"

"Yes. I have come for some information."

"I am surprised that Olaf thinks that I know something he doesn't."

"Not about herbs," Anike told her. She had originally hoped that simply asking for directions to where Hilda lived would be enough but following her encounter with the fish vendor, she felt that she needed to give Ungrid a good reason to help her without revealing her true purpose. "Trollgard is under threat. There is some sort of monster marauding around outside it. I am looking for advice from Hilda the Seer and Olaf told me she lives near here." This was such an unusual and serious matter that Anike felt it would justify someone travelling all the way from Trollgard to seek counsel from the god-touched.

Ungrid frowned. "People who receive Hilda's advice do not tend to be happy afterwards. Nowadays it is only the desperate who go to her. Is this monster so terrible?"

Anike nodded. "It is huge, with a bear's body, the head, claws and wings of an eagle and it is covered in scales which seem to turn weapons aside. A dozen men barely hurt it. We need to find a weakness or people are going to die."

"A harrowling, then? They can be very dangerous."

Anike frowned. "I have never heard that word before."

"No? They are monsters, a blending of normal creatures. Griffins and hippogriphs are better-known harrowlings, but this sounds like a

THE DEMON AND THE WITCH | - 113 -

different sort. I don't know if they have specific weaknesses but I suppose Hilda would be able to tell you."

"We also had a witch in Trollgard a few days ago, but the Arl hanged him," Anike said, feeling that not to mention Gern might look odd and she could see no harm in doing so. "The town has been suffering misfortune lately."

"Witches are bad business," agreed Ungrid.

"Indeed." Anike did not trust herself to comment further. "Olaf thought you might be able to direct me to Hilda. He met her in Ulsvater but said she lives outside it now. He said she was very clever but he did not tell me that people feared her so much."

"I am not frightened of her – well, not exactly," said Ungrid carefully. "I would not lightly seek her advice, though."

"Why not?"

Ungrid toyed with the ingredients in front of her. "There are several reasons. Firstly, she tells people what she thinks without regard for their feelings, and in particular whether or not they want to hear it. More importantly, people think they want to know their destiny but most are disappointed when they find that it is not the future they want. Hilda may tell them about misfortune ahead and then they go on to suffer it, so some believe she brings it down on them."

She smiled ruefully. "When someone visits Hilda, they or their families often need my help afterwards. I can do good business after one of those visits." She paused. "You have to be in great need before risking a visit to a seer but it does sound as if your matter is important enough to justify it."

"Olaf also told me that Hilda had some disagreement with the Arl."

"About ten years ago, she had Oster's complete confidence but something happened between them. I never heard what she did, or what went wrong, but she left town after they argued and went to live in the hills. Even so, Arl Oster used to visit her occasionally but I don't think that he has seen her for a while." Ungrid frowned at her. "You seem like a sensible woman, Anike. Are you sure you want to take this risk rather than seek answers elsewhere? What do you expect to find out?"

Anike thought for a moment. "Some idea of how to end the threat to those I love."

"I pray that the gods look kindly on such a selfless motive and protect you," said Ungrid, "but I doubt that the answer to that sort of question will be simple or easy."

Anike shrugged. "I do not expect it to be." Her motives were not quite as selfless as she had implied and no one could ever be sure what the gods would think. They might nurture and protect humanity but they were still capricious beings, fond of schemes and tricks.

"If you are sure," said Ungrid reluctantly. Anike nodded, and she continued, "You need to travel about four miles south on the river road. To your left, you will see a large white rock – almost square. A trail winds eastwards up the slope behind it. Follow that through into a pass and after about a mile you will come to a plateau. Hilda has her hut beneath the cliff there, near a stream."

Ungrid regarded her keenly. "Knowledge often comes at a price so be sure this is what you want. I suggest you spend a little time thinking about exactly what you are going to ask. It is said that the clearer the question, the less harm comes to you." She shrugged. "I don't know if that is true but you will probably learn more from questions you have properly thought through."

"Thank you, Mistress," said Anike. "I will consider your words carefully." She shifted her bag to her shoulder. "It sounds as if the seer's hut is too far away to reach tonight."

"I would say so," agreed Ungrid. "You may not stay here tonight, though," she added before Anike had a chance to say anything. "I will not risk misfortune settling on my family by sheltering you here. I regret you must find somewhere else to spend the night. You could try the arlberg."

"I respect your decision, Mistress," Anike sighed. The fear of Hilda, or at least the consequences of dealing with her, evidently ran deep in this town. "I wish you a good day." She nodded to the older woman and left the shop.

Outside, Anike considered whether to follow Ungrid's suggestion about shelter. There was still time to leave the town but she did not

THE DEMON AND THE WITCH | - 115 -

want to spend another night outside if she could help it and staying at the arlberg was a sound suggestion. The Arl had a duty to shelter travellers in a town. She could not entirely dismiss the worry that the same fate would befall Oster's hall as Volna's farm though her uneventful night on the road led her to believe there would be no repeat of that first night as a witch. She headed towards the centre of the town and the arlberg.

The suspicion of the seer surprised her but it was obviously deeply ingrained. Given how they felt, Hilda might well have been driven away entirely when she lost the Arl's favour but Anike supposed that the journey of a couple of hours to her hut was enough of a buffer.

Despite the warnings, it was hard for her to see what she had to lose by consulting Hilda. Unless she could somehow rid herself of witchcraft, she would not be able to go home. As yet she had no idea how to do that but finding where the seer lived was a small step in the right direction.

It was starting to get dark. Anike rounded the last corner before the arlberg but froze at what she saw. Bjord was walking out of the gate with Loga at his side. Her ministrations before she left Trollgard had apparently been effective and he looked completely recovered. She ducked back and watched as the pair turned towards the beach. They must have come on the ship that she had seen from the coast road that morning. Bjord could only be here to look for her.

She melted back into the alley and waited until Bjord walked out of sight. Her spirits sank. While news of her was bound to come to Ulsvater eventually, she had hoped for at least another day before a good description of her reached the town. It seemed she had underestimated Bjord's desire to hunt her down.

Going to the arlberg now was out of the question. Bjord would be in and out of it with Loga and probably half a dozen others who knew her, and some of his men might still be inside. Even if no one who knew her was there, Bjord would have told Arl Oster everything he could and if he thought to speak to Ungrid he would find out that she had been in the town and where she was going.

"Excuse me, Mistress." An unfamiliar voice interrupted her anxious thoughts, startling her. She looked round to see a man standing a few feet away, facing her but mostly looking at the ground as he shuffled from foot to foot. He was unkempt, dressed in stained and faded leather and looked vaguely familiar, though not someone she knew from Trollgard.

Seeing that he was not one of Bjord's companions, Anike relaxed slightly. "Yes?" she responded, and a memory slid into place. This was one of the men who had been working on the roof near Ungrid's house.

"Forgive me for troubling you, Mistress, but are you by any chance a herb woman?" The man looked up hopefully before dropping his eyes again.

"I am," said Anike cautiously. His unfrightened but diffident manner told her that he was not a threat.

The man smiled nervously. "Ah, I hoped you might be, seeing as you were a stranger and visiting Mistress Ungrid." He hesitated and then plunged on. "Mistress, my wife is ill. I can't afford Mistress Ungrid's prices – no disrespect meant but she knows her worth, if you take my meaning. But if you could help my wife, we would be very grateful. We can't pay much but we can offer you food and shelter for the night if you could do something to help her, just make her more comfortable maybe."

Anike considered. The man did not look ill, so whatever his wife had was probably not catching, and staying with a labourer had the advantage that Bjord was unlikely to find her. "That seems fair," she said. "I will do what I can to help your wife."

"Thank you, Mistress. I am Jarik, and my wife is Kari."

"Anike," Anike replied automatically then silently cursed herself. Now she knew that Bjord was in the town, it would have been better not to say who she was.

"This way," said Jarik, and led her down a side lane.

"What is the matter with your wife?" Anike asked.

"I don't rightly know, Mistress. She is sweating as if she has a fever, but she is cold to the touch."

"Is she in pain?"

"She moans, Mistress. But you will see for yourself. This is our home." Jarik stopped by a door and opened it. "In here," he said and stepped inside. Anike followed him into the dim interior of the house. It smelt stale and bitter, with an underlying note of decay. A figure, covered in furs and huddled by the embers of a fire, moaned when they came in. Anike stepped forward to get a closer look.

The blow caught her on the back of her head. Pain exploded in her skull and she staggered forward, blinking back tears. Surprise gave way to a flood of anger as she recovered her balance. She turned to face Jarik, who was standing with a club in his hand. Incredulous that this creature had struck her, Anike touched the back of her head and then looked at the blood on her fingers. Uncaring of the pain, she smiled. Despite appearances, she was the one in control.

Then she felt the tip of a knife at her throat, the cold steel pressing against her skin. "If you are quiet, we will leave you here unharmed after we take your money and anything else you have of value," hissed the man who had been playing the part of the sick wife by the fire. "But any trouble from you... well, no one will miss a stranger."

Anike would have laughed at the absurdity of the threat if she had not been so insulted by the attack. "Movement," she cried and an invisible circle of force expanded from her, pushing the knife clear of her skin before flinging both men away from her to strike the stone walls. There were jarring crunches and the clatter of a weapon falling from a limp hand. She watched as both men unsteadily tried to rise. They were as yet still breathing but she had been restrained for too long and was eager to turn the full force of her power on them.

"Wind," she commanded and instantly she stood in the eye of a tornado. Ashes were torn from the fire by the screaming vortex. The furs that Javik's companion had discarded flapped like a great bird as they were caught in the gale and a wind-borne plate struck him in the head. He fell with a cry. Lying crumpled against a wall, Javik looked with wide eyes at Anike, standing tall in the midst of the destruction. He raised his hand towards her in a pleading gesture.

"Lightning," she said, a bolt leaping from her upraised palm to shatter the joists that held the ceiling above him. Large stone tiles fell and his cries of pain were cut off when a piece the size of a shield crushed his head.

The wind died, and Anike strode through the wreckage towards the door, kicking charred wood and shattered pottery out of the way. Despite the violence of the storm, most of the building still stood so she waved a hand at the beams supporting what remained of the roof and called out, "Fire." They blackened and broke as flames spread through them. The roof began to collapse behind her as she stepped out into the lane.

It had only been moments since she entered the house but a crowd had already gathered in the deepening twilight, their faces lit by the flickers of light from the burning building. They stood in her way and she wanted to scatter them.

Now in the open air, with the chaos behind her, part of her whispered that these people had done her no harm. She held onto that thought, telling herself that no one else needed to be hurt, and her burning fury ebbed away. Untainted by the light of witchcraft, she saw that she had not needed to kill to defend herself from the robbers but she had been caught up in the glory of destruction, as she had been at Volna's farm. Now that fierce joy had given way to a feeling of sickness at having brought more death. Confronted with the realisation that she had committed another atrocity, Anike pushed through the crowd of astonished onlookers, desperate to get clear before they realised she was responsible. Picking an alley at random, she fled.

The pain in her head, which had not seemed important when she was in the house, clamoured for her attention but she did not cease her headlong flight. She ran down one alley after another, trying to outpace not only any pursuers but also the memory of her acts. There were already shouts and screams from behind and a loud crash as the house finally collapsed reached her ears. Anike hoped no one had gone inside.

She had to get off the streets, suddenly a labyrinth of closed doors and winding alleys. She took another turn and her path was blocked by the back of the smithy, its slightly slanted roof well above head height. Fighting back panic, she clambered on top of a barrel and leapt upwards to catch the edge of the roof. Desperation gave her the strength to haul her aching body up and roll towards the centre. There were few windows overlooking this building and no one would be likely to see her huddled beneath her dark green cloak now that night had fallen. She pressed herself flat and listened as the noises of pursuit ebbed and flowed, growing gradually fainter. Exhaustion, the aftermath of panic and the pain of the blow to her head caught up with her and she spiralled into darkness.

When she came to, stars were shining brightly through ragged breaks in the cloud. She shivered on the stone roof, hard and cold beneath her. The sound of a familiar voice had dragged her back to consciousness. Bjord was in conversation with someone as they walked in front of the smithy. She strained to hear what he was saying, not daring to move to a better position.

"Anike..." she caught, then, "... destroy this town."

A deep voice responded, calm and steady, though she could not make out the words of the unfamiliar speaker. Arl Oster, she surmised.

Bjord continued, his voice becoming louder as he came closer. "We must hope she doesn't raise up a monster as she did in Trollgard."

Anike felt shocked on hearing this. She felt extremely guilty for the destruction and death for which she had been responsible but the monster had nothing to do with her and she was both insulted and upset at these words. Bjord would not himself have seen it chasing her though surely he would have been told by others who had. While it might be convenient to blame the monster on her, she hoped the town would not be relying on killing or capturing her as a means of defeating it.

It did seem strange that the harrowling had appeared at the same time as she had been cursed so Bjord's conclusion was reasonable, but her hopes of reconciliation seemed more distant than ever.

"We will continue to search for her until tomorrow," the deep voice said, "and even if it turns out that she has left Ulsvater, we will pursue her, though I will not leave the town defenceless."

"The seer won't help her, will she?" Bjord asked, confirming Anike's fears that they knew where she was planning to go.

"Hilda rarely helps anyone much. Not any more." The deep voice sounded regretful.

"The witch has killed people for no reason. The seer might be in danger if she refuses Anike and angers her."

"Hilda can take care of herself. She..." The voice faded as they walked away.

Ungrid must have spoken to the Arl after word of the death of the robbers had got around. There was every reason for her to have told Arl Oster what she knew, and the fish vendor might have come forward as well. With a sinking heart, Anike realised that she had turned Ulsvater into another town where she was known as a witch and a killer. At this rate, if she did not manage to free herself of the unstable power and regain something of her reputation, she would have to move to the other side of Gotlund to escape stories about her. She wanted to go home so much but as things were now that was wishing for the impossible.

She felt less guilt and remorse over the death of Javik and his partner than over what she had done at the farm. She had been defending herself, at least to start with. In similar circumstances, she was sure Bjord would have killed them both and the law would have supported him. However, she was a witch and could never be in the right.

Her head throbbed. Keeping as quiet as possible, she felt in her bag for her elixirs. She found the jar she wanted by touch, checked it by smell and applied its contents to the back of her head. The pain eased as the wound healed though some of the deeper headache remained. She hoped that the blow had not caused long-term harm.

Replacing the jar, she considered her options. The town gates would be closed for the night and her description would have been passed around. All strangers in town would be looked at closely so it would be too dangerous to risk the gates in the morning. She had to get over the walls while it was still dark.

The hunt continued late into the night but eventually Ulsvater quietened as the townsfolk gave up searching for her in the dark.

Anike lay patiently beneath her cloak and waited for a chance to make her escape.

The town walls were some fifteen feet tall with a parapet. They presented a formidable barrier but from what Anike had seen they had been constructed like those of Trollgard, to keep people out rather than in. She had noticed ladders by the gates and stone steps at intervals around the inside of the walls so that the walkway on top could be reached easily by defenders when needed.

There probably would be warriors atop the walls tonight, keeping watch for her. She preferred to avoid the north, where Bjord's ship would be drawn up on the beach. South and east were more obvious escape routes as they led to open country and would be well guarded. The west side was likely to be the quietest, with nothing but a short strand before the river.

She dropped quietly from the roof of the smithy and sticking to the shadows, made her way carefully to the western edge of the town. As she neared the wall, she could see some torches moving above her, indicating sentries on patrol.

It occurred to her that it would be much easier to escape if she could fly again, as she had outside Trollgard. If she had to be a witch, it would be good if it could be of some help. She concentrated, willing herself to rise, but could not feel any connection to the energy inside her. It was like trying to grasp the wind.

After trying in vain for a couple of minutes, she gave up. With no idea how to access the power, she would have to rely on her natural abilities. She located a set of narrow stone steps on the walls and paused at the bottom, listening. She doubted whether everyone on the wall would be carrying a light. Some would prefer to rely on night vision, despite the clouds in the sky.

Hearing nothing, Anike climbed the stairs cautiously, one hand on the rough stone of the wall to keep her balance. She paused every couple of steps to listen. Her head was on a level with the walkway when she heard a voice only a few paces away and froze.

"I heard the witch was trying to find the seer." The voice belonged to a young man.

"Probably to kill her," came the reply in the tone of an older woman. "She must have thought the seer would track her down."

"If she brings down any more buildings, we won't need a seer to find her," said the man.

"We just have to wait for her to try to kill someone else and then we can stop her. It won't be long. Witches can't help trying to kill people," said the woman knowledgeably.

The pair did not have a torch, so Anike could not immediately place them nor see which way they were facing. She turned her head slowly to scan the skyline above the parapet until she picked out their silhouettes. One was looking outward, arms resting on the battlements and the other was facing into the town.

The things they said about her would have worried her a few days ago but now she had come to accept that everyone just assumed that she would kill again. To be fair, she worried about that too. It had become too easy for her to lapse into seeing other people as either getting in her way or nothing more than a collection of flaws, and believe that the only solution was to destroy them. As this thought crossed her mind, it occurred to her that getting away would be a lot easier if these guards were blown off the wall by a sudden gust of wind, but she pushed that idea away. No one would be hurt during her escape if she could help it.

"I will have another look round," said the man. Anike crouched, flattening herself against the steps and hoping he would go the other way, but his footsteps came closer. She silently repeated to herself, "Do not hurt him, do not hurt him," terrified that if he saw her, she would lose control and kill him.

The man passed by, but Anike still felt a tension growing ever more insistent inside her, a fear of discovery and of what she might do if discovered. She could not stay where she was much longer. She sensed that the rising surge of power was on the point of bursting forth to sweep the walkway with fire or something equally destructive. Even though she felt it pulsing through her, she still had no idea how to use the energy to merely take flight again. She had to resist it and get away.

When the young man had gone about a dozen paces along the wall Anike took her chance. In a smooth movement, she bounded up the last few steps, crossed the walkway and vaulted over the wall. Turning and catching the edge so that she dropped only a few feet, she held on facing the stone, took a deep breath then let herself fall the rest of the way, hoping there was nothing beneath her. Even hanging from the top of the wall by her arms, the drop was well over her own height and she felt her right ankle turn as she hit the ground. She suppressed a cry of pain as she came to her feet and put weight on her right leg. What she had intended as a run became a limp. A shout came from above her. "To me! She is here!"

- 11 -

The Seer

No one leapt from the wall after her so Anike dragged herself behind a beached boat before pulling off her boot. She took the rest of the curing salve from her jar and rubbed it onto her ankle. The potent recipe quickly eased the pain and she replaced the boot before rising to her feet. Her ankle hurt as it took her weight but not enough to slow her down significantly.

There were voices on the town wall now. Anike doubted that anyone could see her from there but it was likely that they would organise some pursuit. They might even bring dogs and she did not relish the idea of being hunted. Her best chance was to cross to the other side of the river. There were boats of many sizes beached close by, both facing the sea and alongside the river, but a small boat would stand out on open water even at night. The estuary was too broad to be crossed by a bridge but it would not be a difficult swim for the daughter of a fisherman.

A grating noise told her that someone was raising the bar on the town's west gate. Anike considered plunging straight into the water but did not want to be swept out to sea at night so she decided to head up the eastern shore first.

It was too dark to see how many people had emerged from the town but it did not sound like a large number. The sentinels already on watch might not yet have called for reinforcements since she had not hurt anyone when she had come over the wall.

Trying to pass over the rough sand as quietly as possible and hunching down to keep behind the boats, she headed along the shore. From what she could hear, it seemed that the search was concentrated near where she had jumped, now a couple of hundred paces behind her.

She decided to cross to the other bank before the scope of the hunt widened. The river had narrowed to about seventy paces at this point. After checking that her bag was securely closed, she waded into it and swam across, carried slightly up the river by the incoming tide. Once on the western bank, she splashed upstream along the water's edge to hide her trail from any dogs.

The clouds had held in some of the heat of the day but, soaked through as she was, Anike began to shiver. She knew that cold could be as dangerous an enemy as a hunter so she kept moving, letting the effort warm her limbs. After rounding the first bend in the river, she turned inland. The west bank was wooded, in contrast to the river's eastern side which was mostly bare. She found a hollow and lit a small fire with the flint from her bag. Hanging her cloak on a nearby branch to dry it and hide the light, she warmed herself in front of the flames.

She felt the chill slowly leave her body and considered her next move while she brewed a curative potion to replace the salve she had used on her ankle. There was no sign of pursuit as yet but Bjord would surely be chasing her when daylight came.

They could track her but they would probably also go directly to the seer's home. Even if she got there before them, it was unlikely that she would be finished before any pursuers arrived so she decided to find Hilda's hut first, and then look for a place where she could watch it without being seen and wait for everyone to leave. She finished the potion, sat back against a tree and dozed. She needed as much sleep as she could get.

Dawn lit the landscape. Her clothes were now only slightly damp so she pulled her cloak around her, kicked earth onto the remains of the fire and headed upstream through the woods. She could see that the land across the river rose steeply further to the south. She could not approach Hilda's home from that direction but it would be safer to stay in the forest on the west bank until she drew level with the trail that led up into the hills.

Keeping back from the edge of the trees, Anike walked for another hour, occasionally angling back to the river to look for the white rock Ungrid had mentioned. It was fully light before she sighted it, a strangely regular cube, very pale grey and fifteen feet a side. Slightly rounded at the edges and missing a corner, it appeared both artificial and ancient, completely at odds with the stone around it. Buried partly in the earth by the river bank, it looked as if a long-forgotten giant had dropped a dice as he passed by.

The road ran between the rock and the river. Just south of the rock, a trail branched off from the road and headed steeply up to the hills between two shoulders of land. She found a point with a good view of the rock and trail, climbed a tree and perched comfortably on a couple of larger branches to watch the road.

It was not long before the distant whinny of a horse reached her ears. She looked down the river to see a group of men approaching. Bjord was at their head, mounted on a large grey. Riding next to him was an older man, who she assumed was Arl Oster. His ringmail shone in the morning light and his left eye was covered by a black eyepatch. Behind the two riders came more than a dozen armed men on foot, a very sizeable force. She recognised Loga, the lean form of Tavic and a few others from Trollgard among them. The rest had to be Oster's men, and she was surprised that four of them carried bows. A good bow could cost almost as much as a sword and these weapons, together with the number of warriors and the presence of the Arl himself, showed how seriously he was taking her as a threat. The group reached the white rock and turned up onto the track that led to the seer's home. It appeared they had chosen to start their search for her there.

Anike watched the last of them disappear over the first rise. She could not approach Hilda until everyone was gone so she would have to wait where she was or follow the band at a distance. The men did not seem to be particularly alert and she had not seen any dogs or scouts. She ought to be able to trail them if she was careful. She waited, but no more hunters had appeared after ten minutes so she decided that it was safe to follow.

She went a few hundred paces further upstream then swam back to the east bank. Crossing the road, she went up the steep hill directly ahead of her until the road was hidden by the contours of the land, then turned to the north. After a while, she came over a rise and found herself looking down on the smaller trail that led to Hilda's, running along the bottom of a steep valley some eighty feet below her. Looking to her right, she could see that the valley sides grew steeper as the trail went further into the hills to the east and after about a mile it disappeared over a pass lying between two cliffs.

Anike saw that she would ultimately have to descend to the trail but the cliffs made a good vantage point so she struck out towards them along the side of the hill. She had reached a part where the hillside was steeper when the sound of hooves echoing from the high sides of the pass warned her that Bjord's force was coming back down the trail. She cast about her for some sort of cover. There was nothing nearby except some scrubby bushes and the odd low rock but ahead the hillside became a proper cliff with an edge sharp enough to hide her from the view of someone on the valley floor, if she could reach it.

With some surprise, she noticed that she did not feel worried at the prospect of being seen, part of her welcoming the chance for conflict, and that concerned her. She reminded herself that she wanted to avoid any more deaths, including her own. She forced herself to choose evasion over battle and ran for the cover of the cliff.

A horse appeared on the trail and she flung herself down flat before the rider saw her. She pressed herself down to hide as much of her body as she could beneath her cloak, listening for shouts of recognition, heart pounding. The clatter of horses' hooves on the trail and the distant voices of the warriors drifted up to her. She slowed her breathing, resisting the urge to bring the suspense to an end, to leap up and rain down fire on the men beneath. She strained her ears but heard nothing to suggest that they were climbing the slope towards her. The sounds of boots and hooves on the hard earth slowly died away and she raised her head. The warband was well down the trail towards the river, weapons held more casually than on the way up. There seemed to be the same number as when they had gone the other way and she smiled in relief. She had been worried that Bjord and Oster might have left men with Hilda.

As the group was almost out of sight, one of the men on foot looked back. She thought she recognised Loga as he tugged at Bjord's leg to attract his attention. Bjord looked back but after a moment shook his head and led the warriors down the trail towards the river.

She waited to make sure they were gone then made her way down the steep slope to the trail. Following it uphill to the pass between the cliffs, she found it turned around a shoulder of rock. Before her was a bowl of land with low hills ahead and to the north. Cliffs to the south formed an impenetrable barrier. The trail descended to flatter ground and then veered to the left up the far slope before disappearing into the forest at the crest of the hill.

On the right of the depression, a weathered hut stood close to the cliff, bordered by a patch of worked soil with rows of vegetables on one side and a grove of fruit trees on the other. A brook babbled past, cutting through the trail as it flowed into a small lake on her left. A few chickens scrabbled at the earth and a fenced field held some goats. There was little to indicate that this was the dwelling place of someone who inspired such fear in Ulsvater.

The ground near the wooden building had been churned up by the passage of so many men and horses. Despite her count of the warriors, she had still partly expected a guard but there was no sign that Bjord had left anyone behind. Someone could still have been waiting within the hut, so Anike approached with care before stopping to listen just outside. She heard nothing save the animals, so cautiously put her hand on the door and pushed it open. She peered in and as her eyes slowly adjusted to the dark interior, she saw the outline of a figure sitting at a table. It spoke in a voice cracking with age but still infused with depth and power. "Anike Dareksdottir, come in. I had expected you yesterday."

The outline resolved itself into an old woman leaning forward in her seat, hands folded in front of her on the tabletop. Accepting the invitation to enter, Anike stepped over the threshold and once within she could make out more details. White hair fell over the woman's shoulders like snow on an ancient mountain and piercing blue eyes glinted from her lined face, returning Anike's gaze with intensity and interest.

On the large table in front of her lay a pale hide with lines and circles drawn on it. Scattered on top of the drawing were a dozen or so white pebbles about the size of a thumb. Anike approached the table and when she looked down from the woman's penetrating stare to the pebbles on the table, she could see that each stone had a symbol carved on it. There was something odd about the shape of the stones, slightly angular, and on looking more closely she could see that they were not pebbles at all, but bones. She caught her breath. The woman's demeanour and the display of the bones were subtly menacing.

Energy built within her in response to the perceived threat and she fought down an impulse to shatter the house and burn everything within to ashes. That would be no way to gain the woman's aid.

"You know my name, Hilda, because Bjord Svafnirsson told you," she said slowly.

The woman laughed sharply, a sound like sticks breaking. "Correct! Runes can reveal many things but they provide descriptions more accurately than names."

Encouraged by this response, much less scathing than she had feared, Anike continued, "You knew I was coming before they arrived, though. Well, I am here now. Bjord will have told you what I have done – at least as it appeared to him – and that would lead many people to want me condemned to death. What do you plan to do?" This was direct, but Hilda unnerved Anike somewhat and she wanted to get some idea of what the seer was thinking quickly.

She saw no fear in Hilda's face but neither could she see how Hilda could threaten her or indeed defend herself. She wondered if Hilda was a witch herself but whether she was or not, everything about her implied she was fully in control of this situation and Anike was cautious.

"That was a poor question. Try another." Hilda's confidence was palpable.

Anike was not used to this kind of confrontation. Even Arl Svafnir had not radiated such certainty and she could now see why the people of Ulsvater feared this woman.

She paused to consider her response but Hilda cut through her thoughts. "Our questions do not define us but they do reveal us, sometimes to ourselves." She leaned back, her eyes on Anike's face.

Anike recognised both a warning and an opportunity within these words. What she said next would be important. She wanted to go back to the life she had been living before, when Gern was still just a woodsman, her father had not fallen ill and her greatest problem had been deciding how to respond to Bjord's attentions, but to suggest that she wanted the impossible was not likely to earn Hilda's respect. She recalled Ungrid's advice and decided that asking something about a vague future where she had gained acceptance within Trollgard would not be helpful. She would be better off addressing the most fundamental problem in her life directly.

"Can you tell me how to rid myself of the power that makes me a witch?" she asked.

"That is better," said Hilda. "You have limited options here and it is no easy thing to give up power of any kind. I think you may, in time, learn to improve how you frame questions but this one was both focused and revealing. I do not myself know the answer but in a moment we may seek it together."

Hilda waved her hand at the bones in front of her. Anike followed Hilda's gesture and looked at them more carefully. She had seen the symbols before, on runestones like those at Volna's farm but in the back of her mind was a half-remembered thought that she knew them from somewhere else as well, though the exact memory eluded her.

Hilda touched the hide on which a pattern of lines and circles was drawn. "This represents Yggdrasil, the World Tree, and the worlds it holds. Sit," she instructed, and Anike did so. Hilda touched a white bone. "Each of these runes has a meaning and when they are combined there are yet more meanings. They can tell almost any story about how the world truly is. While not always precise, they are rarely wrong if you know how to read them." Her tone was authoritative and Anike began to glimpse the tremendous power of the seer's craft. The ability to get an answer to any question, even an approximate one, could make a seer valued and honoured but she also knew that life was rarely simple and some truths might be deeply unwelcome.

"Access to such knowledge surely comes at a price," Anike said. "What is the cost?"

"A good question," Hilda replied with a hint of satisfaction in her voice. "I can give you a partial answer but as is often the case with the runes, complete clarity is hard to reach. What I can tell you is that when you use the runes to push aside the leaves of Yggdrasil to see more clearly, the World Tree pushes back. Sometimes the answer itself is sufficient price but in other cases the gain obtained from the knowledge is balanced by misfortune. Tools may seize up or break, illness can strike you or your loved ones, or something important to you will be lost. If you repeat your request, ask more questions too quickly or try for a different answer, the ill luck multiplies. We live in a hard world and the gods do not find it difficult to bring bad luck down upon us."

Hilda's voice lowered. "If you consider that you will probably not be better off overall for seeking the guidance of the runes then that will guide you to an understanding of the cost. Some people will never accept that and will ask regardless of the consequences."

"The people of Ulsvater seem to have learned that lesson," Anike commented drily.

"After many years. But they still come sometimes, and occasionally I am honoured by a visit from someone who has travelled a long way to see me." She shrugged. "The price might be to help an old woman who lives alone with something she cannot do herself. If you recognise that there will be a cost, sometimes you can limit it to a sacrifice of your own choice."

Anike looked at the pattern of scattered bones on the table. "Bjord asked something about me, did he not?"

"Runecasting has rules within its nature and I have more of my own. I do not discuss one person's reading with another, nor do I lie about what the runes tell me." Hilda's voice was firm but without hostility.

"I can see the sense in that," said Anike. "But I can hazard a guess that Bjord cared little about cost and would have disregarded advice about it. He would have asked you where to find me."

Hilda said nothing.

"Indulge my rambling, please," Anike continued. "I do not need you to answer. You would have told him what the runes showed but he did not find me even though he passed me on the trail. If he had been looking properly or he had started back from here a few moments earlier, he would have seen me." She creased her brow in thought. "So he either asked the wrong question or he did not understand the answer properly. Perhaps the cost of the answer was that he would not find me or would look in the wrong place?" She looked down at the runes. "That was what happened, I suspect."

Hilda's face shifted, a slight smile forming like a crack appearing in the bark of an old tree. Anike could not tell if it signified approval or amusement. "If you learn the runes, you will be able to read the answer but the reading will be incomplete without the question. That is the key that unlocks the knowledge."

"Many years of listening to questions and answers could give someone much knowledge and wisdom."

"The more you learn, the more you realise how much you do not know," sighed Hilda. "For example, I have never had a conversation with a witch before."

"So you are talking to me out of curiosity?"

"In part, yes."

Anike felt slighted at this impersonal motive. How dare this woman treat her as if she were a mere object for study? Even as she tensed, she recognised that she was reacting with unnatural sensitivity. It was much better to be met with curiosity than fear and the desire to understand mysteries was a trait she shared with Hilda. After all, the need to learn something had brought her to Hilda's door.

She calmed herself. "Then let us seek some knowledge together. I am ready to ask my question now."

"We shall proceed then." Hilda scooped up the runes and dropped them into a bag. She handed it to Anike, who felt the weight of it in her hand and something else as well, a sort of tingling in her fingers and palm as if the bag were a small creature that had not decided whether she was friend or foe.

"You will need to hold the question you want to be answered uppermost in your mind and heart. If you wish to offer a specific sacrifice, think of that at the same time."

"How would I know if the sacrifice is appropriate? Or sufficient?"

"You won't until the balance is demanded."

"The gods do not make this easy, do they?"

"This is not like buying bread," Hilda said sharply. "Runecasts touch the fabric of the world and respect is mandated. The gods will impose it if it is not offered."

"Of course. I understand," Anike said, stung by the rebuke. "Please go on."

"You do not need to speak the question out loud," Hilda said in a firm but more measured voice, "but it helps focus your mind and unless you tell me what it is, my interpretation will be vague at best. The question is a key part of the reading."

"I understand."

"When you have the question held firmly, draw as many runes from the bag as you feel are right and cast them on the map." Hilda indicated the hide with both hands. "A handful is usual but some cast only a single rune and some many more. Be guided by your feelings."

"Anything else?"

"That is enough for now."

Anike nodded, closed her eyes and contemplated how to word her question. She needed to know how to get rid of her witchcraft but was worried that she would not be able to express her desire precisely enough. She wanted to give the gods as little latitude to make sport of her as she could. She considered asking for the quickest way, or perhaps the best way, but 'best' added little clarity and speed might involve others getting hurt. What she really wanted was a method that did not involve doing any more harm to anyone else and her cast had to answer that concern.

With the true focus of the question clear, she considered the sacrifice. It seemed to her that she had to think about what she would gain from the answer first. If it gave her what she needed, she might secure a semblance of normal life but would probably be committing herself to a dangerous quest or ritual. Possibly, she might receive an unhelpful answer, or one difficult to implement but still worth pursuing. It was hard to know the true value in advance and so judge what sacrifice she needed to make.

Sacrifices punctuated life and were common at festivals, before journeys were undertaken or at the birth of children. Most were performed while prayers were uttered but Anike recalled a legend in which a hero had bargained for knowledge of how to slay a dragon in exchange for a promise to kill the first living thing he met on his victorious return. He had slain the dragon but on his return, his father had rushed joyfully to meet him and the hero had refused to take his own father's life. The gods had punished him by cursing his line so that the firstborn of each generation died as a baby. She did not want to risk that form of bargain.

She had little enough with her to offer – a little silver, potions and herbs as well as her tools – all things she needed, but that was the point. It would be no sacrifice to surrender something she did not need or value. She also had her body and blood. She knew Odin had given up an eye in return for knowledge but while the gods appreciated the spilling of blood, an eye was probably too much to offer. However, proceeding without a sacrifice would leave her too much of a hostage to their whims. Ultimately, she could only do her best when judging the value and just had to make a decision. She had used her healing elixirs a lot on this journey and had little doubt she would need them again. While she could make more, she did not know when she would next have the time or opportunity so she would give those up as her sacrifice.

Her decision made, she opened the bag and slid her hand into it. She could feel the runes, hard against her fingers but also almost alive. Pleasure and disgust ran up her arm as she touched them. The unnatural sensations almost made her withdraw her hand but taking a deep breath, she closed her fingers around the bones and spoke the question she had formulated. "How may I rid myself of the power that makes me a witch, in a way that causes the least harm to others?" She cast the runes and watched them tumble over the map.

The seer leaned forward, her eyes taking in the lie of the bones, flicking from one to another as she studied the pattern. Anike felt her stomach lurch and her hands tremble as she waited for Hilda's reading. She had an overwhelming apprehension that this was not a good result.

Hilda sat back and looked at Anike. "I have never witnessed that question asked before or even one like it, though it can hardly be the first time the gods have heard it. The answer is unusually clear and there is, I am afraid, little room for clarification and none for doubt. The runes tell me that the only way to remove witchcraft from you is by your death."

- 12 -

RUNES

Anike stared at the table. It was difficult to imagine a worse answer.

As her hopes splintered, she felt the desire to lash out. If she could not break the bonds of her fate, she could shatter the building around her. The gift of witchcraft could still find expression in destruction. She started to rise to her feet.

The movement brought home to her the absurdity of her chain of thought and she recognised it as distorted by the energy within her. Witchcraft was no gift. She shut her eyes, willing herself to accept her fate calmly and to try to make the best of her situation. The urge to destroy everything nearby receded and she opened her eyes again.

Her first coherent thought was that she had asked the wrong question. "I just need to put it differently. I asked about the path that involved the least harm to others. Obviously, my death is the answer to that question. No one else would be hurt if I killed myself now."

Hilda raised her hand. "You did not listen properly. The runes revealed that this was the only way to remove the power from you. It was clear. In some cases, the cast does show that the wrong question was asked and it might be worth trying a better one, but there is no indication of an alternative answer here."

As Hilda's words and the message of the runes sunk in, Anike realised deep down that this had not come as a surprise. She had never heard any story about a witch giving up their power, and perhaps more importantly the response resonated with truth. The energy felt like a second heartbeat, so firmly bonded that it had become part of her mind and body.

She fought against the feeling that reducing the runes to ashes would be a very satisfying response and took a deep breath. "That was not easy to hear but I did need to know," she said. "I must remember that all knowledge has some value. I had hoped that there was a way back to my old life and that you could put me on that path. It seems that wish was in vain."

The destructive impulse receded and she realised that she had not made her sacrifice. The pain that the answer caused seemed to be a more than sufficient price but she had made her promise to the gods so she pulled out her flasks of curative elixir and put them on the table. "These are what I offered as a sacrifice. You had better take them," she said, then added "I am sorry, that was ungracious of me. I meant, may I give them to you?"

"I can understand your reaction," Hilda said as she moved the jars to her side of the table, placing them out of Anike's reach, symbolic of accepting the offering.

Anike frowned, wondering what to do next. As her mind turned over possibilities, she asked a tangential question which had been nagging at her. "You said the runes give right answers if you read them properly. Where does this truth come from? It seems too simple to say the answers come from the gods. Odin himself read the runes so who sent the answers to him?"

"I believe the spirits of the Norns select the runes as they spin, measure and cut the threads of fate. They were there before Odin," Hilda told her.

"Believe? Surely you have asked the runes about this sometime in the past?"

"Of course I have, but the answers were exceedingly hard to interpret. I will give you an analogy. One and one make two, do they not?"

"Yes," said Anike, wondering where this was going.

"Why?"

"I do not follow. It is just how it is."

"There is always a reason, a prior cause. The difficulty is that you have no way of describing the reason why one plus one is two. The numbers cannot explain themselves. Runes are like that."

Anike frowned. "I think I understand. Perhaps we can discuss it further in the future, but I would like to ask you about something else.

I felt something strange when I held the bones, almost as if they were alive."

Hilda leaned forwards. "Go on."

Anike thought about the sensations that touching the runes had stirred within her. She found her reactions hard to put into words, particularly since there seemed to be several different impulses. She reached out to touch one of the bones then stopped, glancing at Hilda to see if this was permitted, and pointed at one. "What rune is this?" It seemed to call to her.

"Its name is *Agni*. It is a rune of form and its root meaning is fire," Hilda replied.

As soon as Hilda said this aloud, it was as if Anike had always known it and that she had just needed to be reminded. The rune felt right to her, comfortable and familiar. "Of course," she whispered to herself. As she passed her hand over the table, other runes generated similar feelings of familiarity and reassurance but some triggered the opposite response, subtly but tangibly jarring her nerves and grating at her senses. Yet others felt neither good nor bad, just present, with a sensation of solidity and weight.

"This one?" She pointed at one of the symbols that felt wrong to her.

"This is the rune for water, *Unda*," Hilda replied. Again, the name seemed to release another buried memory but this time the recollection came with a feeling of hostility.

"May I touch these?" she asked and when Hilda nodded, she ran her fingers over the bones, gathering them into piles based on the sensations they engendered. She spread out the group that felt sympathetic and looked questioningly at Hilda.

"*Vata*, the rune for wind or air. *Eneki* is lightning, and *Izik* means disruption or chaos. This one is *Prana*, which represents motion or movement."

Hilda's naming of the runes brought back a memory of Gern attacking her and Anike tried to bring the recollection into focus and recall the words Gern had used. "Keppa," she said. "No, *Kappa*." A ripple of revulsion passed through her. "Is that the name of a rune?"

"*Kappa* means earth," Hilda said, pointing to a rune in the group that had made Anike uneasy. Memory and comprehension fused in Anike's mind. "I heard someone say that word," she explained. She thought of the ice armour that Gern had conjured around him. "And *Ranak* means ice."

"You have been taught the basics, I see," said Hilda.

"Actually, I have not," Anike said, "but as you named each one, I recognised it. The runes have a presence about them. I can sense it, and the memory seems to resonate with it." She indicated the pile of bones in front of her. "This group feels good but this other pile feels wrong, somehow. It is hard to describe."

"Interesting. The runes in the first set are all aligned with chaos – forms like fire, wind, and so on, and runes of effect like destruction, flying, and discontinuity." Hilda indicated the second pile. "These represent concepts aligned with order or law, such as stasis, ice and creation. This final pile contains neutral runes that mostly describe relationships or connections."

Hilda looked up at Anike, her eyes alight with interest. "I feel nothing from these runes. I know their meanings, their aspects and their correspondences, but it is all learned lore. The bones as objects mean no more to me than stone – they are just tools which allow me to read the world. My own teacher never mentioned sensations. It seems that you are different, that something inside you is attuned to the runes or to the forces and concepts they represent."

"The part that makes me a witch," Anike replied quietly. "Even though I could not read them, I saw runes many times before I was cursed and I did not feel anything." Almost without thinking, she closed her hand over the fire rune and she felt the energy inside her respond with sympathy, pulsing with greater power and urgency. On an impulse, she let it go and touched the symbol for ice. Immediately she felt the rising, destructive urge inside her clash with the vibration of the law-aligned rune. The sensations seemed to cancel each other and both faded. She smiled, realising that here was a chance to use the runes to control her inner power. She closed her eyes and visualised the ice rune. A tangible shock ran through her nerves as the ever-present pulse of energy inside her rippled in response, retreating from the image, and her mind seemed clearer than it had in days.

She opened her eyes to see Hilda watching her. "There may be no way to rid myself of this power short of my death, but there could be methods to control it." She smiled ruefully. "Sometimes, it seems, you need to have one road blocked before you can see another path."

"Go on," said Hilda.

"There is some connection between the runes and witchcraft. I can feel the power within me recognising the runes. It is hard to explain, but once you tell me a meaning, it is like you are just reminding me of something I already know. Let me see if I can do it without you naming it first." She thought back to the battle with Gern. He had spoken the word for earth, *Kappa*, but he had used others as well. Sifting through memories, she alighted on the word he had said when she was trapped in the brambles. "*Ert*," she said aloud. "Wait, do not tell me." She repeated the word in her mind, and each time she did so she felt a shudder of revulsion disrupt the flow of force within her, but meaning came back like a distant echo. "It means 'stop'."

"I use the word 'stasis'," said Hilda. She fixed Anike with her gaze. "You say you are not tutored in runes, but many educated people do know a little rune lore and you speak as if you have been."

"My master never used them. He thought they were too vague to use to label plants and until recently I only really saw them on runestones or inscribed onto weapons. Last week, before I was cursed – it seems a lifetime ago now – a witch tried to kill me. I only realised a few minutes ago that he spoke rune names when he attacked. When he said '*Ert*', it felt as if he was draining the life from me."

Anike stood and began to pace about the room. She continued thoughtfully, "This is not quite how I release the power inside me, though. I just say the normal word, 'fire' or 'wind', not the proper name of the rune."

"The runes spoken by this other witch are all law-aligned. Fire and wind are tied to chaos, and could be more malleable," Hilda observed.

"So perhaps it is different for law and chaos," Anike said. "Most of the time, I do not know how to access the power. It is only when I am angry or frightened that I can use it and then it just happens by instinct. Right now, I have no idea how it is done or why it works but I feel that speaking the word is what is needed to crystalise my desires, making them real."

She stopped pacing and looked at Hilda, her expression grave. "I have done some very bad things, actions which I would not have thought I was capable of a few days ago. I did not think I would have hurt anyone save to defend myself or someone I loved but when the power takes hold I want to commit terrible acts, and I enjoy them. It is a little like being drunk. I find myself wishing to destroy those who get in my way, or merely irritate me, and I have to be on my guard each waking moment because I have the power to do it. I am telling you this so that you are clear about the danger that my presence poses." She sat down again and faced Hilda across the table. "With that in mind, will you teach me runecraft?"

The request hung in the air for a moment, and then Hilda laughed. "Your questions are becoming more interesting, though I need no runes to answer this one. I have lived a long time and seen much, but despite all my knowledge I am humbled by what I do not know. I am curious about you, about witchcraft and your relationship with it. Little that is truly novel comes my way nowadays and these old bones can no longer travel the archipelago so it would be foolish of me to turn away the chance to learn something new when it comes right to my door." Her eyes glinted. "Yes, I will teach you if you meet my price."

"Of course there is a cost. I understand," Anike said. "What would you require in exchange?"

"You did not agree without asking that, I see. Good." Hilda raised a finger. "First, you will give me an account of how you became a witch and all that you have done with your power. Secondly, I ask that you share any insight you gain from my teaching or acquire from your own instinctive affinity or perspective." She raised a third finger. "Finally, you will help me look after this place, forage, cook and make such potions for me as I request."

"I did not say I was a herbalist," Anike said.

"No, you did not," agreed Hilda, "but even if the potions you sacrificed were not sufficient to mark you out as one, recall that I did tell you that the runes were better at providing descriptions than names."

At Hilda's suggestion, Anike spent an hour foraging for edible roots from the forest then cooked them into a meal for them both. She noticed that Hilda moved carefully, as if going faster would cause her pain, and while her fingers were precise and sure when she held the runes in her hands, she did not appear strong. There was no doubt Hilda's mind was undimmed by age but her frailty made Anike wonder who tended the neat rows of vegetables outside. It was hard to imagine Hilda weeding them herself.

"How do you manage up here alone?" she asked after she had washed the bowls in the nearby stream.

"I have my ways," Hilda replied, "and every so often someone comes from Ulsvater to help with the heavier work. There are those who live there who are still grateful for advice I have given them in the past and occasionally seekers of knowledge give their labour as payment."

Anike did not question her further but the explanation sat a little uneasily with the attitude of those she had met in the town. She supposed there could be others who felt gratitude, after all in the right circumstances a reading might have made the difference between life and death, but she did wonder if there was more that Hilda was not telling her.

They sat at the table. Hilda had cleared away the runes to show the pattern drawn on the hide lying on the table. She indicated the circles. "These represent the nine worlds and the lines represent paths between them." Anike, sitting opposite, looked down at the hide then up at Hilda's face, vibrant as she started to explain the craft.

"Where a rune falls on the map affects its meaning. There are a myriad of possibilities and it usually takes many years to master the art. The position of each rune and how they are connected carry a different message. Sometimes even I see patterns I do not recognise." Hilda leaned forward and rested her chin on her fingers

"I will be able to set your feet on the path, but you will need to finish it elsewhere."

"The runes tell you that?" asked Anike.

"No. Despite what myths you may have heard, the runes do not tell the future. They only speak of what is. What is to come is not set in stone. Nevertheless, the future, causation and prediction, can be illuminated by craft and intellect." Hilda idly touched the bone carved with the earth symbol. "The runes can show potentials and a well-judged question about these may assist in revealing what is to come. They can uncover a person's intentions too, but that is a fickle area. People are complex and can quickly change their minds or be diverted from a planned course." She looked at Anike, "I knew you were coming to me yesterday, but I could not be certain you would actually complete the journey."

Anike wondered why Hilda had been interested in her before Bjord had come but did not want to interrupt the lesson, so she simply asked, "You can make predictions then?"

"Yes, but not true prophecies. It has been said that the Norns could foretell the future accurately, though that is beyond rune casting as I know it. You may have heard the story of how Odin once went to them to hear a prophecy about Ragnarok. Odin's own skill with runes was not sufficient to tell him the outcome of that final battle."

"Odin is said to have sacrificed one eye for the chance to drink from the well of knowledge," Anike recalled. "In return, Mimir's Head let him drink and he was given mastery of runes and the power of prophecy."

"One and the same thing, perhaps, though after thousands of years we can no longer be sure, particularly as so much knowledge was no doubt lost during Ragnarok," replied Hilda. "In the legends, the Norns have a different role to most of the gods and their gifts may have extended to true prophecy." She sat back. "If the Norns did truly see the future, it was not by reading runes. We can only use them to find a starting point but with a little knowledge of human nature, the predictions can be quite accurate."

She seemed about to say more but suddenly cocked her head to one side as if listening. For a moment, Anike wondered what she had heard over the sound of goats and chickens but then she too made out voices. "Visitors. Two, I think," said Hilda.

"It is unlikely to be Bjord or Arl Oster, then," said Anike. "They would have come back with a larger force or be much more stealthy. Even so, I cannot be seen. If word of my presence here got out, it would bring trouble to you."

"There is no time to get you away from here." Hilda's brow wrinkled. "You could..." Her voice tailed off. "No, we will have to hide you in plain sight." She pulled a ragged fur from a pile. "Wrap that around yourself and cover your hair, then rub some ash on your face and keep your head down."

Anike did as she was told, though she did wonder what course of action Hilda had considered and rejected. The fur stank of decay and sweat. No one would willingly come close, she realised as she tried to breathe through her mouth. Hilda scrutinised her. "Hunch a bit more. Yes, like that. Now go and look as if you are tidying up and as the visitors come inside, take some plates down to the stream and wash them until they leave."

Hilda acted as if she had done this before. It would be a good way to pass close to the visitors but avoid being examined too carefully as they would assume Anike was a thrall and of no significance. She went to the shelves in the rear of the room and began somewhat aimlessly moving the neatly stacked bowls and plates around, as if some of them needed cleaning or tidying.

At the base of a pile of earthenware plates, covered with a cloth, she felt something cold and hard. She unwrapped it to reveal the intricately engraved edge of a silver plate. It was worth a fortune and seemed completely out of place amongst the humble crockery. She quickly covered it again and placed some bowls on top. It was so odd that Anike decided not to ask Hilda about it. The old woman clearly had many secrets but Anike doubted this mystery affected her and it would be disrespectful to pry.

The voices grew louder and there was a knock on the door. "Enter!" called out Hilda, firmly and with authority. The door opened to reveal two men, one thickset and grizzled, the other much younger and slimmer. They had a similar cast to their features, were dressed in green-dyed leathers and had unstrung bows slung on their backs. Even the younger, scarcely out of boyhood, had the weathered look of those who spend most of their time outdoors. Father and son, both hunters, Anike surmised. Word about her might not yet have reached them if they lived away from town, but she still could not risk being identified.

The older man stepped inside, followed by his son. He bowed to Hilda and at a sharp poke in the ribs, so did the younger. While their eyes were still adjusting to the dim interior, Anike scurried forward, a pile of plates in her hands and her head low. The younger man looked directly at her and Anike stooped even further in what she hoped was a subservient manner, then dodged around the two of them as she headed outside. The younger man continued to eye her curiously but Hilda started to speak and he turned away. Anike shut the door and went down to the stream.

She crouched down where she had a good view of the hut. She could hear voices but she was happy to be too far away to make out individual words. She was curious but did not think it was right to intrude on a runecasting that was nothing to do with her.

It was unfortunate that the pair had turned up so soon. She wondered if this bad luck was an additional price to be paid for her runecast but there was no way of knowing. She felt that the young man's interest had been born of a general curiosity rather than arising from any suspicion.

Time wore on, and Anike was beginning to wonder whether she should go back in with the plates when the two men emerged. The young man was smiling grimly, his face was set in a determined expression. The older hunter looked more thoughtful. Once again he paid her little heed but the younger man's gaze lingered on her for a moment before he followed his father up the track leading back towards the river. She shrugged and returned to the cabin.

"This has not been a quiet day for you, has it?" Anike commented as she stowed the plates.

"Life is like the ocean. On some days, it is calm. On others, the waves are driven before storms," Hilda replied.

"Your idea of hiding in plain sight was a good one and they did not seem suspicious. May we continue now?"

"Indeed, and it is time for part of your payment. I wish to hear your account of how you came to be a witch, all you have done with witchcraft and what you have surmised. I have been told a few things but I would prefer to hear it all from you rather than distort your tale by focusing on those parts. I want to know what you choose to emphasise."

Anike considered this and nodded. Bjord would have given one account but Hilda was clearly not going to rely on that. It was impossible to know for certain which events were relevant, as although she assumed the proximity of witch weather had been random bad luck she might even be wrong about that. However, she had to start somewhere so she began with the reason for her journey to Vanir Heights.

Hilda listened intently, in silence for the most part, but when Anike came to her escape from the harrowling, she frowned and leaned forward. Anike stopped, waiting for her to speak.

"Go through the thinking which led you to decide what witchcraft you would use, please," Hilda instructed.

Anike thought back to what had been going through her mind at the time. "I was annoyed that the creature was attacking me rather than the town. I was not afraid, not by then, but I did have to get out of its way and flight seemed natural. I must have thought about stories where witches flew and saw that as a means of escape though I don't actively recall doing that." Hilda's frown remained, and Anike reconsidered. "Knowledge of my capabilities seems to have come to me in the same way as the meaning of runes and I cannot explain that either." Her own brow creased. "It is frustrating that I cannot remember how I accessed the power. If it is purely instinct then I may never be able to control it."

"Ultimately if memory and reason fail, a well-targeted runecast may set us on the path to understanding but we should consider if such enquiries are needed," Hilda said. "Continue with your tale."

Anike did so, concluding with the attempted robbery in Ulsvater.

"Thank you for your account, Anike. I will think on it. We will return to rune lore."

Hilda looked down at the runes on the table, then back up at Anike. It was a moment before she spoke again. "We will start with simple meanings and progress to more complexity when you have comprehended the basics. Runes fit together into patterns just as words combine to make sentences." She slid a few runes together. "Runecastings tell stories, but they are stories about what is happening now, shaped by the question. Remember that, and it will help you understand what you see." Hilda's fingers darted over the runes, sorting them into piles. "We call this group runes of form. They symbolise the elements that make up the world and are the basis of any reading."

Anike recognised fire, movement and wind, as well as the adverse runes for earth, frost and stasis. Hilda named the sympathetic luck rune, *Folor*, the hostile strength rune, *Barak* and the rune for law, *Log*. Two runes related to perceptions. *Osc*, meaning veil, felt good to her in contrast to *Ilun* which stood for seeming.

There was one left in the group and Anike picked it up. It felt slightly more solid than the others and gave her a different sensation, more alien than the law runes but less hostile. "That is *Vit*, the rune of life," Hilda said.

Anike looked at her sharply, startled that the symbol for life should seem so strange to her. As with the other runes, its meaning was clear once Hilda had said its name, as if a jog to the memory was all that was needed to put the concept into words. However, the reaction from within did not provide her with an explanation of the way the symbol for life, something which she thought ought to be more closely related to her than fire, felt so odd. The other form runes all had their opposites, she realised or partly remembered – fire and ice, law and chaos. Only the rune of life stood alone.

Hilda was continuing. "The next group are the runes of effect. They direct the forms." She listed them, touching each one of them as she did so. "Create, destroy, find, fly, transform, warp, discontinuity, light, obscure." The list went on for some time. There were even more in the last group, the description runes, which related to time, distance, relationships and other connections. Anike could readily see why it would normally take years to remember and understand them all, however she found it almost trivial. She only had to be told a name or meaning once and it became as familiar to her as the properties of a plant she had studied for years. Aspects of the forms, such as smoke, also came effortlessly to her. Anike had always had a good memory and her ability to hold images clearly in her mind's eye had been very useful in recalling the properties of different parts of herbs, but this facility with runes was of a different order entirely. She wondered if Odin had felt something similar when he drank from Mimir's Well.

The sun was setting by the time Hilda had taken Anike through all the individual runes, the common pairs and short phrase patterns. As the discussion drew to a close, Anike commented thoughtfully, "This seems too simple. I realise that I have a great deal more to learn but I should not be able to retain everything you told me this afternoon. No one should be able to."

"Your progress is certainly remarkable," Hilda agreed.

"If I had this facility in other matters, I could have been a great skald, travelling the country, relating the ancient stories to the delight of the Arls," Anike said. "I have a good memory but it does not compare with this ability with runes. It is like the antipathy and sympathy I feel with them – the rune names and meanings resonate with witchcraft."

"Let us try something a little more testing then," Hilda said. She laid out a selection of runes in a pattern on the map. "Tell me what you think this means, as a whole."

Anike looked at the symbols and their placement. She recognised all of the runes without effort and then considered how they were arranged. For a moment it was only a jumble of concepts, but then she saw a pattern and discerned the links between the runes. The meanings condensed into a short, simple statement.

"It means, 'There is one here that is touched by chaos,'" she said. "This was not a cast, was it?"

"No, it is just something I constructed," Hilda told her, "but you are right about the meaning. Tell me how you came to that conclusion."

"After a moment, it just seemed obvious." Anike pointed to the chaos and life runes. "I started with the forms. They are joined by the position on the map." She went on to explain the connections she had made between the runes.

"That is an interesting method," the seer said. "I would have read it in this way." She explained her approach. Anike followed the logic but it seemed artificial to her, and she said so.

Hilda sat back in her chair. "I would hazard that we both made a good decision," she said. "We have much to learn from each other."

Anike shrugged. "It just seemed the obvious way to read it." She lifted the life rune. "This one is strange. I would have expected a life symbol to feel good, but it does not. It gives me the impression that it belongs to someone else."

"Traditionally, *Vit* is associated with neither law nor chaos but stands apart as a third principle. It is the only form like that but there is an effect rune, *Vish* – 'heal' – that has the same affinity. It is distinct from the neutral effects like 'transform' that more commonly act on *Vit*."

The sensations Anike felt indicated an underlying truth in the runic affinities that Hilda described as though life was not a part of either law or chaos but something beyond both.

"That's enough for today," Hilda said. "Let me taste some more of your cooking."

Anike marked the progress of the day with extra effort when she prepared the meal and Hilda nodded approval at the delicately spiced dish she prepared before indicating a pile of furs for a bed. As Anike lay down on them, she tried to review what she had learned, but the lore soon blurred and she drifted into an exhausted sleep.

The next morning, she was woken by a shaft of sunlight crossing her face. She opened her eyes to find Hilda already up. "You needed that rest, it seems," said the older woman when Anike sat up. "Let us have something to eat."

Hilda had made no attempt to prepare anything so Anike took those words as an instruction. It was no more than she did for her father and the thought of him alone at home made her sigh. She hoped he was coping in her absence and an unexpected recollection of his cooking entered her mind. There was a reason she had taken over that chore when she was ten.

Hilda's approach to instruction was more discursive than Olaf's and reminded her somewhat of Arl Svafnir, with a lot of meaning lying beneath the carefully chosen words. While her hands were engaged in the simple manual tasks of food preparation, Anike sifted through what she had learned the previous day. The lessons seemed to have settled in her mind overnight and she could recall rune meanings as if she had been born knowing them.

An idea emerged from the growing connections between concepts and thoughts, and she turned it over in her mind. She now knew that runes described the world and she had a link to them more profound than the intellectual one that Hilda had learned. The energy within her reacted to the runes. If she put that together with her own raw power to call forth fire or storm, could she describe these effects with runes, even reproduce them? Could this be a means to bring her power under conscious control? So far everything she had done had been instinctive, responding to what was happening to her without understanding, and those unplanned reactions had led to deaths. If she was ever going to control her power reliably, she would have to learn to use her thoughts in place of her unruly emotions.

She handed a bowl to Hilda. "There is something I would like to discuss," she said and outlined her idea.

Hilda listened and nodded. "It seems to me that there is value in that approach. The connections between your energy and the chaos-aligned runes may be mere coincidence but as the runes correspond with the true elements of reality, it might well be a way to impose your conscious will on your powers."

"The effects of witchcraft seem quite simple conceptually compared with readings from a runecast," Anike observed.

Hilda responded cautiously. "Simple to outline perhaps. There is much detail to consider if you wish to describe the effects properly. Most runecasts are imprecise and need to be carefully interpreted, and what you are suggesting would involve exact definition."

"I could feel the power responding when I pictured images of runes," Anike went on. "This may not work but I need to explore the idea."

"I agree it is worth pursuing," said Hilda. "It could be useful to remember that while all form runes are tied to chaos or law, some of the effect runes are as well. Destruction, flight, and discontinuity are chaos-aligned, though many of the others are neutral and make sense when associated with most forms. However," she added firmly. "You will not be experimenting here. The process and results might be quite destructive."

"But I need your guidance, Hilda," said Anike in dismay.

"And I need my home, Anike. It will be much less dangerous if you come back after your attempts and we discuss what you have uncovered."

Anike thought of Volna's farm and had to accept that Hilda had a point. "I am finding it easier to maintain control now. I have not used my power in over a day."

"You have not deliberately tried to tap into it either."

"True. While I did not try too hard to resist it when the robbers attacked me in Ulsvater, it was still just instinct. But now I am on my guard the whole time." She did not mention the occasions in the hut when she had had to fight to maintain mastery of herself. "It will be a new challenge for me to try to access the energy when I wish to and you are right, I cannot be sure what will happen. I will go into the woods."

"There is a better place you could use, a cave not far from here with nothing inside for you to burn down. There are often hunters in the forest and scorched clearings would attract attention."

"How far is it?"

"Not far for you, a little over a mile to the east. It is easiest to follow the trail for a while, and when you come to a stream, turn south and follow it until you reach the cave."

"Why does no one live there?"

"The cave has very little dry floor, just water and sand, and it is not very inviting."

"It sounds ideal," said Anike, with a touch of irony. "Uncomfortable and wet."

Hilda smiled. "Hard for you to burn down." Anike hoped she was right.

It took Anike half an hour to find the stream. Trees pressed close so she found it easier to walk by the water. As she approached the cliff, the energy inside her began to churn like an angry sea. It had been quiescent all day but now it filled her with a wind of desire, hastening her steps.

Ahead, the banks rose on each side of her to form a narrow gully before opening up into a shallow bowl at the foot of the cliff. The stream came from a cave mouth, a dark hole in the rock face, and just in front was a pile of silver fur. Three dire wolves were lying next to the stream. As Anike caught sight of them, one raised its head and sniffed the air.

- 13 -

The Taming of the Wind

Anike did not hesitate. "*Agni*," she shouted, her hatred of the dire wolves crystalising into a ball of fire that flew from her hand and exploded to envelope them. Howls of pain filled the air as the three wolves were momentarily hidden from sight within the blaze. When the flames cleared, she could see that two of the wolves were burning, fur shot through with orange flame. The third, perhaps shielded by the others, was singed and smoking but largely unharmed. It lowered its head and started towards her, not directly but in a wide circle which would take it out of sight from her position in the gully.

One of the burning wolves rolled on the ground to extinguish the flames while the other headed for the relief of the stream. Whilst hurt, the creatures were still very much alive and she needed to finish them off. She was surprised they had not fled as they had from Gern but was glad they had given her a chance to destroy them. She stepped forward to the mouth of the gully to keep the circling wolf in sight. It was closing, growling deep in its throat as it stalked towards her, teeth bared, very much the behaviour of a predator hunting something dangerous. It was right – she was dangerous.

Ten feet away, it crouched, ready to spring. "*Vata!*" Anike cried as it leapt at her. The blast of wind caught the dire wolf, carrying the creature up into the branches of the tree above it. Leaves were torn from their stems and fell in a rain of green. "*Prana*," she shouted, snaking a thin tree limb around the wolf, holding it fast before it fell. Anike's vision was clouded for an instant by insubstantial shapes dancing across it but they evaporated before she had time to identify them. Above her, the wolf struggled and growled but she paid it scant attention. There would be time to deal with it later.

The one that had been rolling on the ground had extinguished the flames in its coat and was approaching her, eyes blazing with hatred. Anike felt an answering rage. "*Agni*", she hissed. A ring of fire surrounded the wolf and it pulled up sharply, flinching away from the flames. She walked towards the trapped creature, enjoying the terrified howls as it retreated as far as it could without touching the burning circle.

She became aware of the third wolf approaching from behind but it did not trouble her. While its assault would inflict injury, it would not be able to kill her before she had finished off the pack.

Her hand came into her vision as she pointed at the trapped beast and the sight of her unprotected flesh pierced the veil of fire that had taken possession of her. Her survival instinct reasserted itself and she flung herself flat to avoid the free wolf's leap. The beast flew over her and, unimpeded by impact with her body, landed by the flaming circle. It tried to swerve but its momentum was too great and it tumbled through the fire. There was a hiss as the water from the stream soaking its coat boiled away. Its fur caught light again, and it yelped and started to roll on the ground.

The power inside her had dimmed when she chose to save herself rather than continue the assault. Without witchcraft, she could not hope to defeat even one in the open but might be able to defend herself in a tight space. With the dire wolves trapped and distracted, she ran for the cave.

She splashed through the stream into the cave mouth. The roof rose higher than her head and the entrance was at least fifteen feet wide, easily large enough for all three dire wolves to enter. Behind her, the sound of burning faded away as the circle of fire collapsed. At least two of the wolves were now free, so she drew her knife, scant protection as it was. She backed into the cave, keeping her left hand behind her to feel for the walls. There was a crash as the last dire wolf fell to the ground. She could see flashes of silver fur through the undergrowth and took another step back, her foot sinking into the wet sand. The hilt of her knife dug into her palm as her grip tightened around it.

She waited for the attack but it did not come. To her relief, she heard a howl then another, the second sounding farther away. It seemed that the dire wolves had finally chosen to flee. Not daring to relax entirely, Anike looked over her shoulder into the depths of the cave. The shallow stream covered most of the floor immediately behind her. About ten paces in, the cave narrowed and the roof became lower but she could not see beyond that from where she was. There did not seem to be any immediate danger from inside.

She tried to understand what had motivated her to strike first. Something in the dire wolves had aroused such strong hatred that she had wanted to kill, even if she was hurt in the process. That made little sense to her now, but it did appear that the dire wolves felt the same way. Normal wolves would have run when confronted with fire and these same wolves had fled Gern. Neither he nor they had shown any sign of injury when she had first seen them so she doubted that they had attacked him first. Another mystery of witchcraft she would have to unravel in the future.

She had a sudden happy thought that when she got back home she could tell Inge that her husband had read the wolf tracks correctly. She smiled, then felt it drain away as she realised how distant that prospect was. She could return only if she achieved some sort of control over her power.

When she was sure the dire wolves had left the area, Anike sheathed her knife and turned to explore the cave. Near its mouth, the stream was a few inches deep and snaked around a sandbank. Further in, it wound around another sandy area against the other wall. The walls had a few small stone ledges and depressions, just large enough to hold a knife or a candle, but for the most part, they rose smoothly towards the roof.

She took some careful steps into the cave. The roof dropped even closer to her head and as her eyes got used to the dimming light, she could see the cave narrowed to a fairly straight passage. She felt it would be prudent to explore a little further to make sure no surprises lurked within.

Twenty paces in, the stream covered the entire width of the narrowing passage and was getting deeper. The cave roof became even lower and she was forced to stoop, arm stretched out in front of her to prevent her head from scraping on the rock. Confined in an increasingly narrow channel, the stream was pushing harder on her legs, and without the sun to warm it the water was freezing. She shivered. In a few more paces the descending roof would force her to swim if she wanted to go any further. This place was certainly defensible. She could not stay in the freezing water for too long but if the dire wolves wanted to reach her they would have to come at her one at a time. She could clearly see the entrance, lit by the morning sun, but so far in it was unlikely that she would be visible from outside. Satisfied, she splashed through the stream and out of the cave.

Hilda had been right to say that the cave was not a suitable home for men, or any large creature. The floor was wet even where it was not actually under water, but she did not have to live there and it was ideal for her needs – there was nothing that could burn. Crossing to the nearby bushes, she broke off a thin stick and a longer branch that she whittled down to a point to make a crude spear. Enough, she hoped, to fend off a dire wolf in the tight confines of the tunnel.

She stood the spear against the rock wall and, eager to start her exploration of the runes, dragged a small fallen log to the back of the sandbank to make a dry seat. She knew runes could describe the world, but she needed to find out if she could use the language to direct witchcraft.

There was no point in considering law-aligned forms. Her power just recoiled from these so she had to work with chaos runes. She had sent blasts of wind at her enemies so knew air was something she could control, and wind seemed a safer form to start with than fire. She began by tracing the wind rune in the sand by her feet. Just as in Hilda's hut, once it was complete the symbol called to her, resonating on some subtle level with her power.

She thought for a moment, marshalling the lore that was somehow now part of her, then drew a few more runes in the sand with the stick trying to describe how the air would move. Eventually, she had a pattern that seemed to say what she wanted, describing a momentary gust of wind. The collection of runes created a sense of presence in her mind but it was inert. She needed to work out how to activate it, to bring what she had described into reality. Merely writing down the description was clearly not enough – anyone could draw such a pattern. Somehow she had to connect it with the energy inside her.

She let the image of the runes fill her mind and felt the power within her respond and pulse in sympathy. The tension built but there was no release. When she looked away from the pattern she felt the energy subside. It was as if the power flowed like water through channels created by the runes then fell away like the tide sinking into sand when it could not find a way out. She tried again with the same result, feeling her nerves resonating as power surged through her body before receding to leave only a fading tingle.

Then she remembered what she had told Hilda. Both she and Gern had spoken words before the effect had actually manifested. Looking again at the pattern in the sand, she visualised the gust and spoke, "Wind." To her disappointment, nothing happened and the power seeped away. She was still missing something.

She thought back over all the witchcraft she had witnessed or used. She knew that Gern had used rune names and when she battled the dire wolves she too had spoken them, not normal speech as she had done previously. If she was trying to control her power with runes, it made sense to say their actual names. She tried again, letting the pattern fill her mind once more. The power responded, and as it reached its peak, she spoke, "*Vata!*" The air rune seemed to light up in her mind, vibrating in sympathy with the spoken word. The energy channelled by the other runes flowed into and through it. For a moment, Anike thought she had succeeded. The rune pulsed with power, and then its image in her mind shattered with what seemed like a discordant blast from a horn. The force fell back, receding in coils and eddies of power.

Anike frowned as she considered. It was a quite different sensation from what she had experienced when the power just dissipated.

Clearly, the rune name held some significance and was more than a mental cue. She guessed that the discordance meant that the energy was not quite matched to the effect she was seeking, like a badly-made key snapping in a lock.

Even without any tangible results, she was still heartened by her progress. It was hardly surprising that she had made mistakes without any guidance. She would just have to try again.

The problem could be in the pattern she had devised – perhaps it did not describe the effect properly. Hilda had said the runes would have to describe what she wanted completely and accurately. She drew another design from scratch and compared it with the first, looking to see where she had expressed the concepts differently. After further thought, she created a third pattern, incorporating the better elements from each of the first two.

The sun was high in the sky before she was ready for another attempt. Once again, she thought of the effect and let her eyes follow the rune pattern so that it was echoed in her thoughts. The power filled her and she spoke again. "*Vata.*" This time, when the air rune lit up in her mind, the energy coursed through it and out into the world. Instead of the sense of a discordant horn, it was as if a chime had sounded within her. A gust of wind blew, but not where she had intended and her face stung as the wind swirled by her head.

Ecstatic at even this partial success, Anike felt the fire inside her soar to greater heights and in her elation knew she had to express her power even more triumphantly. Nothing short of destruction would satisfy her this time. Like a river bursting its banks, energy flooded through her being. "*Agni!*" she cried. The stick in her hand and the makeshift spear next to her crumbled to ash as she directed fire into them.

The heat scorched her fingers, jolting her back to her senses and she hurriedly put her burnt hand into the stream to cool it. The blaze had erupted in an instinctive, uncontrolled way, in complete contrast to the gust of wind. Despite the pain, she felt triumphant. For a brief moment, she had commanded her witchcraft and neither the fact she had not got exactly what she wanted nor even the subsequent loss of control diminished her sense of achievement.

When the fire had burst forth this time, runes had filled her mind and she realised that instinctively she had placed or painted the runes onto the wood that she had set ablaze. Her excitement grew as she sensed this was how the effects could be directed to the right place.

Filled with renewed enthusiasm, she was determined to try again, and now she was also alert to the risk of being overwhelmed by the power she released. Readying herself for the backwash, she studied the rune pattern, let the energy build again and then visualised the pattern over the stream. "*Vata!*" she said again. Power burst out of the glowing rune in her mind and this time the wind whipped up tiny waves on the surface of the water, exactly as she had intended. She consciously and deliberately quelled the power and stood there, breathing deeply.

She could control it. Consciously tapping into her power was possible, if risky, and it gave her real hope. Witchcraft could be bent to her will.

Until this point, she had not truly believed that she could return to Trollgard, however much she wanted to. If it was possible to master witchcraft, everything changed. Trollgard could benefit from her just as Ulsvater could turn to Hilda. She could accept living away from the town if she could see her father occasionally. As long as she kept a decent distance, that might just be acceptable to Bjord and Arl Svafnir if they could see the advantages and allowed her to pay an appropriate bloodprice for what she had already done. Eventually, she might even earn the town's respect.

In the meantime, her new skill needed more practice. She looked at the runes in the sand again and aimed the breeze out of the cave. "*Vata,*" she said firmly. Energy surged again, and the wind obeyed her. Taking a deep breath, she mastered the flow of power and calmed it. "*Vata,*" she tried again and once more the wind scattered sand as it was directed by her will, but this time she barely held back the backlash of power. She needed to find a more reliable way to contain and quiet the energy once unlocked. The next time, as soon as the force had flowed out into the world, she visualised *Kappa*, the opposing rune which stood for earth. At once, she felt the power recede back to its core, this time more swiftly, seemingly repulsed by the image. She smiled. This was more effective than just letting the energy drain away.

Anike wiped the wind rune from the pattern on the sand and replaced it with the fire rune but instantly realised that the new design did not make sense. She smoothed away the entire pattern with her foot and started again. After another hour, she had a new pattern of a dozen runes that seemed right. She focused on it and pointed her hand at the wall while visualising the effect. The energy flowed, but she held off from speaking the form rune while she let the power resonate inside her and recede. Just as it had with the final version of the pattern for wind, the energy had grown and diminished smoothly and she felt that this rune pattern was right.

She looked at the design again and this time spoke the fire rune, "*Agni*," as the power rose within her. There had been no mistake in her craft and a jet of fire shot from her hand to strike the wall, scattering and rebounding in a myriad of tiny flames. As soon as the fire manifested, she imagined the ice rune, *Ranak*, carved onto a disc of stone. The power retreated, almost recoiling from the image and Anike nodded in satisfaction.

Her success encouraged her to think about other variations. It seemed important to have the rune image clearly reflected in her mind but did that mean she had to be looking at the pattern? She closed her eyes and tried to picture the runes, but found there were too many for her to visualise the entire design accurately. When she concentrated on one part of the pattern another dissolved and no sense of coherent power flow came to her. She persevered, and when she had the entire pattern as stable and clear in her mind as she could manage, she called out "*Agni*," but the energy was too turbulent, breaking apart the image of the fire rune and draining away. The pattern was just too complex but she had come close enough to success to feel that she was on the right track. She recalled the simpler pattern she had devised for the wind. In her mind's eye, she could see it as clearly as if it were drawn in front of her, and when she spoke the word "*Vata*," the wind blew, scattering sand. The key was whether she could see the pattern in its entirety and if it was simple enough, she could visualise it without needing to read it.

She frowned, seeking a better way to describe the patterns she used to create an effect than a clumsy phrase. Some tales referred to witches casting spells and that seemed as good a word as any for rune patterns that channelled witchcraft.

Anike refreshed herself with a long draught of water from the stream. It tasted clean, with a slight tang from the minerals in the rocks it passed through. She was satisfied with her progress even if it was limited, and she knew that to have achieved anything at all in such a short time was remarkable. Her instinctive understanding could only be part of the power itself.

Several hours had passed and the soft sounds of the afternoon drifted over her. Feeling no sense of danger, she walked out of the cave into the woods to stretch her legs. There was enough of the day left to try something more before she returned to see Hilda.

After a few moments enjoying the fresh sunlit air, she returned to the cave and re-examined the pattern in the sand, considering if there were other ways to activate it. She readied herself again and thought "*Agni!*" without speaking it. There was no reaction. She tried again, whispering the rune's name. At that, the fire rune in her mind resonated slightly, but not sufficiently to release the energy into the world. She spoke again, a little louder and again the image of the fire rune glowed, but it was still not enough. Evidently, to manifest the accumulated power she needed to speak as loudly as if she were talking to someone nearby.

Having established this, she sat on the log to eat a piece of bread and she considered what to do next. She had proved there was potential but what she had devised so far was not of much practical use.

Out in the distance to the north, far away, a howl reminded her that the dire wolves could return. She found it difficult to see how Hilda managed – the presence of such creatures was an important reason why few people lived alone outside a town and the hut was well within the range of the wolves. Anike intended to warn the seer about them when she returned to the cabin and decided to ask then how she defended herself. Aside from satisfying her curiosity about at least one of the old woman's many secrets, she might be able to learn something she could use herself in the future.

In the meantime, she wanted to craft a spell to do something that was impossible without witchcraft. She wanted to fly. When the harrowling had attacked her outside Trollgard, she had risen to the top of the cliff and it would be wonderful to be able to recapture that sensation. It would also be extremely useful.

She knelt on the sand to work out the pattern she would need, starting by pairing the runes for movement and flight together and then placing description runes around them. Drawing on what she intuitively sensed, she added more to identify herself as both the controller and the target of the effect, and gave it both speed and duration. She examined the pattern she had drawn and after further thought moved runes around, adjusting the meanings. The sun was sinking towards the trees by the time she was satisfied that the spell said what she wished. It was not particularly elegant, but it seemed clear. She let it fill her mind, and spoke the rune name, "*Prana.*" Energy flowed out of her and suffused her body, surrounding and supporting her more completely than seawater. The excess power in her mind threatened to overwhelm her and she hurriedly suppressed it with the image of the stasis rune.

In response to her silent direction, the force supporting her lifted her a few feet off the ground. She waggled her feet as she floated upward, laughing out loud at the joy of the feeling. Elation flooded through her and she could not help but wonder what she could achieve if she gave herself fully over to the power. She saw the potential to be a force of nature, mistress of the storm. "*Enekt!*" she called out, commanding lightning to burst forth, hammering into the walls and roof. Splinters of shattered rock grazed her skin but she did not care. She drifted out into the open air, knowing that she now had the power to burn down the forest, even tear down the cliffs behind her.

No one could touch her now and she no longer cared about being seen. She rose above the stream, caught sight of the leaf-covered branches swaying in the wind and gathered her will to summon a gale to tear the foliage from the boughs. A pattern of runes flashed before her eyes, so fast that her conscious mind barely had time to register their presence before she cried, "*Vata!*" The closest tree shook as a torrent of air stripped it of its leaves, sending them upward in a fountain of yellow and green.

In the instant afterwards, Anike felt drained and horrified at her senseless act and she shook the fog from her mind. She felt the power starting to build again but this time she pictured the rune of law, *Lǫg*. The flow of force and arrogance inside her was disrupted and she mastered herself, quelling the storm within.

With the throb of power quiescent once more, she was able to enjoy the sensation of merely hovering in the air though she remained on guard against a further surge in energy. She rose and fell, then floated in a circle, testing her new ability. After a moment, the supportive flow suddenly vanished and she fell five feet to the ground with a short cry. Brushing leaves and dirt off her tunic, she got back to her feet. In the intensity of the last few moments, she had forgotten that the effect she had created was only intended to last for a short time. She had not realised that she would have no warning before the spell ceased, and this was something she would need to keep very much in mind if she was flying. She was just feeling her way towards control but she could sense a path ahead and felt much more optimistic than she had at the start of the day.

The sun had dropped beneath the treetops but there was still at least an hour before it was dark. Anike did not want to spend the night in the cave so she set off back to Hilda's home. For the first time since she had left Trollgard, her pace was eager. She wanted to discuss what she had done with the seer and hear the woman's insights, and she was glad to be able to repay her with some new knowledge. She saw no hint of the dire wolves while she made her way back through the forest. With any luck, they had moved on again.

It was twilight when she reached the top of the ridge and looked down on Hilda's hut. She was startled to see a single grey horse tied to one of the fences. There was no rider in sight but the horse was a fine animal with good-quality tack and it looked vaguely familiar. A bow was strapped to the saddle but the quality of the horse suggested that this visitor was a jarl, not a hunter.

She changed direction and left the trail, intending to approach the hut from the side facing the cliff, keeping out of sight of the entrance. It would have been more prudent to wait in the woods but she wanted to know who the high-status visitor who had arrived so late was, and what was being said. If it did not concern her, she could wait until they had finished.

Anike stole up to the back of the hut and pressed her ear against the wooden walls. Inside she could hear a man's voice. "Enough of your prattle, old woman. You lied to me." It was Bjord.

- 14 -

A MEETING OF
OLD FRIENDS

Anike's heart leapt to her mouth. She pulled back from the wall in shock, astonished that Bjord had returned so soon, and alone. She scanned the valley again but there was no sign of the Arl and his followers.

Hilda's voice came calmly through the gaps in the wooden walls, slow and deliberate as if explaining something to a child. "No, I told you what the gods told me through the runes. You are responsible for what you choose to do with that information and for any lack in your understanding."

Hilda gave the impression she was in control of the situation and Anike considered retreating to the forest until Bjord left, but hesitated. Despite radiating knowledge and confidence, Hilda had not displayed any real power. If Bjord was not cowed, in his anger and desire to find Anike he might forget his natural respect for a god-touched woman and attack. Anike could not allow someone else to be hurt because of her. She had to stay close enough to intervene if necessary.

Inside, the voices continued. "Show me more respect, crone! You are talking to a future Arl."

"I know who you are, Bjord Svafnirsson. Your rank means nothing to me. I have been telling truth to Arl and thrall alike since long before you were born."

"You told me Anike was on her way to Trollgard."

"No. I told you Anike was making preparations to return to Trollgard. You should listen more carefully and, more importantly, you should learn to think before you act."

"You presume to instruct me? How dare you talk to me like that?"

"I answer to the gods alone, child."

"The gods have aided me, crone, as I deserve. I am a jarl. Heimdall himself placed my caste above all others and it was he who laid a jarl's duty on us – to protect our people. That is what I am doing. Odin favours me and it was no doubt he who sent the hunters with news that you were shielding a woman here, a woman who could only be the witch."

Outside, Anike frowned. She had not thought that the two hunters, father and son, had paid her much attention. It was a great misfortune that they had carried news of her to Ulsvater – perhaps her sacrifice for the runecast had not been sufficient and this bad luck was part of the gods' price.

Bjord was continuing. "You misled me, and you misled Arl Oster."

"Oster knows better than to take my advice without thinking, something he learned when I lived in his hall and which he has never forgotten."

Bjord was silent for a moment. Anike knew that Hilda had once been one of the Arl's counsellors and had realised there had been some history between them, but she was surprised to learn that she had lived in the arlberg itself.

"Oster told me it was your advice that got you exiled here."

Hilda laughed. "Is that how he put it? Or is that another example of you not listening properly?"

Bjord's voice was tight with barely controlled rage. "You compound your lies with insults. I sent men to hunt along the coast road based on your reading of my runecast. You knew I would do that. You hid her from me."

"You can see Anike is not here."

"Where is she?"

"I don't know." Hilda sounded a little smug.

Listening, Anike realised that Bjord was asking the wrong questions and was too angry to see it. Hilda did not need to lie to frustrate his enquiries.

Bjord was not used to people who had no interest in pleasing or appeasing him and was getting increasingly furious.

"You are vexing me, old woman. You know more than you are telling me."

"I know more than you can imagine, Bjord Svafnirsson."

There was a metallic scrape of a weapon being drawn. Anike edged towards the door, worried that Hilda had goaded Bjord too far. She laid a hand on her knife though she was unsure exactly what she could do with it.

"Last chance, hag. Have you seen Anike?"

Hilda laughed again. "Finally, a better question. You are learning, if a little slowly." She paused, and Anike could imagine her gaze piercing the young man. "Yes, I have seen her," she said.

Anike reached the door and peered through a crack. The inside of the hut was lit by some candles on the table. She could see Hilda standing in the middle of the room, with Bjord a few feet away. As Anike had feared, he had his sword out and it was levelled at the old woman. Anike could not see his face but his body was taut and the blade was steady. Hilda seemed unconcerned but Anike hoped she had something in reserve.

"How long did she stay?" he growled.

"Not long. She did not like what the runes told her. She has gone elsewhere to look for answers." True, Anike thought, but deliberately misleading and Bjord would not be content with that response.

"You lie!" Bjord said, sword arm trembling now. "She was seen here, playing the part of your thrall. Where is she?"

"I do not know."

Bjord raised his sword threateningly.

Hilda said mildly, "It is to be regretted that Svafnir Sigurdsson did not teach his son to listen. What will he think when he finds out that if you hear something you do not like, your reaction is to threaten the messenger?"

Bjord flushed at that, but his sword remained steady. "Then it is fortunate for me that no one will ever know." He tensed to strike.

Hilda's gambit would probably have worked a week before but Bjord had now experienced witchcraft and betrayal. He was driven by a thirst for justice and revenge and, instead of bringing him to heel, Hilda's manner had pushed him too far.

Anike did not dare hesitate. She burst through the door and hurled her knife. It flashed through the space between them and cut deeply into Bjord's forearm as he drew back his sword. He dropped the weapon with a curse and turned to face Anike.

"Coward! You would kill an unarmed old woman?" she cried. Righteous anger fuelled a desire to burn him where he stood. Bjord's eyes widened in surprise when he saw her and then he grinned triumphantly, unaware of how close he was to death.

"A knife, Anike?" he sneered. "Pretending you are not a witch now?"

This did not help Anike to rein in her fury and her rage expanded, encompassing a desire to destroy the hut he was standing in and everything in the vicinity, including Hilda. It took a monumental effort but she denied the surging force within her. Bjord had kept his eyes fixed on her during her struggle with herself and now she met his gaze.

Behind him, Hilda moved backwards with slow, quiet steps but Bjord was not paying her any attention now. He bent and retrieved his sword with his left hand. Anike also backed away, retreating out of the hut to try to draw him away from Hilda and at the same time give herself more room to run.

"I do not want to hurt you again," Anike said, recalling that the last time they had spoken was at Vanir Heights. "I am truly sorry for what happened at the farm and for what I did to you, but that does not excuse taking a blade to a defenceless old woman."

Bjord advanced towards her. "Loga said he thought he saw you on the hillside yesterday but I wrongly judged him mistaken, foolishly believing this old woman rather than my friend – an old woman I now find you hiding behind," he spat.

Anike retreated again, watching him carefully and keeping out of reach of his blade. Bjord followed her.

"You will not escape me this time. I hesitated at the farm because I could not believe you were responsible for that destruction." He held his sword low and steady before him, pointing unwaveringly at her breast. "My heart betrayed me and four people died that night because I withheld my hand. Lives that I could have saved. But though you failed to take my life, you killed that weakness within me by those murders. I will not fail again."

Anike continued to fall back, realising that in a moment he would strike. She could feel her power rising again, enough to burn Bjord where he stood. She only had to unclench her will and it would surge forth to sear the man before her, the man she had grown up with, still tied to her with bonds of blackened hopes. This time there would be no mistake, no recovery. But if she let go, it would be a conscious choice. She had never deliberately unleashed power to hurt someone and if she did so now, she would be no better than Bjord thought she was.

There was no way she could match Bjord physically, even if her knife had not been lying on the floor of Hilda's hut, so she had either to get away or calm him down. "Wait," she said, holding her left hand out placatingly, hoping to reach some part of him that might still have feelings for her.

Bjord lunged, a fraction slower than normal as he was leading with his left side rather than the right, and Anike managed to dodge back so that the blade fell a handspan short of her chest. "I won't make the mistake of giving you a chance again," he said, stepping forward and swinging the sword in a deadly arc towards her head.

Again Anike fell back again, ducking, and the blade missed her by inches. Left-handed, Bjord was slightly off balance and that gave her a chance. She spun round, letting the strap of her heavy leather satchel slip over her head and turning full circle, flung the heavy bag at him. She just registered his sword flash back to deflect it but by then she was already running. She was not sure which of them was the faster, but Bjord had a horse not a dozen paces away and she could not outrun that. Instead of just sprinting away as fast as she could, she concentrated on the pattern she had drawn so recently in the sand, painting it in her mind as she ran. Her focus on escape prevented her fear and anger warping into a destructive impulse and helped her visualise the pattern for flight. "*Prana*," she said, and the movement rune shone in her mind. She leapt upwards and let the spell carry her aloft.

She turned in the air to see Bjord's mouth drop open. Overcoming his surprise, he gathered himself and sprang after her before she rose out of reach, the sword in his left hand slashing towards her legs. She drew up her feet and managed to block his strike with the tough heel of one boot. Bjord landed neatly and jumped again but now she was beyond the arc of his sword and the blow passed beneath her. She headed for the cliff, still rising. She had not forgotten the bow on Bjord's horse and wanted to put a good distance between them before he remembered it too.

Bjord looked up at her and, wincing slightly, pulled a dagger from his belt and threw it right-handed but the pain in his arm sapped his strength and it went low. He then looked back, recalling the bow, and headed for his horse.

She would be fairly safe once she reached the cliff top, but she was not sure if she could get there before the flight spell holding her in the air wore off. She closed her eyes, pictured the pattern again, and spoke the rune, "*Prana*." Power surged through the runic channels in her imagination and out into the world. She trusted she had done enough to reach the top of the cliff, and looked down.

Hampered by the injury to his right arm, Bjord was struggling to string his bow. By the time he had done so, Anike was nearly at the level of the clifftop. He sighted on her, but she willed herself to drift sideways, trying to make herself as difficult a target as possible. The arrow went low in any event, and Anike watched Bjord shaking his right arm as he looked up at her. Before he had time to nock another arrow she was over the cliff edge and safe for the moment. She peered over the lip at him, watching as he sought a path up to her.

He cursed when he saw there was no easy way to reach her and turned to stare at Hilda's hut. After a long moment, he shook his head and mounted his horse. He shouted up to her, "I will catch you, Anike, no matter where you run. If you hide, I will find you. You will never escape and I will bring you to justice." With that, he pressed the horse's sides and set off at a canter in the direction of Ulsvater.

Anike's heart lifted when she saw that Bjord had not chosen to return to the hut to take out his frustration on Hilda. It seemed that shifting the focus of his anger away from the seer and back onto her had made him see how close he had come to committing a dishonourable act. Anike still hoped to talk to him. While Bjord's anger had made reconciliation impossible this time, she refused to give up.

While Hilda had seemed unscathed when Bjord left the hut, she did want to make sure the seer was unhurt but she could not stay after that. Hilda might refuse to shelter her, particularly after Bjord had shown how far he would take his quest for revenge. It would also be the first place Bjord would look on his return and if he came upon her while she slept he would catch her easily, and Arl Oster might also punish Hilda for sheltering her now.

It was nearly dark and Anike knew she would have to find somewhere to sleep. The cliff top was too exposed. South from the cliff, the hills rose steeply and were bare of trees. Her closest shelter was the forest, and Bjord would be unlikely to stumble across her there.

Twilight shaded into darkness. As the light faded the nagging worry that Bjord's rapid departure might have been a ruse to lure her into coming down dwindled. She rose, brought the flight pattern back to mind and said, "*Prana*." Energy surrounded her body, and she willed it to bear her up and, not without some trepidation, drifted forward over the edge of the cliff before slowly descending. She landed at the base and walked up to the hut. There were no sounds of movement, or indeed of anything to suggest what Hilda was doing within.

Anike peered through the still-open doorway. All inside was darkness save for the dying embers of the fire. "Hilda?" she called. There was no response. She took a cautious step across the threshold, listening. There was no sound of Hilda's breathing or indeed any movement at all. Anike found a usable candle on the table – those that had been alight when Bjord had confronted Hilda had now burned down. She bent to the remnants of the fire to light it and slowly surveyed the room. There was no sign of the seer, and Anike frowned.

She was sure she would have seen Hilda leaving the hut. Hilda claimed not to be a witch or, as Anike now thought about it, had implied that she was not, but she might be something else. By legend, draugr – dead warriors and Arls who supposedly left their barrows to wreak revenge on grave robbers or those responsible for their deaths – had a range of powers, including the ability to swim through rock. Hilda appeared anything but dead, revenge-motivated or a warrior, but perhaps she was not actually human either. Anike shuddered at the thought.

She raised the candle high, looking for hiding places in the small hut. Her foot struck something metallic, and she looked down to see her knife skidding across the floor. She bent to retrieve it and found it lying on a wooden board poking out from under a fur which had been dislodged by Bjord's boots. The rest of the floor was packed earth. She wiped his blood from the blade whilst staring at the fur, then tried to move it with her foot but found it was stuck in place. Bending down, she saw it was nailed to a wooden trapdoor. She pulled at the hatch but it moved only a fraction before coming to a halt with a metallic sound – bolted from the other side perhaps. The trapdoor was set in a wooden frame slightly below ground level and a small pile of earth lay against one edge as if it had fallen off when the door was raised. The frame extended well past the door itself and perhaps was part of the structure of the hut. Anike had never seen a trapdoor in a wooden building before, and this was a sophisticated and solid construction. She doubted she could break it without a large axe and considerable effort. The wood appeared old, much older than the ten years Hilda had supposedly lived here and now she came to think of it, the hut looked older than that as well.

She knocked on the trapdoor. "Hilda?" she called. "Bjord has gone." There was no response, but Anike was relieved at having found an explanation for Hilda's disappearance without resorting to the supernatural. She tugged once more on the trapdoor with little effect then let it go. The hidden portal was another mystery surrounding the seer but the presence of a secret passage might explain Hilda's willingness to live alone. The discovery of the trapdoor merely replaced one mystery about the old woman with another. Anike was curious but she had enough of her own problems to keep her busy.

Anike suspected that Hilda would remain hidden until everything had settled down after her visit but even if the seer had been injured, there did not seem to be much she could do about it. Everything suggested that Hilda's continued absence was her own choice so it was discourteous to remain longer without permission, as well as unwise. Her refusal to come out suggested it was not Anike's business any more.

She turned to leave. The candlelight picked out the white bone runes on the table and she went to look at them more closely, wondering if Hilda might have left her a message. When she studied the pattern properly, she decided it was more likely to be the result of a cast. Without knowing what the question was, the best interpretation she could come to was 'Returning to old ground with new knowledge.' It could equally well refer to her or Bjord and it struck her how easy it was for the same words to describe two very different things.

She blew out the candle, replaced it on the table and walked outside, closing the door behind her. Her satchel lay where it had landed after she had thrown it at Bjord, so she picked it up and considered where to go. To start with, she would head for the forest. Sleeping up a tree would be safer than staying on the ground but she would need to build a makeshift platform to stop herself from falling while she slept and she doubted she could make one in the dark. Her alternative was the cave, which was secure though its wet ground made it less than ideal to sleep in and she would need to make something with leaves and branches to raise herself off the wet ground. Hilda knew where it was, of course, but was unlikely to be telling anyone and it would be safe to spend the night there.

She followed the cliff towards the cave. It was very dark beneath the trees near the rock face and she could hear the occasional call of night animals and the rustle of unseen leaves above her. The murmuring of running water came from ahead of her and, with her destination in reach, she started to pick up pace then felt a sense of wrongness and abruptly halted. There was something both out of place and hostile nearby. Even alerted, she barely had time to throw herself onto the ground to avoid the dire wolf as it sprang at her out of the darkness.

- 15 -

The Demon

The wolf went over her. As Anike dropped and rolled, the power rose within her and she made no attempt to hold it back, the brief thrill of fear drowned out by rage. Slamming her fist into the ground, she shouted "*Agni!*" as a pattern of runes flashed through her mind. A wave of flame surged outwards in a circle, scorching the ground until it formed a ring of fire a dozen feet across and as tall as she was. Leaves and branches above her caught alight from the heat of the blaze as she came back to her feet. She could feel the dire wolves prowling outside the circle like pools of unnatural calm in the darkness and she scanned the night, following that touch in her mind.

The glowing eyes of the wolves reflected the light of the circle of fire and their silver fur glinted red when they came close enough for the poor night vision of a human to pick them out. She felt a fierce pleasure knowing that she had a chance to redeem the failure of will that had allowed them to escape their last encounter.

Two of the wolves prowled at the edge of the ring of fire, seeking an opening. She raised her hand and advanced towards them until she was right next to the flames. As she formed a pattern of runes to focus her power on them, she was struck from behind and borne to the ground by the third and largest wolf who had leapt through the blaze from behind her. Claws tore through her tunic and into her flesh and she turned her head to see it open its mouth, trying to snap long pointed teeth on her head. "*Prana!*" she shouted, conjuring a force to fling it away. The wolf howled in pain as it was hurled back through the ring of fire to land a dozen feet outside the circle. It tried to rise but fell back, panting.

Anike got to her feet, ignoring the blood dripping from her wounds. The claws had not pierced anything vital, and she was not in immediate danger of collapsing. The agonising pain was just something that came with having a body now. She was not frightened or even concerned by the gashes in her side but irritated that she had underestimated the wolf and allowed it unnecessarily to injure her. She calmly walked to the edge of the fire circle to enjoy the suffering of the pack leader as it struggled to regain its feet.

She had no warning before the arrow struck her in the right shoulder, making her stagger sideways. Her arm dropped to her side as the wound stole its strength. This was an inconvenience and more importantly, arrows meant humans who could distract her and give the tainted wolves a chance to escape.

Unlike dire wolves, a human did not have a presence she could sense in the night so she had no clear idea where the arrow had come from. Runes flared in her mind, a complex pattern invoking location and light, an aspect of fire. "*Agni!*" she said aloud. A ball of white foxfire blossomed in her hand, then split into seven smaller spheres which shot out into the darkness. In an instant, each had found a target. All of the dire wolves were outlined in pale white flames, burning without heat but making them bay with fear.

Some fifty paces away, four men in a group were similarly surrounded by the spectral fire. Like the wolves, they were unhurt, but they also cried out in surprise and terror. Horrified by the manifestation of witchcraft clinging to them, two fled into the night, one dropping a spear as he ran. The remaining pair gazed after their departing comrades, hesitating, but they pulled themselves together and turned back to her. One held a spear and the other a bow. Without any interest, Anike recognised the latter as the older hunter who had come to see Hilda.

The humans' identity was unimportant but they were a distraction. She would have to deal with them properly after the wolves had been disposed of, but now she would just neutralise their immediate threat. "*Eneki!*" she cried, her voice carrying through the forest as another rune pattern emerged from the depths of her mind to flare for an instant in her consciousness. The two men were each surrounded by a myriad of tiny dazzling flashes of lightning, all but blinding them in the darkness. She watched them draw together, shielding their eyes against the flickering display.

She returned her attention to the wolves. Unfortunately, even the brief time needed to deal with the hunters had given them a chance to escape. One was running in and out of the trees, trying vainly to rid itself of the foxfire by sheer speed, while another was nuzzling the fallen pack leader, who found the strength to stagger to his feet and turned to flee. She drew in power and lashed out with flame, but the pack leader was shielded by his companion who took the main force of the blast. They both howled but managed to limp away, forcing themselves into an uneven run. She gathered her will afresh but by the time she was ready to strike, all of the wolves were well away into the forest, disappearing into the undergrowth. She clenched her good fist in disappointment at being thwarted, then turned to deal with the hunters.

The lightning still crackled around them, depriving them of night vision and confusing their hearing. They stood back to back, one with the heavy spear held in both hands, the other with his bow, an arrow nocked as he tried to find a target. She walked towards them. As she approached, part of her questioned whether this conflict needed to lead to more death but that small voice was drowned out by her anger and outrage that the hunters had dared to attack her.

The archer must have heard her coming for he turned sharply, raising the bow in her general direction, and peered through the cloud of sparks. She was sure he would miss her, but Anike felt it would be amusing to create more confusion and panic before she killed him. "*Agni!*" she said and watched the bowstring burst into flames. It snapped, sending the arrow randomly through the night and the man dropped the bow as it writhed in his hands. His eyes went wide with fear and he pulled a knife from his belt. His companion also turned to the sound of her voice, the blue-white light making his face deathly pale.

The impending doom of the men struck a chord inside her. Only part of her wanted to kill them, the part driven by an arrogant will of chaos and destruction, but deep within a spark of conscience strove to reassert itself, responding to the fear in their eyes. As the pattern of runes to burn the hunters formed in her mind, her core self, the part that valued life, reached out and inserted an ice rune into the pattern just as she said *"Agni,"* aloud. The energy within her recoiled in turbulent currents preventing the conflagration from manifesting. Anike focused on the ice rune, making it glow more brightly in her mind's eye, and she drove back the thirst for vengeance and destruction until the veil of hatred that had been clouding her thoughts and actions tore apart. The power shattered and retreated to the burning core deep inside her.

As the haze lifted from her mind, agony flooded through her, both from the arrow and the gashes the wolf had torn in her side. She collapsed to her hands and knees. The spearman took a hesitant step towards her, levelling his weapon. With pain and defiance radiating from her eyes, Anike raised her head, her face lit by the witchlight and framed by her dark hair, and caught him in her gaze. The hunters turned and fled.

Anike rolled onto her back and writhed as agony washed through her. The men had taken the last of the light with them and in the dark, she pushed herself through the pain and turned her attention to her wounds. The arrow had struck her shoulder bone so it had not penetrated deeply. She braced herself and pulled it out, throwing it onto the grass and holding her cloak against the wound until it stopped bleeding. Now she missed the curative elixir that she had given to Hilda, but she still had bandages and some herbs.

The wounds made by the wolf's claws were high up on the sides of her body, two sets of long gashes, and she gingerly explored them. While both hurt a good deal, one was not too serious. The other, however, was deep and she pressed her tunic against it to try to slow the blood while she felt in her bag with her free hand for some herbs that could help. It was much harder to select them just by smell and touch but eventually she found some woodrose and swallowed it. The flow of blood eased and she wrapped bandages over the wounds then struggled to her feet and headed for the stream and the cave. If she could get even a little clean water, she could make an elixir.

The woods were thinner by the cave mouth and Anike could see a little in the moonlight. She did not want to bleed to death while she waited for an elixir to brew so she cut off the bottom of the cloak with her knife and washed it in the cold water then bound up her shoulder and sides. A dark stain of blood spread through the fabric but the cloth and icy water soon staunched the flow.

Alive but weak, she pulled out her cauldron and then hunted for her tinderbox. It wasn't there, and she swore. It must have fallen out of her bag while she was looking for the herbs. While it was probably just lying on the ground near the site of the battle, there was no chance she would be able to find it in the dark.

Without a proper elixir to heal her wounds, there was no option but to rest until it was light enough to search for the tinderbox. She dared not sleep outside in case the wolves or the hunters came across her, so she retreated into the cave and sat on the log, her back against the wall. Her strength was spent. Closing her eyes, she put her head back and tried to sleep but the pain prevented her from dropping off for more than a few minutes at a time. Her rest was poor, and the few dreams she had were filled with blood and fire.

Some hours later she returned to full consciousness. No longer able to rest, she cautiously stood up and stepped into the night air, taking care not to re-open her wounds. A faint pink was colouring the sky to the east, though not enough to pierce the canopy of trees.

In truth, she doubted that the injured and terrified dire wolves would come back yet and the hunters had probably been tracking the dire wolves. After last night she did not believe they would deliberately seek her out as they had seen the terrifying effect of her power firsthand.

Dawn was approaching and though it was not really light enough to hunt for the tinderbox, or even for herbs, Anike started looking anyway. If she could not rest, she might as well do something useful, so treading carefully to avoid any slips in the dim light, she set off toward the scene of the night's battle.

Once it became light enough to see the scorches on the trees and in the undergrowth, it was not too hard to locate where she had been attacked. The arrow she had pulled from her shoulder lay on the ground, and nearby she found her tinderbox and several small pouches of herbs. She packed them carefully away and turned to head back to the stream but with the scars of destruction all around her, she could not help thinking about the witchcraft she had used during battle.

She had noticed some rune patterns flash through her thoughts when she was out of control and they had been extremely complex, more intricate than those she had worked on in the cave. She had no idea how she had been able to create effective combinations so quickly, nor why she could not now recall them. She had not noticed rune patterns forming spontaneously in her mind when she had burned the farm or when she had encountered the dire wolves by the cave though, looking at her memories afresh, she did recall blurred flashes in her vision when her witchcraft manifested, something she had not quite comprehended or paid attention to at the time, which could have been rune patterns. What she had supposed were purely instinctive manifestations of power could actually have been the product of conscious thought, but if so, how had she known how to create them? And how had she known what she could achieve? It had never crossed her mind that she could mark enemies with foxfire before she did it.

The sky had brightened in the east and the woodland birds had woken to fill the air with their song as Anike mulled over those thoughts while walking back to the stream. In the strengthening light, she came across a patch of jarl's narrowleaf, the same herb that she had given Bjord after their fight with Gern. She knelt to pick it up gratefully and started to chew some. Immediately, its vitality flowed into her and some strength came back into her limbs.

As she walked on, another odd thing nagged at her. During the battle with the dire wolves, the words she had spoken aloud had been rune names but before seeing Hilda she had used normal words. At the time the invoking word seemed right, whether or not it had been a rune name, yet when she had devised rune patterns to make herself fly or conjure winds, only the rune names had worked.

Trying to make sense of the apparent anomaly, she thought back to the times when she had used witchcraft, concentrating on the words. Most of those events were associated with things she deeply regretted and did not want to think about anymore, but the escape from the harrowling was a memory she could examine without guilt. She replayed that encounter in her mind, trying to recall the exact moment of invocation. Was there a distinction between her thought and the sound of speech? She concentrated, thinking about the sound of her voice in the wind as she stood atop the cliff and shattered it. When she really focused, she could tell that even though the idea she had expressed was 'movement', her voice had used the rune name '*Prana*', and she had not even realised it. The meaning had been so clear in her mind that she had not noticed what language she was actually speaking.

She walked back to the cave, picking a few edible roots along the way, and found some bright blue bellflowers which she could make into a powerful restorative. When she reached the stream, she built and lit a fire before filling the cauldron with water and adding herbs. While it boiled, she considered another aspect of the encounter with the harrowling more carefully. She recalled that she had thought it a creature to admire for the merger of the animals that made it up, and even liked the wound it carried, specifically because that marred its symmetry. In contrast, her perception of the dire wolves was filled with an unreasoning hatred. In both cases the attitude she remembered felt natural at the time but foreign to her now. These thoughts, this perspective, seemed to belong to someone, or something, else.

Anike rebelled against the obvious conclusion. It had been hidden by her failure of imagination but the signs were all there. Her sense of right and wrong had been so distorted that she had considered killing people she had known for years. There was knowledge inside her that she had never learned. When the energy was coursing inside her she could devise rune patterns instantly but she could not remember them afterwards, and she had used them to do things she never imagined possible, not mere random outpourings of raw energy but complex effects. When she was out of control she had no regard for pain and little for her own safety. It was almost as if her body was a horse being ridden by someone else.

There, inescapably, was the reality she had been blind to. It was not merely energy that had entered her when the ball of fire had struck her in the mountains, but an alien will and mind, a being bent on destruction and chaos, now indelibly fused with her. Anike recognised the demon inside her for the first time and as she saw it for what it was, it struck.

- 16 -

The Prison of Ice

The demon seemed to feed on the fear and horror Anike felt on its discovery. Fire blossomed within her mind as it followed the path carved by her emotions up into her consciousness. Shifting images of lightning and flame hammered into her as it abandoned subtlety and misdirection and struck with the raw energy of chaos, trying to break down the walls of her being. She reeled, her body sagging sideways and slumping down next to the stream, but she barely noticed as the phantom storm tore at her spirit. The demon was an insubstantial, shifting pattern of force all around her, lashing her with images of destructive energy. She sensed flickers of thought coming from it, too alien to comprehend beyond a wish to destroy.

She drew her consciousness back and into itself, trying to regain her bearings whilst she shielded herself. In the face of the unearthly onslaught, she gathered her mind and will, and rallied. Energy beat upon the walls of her consciousness but despite the fury around her, the core of her being held firm.

Now she could see the demon for what it was, not just a wellspring of power but a malevolent chaotic being, its previous insidious approach had been blunted and it was trying to shatter her will and take control by force. It struck at her again and again, its power translated into images of storm and flame trying to tear her apart, but Anike felt herself recovering, strengthening despite the furious assault. She realised that for all the demon's energy and fury, she was the stronger. It had never been able to dominate or overpower her, only to exploit her regrets and insecurities or warp her views and perceptions with promises of triumph and power, and now she understood its nature it was getting desperate.

She conjured up an image of the rune of ice and pushed it towards the centre of force that was the demon. It recoiled, then turned its assault against the rune, surging against the image. Anike concentrated, holding the symbol clear and solid in her mind, and the demon fell back like a wave that had broken against the shore. She visualised a chest of ice, lid open, beneath it and cast the ice rune at the fiery centre of its being. The demon seemed to shudder and recoil at the impact, and Anike surrounded it with more images of law-aligned runes, forcing it down into the chest. She slammed the lid down, then bound the clasp shut with the rune of law. The demon threw itself against the sides of the confining image, time and again, but was unable to break the prison of her will. Caged and defeated, it eventually subsided into a quiescent state, its pulse of power muted by her new defences. Anike inscribed images of the rune of ice on the chest and the image persisted even when she tentatively withdrew her concentration as if it were being sustained by the forces represented by the runes.

Opening her eyes, she found herself lying face down on the grass. The dappled sunlight fell across her body as the new day dawned. Inside, she could still feel the demon struggling against its bonds but the whispers that had threatened to distort her perceptions seemed much quieter than before and her mind was clearer than at any time since she had been struck by the ball of fire.

Wiping grass and morning dew from her face, she rolled onto her back and took stock. If she accepted Hilda's runecast was still right in the light of what she now knew, she and the demon were joined together until her death. A being that wanted only to cause chaos and destruction was now part of her.

There was one consolation. She had not killed anyone herself. From the lightning that struck down Bjord to the collapsing of the roof on the robbers in Ulsvater, it had always been the demon. It might have used her situation or memories to give it ideas, or perhaps she was just placing her own interpretation on its actions but they were its actions and not a result of any choice of hers. Her failing was not, as she had previously thought, a sudden inability to control suppressed emotions but that she had not recognised the existence of the demon earlier. The danger was not over – even now she could feel it testing the strength of its prison – but recognising her enemy took away its biggest advantage.

Of course, whatever the effect on her conscience, it probably did not matter much to anyone else if it was her or the demon who had committed murder. Even in her relief, she knew it would be naive to believe that all her problems were solved and that it would be simple to re-establish normal relations with her father, Olaf, or more pressingly, Bjord. It was hard to imagine a conversation starting with 'I did not strike you down with lightning – it was the demon within me,' ending well.

She now realised that all the times in the past week when she had regarded buildings as confining or had held people in contempt, it had been because the demon had been distorting her values and encouraging her negative emotions. As she thought back, she could now recognise the moments when it had dominated her, mostly at times of passion or danger or after she had deliberately tapped into its power with the runes.

The demon's energy was ever-present but she could not sense its thoughts or feelings now – she didn't seem able to unless it was trying to influence her. When it had been in control, it seemed to think in runes, certainly when it came to using its power to affect the real world.

Its merger with her had to be related to the witch weather. Might it be that the ball of lightning had taken her somewhere where the demon had joined with her? Now she thought about it, that did not make sense as her body had not vanished in the storm – Bjord had carried her to Volna's farm. Instead, it seemed more likely that the demon had been formed during the witch weather. Could that sudden storm have been a crucible in which it had birthed, and if so did all such storms mark the coming of a new demon? Presumably, the demon itself knew, but any answers were locked away from her. Hilda might be able to retrieve them with her runes now that Anike had a better idea of what questions to ask, and she herself might even be able to do this if she acquired a rune set of her own. It would be disrespectful to use Hilda's rune bones without her permission, and she had a sense that the gods would ask a high price for answers using stolen runes.

Since the demon was irreversibly bonded to her, how to deal with it was more important than where it had come from. She could kill herself, of course, and that would presumably end it. When Gern died, his demon had not been released or passed into anyone in the crowd, so it had probably perished with him. It was dangerous to make assumptions, she reminded herself – after all, Gern had commanded frost and earth, forms tied to law, whereas her powers were allied with chaos. Vague memories of the witch who had burned down the town market when she was a child came back to her. There had only been the one, no successor after the Arl had executed her, so it seemed likely to Anike that her own demon would die with her but suicide was not something she wanted to consider until she had exhausted all other possibilities. Suicides went to Niflheim which was not where she wished to spend eternity.

Knowledge surely gave her power. Awareness of the demon, and her increased skills in containing it with images and runes, made her position better, not worse, and she knew it was not strong enough to simply overwhelm her will. It had to rely on manipulating her. Anike was not sure if it was actually reading her thoughts but rather thought it was layering its view of the world over hers whilst at the same time it had magnified her own destructive emotions. Now that she was forewarned, she felt much more confident about detecting its influence should it escape its imprisonment within images of ice.

The idea of immediate suicide was now well behind her and she needed to recover her strength. A stab of pain in her side reminded her that she was still injured so she turned her attention back to her herbcraft. She started a fire and began to brew an elixir strong enough to cure deep wounds from the plants she had harvested before the battle with the demon.

While she waited for the potion to be ready, she decided to see if her understanding of her invader would affect what she could achieve through witchcraft, and whether she should still try to use it. She had resisted it many times before and now bound it, so provided she was careful she saw no reason why she should lose control if she drew on its power again. She felt the pulsing energy of the demon quicken as her attention touched it but the throb of power was deadened behind the images of law confining it deep within her.

She scratched the now familiar pattern for wind into the sand with her knife and let it fill her mind, at the same time raising the figurative lid of the chest containing the demon. "*Vata*," she said aloud, picturing the runes as she read them. The demon's power flowed, or perhaps was drawn, through the rune pattern and outwards through the wind rune and a blast of cold air swirled through the cave.

She quickly forced the struggling being back into the prison with an image of the earth rune. The process was tricky the first time, and she sensed that a lapse in concentration risked releasing the demon, but holding it under control while she gathered her will again was no harder than it had been the day before. Visualising a succession of images, first chaos to draw on the demon's power then law to confine it, should become easier with practice. She cautioned herself against overconfidence but it did seem that she still had control.

It was just over an hour before she could drink the potion. She watched her flesh knit back together and once the final vestiges of her pain had been banished, her thoughts turned to her home. While she still wanted to live near Trollgard if she could somehow reach an accord with Arl Svafnir, she could not install an entity bent on destruction within the heart of her community. Regardless of whether or not she had to leave the area, she did want to tell her father what had happened and it was not a message she could trust someone else to deliver, even if she could have found anyone prepared to carry it for her. Her father would undoubtedly have questions which that person would not be able to answer. She needed to talk to him herself.

It would be hard to enter Trollgard safely, and there was a good chance she would require witchcraft to do so. She needed to be able to fly faster and for longer to be able to get over the walls undetected. The spell she had already created was useful but it only let her move slowly, and that left her vulnerable.

Without a written image in front of her, she could only hold fairly simple patterns in her mind's eye clearly enough for them to channel the demon's power, and they could only create relatively weak effects. The levitation spell she had used to escape Bjord was at the top end of what she could achieve with an image drawn straight from her memory. Judging by last night, witchcraft could achieve a lot more than mere destruction, but more powerful or subtle effects would need more sophisticated patterns that would have to be written down.

She lit a fire just outside the cave and then took a blackened stick from it to sketch runes on the cave wall, starting with the flight spell she already knew then extending it to increase its duration and speed. The sun was high in the sky before she had a pattern she was happy with and prepared to test, a spell which she thought would enable her to fly at the speed of a galloping horse and last for many minutes. She focused and firmly said, "*Prana.*" The power flowed from the demon, but this time it did not reach the external world. It was as if the pattern had created a set of deep channels and there was not enough energy to fill them. It seemed that this spell was beyond her, or rather the demon's, power.

It was important to know that the demon did have limits, though that was obvious when she thought about it. She had not reduced the house in Ulsvater to dust nor incinerated the dire wolves with a single blast of flame. Witchcraft had constraints, and she returned to the pattern with that in mind, scaling back the effect. After another hour she was ready for a second attempt, this time with the pattern describing her speed being as fast as she could run. Now that she had a better idea of the demon's limitations, she had to pay attention to the power needed to achieve an effect. When she concentrated, she could sense that the rune patterns had a weight of sorts within her mind, an indication of how much power was needed to make the spell work. She assumed the demon sensed this instinctively and she was sharing its perceptions in some way.

She could feel that her revised design required less energy and this time the spell worked. The force surrounded her once more, as powerful as that which had lifted her out of the way of the harrowling at Trollgard. She willed herself out into the woods and flew around the nearby trees at a brisk pace before returning satisfied to the cave.

She marvelled that she had accomplished so much in so short a time. Some part of the demon's knowledge must be merged with her own for that to be possible and she hoped that the understanding was free of its warped influence.

A pattern drawn on the cave wall was not mobile. Ideally, she would have liked to use ink and vellum to record it but those were rare items. Olaf had some diagrams of plants, and Arl Svafnir had his large map, as well as a collection of boat and building plans, but she did not know where to find blank sheets and she could hardly go to the markets in Trollgard or Ulsvater and ask around.

For the present, she could make reasonably durable patterns on cloth using dye. She did know some plants that were good for colouring clothes though she had not had much use for them before. It would be simple to find some and stain a pattern into the lining of her cloak. Some people entreated the aid of the gods with ostentatiously dyed or embroidered runes on their clothes or engraved them on weapons, but she could ill afford the attention that would draw and would have to conceal the pattern.

Satisfied that she could use the demon's power and still retain mastery of herself, and alert for any sign of man or monster, she set out to gather some suitable plants. After a careful search, she came across some dark arlberries which she could make into a reasonable dye. It would not be permanent but should last for weeks before fading. She gathered the berries in a fold of her cloak and took them back to the cave where she crushed them to release the dark juice and mixed it with a little charcoal from the fire.

After she had washed the blood out as best she could, she used a stick to copy the flight pattern onto the lining on the right-hand side of her cloak. She felt confident that she would be able to get in and out of Trollgard, something that would have been almost impossible without witchcraft. She could fly more swiftly and with greater stealth than she could walk and passing high over the walls at night would avoid the greatest concentration of watchers.

She regarded the flight pattern critically. The marks were not perfect, but the pattern was clear enough for her to read and understand. She let it dry while she contemplated what other spells she would need. A useful ability would be to move objects without touching them, another would be to make an object glow with foxfire in case she needed a light source. She set to work on these, drawing patterns on another part of the wall. After another couple of hours, she had two designs that she felt would work. On trying them out, she was able to surround a small stone with light, and then make it fly slowly through the air. These spells were simple enough to use without the written pattern in front of her as she could visualise them clearly. Finally, she created a spell to conceal herself within a cloud of smoke, which she dyed into the left-hand side of her cloak lining.

The sun had long passed its peak and Anike began to think about moving on. She had not heard any sounds of men but a few scouts could move quietly. She briefly considered heading directly east through the forest but that would be hard going, and through an area she did not know, so she decided to head towards Ulsvater and then on to Trollgard, keeping in the fringes of the trees.

Once she was sure the dye had dried, she splashed water onto the wall to wash the patterns away. There was no need to leave such clear evidence of her presence. She packed away her cauldron and herbs, scattered the remains of the fire and set off.

She headed north, following the stream away from the cave until well after she had crossed the trail that led back to Hilda's home, then she turned east. When she reached the borders of the forest, she turned north again, staying twenty or thirty paces back in the trees.

She thought she heard the sounds of men in the distance behind her but the noises were faint and she could not be sure that she had not imagined it.

The sun had set and it was getting dark when she reached the top of a hill and looked down towards Ulsvater. At this point, the forest was about half a mile from the town and it was possible a sharp-eyed watcher would spot her if she left the woods. She did not want to walk through the unfamiliar forest at night if she could help it as there was too much risk of injury or getting turned around, so she decided to stay between the trees until it was fully dark and she could safely continue in the open. She settled down with her back against a tree trunk and waited, keeping an eye out for unusual activity in the town.

The sky darkened slowly to black, and then the moon rose, giving just enough light to let her see the ground. She could have sworn it was too dark to see anyone in the trees but as she stood up, an arrow buzzed past her cheek.

− 17 −

HUNT AND QUARRY

Anike threw herself to the ground. There was a curse from deeper within the forest, perhaps fifty paces away. Someone must have found her trail and tracked her. Bjord's familiar voice shouted, "You missed!" in accusatory tones and there came the sound of men pushing their way through the undergrowth.

Fear washed through her and she felt the demon struggle at its bonds, but the image of the prison held. She forced herself to think. A large force would have made more noise so there could only be a small group of men behind her – Bjord with some of Oster's hunters, she supposed – and Bjord was no woodsman. She could hear them struggling towards her now and only had a few moments before they reached her. If she ran through the forest, the sound of her crashing through undergrowth in the dark would give her away. If she went out into the grassland, she would be an easy target in the moonlight.

Instead, she felt along the ground until her hand closed on a loose stone which she drew back under her cloak. Holding it tightly in her hand, she concentrated on a rune pattern and spoke, "*Agni.*" The stone was surrounded by a cold white fire and Anike shifted slightly so she could see the flight spell she had dyed into the cloak. She hoped the light was concealed, but some of it must have escaped as she heard a voice call out, "Over there!" It did not sound far away but she resisted the temptation to look around and focused on the runes. "*Prana,*" she said aloud and felt the energy surround her, ready to carry her away, then cried out in pain when an arrow flew low through the bushes and struck her left shoulder. Part-formed, the image of the stasis rune wavered in her mind and the demon surged forward, struggling for freedom and control. Bjord was less than a dozen paces away, pushing through the foliage with his sword drawn. She was caught between the twin fires of Bjord and the demon, unable to focus on one without leaving herself open to the other.

The blood welling from her wound felt hot on her skin and the bitter taste of fear was in her mouth. With the demon hammering at her from within, it was all she could do to hold it back and hurl the fire-lined stone towards Bjord, hoping to distract him and steal his night vision. It worked better than she had hoped. He flinched back, dodging away from the unearthly fire. In that moment of his distraction, Anike gathered what remained of her will and repelled the demon with an image of the rune of ice. It recoiled, and she could feel its fury as the rune drove it back. In the space she had created, she managed to direct the force of her flight spell upwards and her prone body lifted rapidly towards the overhanging branches. "No, you will not escape again!" Bjord shouted.

Another arrow grazed her leg, drawing a deep gash in her flesh and she stifled a cry as she rose into the foliage. Hidden for a moment by the leaves, she turned her focus back to the demon, which was taking advantage of her distraction and flowing past the dissolving image of the ice rune. Urgently, she visualised more law-aligned runes and flung them into it, forcing it to withdraw again in a cascade of sparks and cinders within her mind. With the demon in retreat, Anike sent herself up between the branches then in a long arc out towards open ground.

Knowing that she might not have long before she passed out from loss of blood, she clamped her cloak hard over her shoulder wound to staunch the flow. She could not sort through the elixirs in her bag until she was on the ground and she needed some distance from Bjord before she dared land.

The demon was rallying and with pain flooding her body and mind, she could not focus sufficiently to confine it properly. Flying in a shallow dive, she closed her eyes to concentrate on the inner struggle. With the dwindling embers of her will, she held back the demon's flame and storm with images of ice and stone until the grass brushed her hands. She let herself fall onto the ground and formed the law rune in her mind to keep the demon at bay while she desperately shook out the contents of her bag. She hunted through the potions until she found the one she needed, and drained it in one swallow. The pain evaporated as the numbing potion took effect, and her mind cleared. Without the agony from her wounds sapping her will, she strengthened the image of the law rune, forcing the demon back into the box of imagined ice, and slammed the lid closed.

Although it had suppressed her pain, the potion had done nothing to heal the wounds themselves. She had only brewed enough elixir that morning to cure the injuries she had sustained the night before. She bound bandages tightly around her shoulder and leg. Getting to her feet, she took a tentative step. Her leg held her weight but she needed to find more herbs, and soon.

The forest was a few hundred paces away and from its edge came two short blasts of a horn. Someone had lit a torch and was signalling with it. In the distance, the town gates groaned open and a warband marched out into the night, accompanied by the baying of dogs. Bjord must have had this ready. Arl Oster was giving him a lot of help, clearly taking her presence within his domain rather seriously. The dogs were a new threat though they worried her much less now that she could fly.

She had to do something about her wounds, particularly the one to her shoulder. She could pass out from loss of blood. Perhaps worse, the pain had interfered with her ability to restrain the demon and that added to the urgency. Until her will had been sapped by her injuries, she had not found it hard to maintain the prison and re-cage the demon after she cast a spell, but if she weakened much further she might be unable to prevent it from escaping its bonds and using her to attack the hunters.

A howl from one of the dogs carried through the night and galvanised her into action. She flung everything back into her bag. Walking would take too long so she spread out the cloak and read the flight pattern again. The demon struggled, but with the pain masked by her potion, Anike held it at bay and took to the air.

The herbs she needed could be found in the most wooded areas and she would gain time if she could put the river between herself and her pursuers. She passed low over the ground and then the water to land on the far bank. Safe for the moment, she took the time to bind her wounds properly. The potion she had drunk gave her the illusion that she had recovered more than she actually had and it would be easy to overestimate her endurance or aggravate her condition.

It was not yet midnight, and even in the summer it would be many hours until dawn. The moon gave some light but it was not enough to hunt in the forest for plants. She looked through the contents of her bag. There were some herbs she could combine into another elixir to provide strength and, in the absence of anything better, she found a thicket and started to brew it, hoping the trees would hide the light of the little fire. There were sounds from the other side of the river as the hunters scoured the eastern bank and it would not be too long before they decided to cross after her.

The potion was nearing completion before the creak of oars carried over the water to her. As soon as it had cooled enough to drink, she downed it and headed further into the trees. The effect of the numbing elixir was starting to wear off and while the vitality potion allowed her to keep going, the pain from her wounds was starting to intrude. She could not rest with the dogs on her trail but was wary of using witchcraft and giving the demon a chance to overwhelm her in her injured state. She did not dare to try to fly again.

At first, she had little aim but to get away from the river and it was hard going through the undergrowth. Eventually, the sky began to lighten as night gave way to pre-dawn. The growing light was enough for her to make out some of the larger plants and she used where they grew to guide her towards the herbs she needed. Even following these clues, the sun was rising before she was able to find a small patch of bloodmoss. The baying of the hounds reached her again as she was gathering it. She quickly thrust the moss into her bag. She turned south, trying to increase the distance between herself and the pursuit while looking for a safe spot where she could brew her potion.

A few moments later she felt blood running down her thigh. A branch had caught in the bandage and opened up the leg wound. She stopped, discarded the blood-soaked cloth and listened. The dogs were getting closer but the wound could not wait.

She wrapped a new bandage around her leg. The hounds' baying was louder now, and she could hear men's voices. Even with her wound bound again, she could not run and she needed to get far enough ahead of the hunters to work her herbcraft. She laid her cloak on the ground to view the flight pattern but her focus was blurred by fatigue and blood loss, and the details of the runes slipped from her mind as she tried to activate the pattern. She took a deep breath to steady herself and tried again, frowning in concentration as she stared at the pattern on the cloak. This time she held on to the meaning of the runes and felt the conjured energy support her. The demon struggled hard as she tried to re-cage it after casting the spell, sensing her weakened will. She barely managed to confine it.

When it was locked away, she rose into the air just as a shout of "I see her!" rang out. A bowstring thrummed, though she never saw where the arrow went as she dodged back and forth between the trees. In a moment she had lost sight of the pursuers but they were far too close. She could hear men crashing through bushes but they could not match her speed aloft and fell behind. She rose up through the canopy to get her bearings, then turned sharply east, hoping to throw them off track. The river was closer than she had thought and there was no sign of the hunt on the other bank. Crossing back would gain her time. It was hard to swim in armour and no bowman would want to ruin his weapon by soaking it so they would need to have boats brought up from Ulsvater.

For a moment, looking down on the forest from above with the bright river shining in the morning light as it wound through the wide valley, she could appreciate how beautiful the land was. She could almost forget that beneath those trees her pursuers were scurrying like so many insignificant ants. She smiled grimly, recognising the demon's influence. Her control was weakening so she re-imagined the prison, strengthening its walls and felt the insidious thought evaporate.

Above the treetops, she travelled east for a few moments then dropped between the branches to skim over the bushes. The flight spell ended just as she reached the edge of the forest and she limped the last few paces out into the sunlight. A grass bank sloped gently towards the river a few dozen paces away and a long way downstream she could see half a dozen boats pulled up on the bank on her side.

She needed to cast the flight spell again so she spread her cloak at the river's edge and stared at the pattern. It swam in and out of focus and only then did she understand how truly drained she was. "*Prana*," she said knowing, even as she spoke the word, that she did not have sufficient clarity. The spell failed.

A horn sounded from the edge of the forest. Looking back, she saw a pair of hunters emerge, one with the hunting horn in his right hand and a leash holding a fierce-looking hunting dog in his left. The second man had a drawn bow and had trained its arrow on her. "*Prana*," she tried again, more urgently, but still could not focus on the rune pattern clearly enough for the power to do more than churn in turbulent arcs within her. It was an effort to remain standing and her left leg threatened to give way at any moment.

Before she had time to do anything else, Bjord stepped out of the forest, half a dozen men behind him, one holding back another dog. Bjord too had a bow drawn and his arrow pointed straight at her heart. "Anike!" he called. "Surrender or die!" His men fanned out as they advanced towards her across the open ground, some also armed with bows and the rest with war darts. The dogs strained at their leashes, growling and snapping.

Anike saw the choice he offered as between a quick death and a slow one. A week ago the habits of obedience and conformity would have led her to surrender, but with all she had been through she no longer felt limited by other people's expectations. She would not live past the Arl's trial even if Bjord, bitter from her betrayal, let her survive long enough to face it.

The other spell dyed into her cloak was simpler than the flight spell and she looked down at it as she raised her hands in pretend surrender. She had only one last chance to hold the runes clearly in mind, and she marshalled her will. Even as she let her left leg collapse beneath her, she read the other pattern on her cloak and named the fire rune, "*Agni*." Her concentration held and a cloud of smoke formed instantly around her, extending outwards for at least a dozen paces, hiding her from sight as she fell to the ground. An arrow shot through the space her body had just occupied.

The last of her strength had been used to maintain the rune pattern in her mind long enough to cast the spell. In her fatigue, she had been unable to focus enough to imagine a law rune to re-cage the demon, which sensing her weakness and its opportunity, burst forth and its fury burned through her mind.

Overwhelmed by the demon's will, Anike was once again in thrall to its desire to sow destruction and chaos. "*Agni*," her body called again, and a semi-circle of fire formed about her and expanded outwards in a wave, lighting the smoke with an eerie orange glow. Shouts of fear and pain reached her, and the baying of the dogs turned to terrified yelping. The demon's pleasure at the sounds of chaos beyond the smoke washed through her as it let its power build up again.

Bjord was shouting orders to his men to re-form and advance and as he started to bring some order to them, she was carried along by the demon's desire to bring more chaos.

Another arrow hummed through the smoke and she knew that while it wanted to see the panic it had caused, the demon did not want to expose her body to a hail of missiles while it was so injured. Her mouth said, "*Vata*," and she was surrounded by a tightly bound whirlwind. A war dart that found her through the smoke was flung away by the tornado before it touched her. The smoke swirled but did not disperse, held in place by the spell that had created it. Ignoring the pain and weakness in her leg, her body stood up.

THE DEMON AND THE WITCH

Anike tried to struggle against the demon's control but her will faltered in the face of a fear of becoming helpless if she did manage to restrain it, and she was unable to resist the demon's purer desire for destruction. She felt her own consciousness being warped so it was harder to tell where she ended and the demon began.

"*Prana!*" her body shouted, and she rose into the air above the smoke cloud. Below her, she could see those who had been her hunters, who were now her prey. The dogs and some of the men had fled in panic but more warriors holding war darts and axes had come out of the forest and were advancing uncertainly from the trees. Bjord had drawn his sword and was waving it in wide arcs as he stepped towards the smoke's edge. His bow still held in his left hand and he had an expression of grim determination on his face. He looked up at the sound of her lifting out of the smoke, clothed in the whirlwind.

"Bring her down!" he shouted, dropping his sword and pulling an arrow from his quiver. A war dart from one of the other men flew beneath her while Bjord drew his bow and sighted on her. Anike felt amusement at this. The weapons of wood and string were so flimsy that they almost begged to be destroyed. "*Agni,*" she called and laughed. Flames incinerated the strings of all the bows that she could see.

Struggling to regain her own identity, Anike could feel a slight loosening of the demon's control over her in the moment after it used its energy for each new spell, but its destructive purpose was unabated and its strength returned quickly. She hovered as the power built again, watching the despair and frustration in the faces below her as war darts hurled at her were brushed aside by the shielding winds.

Thus far her actions had been primarily defensive but now she was flooded with the demon's impulse to cause some real harm. The hunters were spread over a wide area, between the smoke cloud and the forest, too far apart to be caught in a fireball such as it had used on the dire wolves. Instead, she cried "*Eneki,*" and conjured bolts of lightning to flash from her hands down at the warriors. Half a dozen men cried out in pain, staggering and reeling under the assault, and many of the rest stepped back in fear. Anike deplored the needless suffering but part of her did want to hurt these men enough that they would leave her alone, and this ambivalence was making it harder for her to oppose the demon.

As she fought half-heartedly to recover control of her body, the demon drew in more power and a rune image flashed through her mind. "*Vata*," she called out, and vortices of air lashed more of her attackers. She saw drops of blood fly from shallow cuts on her foes' exposed skin and realised that the demon had somehow formed blades out of the air. With most of their number hurt, and all terrified of her power, the collective courage of the hunters broke and they ran for the forest leaving Bjord alone standing his ground.

He stooped to pick up a fallen war dart. She looked down at him, registering the terror in his wide eyes and the tremor in his hands before his jaw clenched again in a mask of determination. He mastered his fear, sighted, and threw.

Anike thought that he had missed, but he had anticipated how the winds of her shield were whirling. The dart was pulled sideways and its shaft bashed her injured leg. She felt the demon's indignation that he had inflicted even that small injury now it was free to use its powers. Anike saw the outline of the demon's intent in the rune pattern that formed in her mind. It was going to cast a lightning bolt onto him as it had done at Volna's farm.

Bjord knew nothing of the demon and could not know she was not his true enemy. He did not deserve to die for trying to defend his people. Overcoming the vestiges of her resentment that he had hunted her so doggedly, her will crystalised around a refusal to let the demon try to kill him again and she found the strength to deny it once more. She flung a water rune into the pattern of the demon's spell and the energy it was about to manifest collapsed. While the demon reeled, she held the image of the rune between them and she forced it into retreat. It struggled, sparks flying from it as she purged its influence from her thoughts and finally bound it within the chest of ice. Clear-headed again but weak from exertion and blood loss, she turned away and flew out over the river, looking back to see Bjord alone on the bank, staring after her.

The spell the demon had used did not allow her to move as swiftly as the one she had devised so she passed over the water at little more than a walking pace. Without the demon's influence dominating her perceptions, she was acutely aware of her body's limits and of the pain lancing through her shoulder and leg. She was glad that the demon had not killed any of her pursuers but some had been badly injured and they would be looking for revenge once they regained their courage. She could see Bjord heading downstream towards the boats, but she had bought time.

She was ten paces from the eastern bank when the flight effect suddenly expired, dropping her in the river and her shriek was cut short by the water closing over her head.

- 18 -

BURIED SECRETS

Fighting her way back to the surface, she gulped a lungful of air before the current drew her under again. Her injured arm was not strong enough to support her, and blood seeped from her wounds to be carried away downstream. Fear and desperation grew within her and she sensed the demon trying to ride those emotions back to freedom.

She forced herself to relax. It was not far to the bank and she allowed the river to support her as she kicked out with her good leg, using her awareness of the law-aligned water around her to help resist the demon. A few strokes later she felt the river bed beneath her feet and pushed herself forward to collapse on the bank. She lay there trying to recover her strength, blood seeping through her clothes.

She knew she could not rest like that for long or she would never have the strength to move again. Fighting back exhaustion, she forced herself to sit up and open her bag. She poured the sodden contents onto the ground and picked up the bloodmoss, hoping that the brief exposure to river water had not ruined it.

The east bank of the river was bare of large trees but there were rushes and some scrubby bushes. She crawled to the nearest and cut some branches, laying them on top of reeds to make a fire. The moss went into her cauldron and she started to brew the potion. Every so often, she glanced up to check for pursuers. She could no longer see Bjord on the opposite bank and wondered if he had reached the boats.

The pain in her arm was becoming more intense and she had to resist the urge to rush. The water started to boil and she added more herbs, counting to herself to ensure she took the time she needed. In the distance, she could see a single boat crossing the river. Her eyes started to shut, and she jerked them back open. If she slept, she might never wake. Minutes passed and the potion started to change to a deep blue. Once it was done she would be able to cure herself and use witchcraft to escape.

She laid out her cloak so that she could use the flight spell as soon as the elixir was ready. Her breath caught in her throat when she saw that the dye had started to run and that some of the runes were obscured by bloodstains, ruining the sense of the complex pattern.

Anike stared at what was left of the spell. Almost a quarter was blurred or covered in blood, and it was not complete enough for her to read. The spell she had used to drift out of Bjord's reach at the cliff was simple enough that she did not need to see it written but it could only move her slowly. If any bowmen reached her, she would be in range for far too long. Briefly, she considered looking for somewhere to hide but she could barely walk and there was nowhere within sight. She somehow had to replace the pattern.

She could not see anyone coming up the river yet and after the rout on the opposite bank, she hoped any pursuers would be cautious in their approach, so she still had time. It was fortunate that she had only recently created the spell and remembered how it was constructed and which runes were missing. She just needed to find a way to mark the cloak. Looking around, she saw the answer within reach. Holding the cloak down, she took a charred stick from the fire by its unburnt end and started to re-draw the missing runes with charcoal, using a succession of blackened twigs. The pattern did not need to hold long – it just had to be clear enough to read.

She paused her work on the runes to attend to the potion. It was now a clear blue and she only had to add a handful of waygrass to stabilise it. Glancing up, she spotted three horsemen in the distance and did not doubt that one of them was Bjord. The potion would take a few minutes to cool and it would be a near thing. She hastily pictured the water rune before her anxiety gave the demon another chance to escape.

She reached for a stick and finished the pattern on her cloak before looking up again. The riders were getting closer and she grabbed the cauldron, poured its contents into a cup and swallowed a large mouthful. Tears welled up as the elixir scalded her throat but she felt her wounds begin to close and the pain receded. She downed the rest.

The riders were nearly within bow range. With no time to improve the pattern, Anike read it as it was. "*Prana!*" she called, hoping the design was clear enough. Power and relief flowed through her as the demon's energy was channelled into the spell. She slammed it back into its prison then shoved the cauldron into her bag and grabbed her cloak.

She willed herself backwards over the water and then upwards. At extreme bow range, Bjord sighted on her but she shifted direction and his arrow went wide. She headed directly out into the river putting distance between them and with more time to react, she easily avoided the next shot. Moments later she landed on the west bank and was hidden in the woods.

Unless there were hunters on both banks now, she was almost certainly safe. From the shelter of the trees, she watched the riders turn back towards the town, thwarted in their attempt to reach her by the wide river. If Bjord was persistent, he might cross back to her side but that would take an hour or more and this time she had not left a trail that dogs could follow.

Safe for a while, she reflected on the events of the morning as she brewed another potion to restore her strength. Pain and fatigue had sapped her will, in sharp contrast to the demon which seemed unaffected by any strains on her body. The potential for it to escape while she was weakened gave her additional incentive to avoid being wounded and she knew she would have to keep a reasonable stock of healing potions to hand from now on.

It was clear that Bjord was uninterested in any sort of reconciliation and each time they met she had fuelled his hatred. He would think that she had shown weakness by running from the last encounter even though she was winning and take it as evidence that he had exhausted her power and forced her to retreat. Unfortunately, the demon had no interest in inflicting a non-fatal but conclusive defeat on Bjord, and while it did seem to enjoy chaos at the start of each fight, the fate of the robbers in Ulsvater made it clear it had no compunction about killing. A battle was not going to end up with Bjord and her being able to talk and unless she could find some other way to get him to listen she would be unable to bargain over a bloodprice so she could live near Trollgard. If she could not do that, she would have to accept being driven well away from the coast, to where news of her actions had not reached.

Obviously, she could not say with Hilda. It was too dangerous for both of them. Going further afield meant abandoning her father but she did not see any other choice if Bjord remained hostile. It would be hard for her to do that and she could not bear to leave without explaining everything to him face to face. She had to see him first.

She did want to check on Hilda before she went back to Trollgard. The old woman had behaved with great assurance but her disappearance after Bjord's assault was a mystery. Anike recognised that part of her desire to see the seer again was born of curiosity, but she felt guilty as well. She had brought trouble on Hilda and she would feel better if she could assure herself that she had done no lasting harm. If she travelled through the fringes of the mountains rather than try to get to the road again, she could pass by the hut on her way home. It would be all but impossible for someone who could not fly to travel along the top of the cliffs that looked over the forest so she was unlikely to be troubled or identified. She wished she had thought of going that way sooner.

Anike took a little time to properly dye the flight spell back into her cloak and brew another invigorating potion to restore her strength. She hiked upstream until she could fly back across the river to land near the white rock. There were no more signs of hunters and the only movement on the road she had seen was a small party of men with pack mules, plodding towards Ulsvater from the south.

She followed the track up from the white rock then veered up the side of the hill, a route that would take her up to the cliff where she could look down on Hilda's home. If men were waiting for her, it would be foolish to approach at ground level.

She made her way along the clifftop until she was above the hut. Everything seemed quiet and peaceful, though the ground near the building was churned and broken by the passage of men and horses. No smoke arose from the hut and the door was open. As she was lifting her cloak to read the flight spell, movement near the entrance caught her eye and she pulled back from the edge, then cautiously peered down, flat on the ground.

A white-haired man was leaving the hut, and she could see the bow on his back. With a shock, she recognised Masig Valisson, the hero in Arl Oster's service whom she had last seen just outside Trollgard. His presence here was unlikely to be a coincidence. She tried to keep as low as possible. It struck her as odd that he had not been with Bjord and Oster earlier, as a man with a lifetime of experience should surely have been called on to find a witch. She shrugged. Some of what he had said to her outside Trollgard made her think he would not have enjoyed hunting her. He did not seem to think as other men did.

Masig looked around and Anike thought his eyes passed over her for a moment, but he gave no sign that he had seen her and set off up the trail back towards Ulsvater. She watched until he was well out of sight, then cast her flight spell and flew down to the hut.

She saw the dried remains of muddy footprints on the threshold, more than would have been left by Masig alone, but heard nothing to suggest anyone was still there. She knocked on the open door and waited, but there was no response so she went in. The floor was far messier than it had been, with scattered furs and chairs on their sides. The cupboard and the stores did not seem to have been touched, and she could see the cloth wrapping of the silver plate still poking out from under the pile of earthenware. She supposed that Oster's men had come looking for her and had just checked for places large enough to hide in. Oddly, she could see no sign of the runes, either on the table or scattered on the floor, and while she would have understood if they had been spilt during a search, it seemed strange that they were the only things that had been taken.

In any event, there was no sign of Hilda. Anike went to the trapdoor, still hidden beneath the fur rug, and pulled. It remained firmly shut, which surely meant that Hilda was still on the other side and had not been taken by Oster and Bjord. She called the seer's name but no answer came.

Looking around the cabin again to confirm that there was no other hiding place, she bent to examine the trapdoor more carefully. It was old, hinged to open upwards, and its only feature was a neatly crafted wood recess that served as a handle. It shifted only a fraction of an inch when she pulled it, so it had to be bolted on the other side.

She took out her paring knife and ran its thin blade along the gap between the door and the frame until she found the bolt. Drawn both by a curiosity about the trapdoor as well as a desire to confirm that Hilda was not harmed or trapped, Anike decided to open it. She rested the blade gently against the bolt and brought the spell for movement clearly to mind. She wrapped the runes around the bolt with her thoughts and spoke, "*Prana.*" Energy flowed from her, and she willed the bolt to move. There was a faint scraping sound as it slid back and she lifted the trapdoor to reveal a ladder leading down a wood-lined shaft to a passage which seemed to head towards the cliff, its floor about fifteen feet below ground level.

Anike found a candle, lit it with her fire strike, and descended the steps. She felt very aware of the weight of the earth enveloping her so completely. A sensation of dread crept through her before she realised that it was the demon's reaction to being surrounded by a law-aligned element seeping into her thoughts. Once she understood where the feeling was coming from, she was able to push it out of her mind and looked down the passage. By the light of the candle, she could just make out that the walls and ceiling were made of tightly packed earth, supported by thick posts and beams of ancient oak. It had clearly been built many years ago but with great skill and care. It was tall enough for her to stand upright and sloped slightly downward.

She had followed it for about forty paces and thought she was probably now beneath the cliff when she came to a door. It was also made from stout oak and bound with bronze, with a lock and a small closed hatch at head height. Anike had never seen a lock on a door before, only on chests containing something extremely valuable. The bronze bands running around the edge and across it were slightly discoloured and pitted with age. She tried the door and was not surprised to find it as unmovable as the cliff itself.

It was set into a wide frame, also made from bronze-covered wood, and try as she might she could not get her knife more than an inch into the gap. Her movement spell was entirely unsuited to release a complex mechanism like a lock so there was only one thing to try. Hoping that it was only the seer who could hear her, she knocked hard on the wood. A dull boom echoed through the passage, a testament to the weight of the door. She waited a moment, then knocked again, and called out "Hilda, are you there?" She was raising her hand to knock a third time when the little hatch opened abruptly and Anike found herself looking into Hilda's bright blue eyes.

"You had better come inside," said Hilda, and the hatch snapped shut. There was a slow grating noise as the bolts all around the door slid back. It opened ponderously, and Anike stepped through to find that the passage rose steeply upwards for a few paces and then opened out. Her mouth dropped open when she saw what lay beyond, and she stood transfixed as Hilda shut the door behind them.

Beyond the short cutting leading from the door was a great chamber. A cold white light illuminated a gallery about the same size as the Arl's hall. The stone walls were worked so finely that they appeared smooth, with straight lines leading to soaring curves and arches rising far above her. At the sides were alcoves with seats that seemed to grow from the wall. Everywhere subtle intricate patterns decorated the stone.

No human had made this chamber. No human had the skill.

The light was radiating from crystals, some high in the wall above her while others, set into the walls within the alcoves, gave off a paler light. The illumination seemed bright when compared to the candle but when her eyes adjusted Anike could see that it was more like twilight.

At the far end of the chamber, a broad passage stopped abruptly after a dozen paces at a solid but unadorned wall but the beauty of the construction was marred at that point. An irregular passage, a pace wide and a few paces long, had been chipped out of it.

Hilda's runes lay on an elegant stone table which dominated the centre of the room and next to it, an incongruous pair of rude wooden chairs and a pile of furs had been placed. Anike stepped forward into the centre of the chamber and turned in a slow circle to take in the beauty of the whole construction. There was a mound of old, packed earth on the side she had entered by and the gully she had walked through led beneath it, below floor level. Behind the earth mound, a tiny uniform gap in the wall formed an arch some twenty feet high, perfectly divided into two. Anike realised that the earth mound was partially blocking a pair of enormous doors in the cliff.

Above the arch, translucent crystals surrounded a great picture carved into the rock, a bas relief showing men gathered around a giant on a throne. The light, which Anike now saw was daylight, passed through the clear crystals, sending shadows across the scene.

She noticed that Hilda was watching her. "What is this place?" the young woman breathed.

By way of response, Hilda indicated the chairs and they sat. Closer up, Anike could see that the carvings on the table were blurred and cracked in places, and wondered how many years had passed since they were first engraved. She remembered her manners. "Thank you for allowing me into this place. I am glad to see you are well. I was concerned, particularly when I saw Masig Valisson leaving just now."

Hilda smiled. "Masig and I have known each other a long time. I am well, but I anticipated trouble when Oster and Bjord came to see me for the first time. It was clear you would bring a storm with you when you finally arrived, and the need to spend a few days in here to avoid the worst of it did not come as a surprise. Did you do much damage to my trapdoor?"

"None, actually."

"Oster will be pleased about that. He would not want to go to the trouble of having it repaired."

"Arl Oster knows about this place?"

"He was the one who showed it to me. He will probably come himself once the excitement has died down after you leave, but in the meantime, he asked Masig to visit and see how I was."

Anike wondered briefly if Hilda had deduced her plans or seen them in the runes, but was also interested in Masig, whom she had found surprisingly thoughtful for a warrior when they had last met. "I did not see Masig with the men who were hunting me," she noted.

"No, you wouldn't have. Masig did not approve of that. But he remembers you and asked me to pass on his regards if you came by."

"Why did he do that? I would have thought his interest would be in serving Arl Oster."

"That would be something for him to tell you if you meet him again," Hilda said.

Anike recalled her discussion with him outside Trollgard after Gern's trial. "He seemed almost regretful when Gern was put to death," she said. "I wonder if he has some interest in, or perhaps a use for, witches."

"As I said, that is something you would have to discuss with him."

While Anike would have liked to pursue it further, that subject was clearly closed as far as Hilda was concerned. She knew better than to press a woman so used to keeping the secrets of others. Fortunately, there was a great deal more to interest her, such as the vast stone hall in which they sat. "This chamber," she gestured around her, "was made by dwarves? What purpose did it serve? It seems strange for it to be here, isolated and hidden." She looked around, trying to discern the builders' intentions. "Was it a shrine?" Her eyes settled on the crystals in the alcoves. "And why do they glow? That is not sunlight."

Hilda laughed. "You have a curious mind, and I will tell you what I can. We are not in a great hurry, however, so you have time to complete your side of the bargain and tell me about your insights."

Anike's obligation to Hilda had not been at the front of her mind but Hilda had a right to ask her to fulfil it. It would have been dishonourable to return to Trollgard without doing so as it was unlikely she would ever have another chance. She had learned a good deal that could interest the seer and she wondered how much to say and where to begin. It was doubtful that she could ever find an appreciative audience for her revelation about her demon but Hilda was more likely to hear her out than anyone else.

She explained what she had discovered about the rune patterns and manifesting effects. "I used witchcraft to open the trapdoor," she said by way of example.

Hilda smiled. "I see you have achieved a measure of control. Show me."

At Hilda's instigation, Anike bewitched a small stone and lifted it into the air while the old woman watched on carefully. She showed the seer the patterns she had dyed into her, now rather battered, cloak. Hilda read them, eyes alight with interest. Anike explained how she cast the spell, and the seer attempted to trigger the smoke effect herself, looking carefully at the pattern and speaking *"Agni,"* in a firm voice. Anike watched with interest but was not surprised when nothing happened.

Hilda leaned back and smiled ruefully. "I see the principles but even if I were to devise a spell myself, I would have no way to test it. Still, as a mental exercise, it could be very interesting to try. Wait a moment." After digging around in the pile of furs, Hilda produced a flat black slate, a little bigger than a plate, and a small white stone. She drew a rune on the black stone with the white one. "Slate and chalk," she said. "I use these to help work through complex rune patterns. Show me the other spells you created."

Anike wiped off the chalk with her sleeve and drew the other patterns in turn. Hilda nodded at each, as her eyes swept over them, taking in the detail. "Yes, this is very interesting. I suspect they could be phrased more elegantly and work more efficiently, but I will have to leave that development to you. What I see as improvements to the pattern might not work at all." She folded her hands. "Did you obtain any other insights?"

Twisting the ends of her hair with her fingers, Anike hesitated, then began to speak. "Yes, I have found out that witchcraft is not really my power at all. There is a demon inside me, a spirit of fire and chaos, and it is what casts the spell. All the times when I used witchcraft before I started working on the patterns I have just shown you, it was not me at all but the demon acting through me. I originally thought it was just power escaping, distorting my judgment like a drug, but the truth is much darker. The rune patterns draw on the demon, channelling its power to perform the action the runes describe, and each time I have to cage it again with images of law." Anike looked up to see Hilda's reaction.

The seer was silent for a moment, regarding Anike with her blue eyes. When she spoke it was in a surprisingly warm tone though Anike could sense tension in her posture. "That cannot be an easy thing, knowing you carry an invader and a passenger, which is constantly looking for a chance to use you for its own ends."

Anike frowned. "It is always in the back of my mind, looking for a way in. It can alter how I see things but now that I have recognised it for what it is, I am finding it much easier to resist. It wants to destroy, to tear down structure and order but beyond that, I cannot understand its thoughts though sometimes its emotions filter through. I can feel its hatred of the dire wolves and its contempt for humans. I think it has greater access to my thoughts but I am not sure about how much it really understands."

"Someone watching you would not see the spirit itself, I take it? It would seem to those around you that you were choosing to use witchcraft yourself."

"I think something might show in the eyes if you knew to look for it," Anike replied, thinking of Gern. "But it would not be obvious that the demon was in control, and to start with it and even I did not suspect I was in thrall to another being. I thought the power had lowered my inhibitions and allowed my baser instincts out. That was why it took me so long to realise the truth. It was not until the demon did something I had never even imagined that I realised that another intelligence was channelling power through my body."

"This does explain the destructive behaviour witches are known and feared for." Hilda seemed to relax slightly. "I cannot see any practical use for the knowledge yet, but this is fascinating to hear. It may actually be worth the trouble you have brought with you." She smiled. "It will be hard for most people to accept, though. I cannot see the news that you are carrying a demon bent on destruction endearing you to those that you meet."

"I have come to the same conclusion," said Anike drily. "Do you have any idea where the demon came from? I thought it might have been birthed during witch weather."

"I'm afraid I do not know, but that is as likely an explanation as any. The name 'witch weather' is very old and may reflect forgotten knowledge of a connection between the storms and witches."

Anike wondered about the witch weather that her father had told her marked her birth. Was that just a storm, or had a demon been born when she was and if so what had become of it? Could it somehow have made her more susceptible to the demon at Vanir Heights, or was it even connected to her mother's death? She shook her head. There were still so many unanswered questions.

"I could read the runes for you again if you want to know more," Hilda offered, reading her expression.

Anike thought about that. "No. Thank you. I am going back to Trollgard to see my father one last time, then I will have to find somewhere new, perhaps on the other side of the mountains. I think you anticipated that. If the origin of the demon is truly significant, the answer could come with a great deal of bad luck and I really cannot afford that right now."

Hilda nodded. "When everything has quietened down, perhaps you could try the cast yourself," she suggested.

"I may do that when I get the time," Anike looked around her. "You were going to tell me about this place."

"Yes, though you may find it a less interesting tale than the one you have just told me." Hilda waved her hand expansively at the large chamber. "As you have guessed, this is dwarven work. The history, as told to me by Oster, is that this was an entrance to the underground dwarven realm, Svartalfheim, dating from a time before the dwarves came onto the surface in force."

Anike glanced around again. "But there is no way out," she said.

Hilda pointed to the back wall and the passage that had been crudely cut into it. "That passage used to descend to Svartalfheim. The dwarves sealed the entrances when they retreated from the surface, and you can see the differences between that stonework and their original work. It is more recent and less elegantly constructed, though still very solid."

"And that rough alcove?"

"At some point, shortly after the dwarves abandoned the surface, there was an attempt by humans to break through so that they could explore the dwarven realm, to look for treasure perhaps, but the wall proved too strong. After that, the Arl of the time buried the chamber entrance but built the door you came through, preserving this as a secret refuge in case of war. The trapdoor, I am told, was originally hidden, buried a few inches under the ground. The hut is more recent."

"Why was the entrance placed here? It is not particularly close to the town."

"This chamber predates the stone town in Ulsvater, though there may have been an older settlement where the town now stands. The dwarves built the stone town when they emerged onto the surface and they made another entrance to Svartalfheim from what is now the Arl's hall. They sealed that passage too. There is no entrance chamber there, just a large stone set into the ground, capping the deep chimney underneath." Hilda stood and looked down at Anike. "Oster's ancestors have been Arls at Ulsvater from that time on, and the secret has been handed down, father to son, through the generations."

"So how is it that you know it then?" Anike put her hand to her mouth. "I am sorry. That was impertinent."

Hilda waved the apology away. "Oster and I are very close. I have known him since he was a boy. When we decided it would be better if I did not live in the hall, he brought me here, showed me this place and shared its lore with me."

"Why are you telling me all this?"

"Oster wishes this place to remain a secret. If I did not explain it to you, you might try to discover more from other people, and that could bring others looking for it."

"Oster is trying to kill me. Why should I keep his secrets?"

Hilda's gaze was suddenly cold. "It would not be honourable to betray my trust in you."

Anike winced at the rebuke. "I apologise. You are right, of course. I am not used to being hunted and I was in danger of letting it affect my judgment."

"Unfortunately, Oster has good reason for hunting you, as does Bjord." Hilda's tone softened. "Bjord will remain your problem, but I shall talk to Oster in due course, and with you gone from his domain his pursuit of you will end. You should not have to talk to him again, so the question of this chamber need never come up."

Anike reflected on the implication within those words. Hilda had given her a powerful secret that she could use to protect herself against Oster. He would not want to give her a chance to reveal the existence of this place in public and she could do that if he put her on trial. It might not stop him from having her murdered but she supposed Hilda had judged that unlikely.

"Why did Oster move you out of the hall to here?" She sensed another secret.

"That is between me and him," Hilda said, without hostility but there was a note of finality in her voice.

Anike accepted that this subject too was closed and glanced around the great room, trying to decide what else she should ask before she departed. Her eyes lighted on the peculiar crystals in the wall, and she went over to one of them, bringing her hand up to it. It gave off a dim light with a slightly blue tint, but no heat. "What are these?" she asked.

"Oster called them glowstones." Hilda came to stand beside her. "They absorb light and heat, and they can glow for hours if the day outside has been bright. They are a natural rock found deep underground and brought here by the dwarves. Probably not a great wonder by their standards, but they make life in here a little easier."

Anike touched the stone. It was cold, colder than she expected, and it brightened at her touch, a ripple of light travelling across the surface. "Even the heat of your body is enough to create a little light," said Hilda.

Anike lifted her hand away. She supposed the stone could be valuable but had no desire to disturb it. "This is a wondrous place. It is a shame that there are no dwarfs left on the surface these days."

"I doubt many would agree. The dwarven rule was harsh, by all accounts."

"Even so, there is much we could learn from them. They brought us the secrets of steel and of working stone, and I doubt they shared all of their lore."

"We can learn much from many people, Anike, it just takes an open mind. I have certainly gained from my association with you."

"As have I, Hilda."

Hilda crossed to the central table and picked up the slate and chalk. "Take these with you. I think you will find more use for them than I will."

"Thank you." Anike gratefully put the two stones, black and white, into her bag. She took a last look round, turning to embrace the old woman before she moved to the door. "Take good care of yourself, Hilda."

Hilda smiled. "You as well, Anike. Stay safe."

Anike returned through the passage and up the ladder to the hut. She closed the trapdoor behind her and arranged the furs carefully on top before leaving. Looking at her cloak once more, she gathered her will and firmly spoke, "*Prana*," resisting the demon and channelling its power. She rose into the air and started her journey to the town which had once been her home.

- 19 -

The Siege

It took Anike several days to return to Trollgard. She had started by walking along the top of the cliffs and enjoyed the view of the forest and the sea to the north. As far as she knew, no people lived in these mountains, but there was plenty of life. Goats, rabbits and small birds moved through the gorse and heather, and a few plants she had never seen before nestled in the grass. In places, the terrain was too difficult to cross on foot and she had been forced to use witchcraft to fly over some of it.

Occasionally she saw a larger animal. A puma scattered a flock of mountain sheep and in the late afternoon of her first day, she saw something in the distance. It was sleek, grey and larger than a dire wolf so as the sun set, she found a broad ledge some fifty feet beneath the top of the cliff and flew down to spend the night there. In the small hours, she regretted this choice of resting place as her battered cloak gave scant protection against the wind blowing onto the exposed rock face, and she slept badly. When twilight deepened at the end of the second day, she descended all the way to the forest.

The journey had given her time to think more about what she could do with witchcraft and she used the slate to develop several spells. On the second night, having stacked the wood she had gathered in the forest, she devised a simple pattern she could hold in her mind for igniting wood even if it was green or damp, and used it to start a fire. Had she been close to a settlement, she might not have risked releasing the demon for something she could easily do by hand but there was minimal risk so far from habitation. Every casting of a spell meant a battle to contain the demon and while she did not enjoy these, they did give her a chance to sharpen her mental skills far away from anyone she could hurt and her handling became surer with practice. The demon had not even come close to taking her over since she had left Hilda, but she wanted her control to be absolute when she reached her home again.

Two complex spells were now dyed into the sleeves of her tunic and she could conceal the patterns against casual inspection by keeping her arms within her cloak. The demon had provided her with ideas for some useful effects and while she knew that in time she would be able to construct more original spells, for the moment she was still largely ignorant about the limits of her craft. Knowing it was within her power, she worked out a pattern to protect herself from war darts and arrows with a shield of wind. The other effect was simpler but something she anticipated having to use when trying to enter Trollgard at night – a spell to extinguish fires that she could use on the torches of any sentries.

As she travelled towards Trollgard, the forest began to look more familiar. She was not in a great hurry so she took time to replenish her stock of herbs along the way and the pauses in her journey grew longer as she brewed new elixirs. On the fourth day of travel, she had gone far enough to the east and turned north through the forest towards Trollgard. She had avoided the main paths but had not heard any sounds of axes, or indeed any indication of human presence, so she was cautious as she came to the edge of the trees and looked down on the town.

Armed men stood on the walls, twenty or more perhaps, but the wood town seemed unnaturally still even though the gates stood open. Apprehension at the strange scene replaced her pleasure at seeing her home again. As she looked more carefully, she saw that many of the wood town buildings had been toppled and lay like piles of discarded sticks on the ground. The livestock seemed to have gone too, and a sense of foreboding lay over the whole area.

A roaring screech came from the forested edge half a mile to the east and the harrowling burst from the trees. It spread its wings wide then ran towards the town, picking up speed as it did

THE DEMON AND THE WITCH

so. It seemed to be making for the gate. A brassy call of horns sounded on the wall as the creature broke cover.

Anike now saw what she had initially missed – half a dozen people searching through the ruins of a partially collapsed building outside the wall. On hearing the warning, they ran for the gate. The speed of their reaction suggested to Anike that she was watching a practised response.

In the half minute it took for them to reach the stone town, the harrowling had covered most of the distance from the forest. The gate closed behind the fleeing townsfolk and the monster pulled up, screeched in frustration then it seemed to gather itself, spreading its wings wide. Anike did not believe it could fly – it had not pursued her up the cliff when she had fled the town – but it could leap and she feared that it might be able to get over the wall.

It appeared that the defenders had anticipated the harrowling's action. Half a dozen arrows flew towards it as it charged, some bouncing off its scales but the rest striking its wings and lodging there. It hissed and closed its wings, shaking the shafts loose, and slammed its massive shoulder into the gate. The wood boomed at the impact, scattering splinters onto the harrowling's back, but it held and the creature bounced back a few paces. War darts and arrows rained down on it and it turned away with a final screech of frustration. On its way back to the forest, it paused to rake through the ruins where the townsfolk had been scavenging, perhaps to see if anyone was still hiding there. Anike could see that it was still limping slightly, just as it had been when it chased her. Once the creature had disappeared back into the trees, the town gates opened and some people emerged cautiously, returning to search through the ruins.

She was surprised that the harrowling had not been driven off or killed while she had been away, but it did not even seem to have been seriously hurt. The wood town looked abandoned and she assumed that those who lived there had sought shelter behind the town walls.

As the gates were now open, she considered making her way down to one and slipping inside but with only a few people in the wood town, there was not enough of a crowd to lose herself in. With her torn and bloodied clothes and unkempt hair, she might not resemble the woman who had left Trollgard a week before at a casual glance, but anyone who gave her a second look would recognise her. She would have to wait until dark.

Cocking her head to one side, she could just make out the sound of the monster in the distance. It was not stealthy in the forest so she would have plenty of warning if it came back. She settled down under a tree and watched the amber light of the sun fade as it sank towards the west. Its last rays brought a golden fire to the crests of the waves rolling onto the beach and the light danced on the water until the sun finally sank out of sight. It was almost possible to become lost in the view and forget about recent events but as the darkness flowed over the town in the sun's wake, she put aside any thoughts of rest and focused on how she would get to her own home without being seen.

When the dusk had deepened, she walked to the edge of the ruins of the once vibrant farmsteads and shook her head in disbelief at the destruction that the harrowling had caused in only a week. A few buildings remained intact but many were little more than piles of kindling. Anike definitely wanted to be behind stone walls when the monster returned. She hoped it did not function well at night.

Occasional torches dotted the parapet on the landward side of the town. Crouching down behind one of the wooden walls that remained standing, she conjured light onto a piece of wood and read the flight spell on her cloak. She flew silently, keeping close to the ground between the ruined houses until she reached the seaward side of the town. There were no watchers on the side facing the beach so she flew along its base almost to the north gate, glided up and over the wall then dropped quickly to the ground inside. Crouching in the shadows, she looked about her to check she had not been seen. The streets were quiet but from the houses came the sounds of families bringing the day to a close. She waited, listening and watching for any sign of alarm, but when none came she drew her hood over her head and started down a lane. A few turns past familiar houses brought her to her home and she sighed in relief. She opened the door.

Inge, who had been sitting at the large table in Anike's home, jumped up and spun about, her golden hair flaring out. Her eyes widened and she opened her mouth to scream.

"Shh!" Anike whispered urgently, stepping inside and pulling the door shut behind her. Inge took a step back, eyes darting from Anike to the corner where Darek's axe stood against the wall. "Anike?" she quavered.

"Yes, it's me. I know I look terrible. But it is so good to see you again." She stepped forward, opening her arms to embrace her friend.

Inge paled and stepped away, anything but reassured. "Have you come back to kill us too?" she asked in a small voice. She took another pace back.

"Of course not!" Anike said in astonishment, coming abruptly to a stop and lowering her arms. She should not have been so surprised. Bjord would have spread his story of how she had attacked him but she had not expected to see Inge here and had not considered how her lifelong friend would react. She had wanted to see her father first. Uncertain as to where he was, she glanced around the house, but Inge still looked to be on the point of screaming and Anike needed to calm her down.

A muted thought that the obvious course of action was to kill the girl tried to insinuate itself into her consciousness. She ignored the demon's attempt to subvert her, raised her empty hands and took a careful step backwards. "Inge, I do not know exactly what you have heard but I am not going to hurt you or kill anyone."

Inge watched her, poised like a deer ready to spring away at the first sign of danger. "I can still scream, you know," she said.

"I know you can, but there would be no time to say goodbye properly if you did."

"So you do want to kill me, just slowly." Inge shrank back even further.

Anike thought about the words she had used and nearly smiled at how Inge had misunderstood them in her panic, but caught herself in time. "No, no," she said, as consolingly as she could. "I am the one who is leaving. Look, Inge, give me a chance to explain. Sit down. Please." She gestured to one of the chairs by the table, and slowly walked to the other and sat herself. Inge's eyes again measured the distance to Anike, then to the axe against the wall, before she sat cautiously on the edge of the other seat. Anike was not sure that Inge could even lift the axe.

A snore came from the sleeping platform above. The familiar sound dispelled Anike's anxiety about where her father was so she gave her friend her full attention.

Still tensed like a frightened animal, Inge was watching Anike carefully. "Arl Svafnir announced that you were a witch and that you slaughtered some farmers, and Bjord told us how you killed even more people in Ulsvater," she said.

"Inge, I was out of control when those things happened, even after I left Trollgard, but I promise you that everything is different now." She leaned across the table and reached out her hand but Inge pulled away. "Look into my eyes," Anike continued. "I am still the same woman that I was last month. I was cursed, and I was overwhelmed by it. I admit that. On Vanir Heights, a power I had never wanted was poured into me and I could not stop it from bursting out."

"Anike, you killed people!"

"I know." Anike's mouth tightened. "But it was an accident. Listen. When I was in the mountains, there was witch weather and a ball of fire fell from the sky. It was going to strike Bjord, so I pushed him out of the way and it hit me instead. Its power passed into me." Anike doubted that telling Inge about the demon would help calm her at that moment. "At first I could not control the energy at all. It just exploded out of me and that is what struck Bjord down, and those other people on the farm. Believe me, Inge, it was all an accident, a terrible catastrophe."

"If it was all an accident, why did you run?"

"I was frightened. I thought I had killed Bjord until he was brought here. Arl Svafnir was angry enough that Bjord had followed me and if he had found out I had used witchcraft on his son, he might have killed me without even a pretence of a trial. Who would have believed me if I had said it was an accident and even if they had, who would care?" Anike held her friend's gaze. "And I was still dangerous to be around people back then. When I returned from Vanir Heights, I was barely hanging on. I had to leave, to try and find some way to get rid of the curse. While I could not manage that, after some time and a lot of effort I got to the point where I was sure it was safe enough to be able to come back, just for a short visit."

"Visit?"

"I am not staying, Inge. You are my best friend, and look how frightened you were when you saw me and to be honest, I do not blame you. And Bjord hates me now. He opened his heart to me on the mountain and I betrayed him immediately afterwards. He will never accept it was not my decision."

She looked up at the bed. "I only came back to see my father and explain everything to the people I care about, and to say goodbye. Why is my father still asleep?" She and Inge had not been quiet and her father had not stirred.

Inge's expression turned from fear to worry. "Olaf made a sleeping draught for him. He did not take the news that you were a witch very well, and some people think that he was involved in what you did, though more are sympathetic to him for having put up with you. I have suffered too, as everyone knows we were close," she added bitterly, a spark of her old spirit showing through. "Anyway, after he learned what you had done, your father could not face work and now just sits there by the fire. Arl Svafnir was harsh with him too, at least to start with. You were right about him being very angry, and your father was the easiest target."

Anike clenched and unclenched her fist under the table where Inge could not see it. "I was not a witch until I went to Vanir Heights and I hardly had time to speak to my father before I was forced to run. I did not even tell him I had become a witch. Arl Svafnir should have been fighting the monster rather than persecuting an innocent man."

"So that was why you set your monster on the town – to keep everyone away from your father? It certainly stopped the Arl coming to see him."

"What do you mean, 'stopped him'? And it is not my monster – I do not know where it came from."

"Really? Everyone says you made it and set it to punish the town." Inge frowned. "Arl Svafnir was seriously hurt in battling it, so badly that some thought he was going to die. Olaf saved him but he is still abed, unconscious most of the time. Olaf says he will recover, though." She looked at her hands. "Others were not so fortunate."

"I am sorry to hear that, Inge. I truly am, but the harrowling is none of my doing. It tried to kill me too." Anike stopped suddenly, for even as she spoke she recalled how the demon had admired the creature and a suspicion that it was somehow connected to her formed in her mind. She pushed it aside and stood. "I need to talk to my father. You gave him enough of the sleeping draught to last him through the night?" Inge nodded. "I will need to wake him then. Before I do, tell me what else has happened. What has the monster been doing?"

"It's been coming every day since you left. It ate a lot of the livestock from the farms outside and destroyed most of the wood town buildings looking for more. Everyone who lived there has come behind the walls to stay with family or camp in the marketplace. The creature still tries to catch anyone it sees outside the walls and no one has been able to seriously hurt it. We have lost six warriors and it has injured a dozen more. Siv organised a defence and managed to stop it getting into the stone town so far but everyone is worried it will break in."

Anike imagined the creature tearing its way through the market and shuddered. "It would be a disaster if that monster breached the walls," she agreed.

Inge pulled her hair back from her face. "People are terrified, but Bjord came back the day before yesterday, boasting that he had left you mortally wounded and that he will do the same to the monster. That has given people hope, though you don't look mortally wounded to me. But he plans to lead an attack on it tomorrow."

"No doubt he will try but if his father failed, I doubt he will succeed and he could get more people killed. It sounds as if everyone here is at risk. Perhaps you should come with me when I leave, you and your husband?"

Inge looked frightened. "I would prefer to take my chances here. Even if we got past the monster, I don't want to travel with a witch. I am sorry, Anike. You say you are in control now but how can I know that for sure? You could kill us in our sleep. Or when we are awake."

While no longer on the verge of panic, Inge was still trembling and she kept looking away. Anike now doubted that mere words would change her views any further. The fear of witches and the belief that they were nothing but ruthless killers was too deep-rooted to displace by argument, but there could be another way.

"I will prove myself to you, and to everyone else," Anike said with sudden determination. "I will kill the harrowling for you."

- 20 -

GATHERING CLOUDS

Inge's eyes widened. "Do you really think you can kill the monster, even though all our warriors have failed?"

"I can certainly try and yes, I believe I can." Glimmers of a plan were forming in Anike's mind. She had spoken in haste but the demon had not felt threatened by the harrowling, only irritated that it had to deal with it. Now she had access to the demon's power she should be able to defeat it herself and if things went badly she could certainly escape. "If I succeed," she continued, "all of Trollgard will be able to see that I still want to help the people here and I can use witchcraft to protect the town."

She stood up, her eyes alight with sudden hope. "Perhaps Bjord and Arl Svafnir will even let me pay a bloodprice and stay close by. Not in the town itself but somewhere not too far away. Inge, if I can kill this creature, I may not have to leave at all."

Inge's face did not reflect Anike's enthusiasm but she managed a small smile. "Perhaps," she said.

"Well," Anike told her, "even if the town and the Arl do not want me back, defeating the monster can be my parting gift. But I believe Arl Svafnir is pragmatic and he will see me as an asset."

Inge looked doubtful. "He hates witches, Anike. I think he is afraid of them, and he destroys things that frighten him."

Bjord was like that too, Anike thought. He had been frightened of witchcraft but had pursued her despite his fear. She doubted that he would want her anywhere nearby, but he was young. Arl Svafnir had looked after his domain for many years with shrewdness as well as prowess in battle. She recalled how he had manipulated her during Gern's trial. He was a complex man and there was a good chance he would reassess witchcraft if she could show him its potential.

She was about to reply to Inge when a voice came from above. "Haven't I told you not to take risks, child?"

"Father!" Anike cried, running over and taking the ladder two steps at a time to envelop him in a hug.

"Now, girl, I need to breathe," he said as he held her close, then drew back to look at her face. "I thought you were dead, Anike. I am so glad to see you again." Then he frowned. "You can't stay here, much as I would like you to."

"Inge has told me what the town thinks about me, Father, but I have a plan to change that."

"I heard, but I thought I was still asleep and having a nightmare. Don't do it. You would just be throwing your life away."

Her safety was always her father's first concern, but that was hanging by a thread anyway. If she ever was to change that, she had to show that witchcraft could be used for something good. The best anyone thought of Gern was to wonder why he had suddenly revealed his power, and Svafnir had suppressed even that but if she could portray witchcraft in a positive light, acceptance might follow. People admired and respected skilled warriors and they were dangerous too.

"Father," she said, "I have done some terrible things but they have been accidents. I never wanted to hurt anyone but it took too long for me to learn how to control my curse. The power escaped before I could stop it. I left to search for a way to rid myself of it. My journey did not lead where I hoped but I did learn enough to control the power. I would never have risked coming back if I was any danger to you."

Telling her father about the demon and everything else that she had been through could wait. Inge was nervous enough already and even if they could accept the truth of what a witch was, Inge in particular might tell others who would not be so tolerant. She also had the sense that talking about the demon could give it strength and she did not want any risk of losing control in her home.

Anike let go of her father and returned to the table. "I saw a seer in Ulsvater. She helped me understand myself better and I learned that while I was always going to be burdened with witchcraft, I could control it." She fixed Darek with her gaze. "I want everyone to see that I can do more than bring disaster. I really think that I can defeat the monster but even if I have to retreat, I will have shown the townspeople I tried and am not their enemy. I want to stay here if I can but I have to kill the monster first. I can offer the Arl its death as bloodprice for my attack on Bjord. That might be fitting."

On the other side of the table, Inge shifted nervously. "You are wrong about one thing you said, Anike," she said in a small voice. "You are not the same person you were. I have never seen you so forthright." She did not sound happy about it.

"Is that not a good thing, Inge?" asked Anike.

"I just think you would be less frightening if you were less sure of yourself. Like you used to be."

"That wouldn't help, Inge," Darek said, coming down the ladder to join them. "People would still be afraid of her." He turned to Anike. "Forget the monster. It is too dangerous and I won't have you taking such a risk."

"Was I really like that, Inge, cautious and uncertain?" said Anike. Inge nodded. "Oh. My father is right, though. If I appear like that now, it will seem to be a trick. It will not stop people blaming me for the harrowling either."

"Harrowling?" asked Darek.

"That was what a herbalist in Ulsvater called the monster."

"But surely its appearance is connected to you," said Inge, carefully watching Anike's face for her reaction. "I cannot help thinking that your curse and the monster are linked. They are both such strange things, and its first attack was on Volna who was bringing news of your witchcraft to the town." She looked at her hands, probably regretting she had spoken. "I am sorry, but it does look very suspicious."

"I can see that," said Anike ruefully. "It was not my doing, but I agree that the timing seems too similar to be a coincidence." She paused, considering. "I wonder, the harrowling is part bear, part eagle, and part something with scales, yes?"

Darek nodded. "Fish scales, I think." He would recognise those, of course.

Anike nodded. "And when it first attacked the town, it had a wound on its right leg?"

"It still has it," Inge said. "The scales have not grown back over that part of it, though the injury seems to trouble it less now."

"When I was on Vanir Heights, I saw a bear with a wound in the same place. There was an eagle in the sky overhead and fish in the pool by the waterfall. I think that the creatures were joined together at the same time as I became a witch, and the bear part is still wounded." She frowned as she remembered applying the salve, healing the bear enough to get out of the ravine. She had not created the harrowling but might have helped to release it. It was something else for which she needed to atone.

Darek spoke again. "You still can't fight it, Anike."

"I can," she said. "I cannot just wish it dead or anything like that, but I know I can hurt it and I can stay out of its reach while I confront it."

"How can you be so sure?"

"Father, I can fly." He stared at her. "Really, I can. If anything goes wrong, I can get away easily. The monster cannot fly, despite its wings."

"They do help it jump, though," Inge said. "That is why everyone is worried it might get over the wall."

Darek looked grim, his old stubbornness emerging. "Anike, I have seen how strong and fast this creature is. I can't let you do this. I would rather you leave and find refuge far away than take such a foolish risk."

Anike laid a hand on his arm. "I know you want to keep me safe, Father, but this time I can protect you. There is very little of the wood town left now. How much longer before the harrowling really tries to get over the walls? If it succeeds, no one in the town will be safe."

"Once inside, we can trap it," Darek said.

"Perhaps, but at what cost? This is a much better way. I want to do something useful with this power. I need to do this, not just for Trollgard, or even for how it looks to everyone else but how I feel about myself." She looked at him. "Do you understand?"

"No," Darek sighed despairingly. "But I see your mind is made up."

Anike looked from him to Inge, who was now looking concerned as well. A warm feeling spread through her knowing that deep down Inge still did care, but her pleasure was overtaken by a dawning appreciation of the size of the task she had taken on. Warriors had lost their lives fighting the harrowling, but she was prepared to take the risk to protect those she cared about and for the chance of a future in Trollgard.

The spells she had devised so far would take her some way but she was conscious that there were gaps in her armoury. She had spent a little time working on a pattern for a firebolt during her journey back to Trollgard, but it only had a short range. She had wanted something to protect herself but had not completed the design as she had been uncomfortable creating a spell which had no purpose except to harm. Now she would have to finish it and she also needed something which could strike at the harrowling from further away. "I have to prepare," she said. "Inge, will you go and fetch Olaf, please? I would like to talk to him and I do not want to risk being seen in the streets."

"I think he was disappointed in you," said Inge. "He may not come."

"Tell him I am going to kill the harrowling," said Anike. "That should make him put aside any doubts long enough to talk to me, at least. And please ask him if he has any blank vellum and ink that he can spare."

Inge frowned, then nodded and left. After she had gone, Anike turned to her father. "I missed you so much," she told him, "and I never wanted you to suffer because of me."

"I didn't believe it at first when the Arl told me what you had done. How could the daughter I had raised be a witch? But Bjord came with him and told me what had happened to him so I had to believe it."

"I wish with all my heart I had not attacked anyone but Bjord could only see from the outside. He could not look within me and understand what was really going on. If I had the control then that I do now I would never have hurt him. I just hope that after I kill the harrowling, I will be able to explain that I never wished him any harm."

Darek looked at her. "I am proud you are not giving up and that you are brave enough to face this creature. Your mother would have been proud, too." Anike knew he was feeling overwhelmed. He rarely mentioned Isolde at all.

"Even so," he continued, "I still wish you would give up this plan. After Arl Svafnir and Bjord came to tell me what you had done, I thought I would never see you again. When Bjord returned yesterday and announced in the market that you had fled, gravely wounded, it felt as if I had died myself. Now that I have just got you back, I do not want to lose you."

"You are not going to, I promise you that. If it looks like I am not going to win, I will retreat." She reached out and took her father's hand in hers. "But if it goes well, I may be able to stay close enough for you to be able to visit me."

"I hope so, child. I really do."

"Then pray for me, and for Bjord and Svafnir to see things clearly. Now, I have to prepare."

Anike smiled at him, crossed to her small work table and took out her herbs and cauldron. She would need both witchcraft and herb lore to defeat the harrowling. "This is going to work," she said aloud and wondered if she was trying to convince her father or herself.

The door opened and Inge came in, followed by Olaf. "Inge told me that you had come back, and what you said." Olaf closed the door carefully behind him. "It is good to see you again, Anike. I had feared the worst."

"It is good to see you too, Olaf. I missed you." She gave him a hug. He froze for a moment before returning it.

"Inge said you had seen a seer. Was that Hilda of Ulsvater?"

Anike frowned at his choice of words. Olaf knew exactly where she had planned to go, then she realised that he had sensibly not told anyone about their discussion. With so much ill feeling against her in the town, any hint that he had helped her could have ruined him.

"Yes," she sighed, unable to blame him. "With her help, I learned to bring this curse under control. I wanted to be rid of it completely, but when she told me that was impossible I had no choice but to learn how to control it. We discovered that witchcraft can be channelled with runes and now I can do much more than just let the power boil out of me."

"Control witchcraft with runes? How?" asked Olaf, sounding surprised.

Anike lifted her cloak to reveal the lining. "It is a bit tattered, but you can see the pattern." Despite all that had happened, a thrill of pride ran through her as she showed her master what she had done.

Olaf bent over the cloak. "Remarkable. I see something about movement here – and flying? I always found runes somewhat difficult myself so I never spent much time learning them."

"Yes. Using this pattern, I can fly." Olaf looked doubtful. "You will see tomorrow. I will use it when I fight the harrowling. Flight will give me an edge no one else has." She looked at Olaf. "I can stop myself from releasing the power accidentally now but to defeat the harrowling, I need to devise some more patterns and they have to be written down. That is what the vellum is for."

"You really can hurt it?" asked Olaf.

"I think so, yes."

"I hate to think about what witchcraft that dangerous could do to a person," said Olaf sombrely. "Or how it could corrupt the caster to use it in that way."

"And I have no intention of finding out, Olaf," Anike told him. "It is just for the monster, nothing else."

"I hope so, but once learned, you will always have that knowledge as a weapon."

"Is it any different to having an axe or a bow, Olaf? It is how I choose to use it that is important."

"I acknowledge that deeds are crucial, but they can change you as well as reveal what you are. Just because you can do something, does that mean that you should?" He shrugged. "I hope this works. The town chafes under the siege this monster has imposed on us and it was beginning to look as if it will cost many lives to bring it down."

"I plan to prevent that." Anike sat at the table again and Olaf took a seat opposite her. "I want to give myself the best chance to defeat it. Tell me a bit more about its habits. Does it come every day?"

"Yes, sometimes twice but not at night, at least not so far. Siv followed it once and she said it sleeps on an outcropping of rock in the forest, difficult to approach in large numbers without waking it."

"Has anyone managed to injure it?"

"Slightly. The scales are all but impervious to weapons but it is sensitive around the neck and wings. While it cannot fly, it does run very fast in a straight line. It is slower on turns but more agile than one would expect for something so big."

"Is it frightened of fire?"

"No. We tried to scare it with torches and flaming arrows, but they have no more effect than steel."

Anike frowned. She had hoped that the harrowling would act like the dire wolves and panic in the face of fire. Still, she had more than just flames at her command.

"I will have to face it tomorrow," she said thoughtfully. "Any longer and Bjord might find me here. In any case, I need to act before he risks any more lives in battle. Olaf, may I have the sheets of vellum? And could you let me have two potions? One to numb pain, and one to heal wounds, please." She did not want to risk the demon gaining control if she was injured.

Olaf held out the vellum but when she reached to take it, he held on. "Anike, why didn't you... never mind." He released his grip, but his face was hard.

"What did you want to say?" she asked, as she took the sheets.

"It will wait," he said. "I will return with the potions before dawn."

"Thank you, Olaf," she said smiling at him. He half returned it before he headed for the door.

"I must go, too, Anike," said Inge. "It is late, and Drakna will be worried."

"Of course, Inge." Anike took her hand. "This will all work out but please do not tell your husband I am here. Not until tomorrow."

Inge froze at Anike's touch, but only for a moment before squeezing Anike's fingers in return. "I know it will, Anike and I will say nothing, believe me." Anike watched her close the door behind her, wondering if she would indeed keep silent but knowing there was nothing she could do about it now.

When they were alone, Darek took the chair opposite her. "You may not have intended to use witchcraft on people, Anike, but you still did it. This is not like accidentally letting a rope snap back on a boat and breaking a man's arm. Killing by witchcraft is a crime, whether you meant it or not."

"I carry the guilt of those deaths because I was not strong enough to stop them. If I can defeat the monster, that may help how I feel." She shifted uncomfortably. "Bjord told me that I killed four people at the farm. I am ashamed to say that I only remember two being hurt, apart from Bjord, but I suppose that the others were caught in the burning buildings. But now, I need to look to the future. I have to prepare for tomorrow."

"Is there anything I can do to help?"

"Yes. Can you sharpen my knife, please? I may need it." She hesitated, then plunged on. This was no time to hold back. "I know you kept my mother's armour. Would that fit me?" When she was a child, Darek had often taken Isolde's leather armour out and just stared at it. She knew he valued it, but the last week had made her more aware of injury than years of herbcraft, and she felt she needed some protection.

Darek looked at her for a long moment, then nodded. He went to a corner, opened an old chest and lifted out a suit of leather armour, faded but intact. He handed it to Anike, who put it on. Some of the thongs were frayed, and her mother had been a little stouter but on the whole it fitted her quite well.

Darek fussed over the bindings, keeping his face lowered, trying to hide his tears. "I hoped you would have a life where there was no need to wear this, but Isolde would have been proud of your taking a stand to help others. I am too." He blinked to clear his eyes and turned to the table. "Now, take it off so that I can fix it."

Anike had not worn armour before and struggled out of the leathers. The suit felt tough but flexible and should not slow her down. She watched her father, dexterous even with his single arm, deftly measure and cut new thongs, then turned to her cauldron to boil some water. Despite her brave words, she knew this would not be an easy battle. The harrowling was much bigger than a dire wolf and its scales looked more resistant to fire so it would take multiple strikes to bring it down.

She set an elixir to brew then pulled out the slate and chalk, Hilda's last gift, and began working on the spells. She weighed her options. The demon had used lightning to shatter the roof beams above her attackers in Ulsvater, and she believed that would be more effective against scales than fire.

She set to work devising the spells she would use. Olaf was right to be concerned that she was making weapons against which even seasoned warriors would have no defence, but it was necessary. Hesitation might lead to injury or fear and let the demon gain control, and she could not risk it attacking the town as well. If that happened, she could hurt people she knew and loved as well as lose any hope of reconciliation with Bjord and the Arl.

She worked into the night. Darek repaired the armour and then sat looking at her, ale cup in hand, as if trying to fix her in his memory until at last he dropped off to sleep. Anike drank a freshly brewed potion to keep herself awake. Eventually, she had done most of what was needed and closed her eyes, intending to rest for a moment before working on the final potion, but before she knew it she was woken by Olaf gently shaking her shoulder.

"The sun will be up soon," he said.

Opening her eyes reluctantly, Anike could see the grey pre-dawn light seeping under the door. "Did you bring the elixirs?" she asked, struggling back to wakefulness.

"Here is the numbing potion, and I have these jars of salve for wounds," he replied. "I hope you will not need them but it's not too late to change your mind. Are you sure about this course of action?"

"I am. I grew up wanting to help people in this town and from you I learned to heal them and take away their pain, one at a time. Now I have a chance to help them all. I know that a witch can be a force for good even if Bjord and Arl Svafnir do not see it yet."

Olaf frowned, glanced up to check that Darek was asleep, and sat down. "Now that I have you alone, Anike, I do want to ask you something."

Anike saw no trace of a smile on his face. "Yes?"

"When you told me you were a witch, why didn't you also tell me you had killed people?"

Anike shifted uncomfortably and dropped her gaze. "At first I planned to, but Fenris' reaction unnerved me. I was frightened that you would not help or even hand me over to Arl Svafnir. At the time I thought I had killed Bjord too." She looked up again. "I had just worked up the courage to tell you but Tavic interrupted, and there was no chance after that. I am truly sorry."

"You should have told me," said Olaf firmly. "How can people trust you if you keep important matters from them?"

"I do realise that, but it did not seem the best way to start our conversation, and I truly did intend to say something when you had recovered from the original shock."

"You must have realised I would have wanted to know everything when I was deciding what to do about you." There was no mistaking the accusation in Olaf's voice.

"Yes, of course I knew that. I am sorry. I just did not want to run the risk, and I needed your help."

"So, you deliberately hid something important, in effect lying to me, in order to manipulate me into helping you. The ends justify the means?" asked Olaf.

Anike swallowed. "I know I should have trusted you rather than assume you would be prejudiced."

"It would hardly have been prejudice since you had hurt people, would it?" said Olaf, flushing red. "You, or rather the people of Trollgard, were lucky."

"No one in Trollgard was hurt."

"You think that makes a difference?"

"No. I am sorry. I was frightened of what I could do and what I had done, and I could not cope with you being afraid of me too."

Olaf took a deep breath, visibly calming himself, and when he spoke again it was in a softer tone. "I can see that it was hard for you but you chose a path that put more people at risk. Had I known, I would never have allowed you to go to the Arl's hall. You took far too much of a chance."

"I know, but I could not say anything without Tavic hearing," Anike told him, wanting to bring this conversation to an end. She glanced at the light spreading out under the front door. "You need to be gone before anyone knows that you helped me."

Olaf looked at her. "I hope your choices will be made with more honesty from now on."

"I want you, the Arl and the whole town to see the truth about what I can do, and I am prepared to take the risk that comes with battle if it gives me the chance to be accepted in Trollgard," Anike said.

"You really want to stay here, despite everything?" Olaf looked surprised. "It will be even more difficult than you realise."

Seeing Darek was still snoring, he leaned forward and lowered his voice. "I am going to tell you a secret that you need to hear if you plan to convince Arl Svafnir to let you stay. Many people have good reason to be afraid of witches, including me. Svafnir and Bjord have a personal reason. You were only tiny at the time but you know that my wife and son were killed in a Larten raid. Svafnir lost his wife Elin, Bjord's mother to witchcraft, in the same raid. She was killed by a witch supporting the Larten raiders and, to make matters worse, he got away."

Anike bit her lip. "And Bjord knows this?"

"Yes, I believe so, but Svafnir did not want the details to become common knowledge. He was worried that Trollgard would panic if it was known that the Lartens could command witches. But I knew. I tried to save Elin but she was already dead, without a mark on her."

Tears filled his eyes, and Anike could see him struggling with the pain of the memory. It sounded as if he had known Elin well and being helpless before a force he could not understand despite his years of knowledge and experience could only have made it worse. Anike had felt her life start to drain away when Gern used the stasis form on her. She shuddered at the memory, and pity for Svafnir's wife welled up inside. Bjord and Svafnir's implacable hostility was only to be expected.

"Why did you not tell me this before, Olaf?" she asked. "You lectured me on not being open with you, and this is important." She felt anger, her own and the demon's, rising.

Olaf looked abashed. "I am sorry. I had not realised that reconciliation was part of your plans. You only talked to me about fighting the monster."

"I still need to try," Anike said, recalling that Olaf had not been there when she had told her father and Inge she wanted to stay, and calming herself. "That was a long time ago and perhaps Arl Svafnir will see me as the Larten chief saw that witch."

"I pray that everyone likes what they see," Olaf said quietly.

Anike rolled the vellum up, pulled out a backpack from under the table and packed the scrolls and potions into it. "I will need a pack horse if I try to take anything else," she told Olaf, trying to lighten the mood. Olaf gave her a token smile but he was clearly still upset. Anike trusted he would come round in time and went to shake her father awake.

"It is nearly dawn," she told him when his eyes opened. He peered at her groggily from the chair where he had spent the night.

"This is not goodbye," Anike told him hastily. "I will be back. Now, help me into the armour." Darek lifted the leather suit over her head and pulled the thongs tight, then stood back and looked at her. "Isolde will keep you safe," he said.

"She will, Father." Anike hugged him. "You will not see me until the monster appears, but come to the wall when the horn sounds." She smiled at Olaf and spread out her cloak. "*Prana*," she said, reading the pattern, and felt a rush of pride at showing what she could do to these two men who had, in their separate ways, raised her between them. Feelings of triumph flowed through her, empowering her will far beyond anything the demon could oppose. She rose into the air to their gasps of amazement and flew to the door, opened it and rose into the brightening sky.

She knew that she had hurt Olaf by not trusting him with the full horror of her actions, and he had every right to feel that way. Her explanation as to why she had not told him everything sounded weak, even to her. She hoped that she was not repeating the mistake by keeping knowledge of the demon from him as well, but she was not ready to reveal that yet and the reason why she lost control ought to make little difference. The important thing was that while she had failed in the past, she would not do so again.

She was grateful that Olaf had told her how Bjord's mother had died. Arl Svafnir had given the impression that he knew quite a lot about witches and it made sense that he had studied them after his wife's death. His attitude might be coloured by experience and preconception but if she could make him recognise his own bias, perhaps by unexpected heroism, she hoped she could reach him.

She landed at the edge of the wood town amongst the ruined buildings. It might have been safer on the town walls, but she did not want to be attacked by misguided townsfolk, nor did she want the demon to choose them as targets if it somehow escaped her control. She also rejected battling the monster in the forest where it would be slowed by the trees. She needed an audience to show the town her worth. The wood town was not the safest choice of a battleground but it best met her needs.

Shattered buildings surrounded her and she tried to decide which to use as a base. She doubted that the monster would fall quickly so she needed a place from where she could retreat if she had to, and which had already been scavenged so she would not have to deal with any townsfolk while she waited. She found the remains of a farmhouse at the edge of the town that seemed suitable. It had two walls still standing and a ramp to the top of them, formed by a tangle of beams that had once been its roof. Its barn was in a similar condition and could serve as a fallback position. She laid the vellum sheets with the first spells she planned to use near the top of the ramp and weighed them down with stones, then crossed over into the barn where she set down another spell, together with two flasks of elixir. Satisfied, she went back to the ruined farmhouse. From the top of the ramp, she could see both the town walls and the edge of the forest in the brightening morning light. She did not know how long it would be before the harrowling appeared so she climbed down into the ruin to wait out of sight and began to chalk the beginnings of another spell on her slate.

It was mid-morning when she was interrupted by a screeching coming from the forest. She clambered up the sloping timbers to get a good view. Three hundred paces away, the harrowling was emerging from the trees.

- 21 -

STORM AND FURY

Anike quickly drank a potion to banish any fatigue from lack of sleep and looked down at the pattern drawn on the vellum. "*Eneka!*" she said, calling lightning from the clear sky down onto the harrowling.

The bolt of electricity hit it in the back, striking incandescent sparks from the silver scales. It roared in pain, staggering under the shock and came to a halt, its head whipping around as it sought the source of the attack. Anike slammed the demon back into its prison with a water rune, ducked down out of sight and waited the few seconds she needed for her well of energy to refill. A moment later, she raised her head so she could see the harrowling again and repeated the spell. Once more, the monster was outlined in blue-white energy which singed feathers and drew another screeching roar but it screamed defiance and scanned the ruined wood town for its attacker.

Anike called a third strike from the sky. The harrowling crouched, bracing itself against the force of the bolt and its piercing eyes swept the the area to light upon her. Its head became still and then it folded its wings and charged. A spell which could reach so far had to sacrifice intensity for range and while Anike had not been confident that she could bring the creature down before it saw her, it had located her more swiftly than she had expected and now it was rushing towards her like an avalanche.

Lifting her cloak, she cast the flight spell and felt the supporting force gather but she stayed where she was and watched as the monster bore down on her. She tried to ignore how large it was, its claws easily the size of her head. Picking up another piece of vellum, she waited until it was a dozen paces away before she raised her hand, read the pattern and shouted, "*Agni.*" Fire flew from her palm to engulf the harrowling's head and chest. Feathers charred and the creature bellowed, throwing its head back as it pushed through the flames. Despite the obvious pain, it recovered and regained its stride.

She had expected the fire to have had more effect and was taken aback at how quickly it resumed its charge. Almost too late, she flung herself backwards off the wall and out of its path, then soared outward and up. The harrowling pivoted with frightening agility and lunged forward to where it had expected her to land. Its wings passed beneath her as its shoulder crashed into the wall of the house, smashing it into splinters. Anike watched what remained of the structure collapse, burying the vellum sheets she had laid out there. Looking down at the jumble of timber, she could see little chance of quickly recovering her spell for calling down lightning so she would have to continue the fight up close. While the harrowling shook the debris off its back, she drank the numbing potion, knowing that she could ill afford to be distracted by pain.

She glanced at the town walls and saw that a crowd had gathered behind the parapet but there was no time to pick out the faces of her father, Bjord or the Arl. She turned her attention back to the monster.

The harrowling raked vainly through the shattered wood with a claw then spotted her hovering above. It hissed like an army of snakes and she fought down the impulse to fly to safety, instead pointing at it while reading the vellum she still held. "*Agni,*" she said again, and once more fire lashed from her hand to strike the monster's head and back. She felt a strange elation and whether it was the thrill of battle or if the demon was happy to let her continue to cause destruction, she was having no difficulty staying in control.

The harrowling crouched, then gathered itself, wings lashing in a thunderous clap as it launched itself upwards in a great arc. Its neck stretched towards her, razor-edged beak open wide. Again, Anike had underestimated the creature. She had thought the harrowling's wings good for little more than show and herself well out of reach. With impending death surging towards her and no chance to think, she let herself drop away from the monster's beak but an instant later realised her mistake. She had brought herself within reach of its talons.

At the peak of its leap, the harrowling struck at her. She frantically willed herself to fly to the right and felt the wind of the claw's slash as it passed within an inch of her shoulder. An instant later, her relief turned to panic as she was slammed to a stop by the neck. The claw had caught her trailing cloak and she was dragged down as the harrowling fell back towards the earth. Gasping for breath, she instinctively grabbed the cloak with both hands to try to pull it clear of her throat, dropping the vellum as she did so.

She just managed to pull her head down and out of the cloak's choking grasp before the monster came down onto another ruined building. The wind exploded from her lungs as the harrowling dragged her through a wall, and the cloak was torn from her hands. She tried to break her fall with witchcraft and will but struck the ground hard just as the creature's rear legs slammed down a pace away. In a frozen instant, she saw the pink flesh of an almost healed wound through a gap in the scales before the creature's muscles bulged as it tried to stop and turn on her again. Shaken, but thankful that her mother's armour had saved her from serious injury, she used the flight spell to lift off the ground and head back towards the ruins of the house where her spell patterns had been buried.

Roaring furiously, the harrowling pivoted and came after her again, spreading its wings to regain its balance and scattering broken timber, but favouring its left leg. She now had no doubt that the bear from the mountain had somehow been merged into this creature. The wound she had treated was in exactly the same place on its leg as the gap in the harrowling's scales.

Her cloak was still impaled on the beast's claw, but her flight spell would last a little longer. She wound her way between the remains of the buildings, trying to get back to her second cache. The monster could run faster than she could fly once it built up momentum but by weaving between ruins and changing direction she was able to stay ahead of it. She managed to gain something of a lead, though not enough to give her time to put her next plan into action so she went past the barn where she had left the last of her spells and potions. Turning to face her pursuer, she hovered in front of the next farmhouse, level with the top of the wall.

The harrowling sprang at her again. This time she was ready for it and shot straight upwards. It craned its neck back and snapped at her as it passed underneath. She drew her legs up and dived over its back, and the beak closed on empty air.

The creature crashed through the wall behind her. Before it could recover and turn its attention to her again, she swooped towards the scrolls and potions she had left in reserve. Coming to a halt within the broken walls, she snatched up one of the vellum sheets and a flask and turned to face the harrowling again. The creature was shaking off the remains of the building and turning to face her once more.

She pulled the stopper from the flask, then concentrated on the pattern and said, "*Prana*," to surround the flask with force so she could move it with her mind. The monster screamed and leapt again but she flew left to evade it and hurled the flask towards its head. The harrowling ignored the small missile passing by and turned to track her. Anike halted the flask in mid-air and made it hover behind the creature's head as she drifted slowly back and away. The harrowling gathered itself to leap and opened its beak to scream at her again but as it did so she willed the flask to fly into the open mouth. The harrowing choked and hissed and snapped its beak shut. Anike lifted straight up, out of its reach, and waited for the elixir to take effect.

The potion was a concentrated form of the sleeping elixir she had used on the bear at Vanir Heights. She had anticipated that witchcraft alone might not be enough to defeat the harrowling and hoped that herb lore would make the difference.

The monster's head swung up to look at her, its eyes starting to lose focus as the drug took effect. She retreated to where she had dropped the vellum with the firebolt pattern but as she reached it the flight spell came to an end and she fell to the ground, landing hard on her left arm.

With any pain masked by her potion, she rolled to grab the vellum and came to her feet to face the harrowling. It was trying to charge, but could only stagger towards her, opening its beak to strike. "*Agni*," she shouted and fire flashed from her hand and down its exposed throat. It roared in agony, clawing futilely at its neck, then fell sideways and crashed to the ground. Its limbs flailed weakly until, with one last shudder and wracking gasp, the rise and fall of its breathing ceased and it lay still.

She stared at the corpse, scarcely believing that she had slain the monster. Exultation in her triumph blossomed as the victory sank in but the heady feeling of achievement became tinged with regret. The animals that had been merged into the harrowling had been as much victims of the witch weather as her.

The town wall was now lined with people. They seemed to be frozen in shock, perhaps still unable to comprehend her victory or accept that witchcraft had been used to help them. Now she was able to pick out Bjord, Siv standing tall beside him and on another part of the wall, she saw her father standing with Inge and her husband. Olaf was a little way away but though she could make out Rogar and Tavic's slight form, she could not see the Arl.

The crowd seemed stunned, unable to decide what to make of what they saw. One man raised a cheer but even as that lone voice rang out, someone else on the wall loosed an arrow at her and she ducked instinctively as it flew over her head.

Other warriors on the wall were looking at Bjord for instructions. The Arl's son had a bow in hand himself, but he had not drawn it. Anike had not really expected instant acclaim considering what she had done when the demon had been in control, but she had hoped for something better than an arrow. She took refuge behind the skeleton of a wall.

Bjord looked left and right down the line of watchers, possibly gauging the mood. She realised that no one had shot at the harrowling while she fought it and suspected he had ordered them to wait, seeing this as a battle of two evils and that he would be better off whatever the outcome. The eyes of the dead monster seemed to mock her for believing that her demonstration of power would lessen the fear she inspired. Her cloak was still impaled on its talon, like the banner of a foe defeated at the cost of its own life.

On the wall, Bjord was now yelling orders. The words "witch" and "surround" reached her ears but the rest was lost in a swell of other voices. She peered round the nearest corner to see people pushing past each other on the wall, some trying to follow his commands and reach the steps to come down but others pressing forward to look out over to the ruins towards her and the dead harrowling.

It was not part of her plan to allow herself to be captured before she had a chance to talk to Arl Svafnir. If Bjord caught her, she would be held like Gern had been, bound and gagged until her trial, and her fate would be sealed. She needed a position of strength to negotiate.

The town gates groaned open to allow a large party of warriors through. She had expected that, and she had to take this chance to talk to Bjord. Retreating now would ruin the impression of strength and control she wanted to convey but she had to be prepared to defend herself and escape. She slipped back to the ruined house where she had started the battle and dug the spell patterns out from beneath the fallen timbers before making her way to the mound of the harrowling's corpse. She bent to retrieve her cloak, still impaled on the sword-like talon, and hesitated. An irrational fear that the enormous creature might still be alive swept through her before she gritted her teeth and pulled her cloak free. It was rent on the left-hand side and the tear had destroyed the smoke pattern beyond repair, but the flight spell was still intact.

She did not want to be surrounded or give anyone the chance to creep up on her while she talked with Bjord. It would be too blatant to use witchcraft to rise into the air – that might well provoke a confrontation. She wanted reconciliation, not another fight. With a start, she realised that the obvious location was right in front of her. She prodded the harrowling with her boot, just in case, and then clambered up to stand on its back beside one of the great wings. From there she could look down on Bjord and he could not ignore her victory.

Bjord was at the head of a group of a dozen warriors, some of whom seemed more than a little hesitant, and Siv was leading a few more on a more circuitous route to cut off any retreat. There were archers in both groups, but while they had arrows nocked, they had not yet drawn their bows. Svafnir himself was still nowhere to be seen.

She let them come closer, then read the flight pattern. "*Prana*," she said slowly and distinctly, letting her voice carry. The demon made a brief bid for control, trying to exploit her anxiety about meeting Bjord again, but she quickly subdued it.

Several of the approaching men paused when she named the rune, looking uneasily about them but as nothing appeared to happen they resumed their advance, though even more cautiously. She shook out her sleeves so the patterns of runes on them were clearly visible and waited for Bjord to come close enough to hear her.

"My lord, Bjord Svafnirsson," she said formally, choosing her tone carefully to show respect but not fear. "I offer you and your father the death of this monster as tribute and bloodprice for my assault on you."

Bjord held up his hand and the archers took up positions behind him, arrows nocked and bows at half-draw. The other warriors held war darts ready to throw and stood with shields raised. Bjord himself had not reached for a weapon but he had his bow held loosely in his left hand.

Anike waited for her audience to finish positioning before she called out again. "Good people of Trollgard, I have killed the monster that was bringing destruction to our town. For your sake, my friends, I risked my life. I love this town and all I want is to be accepted once more."

Bjord called back to her, contempt in every word. "You used witchcraft and poison. You have shown yourself to be without honour or scruple and there are no depths to which you will not sink. You are a murderer!" He shook his fist at her, his gesture matching the fury in his voice. "You cast lightning around the town just as you flung it against me when you tried to kill me."

"My lord," Anike riposted, "you saw that I directed the lightning against the monster, not the town. What happened at the farm was a terrible accident. I do not deny what I did but I regret it more than I can say. Today there were no accidents. I can control my witchcraft now, and I brought the monster down without putting anyone else in danger. There will be no more mistakes and if you will allow me, I will use it in service of this town in future."

"Your attack on me was no accident! I looked into your eyes and there was nothing there but fury and hatred. Death and destruction are all that witches bring. You waited for your chance, first against me then by setting this creature on the town, and now you dare to suggest that undoing a terror you created could earn you a place among us? That was your plan all along. You waited until the town was at its most desperate and then returned, pretending to be its saviour. You want us to welcome you back so that you can betray us again and strike at our hearts from within." His voice rose with barely controlled rage. "It will not work, I tell you. You will not fool me twice!" There were shouts of agreement from the warriors behind him.

Anike had realised that this would not be an easy confrontation but was unprepared for how quickly Bjord had woven a narrative in which her triumph was just part of a larger plot. She stole a glance behind to check where Siv was and saw her standing only twenty paces away amid her warriors, her bow in her hand. She regarded Anike coolly.

Not yet ready to give up, Anike tried a different approach. "It is for your father to enforce the law in Trollgard, not you," she said clearly. "Let him say if he accepts my offer of the monster as bloodprice and as atonement for my accidental injury to you, something for which I am truly sorry. Allow him to set a fair price for the tragic deaths and all the harm I have done."

"I do not need my father to tell me that no price suffices for those deaths or for wielding such dark powers against his heir, nor for the destruction your creature caused." Bjord gestured to the dead monster. "You have the temerity to stand there, proud of being a witch and trying to cow us into submission. I say no!" He lowered his voice, his words full of menace. "I will bring you to my father in chains, or he will pass judgment on your corpse."

The voices of approval and agreement rose again. Anike could see that the only thing holding back their attack was dwindling fear, or perhaps a sliver of hope that she would surrender without a fight. If Bjord were to give the order or raise his bow, that would end their restraint. If she were to use witchcraft now, that too would trigger an attack. To make matters worse, the demon was once again struggling for release, trying to convert her apprehension and disappointment into fear and anger, and at the same time magnifying her confidence in her abilities.

The situation was spiralling out of her control. Bjord's impassioned leadership was ruining any chance of a moderate response. She should not have been surprised. His good opinion of her had been shattered at Volna's farm, and crushed further by every subsequent meeting until his hatred was set in stone. In some ways, it was as if he too had a demon veiling his thoughts but one of his own making, and now any trust or affection he had once felt for her was buried deep in the shadows of his mind.

Seeing that she would not be able to gainsay his pre-judgment, she tried to circumvent him. "Siv, hear me and take my words to my lord and yours, Arl Svafnir. The gods gave you strength, and the wisdom to use it justly but that wisdom did not come fully formed when you lifted the haft of your first axe. Did you never hurt anyone by accident in training? The gods have given me a different kind of strength and after my first mistakes, I am trying to use it in service of Trollgard. I only seek the chance to do what is right."

Siv looked at her, her expression cold and calculating, then slowly brought her bow to full draw. "If you wish to do what is right then, as my lord Bjord says, surrender yourself to us for trial now. If not, you will die where you stand." She took aim at Anike's heart.

The warriors responded to the rising tension. "Surrender, Anike!" called Loga with a note of pleading in his voice, but another man cried "No, kill her!" and was echoed by others. Looking at them, Anike realised that the mood had become too hostile for her to remain in Trollgard. Even if Arl Svafnir allowed her to stay, she would always be seen as a threat. Any misfortune would be blamed on her and any visitor to her home might have come to kill her, confident that the law would support them. Her plan had failed. Exploiting her despair, the demon fought for its release and the struggle must have shown in her expression, for Tavic shouted, "Beware! Witchcraft!"

Holding the demon back, Anike lifted her left arm and read the pattern on the sleeve even as Bjord shouted "Kill her!"

"*Vata*!" she cried, dropping to a crouch as the tornado formed around her. Arrows flashed towards her, only to be caught by the vortex. Some went over her head and others were flung clear but the wind could not entirely shield her at such close range. One cut open her cheek, and another stuck into her back though her armour slowed it enough to prevent a mortal wound. The potion she had taken earlier insulated her from pain but under the impact she still staggered forward off the harrowling's back. The warriors' cheers turned to cries of astonishment and frustration when instead of falling, she was borne aloft by the flight spell.

Moving swiftly and surrounded by the shield of wind, the arrows did not touch her as she climbed higher and headed for the forest. Some of the warriors started after her but the trees lay uphill from the town and they could not match her pace. She heard Bjord call out to them to let her go, promising them that their chance would come.

She landed amongst the trees at the wooded edge of the forest. Even a few paces in, she was invisible to anyone on the walls but still had a good view of the town. She looked back sadly. Now beyond the reach of any immediate threat, she opened her bag, pulled out the arrow from her back and applied salves to her wounds. The elation she had felt melted into anger and hurt. Overwhelmed by the uncompromising rejection by Bjord and the townsfolk despite her triumph over the harrowling, she choked back bitter tears. Svafnir himself was beyond her reach now. Bjord would carry his own story to him, one in which she was the villain.

Taking a deep breath, she calmed herself. She realised that the demon was magnifying her negative emotions, trying to create a means of escape. This time its influence was harder to suppress because she truly did feel rejected, and she reinforced its prison with layers of ice and stone so that she could think without interference. She had done all she could to show that she was in control, that she had grown and reformed since she had committed her terrible crimes and was willing to atone for them. Her hope had been to demonstrate both strength and humility, but it had not been enough.

Gradually, she felt the anger leave her. She had let her expectations run away with her. The day before she had only wished to say farewell to her father and she had done that, and more besides. She had managed to see Inge and Olaf as well and there was no one else she needed to say farewell to. She had saved lives and she could take satisfaction in that, regardless of what others thought her reasons were. She could be content with what she had done.

She sat down with a back against a tree trunk and smiled ruefully. Heroes in sagas often confronted monsters to save others or for glory with no thought of gain but they usually received appreciation if they triumphed, whatever nay-sayers there were before. In those stories, the defeat of the monster was the conclusion, but the people of Trollgard believed a witch would always be a threat and it was only too easy to let fear dictate their response.

Looking down on Trollgard, she wondered if there was still any chance the town would ever accept her. The battle with the harrowling had been intense and emotions had run high. While Bjord would not forgive her, the Arl might have a different view.

But she knew that was just a dream now, and she ought to leave. The road to the east led to Skellet, another town on a river mouth a bit further away than Ulsvater. Further south, Gotlund contained yet more settlements with their own Arls, and many miles west lay Ingernak, the capital. Not for the first time, she wished she had a copy of the map hanging on Svafnir's wall in the arlberg, or at least had spent more time studying it. The news that she had killed the harrowling would spread, no doubt entwined with the tale of how she had created it in the first place. If she went, she would need to outdistance that, which meant going further than the nearby towns.

There had been no attempt to pursue her, probably because Bjord was aware that she could disappear into the forest all too easily and for now the people of Trollgard seemed more interested in clearing away the harrowling's body. They had collected wood from the shattered buildings and built a pyre around the creature. Anike watched the activity but realised that she would have to tear herself away before attention turned to hunting her down. East seemed the better direction as no one in Skellet would know her by sight and she should be able to pass through without much trouble.

No doubt Bjord would search her father's house and she hoped he would not discover that she had already been there. That might cause trouble for Darek, perhaps for Inge too, but going back would implicate them more surely than staying away. She could not manage every detail herself anymore. She had to have faith in them to live their own lives.

Flames now surrounded the harrowling's body and people were singing and dancing round the fire. She was glad that she had done something they could celebrate, even if it was that a witch had now destroyed a monster she had created.

Anike continued to wonder how exactly the creature had been formed but, like the origin of the fireball that had created the demon, it was a mystery beyond her present understanding. The demon's feelings towards the harrowling were in complete contrast to how it regarded the dire wolves, despite the monster's obviously unnatural origins. She wondered if the circumstances of their creation, perhaps arising from the witch weather in different ways, was the reason. So much about witchcraft was unclear and the stories and lore that she knew held only fragments of truth amongst a great deal of confusion. She sensed that what she had puzzled out for herself so far was only the surface and what lay beneath might, ultimately, be very important. Perhaps there were wiser loremasters somewhere who knew more and now she had a chance to seek them out.

Anike felt the solidity of the trunk against her back. Unconsciously she had selected a tree that she knew well. The leaves whispered above her in a comfortable tone. She had sat in this spot many times before, sheltered beneath the green canopy. Often she had rested alone on the way back from gathering herbs in the forest, but sometimes she had sat her with Inge and once with Loga. She had climbed the branches and skinned her knees.

There was a good view of both the town and the beach. She could pick out rock pools she had paddled in, and she fancied she could even see her father's boat. The harrowling had destroyed much of the wood town but the stone town was solid and familiar. She looked down on it, until a cloud of smoke from the fire drifted over the scene, covering it in a grey haze where edges became less certain.

With the harrowling gone, they no longer needed her and she could leave without any sense of guilt. It would not be difficult to remain out of sight in the forest while she skirted the town, and then she could join the east road out of view of the walls. Once on the road she could swap information with travellers coming the other way, find out more about Skellet and learn what lay beyond.

People were sifting through the ruins, sorting wood and even starting to rebuild in some places, and her heart lifted at their strength and resilience, then she noticed a lone figure making its way up from the town, broadly following the line she had taken in her flight. She blinked in surprise when she saw who it was. She had expected Bjord or Siv to come after her, or perhaps a hunter, but it was Inge who was climbing the slope towards the forest. She was moving hesitantly, occasionally looking over her shoulder. Anike checked the town again and while no one was following her friend, she could see people watching from the wall. She recognised Bjord and next to him was the tall figure of Siv. Inge reached the edge of the forest about a hundred paces from where Anike was waiting and stopped. "Anike, can you hear me?" she called out, looking around anxiously.

Confused, Anike made her way through the trees, keeping back from the open ground, until she was about twenty paces away. "Inge," she called.

"Anike!" cried Inge. "Bjord has seized your father. He made me come to try and find you. If you don't surrender to him by midday tomorrow, he will have Darek tried as a witch!"

- 22 -

TRUST

Almost unable to believe her ears, Anike shook her head. "He cannot do that. My father has done nothing. He is no witch!" She tried to process what Inge was telling her.

Inge was on the verge of tears. "Bjord is saying that Darek is a witch too and that he prepared and trained you in secret."

"He knows that is a lie," said Anike angrily. "He is just saying it to give himself an excuse to threaten me. I thought he was misguided, but still an honourable man. It seems I was wrong."

The demon rode her anger towards her consciousness, stoking her righteous fury and filling her with certainty that she could and should destroy Bjord. His puppet, Inge, was no better, mouthing some excuse for him. With an effort, Anike placed more bonds on the demon leaving her with only her own anger and she was able to focus on what her friend was saying.

"There is only your word about how you came to be a witch, Anike," Inge was pointing out tremulously. "Does Bjord even know what you told me – I mean that it was a ball of lightning on Vanir Heights that was responsible? I don't think I heard you say that when you were pleading with him."

Anike struggled to keep her breathing steady and thought back to her few brief and frantic conversations with Bjord. Now that Inge mentioned it, she realised that the fireball had never come up. Bjord had been with her, after all, and its role in what had happened seemed so obvious that she had not said anything about it. Surely he had realised that had she not pushed him out of the way, he would have become the witch rather than her. She sighed. "Perhaps not, but he was there when it happened and he has known me almost as long as you have. My father used to be one of Arl Svafnir's close friends. Bjord cannot really believe he is a witch." She paused. "It is a vicious and cruel tactic, but it is cunning."

"I know your father is innocent, Anike," said Inge. "You can't let him be put on trial." She gulped, and tears welled up in her eyes as what little remained of her composure broke. "I think you have to give yourself up," she stammered, her gaze on her feet.

Anike looked at her sharply. "Did Bjord tell you to say that?"

"Yes." Inge was struggling between sobs. "Please don't kill me." She wiped her eyes and nose on her sleeve. "But you have committed crimes and your father hasn't. I don't believe he is a witch, but I am sure Bjord will put him on trial regardless unless you surrender yourself to him."

"Inge! I can't believe you want to see me executed."

"I don't!" Inge's hesitation had been so brief that Anike would have liked to think she had imagined it. "But a trial will still give you a chance. And your father will be saved!"

"If he was interested in the truth, of course my father would be absolved and I would have nothing to worry about. That would hardly be a threat and it would not give Bjord any leverage over me. No, I cannot be sure that any trial will be fair." She stared at Inge, struggling with her friend's willingness to go along with Bjord and his dishonourable scheme. Inge was trembling and could not meet Anike's eyes, her gaze darting around her as if seeking a way out. Anike watched the conflict of emotions on her face, uncertainty, loyalty, and most of all, fear – fear of Bjord and, even more, of Anike herself.

Anike sighed as a wave of sympathy washed over her. Inge had placed her trust in the Arl's justice and was using it as a lifeline in her shifting world and as a sop for her conscience. She spoke gently, trying to keep any feeling of hurt or betrayal out of her voice. "This is a strange time for all of us, Inge. I know this has been a shock for you, and I understand how hard it is when you are caught up in events and do not know which way to turn."

Inge looked at her, eyes suddenly hopeful.

"Tell me," Anike continued more thoughtfully, "did Bjord announce the deadline to everybody, or did he just tell you?"

"I was at your father's house when he came with Siv and Rogar and some others. After they took him to the arlberg, Bjord sat down with me and told me to tell you that if you do not come by midday tomorrow, he will put your father on trial."

"Did he know you had seen me?"

"Yes. He asked me," Inge stuttered. "I had to tell him."

"Of course you did," sighed Anike. It was too much to have expected Inge to protest when the Arl's heir could condemn anyone connected with her.

She looked away and considered her options. If she did what Bjord wanted, it would save her father's life but would break his heart. He would be consumed by the guilt of knowing that he had been the cause of her death. Despite Inge's feeble protestations, she was sure how her own trial would end. She could attempt to rescue her father but that would be dangerous, and it would likely mean permanent exile for Darek as well as herself as Bjord would simply recapture him if he stayed in Trollgard. Finally, she could just leave and trust that Arl Svafnir would behave with honour and release her father. There would be no reason to hold him as a hostage if she were not around to succumb to pressure.

"Are you going to surrender?" Inge asked anxiously. "Will you give yourself up and bring this to an end?"

Anike knew Inge would repeat everything she said, so she replied carefully. "I do not believe Bjord will actually put my father on trial. I think it is a bluff. Taking someone for ransom is one thing, but it is quite another to condemn a man who has obviously done nothing wrong. No, I will not hand myself in. I did the town a great service today, and I do not intend to pay for that with my life. I will just leave, never to return to Trollgard and trust in Bjord and the Arl to act fairly and justly. Bjord may hate me now, but when I am gone he will come to his senses."

It cut her inside to lie to Inge, so she turned her face away. "I will go south, over the mountains, far beyond Trollgard's domain. I am very sorry to have brought this pain down on you, Inge, but once I am gone, your life should return to normal again." She looked over her shoulder towards the town. "If you get a chance, tell my father I love him. He knows, but please tell him anyway."

She looked back at Inge and let her gaze linger on the tearful face framed with golden hair, taking in its details for the last time. She wanted to hold her close, tell her everything would be alright and comfort her, but Inge was trembling, ready to flee, and Anike knew their friendship had not survived her fear. "Goodbye, Inge," she said.

Inge stared at her. "Goodbye, Anike," she said in a small voice, as if undecided if she was relieved or sad, and just watched as Anike walked away into the forest.

Anike did not know if Svafnir was well enough to make any decisions and she no longer trusted Bjord would act honourably. Despite what she had told Inge, she had to take the threat to her father seriously. While she was sure that Bjord's main aim was to hold him as a hostage and so could release him when it was known that she had left the area for good, he might truly believe that her father had kept her witchcraft secret for years and was a witch himself. It would only be a short step from that to finding some little thing her father had done which could be seen as an act of witchcraft. It might even be suspicious that Anike had been born during witch weather.

The last few hours had hammered home to her that belief was interwoven with perspective and that people could be prejudiced by the passion of a powerful man. Even if Svafnir himself did not believe that Darek was a witch, he might not wish to gainsay his son and hold the trial to show both support for Bjord and his own intolerance of witches. She could not abandon her father. She had to get both of them away from the town.

Her tale that she was leaving, relayed through Inge, might make Bjord lower his guard a little, making it easier to rescue her father. She needed any advantage she could find. Inge would not have lied to Bjord for her, but deceiving her friend in what was probably their last ever conversation had been painful. Inge was now well out of sight and Anike stopped. She closed her eyes and tried to hold back her tears. For as long as she could remember they had been friends and while she understood her childhood companion's fears, the loss and betrayal still tore at her.

Blinking to clear her vision, she started walking again and headed east. After a while, the rhythm of her steps settled her and she was ready to plan her father's rescue. She slowed her pace and began to think through her options.

He was probably held in the Arl's hall. It was the obvious place, in the centre of the arlberg and under Bjord's control, and it was made of stone so she could not burn it down. She could not assume that Bjord would accept the tale of her departure at face value, so he might still expect some sort of rescue attempt and keep a guard in place. It would be a bonus if he reduced it after hearing Inge's report but he certainly would not release her father until after the deadline had passed.

After she had freed her father from Bjord, she would have to get him out of the town and that might not be easy. He could be unwilling to leave, not realising how much danger he would be in if he stayed, or he could have been injured and unable to walk far. His fishing boat was her best option. They could sail to Skellet, then up the river to find somewhere else to live.

It was unlikely that she would get through the entire rescue without being seen but she could limit the risks. Bjord knew she could fly and would realise that there was little chance of stopping her from entering the town, but the arlberg was a different matter. He would know she had to go to the hall and could set watchers there but while they would probably be alert to start with, by the middle of the night their doubts that she was coming ought to have grown and they should be less careful. It would also be easier if Bjord himself was asleep and surely he would not stay awake all night.

She found a thick cluster of bushes to the east of the town and settled down to prepare the spells she would need. It did not take her long to reproduce the smoke pattern that the harrowling had torn, dying it into the front of her tunic this time, but she would need some new spells too. Bjord had a greater knowledge of her capabilities now, and he was surrounded by many loyal followers. Above all, he had her father.

What she needed was an unexpected way in, and for that she had a plan. The demon had brought down a cliff on the harrowling using the movement form but it had not moved tonnes of rock directly. It took only a few moments' work with the runes to confirm this was far beyond the demon's power. Instead, it had destroyed enough to create a crack and let the cliff sheer away under its own weight. She could adapt that effect to disintegrate small areas of rock. Bjord would not be expecting her to make an entrance through solid stone.

It was nearly dark when she finished the new spells and she lay down to rest for a few hours, selecting an uncomfortable position so that she would not sleep through the night. She could mask any fatigue with potions long enough to rescue her father.

As she had intended, Anike woke several times and on each occasion checked the position of the moon and stars. When her eyes opened for the fourth time, she judged it to be well after midnight so she made her way on foot down to the treeline. Only a few clouds drifted across the field of stars above her. The moon hung low in the west and covered the land with a silvery light. It was bright enough for her to read the rune patterns but it would also make it harder to hide.

Cautiously she approached the fringes of the ruined buildings of the wood town, alert for any sign of ambush or even of people who had returned to the remnants of their homes, but the night was quiet. Once she had passed the first collapsed house, she paused to read the flight pattern and rose a few inches above the ground to flit between the broken buildings, then soared up and over the wall. Torches flickered where the arlberg abutted the town wall to the east but if there were watchers elsewhere she could see no sign of them.

Keeping just below roof level, she headed towards Olaf's store. Reluctantly she had decided she needed help and he was the only person she could turn to. Rising just above the buildings, she avoided the market, still filled with the tents of the people displaced by the harrowling, and dropped silently to the ground outside his shop. She heard nothing inside and pushed at the door, only to find it did not move. Checking that there was no one paying attention to her, she visualised the pattern that allowed her to move objects. She was so familiar with the inside of this door that she knew exactly how it was secured and did not need to see or feel the bar to cast a spell on it. She placed her hand against the wood, intoned "*Prana*," then moved the bar out of the way and went in.

Fenris came padding out from the rear of the building as Anike was closing the door behind her. She had forgotten about him, but now recalled how he had reacted on the last occasion he had seen her. She waited, holding the demon's prison closed to prevent it from attempting to strike at the dog. To her surprise, this time Fenris did not bare his teeth or snarl but wagged his tail as he used to do. She blinked in surprise, relaxed a little and held out her hand for him to sniff. Inside, the demon suddenly hammered against the images that confined it, and the dog pulled away, ears laid back. Anike reinforced the bonds holding the demon and Fenris relaxed again, though she thought she saw some suspicion in his brown eyes as she ruffled his ears. Many animal senses were much more acute than human, and she wondered if the demon's influence made her give off subtle cues that the dog picked up or if it was more direct, akin to the sensation she felt when touching a rune. Once again, she was reminded how little she knew about the demon.

Hand resting on Fenris' fur, she walked towards the back of the shop.

Olaf, knife in hand, had emerged from the doorway ahead of her, rubbing his eyes. He put the blade down when he saw it was her. "What are you doing here, Anike? Inge told me that you were leaving." Fenris went over to him and pressed against his legs.

"I wanted Bjord to believe that," she told him. "I need your help again, Olaf. Inge said Bjord was holding my father. Do you know if he is in the arlberg?"

"I believe so. The news is all over town, accompanied by a whole flock of speculations as to why."

"Inge said my father is going to be tried as a witch himself," said Anike grimly.

"She told me that too, but Bjord has not announced it. I think he is waiting to see if you hand yourself in. If you did, he could release Darek quietly, but if he announced a trial it would be hard to back down."

"You do not believe my father is a witch, do you, Olaf?"

"One of my oldest friends? Of course not, and I doubt that Bjord does either."

"What makes you think that?"

"He talked to me before he went for Darek and asked about you, and in particular how we felt about each other. I think he was trying to decide whether he could justify taking me as a hostage too, but I gave him the impression that I now strongly disapproved of you."

"I see. Could you denounce him?"

"It wouldn't do much good at the moment, since Darek is just being held without a specific reason." Olaf paused. "If your father had actually been put on trial, of course I would have spoken up." He looked at her thoughtfully. "But it seems that that will be unnecessary now. Since you are here in the middle of the night, I assume you plan to rescue him. You would have come during the day if you meant to give yourself up."

"Yes. While I hoped Bjord was bluffing, I could not take that risk. He is so consumed with his need to pursue me that I think that he might go through with the trial."

"I suspect you read him correctly, Anike. He is obsessed with catching you, and he is likely to strike out at those close to you in anger if he can't. Hate is an emotion that binds people as closely as love and there is a smaller distance between them than you might think."

"I know he feels betrayed. Just before I pushed him out of the way of the ball of lightning, he said something about his feelings for me. There was no time to discuss it further though and I have no idea what I would have said, but he feels he has made himself vulnerable. It did not help that the next thing I did was throw lightning at him."

"Attacking him has made things worse but as his mother was killed by a Larten witch, you would have always struggled for acceptance."

"Well, there is no coming back now," she said.

"I was surprised you even considered staying where everyone knew what you were, Anike. It was a brave thing to attempt."

"That ambition is gone now," she told him. "I have no place here, and given what Bjord has done, I cannot risk leaving my father here either. That is why I need your help."

"You are not planning to hurt anyone, are you?"

"Of course not. I just want to escape with my father."

"What do you want me to do?" asked Olaf.

"We would be quickly caught if we fled through the forest, so we will need to take my father's boat. Can you get it ready to sail?"

Olaf frowned. "I will do it for your father's sake. He is no witch, has hurt no one, and whatever reasons Bjord has for his pursuit of you, he should not have used an innocent man as a weapon."

"Thank you, Olaf. I do appreciate this."

Olaf looked down and scratched Fenris' ears, then raised his gaze to meet hers. "There is another option, of course. You could give yourself up to Bjord."

- 23 -

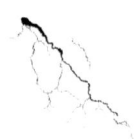

SMOKE AND STONE

Anike looked at him aghast. Olaf saw her expression and hesitated for a moment, but then pressed on. "He would release Darek, and when it comes to your trial it would be Svafnir who would judge you, not Bjord. You did kill the harrowling, and a whole crowd saw you fly away afterwards without hurting anyone. That was not something Gern could say. It should serve you well."

Anike stared at him. "Svafnir will never undermine Bjord over this. I would be taking a huge risk if I did that."

"It would save your father, and Arl Svafnir is fair. He might not order your execution or you might even be able to escape using your witchcraft. Attempting to rescue Darek is not safe either, you realise? You or he might be killed or injured, and what happens if you lose control again under pressure? You might kill a lot of people without meaning to."

Anike bridled, then felt the demon draw on her anger and took a deep breath to calm herself. "I am in control, Olaf. I do not need to be feared, and no one is going to get hurt. Yes, there is some risk, but how do you think my father will feel if I just give up my life in exchange for his?"

Olaf sighed. "You are right. He would blame himself, and that would take him somewhere very dark. He would hold himself responsible if anything happened to you." He stood. "I will find a way to talk myself past the gate guard, perhaps tell him that I have to look for a rare plant that has to be picked before dawn."

"That should work." Anike smiled, trying to ignore the unsettled feeling that had come when her master had suggested handing herself in, and got to her feet too. "Thank you. I will be a little over an hour, I imagine. I will have to move slowly so that I do not give myself away." She hugged Olaf, who stiffened then put his arms around her somewhat awkwardly.

"Fenris will miss you," Olaf told her. "And I will have to find another apprentice."

"You will not find that difficult," she said, blinking back tears. "Will an hour be enough for you to ready the boat?"

"I should be finished by then. It isn't as if I need to sail it anywhere."

"You do not have to wait once you have prepared it."

"I think I had better stay, though," Olaf replied. "Just in case there is anything I need to take care of. Good luck, Anike."

"I will see you soon, Olaf. Thank you." Anike slipped out of the door and ducked into a side alley. In a silver patch of moonlight, she invoked the flight pattern again and flew towards where Bjord held her father hostage.

She landed on the gable end of a house, lay flat and studied the arlberg and its defences. The far wall, bordering the wood town, was lit with half a dozen torches and three figures paced between the pools of light. The gate was less brightly illuminated by a single torch and another watcher stood beneath it, shifting from leg to leg. A further guard walked slowly along the wall adjacent to the stone town. Down below, next to the closed main door of the Arl's hall, two more men sat on a bench beneath yet more torches, long spears resting against the wall beside them. Occasionally, they exchanged words in low voices but did not seem to be particularly alert.

There was a lot of light and the unusually large number of guards suggested that Bjord had not believed what Inge had told him, but it was late and fatigue had taken its toll. If she was lucky, the obvious weariness of the men outside would be matched by those undoubtedly also waiting inside the hall. Reminded of her own condition, she drained a potion quickly to give herself energy, followed by another to numb pain. Olaf's comment about the possibility of further injury was fresh in her mind.

The smoke spell was now dyed onto her tunic, and though it could be useful should she be discovered, it would not help her approach undetected. She waited for the two men at the door to begin talking again, then read the rune pattern she had dyed onto her left sleeve. Whilst holding her other arm in front of her mouth to muffle the sound, she focused on the torch by the gate and spoke, "*Agni.*"

Her witchcraft snuffed the flame out. The guards' reaction was immediate. The one closest to Anike drew an axe and moved towards the gate while the watcher there started and hurriedly looked about him. One of the men by the door called up, "What is going on up there?" Anike could see that they were jumpy, no doubt fearful of meeting a witch in the dark. Both of the men by the door stood and one turned to bang on it before the other stopped him. "It's just the wind." He called up to the gate guard. "Relight the torch."

Sparks blossomed as the man struck flint and tinder. Trusting this was holding everyone's attention, Anike cast the flight spell, again muffling her voice with her sleeve. Swiftly and silently she flew high above the wall to land on the roof of the hall and settled into the deep shadow of the chimney.

Bjord had not thought he needed a watcher spending a very uncomfortable night there, clinging to the steep slope. The roof was made of thick stone tiles and the chimney itself did not provide easy access to the inside of the hall. It was wide enough for someone to climb down but she recalled, from happier times when she had played with Bjord, that there was a solid steel grating fitted to stop raiders from using it and she could not breach it with the spells she had, at least not quietly.

The stone tiles deadened sounds from within but a little noise came up through the chimney. When she peered down, she could see the fading embers of the cooking fire beneath her. She strained her ears, but even though she could not make out any conversation over the cracks from the cooling wood, it did not mean that everyone was asleep.

If Bjord had considered the shuttered windows and barred doors to be her only way in, he had underestimated her. Crouching down again, she pulled a piece of vellum out of her bag and placed it so that the moonlight illuminated the runes. Keeping her body in the shadow cast by the chimney, she muffled her voice with her cloak and laid her hand on a tile next to her. "*Prana.*"

Cracks ran through it, multiplying and branching until the stone crumbled silently to dust which was borne away by the spell to scatter across the roof. The gap created was not quite large enough to allow her to pass through but now she could see inside. There had been no noise while the tile had disintegrated and she doubted that anyone had been looking up, but nevertheless she waited and listened for shouts of alarm before peering down into the hall. Flickering torchlight cast an uncertain light throughout the chamber.

Bjord had not been taken in by the story she had spun for Inge and a considerable force awaited her. In addition to a few thralls clustered together in the cooking area, there were a dozen armed men and women in the hall. Half were stretched out on bedrolls while the rest were sitting in a loose circle with weapons at their feet or on a large table nearby. Darek lay on his side in the centre of the circle. He had been placed on some furs and from the slow rise and fall of his chest, she could see that he had managed to fall asleep.

The warriors spoke to each other in low voices, and from time to time glanced at the double doors leading to the courtyard. Anike recognised the grizzled face of Rogar amongst them. A great axe lying next to one of the sleepers marked out Siv, but she could not see Bjord so guessed he was in his private chamber at the side of the hall. No doubt he could be roused within moments if she was seen. She had hoped for less vigilance but remained determined to rescue her father, and to do it without seriously harming anyone in the process.

None of the warriors below had noticed the missing tile in the roof. Sliding as far away from the gap as she could whilst remaining in shadow, she covered her mouth with her sleeve again and used the spell on the vellum sheet to destroy another tile, making the hole big enough for someone to pass through. Heart pounding, she waited for a cry of warning from below. When none came, she peered over the edge again.

Now she had to kick the hornet's nest. She drew a small stone from her bag and carefully tossed it onto the table covered with weapons. It clattered on an axe blade, striking a sharp note which cut through the muted tones in the hall.

"What's that?" one man asked, looking around.

Rogar stood, placing his hand on the hilt of his sword, and peered about him, scanning the room. He cocked his head to one side. "Wake Siv," he said to the man next to him, who Anike saw was Slad.

"You wake Siv," muttered Slad irritably, but he did as he was told and nudged the woman's recumbent form with his foot. Instantly her hand went to her axe and she came to a sitting position. Slad took a prudent step back. "Tavic, check outside," she said, coming to her feet so fluidly that Anike doubted she had been asleep at all. Tavic headed for the door, and all around men reached for weapons. Her father was waking from his fitful sleep and looking about him groggily.

It had been a risk to put the guards on the alert, but it probably made little difference if a dozen were awake or half that, and she needed the cover of noise they would make. Anike flipped the sheet of vellum over so that she could see the other side. Her next intonation of "*Prana*," went unnoticed in the clamour of men readying themselves for battle. Even though she could not use it yet, she had to place the flight spell on her father while she could still see him.

Tavic had opened the door and disappeared down the short corridor leading to the courtyard. He had the attention of most of the hall as he lifted the bar. When Anike heard the outer doors groan open, she looked at her left sleeve and read the pattern, "*Agni*," her voice lost once more within the tumult beneath. All of the flames in the chamber winked out at her command and the hall was plunged into darkness save for the glimmer of moonlight from the doorway.

Shouts of alarm and confusion echoed through the building, punctuated by curses as men tripped and stumbled. Silhouettes flitted across the dimly lit threshold as warriors sought the exit, whether in panic or to engage the supposed threat. Anike concentrated, no longer able to see her father but still able to sense the spell she had cast on him. She lifted him off the floor and towards the roof where she waited.

Her father then chose to do the obvious thing she had not anticipated. "Help!" he shouted.

Anike bit back an oath and whispered down to him as loudly as she dared, "Quiet, Father!" but her voice was lost in the chaos below. "Help me!" called Darek again as he drifted higher. There was the sound of booted feet below him now, and sparks flew in a corner of the hall as someone tried to light a torch. She could see his arm flailing about him, trying to grab hold of anything to stop himself from rising higher. Stealth had to give way to haste. "Father, this is a rescue! Be still!" she hissed at him urgently.

"Anike?" Her father's voice sounded on the edge of hysteria.

"Who else would it be? Stop struggling!" She concentrated and lifted him towards her.

"The roof! She's on the roof!" Siv shouted from below. A torch flared into life within the hall, followed by another. The orange light framed Darek as Anike guided his body through the hole, but the relief on his face at seeing her suddenly turned to pain and he gasped. The war dart that had struck his back was pulled free as it caught on the edge of the gap, tearing through his flesh.

Anike clenched her fists on seeing this pointless strike against him, but she suppressed her anger. She could not afford to give the demon an emotion it could exploit to subdue her. A single wound from a war dart was not usually life-threatening, but it would be better to deal with it sooner rather than later. The patch of blood on his back was spreading through her father's tunic. She set him on the roof in the shadow of the chimney, pulled a potion from her bag and thrust it at him. "Drink this, then hold on to the roof. The spell will end in a moment and I do not want you to fall before I recast it." Darek drank the potion and sighed with relief.

As Anike retrieved the vellum from the roof, movement flickered in the corner of her eye and she ducked as an arrow struck the stone above her. One of the men on the wall had moved round to sight on her and as he reached into his quiver again, she saw more warriors ran into view on the ground. Some of them had bows too, including Bjord and Siv who had both come outside.

She bit her lip. They were too vulnerable on the roof. If she tried to lift off now, she would make a good target for arrows and her own flight spell would not last much longer, nor was it powerful enough to support both her and her father. She looked at Darek and placed a hand on his arm. "Keep low," she told him and read the pattern on her sleeve.

"Kill her!" yelled Bjord from below, and loosed his arrow even as Anike shouted "*Vata!*" to conjure the wind shield. The arrow hummed through the night before being tossed aside by the vortex of air, as were the three that followed from the other bows. Anike tried to shield her father with her body, pressing them both back against the chimney. The wind provided protection, but she knew a well-judged or lucky shot might still get through and she needed a few moments for her well of energy to refill enough to power new flight spells. That delay might prove fatal. Siv, in particular, was an excellent shot and Anike's shoulder blades began to tingle in anticipation of an arrow. They could not remain so exposed.

The flight effects needed the most energy of all the spells she had devised, but she would be able to cast others a vital few seconds earlier. Putting her head to her father's ear so that he could hear her over the wind, she said, "When it goes dark, climb into the chimney and wait for me." She tried to keep her voice steady and Darek nodded, looking up for a handhold. Anike flinched away from another arrow, then stood, letting the moonlight fall on the runes on the front of her tunic. "*Agni,*" she called out, and the air above the roof filled with smoke, blotting everything out. Darek coughed, but she heard him start to climb and relaxed a little. Once within the chimney, he would be safe from arrows even if they were loosed blind into the cloud and while bowmen might aim at her by the sound of the whirlwind, it would be the purest luck if she were hit.

She could not read her rune patterns while within the smoke but with her father safe for the moment, she was free to move. She was starting to rise towards clear air when her flight spell expired and she fell back to the roof and started to slip towards the edge. Scrabbling in the dark for purchase, her fingers found the lip of the gap in the tiles and she just succeeded in bringing herself to a halt before she slid off the roof. Darek's voice came from above her, "Anike, are you safe?"

"I am fine," she called back. "Just wait and be ready to hold on to me when I say." With the wind and arrows singing around her, she doubted that she could hold even her simpler flight pattern in mind clearly enough to use it, so she pulled herself up and into the hole. She hung for a moment by her hands then let herself drop, falling through the smoke into clear air before landing on one of the large tables. She bent her knees and rolled off onto the ground. The hard landing had probably done her some injury but she felt nothing, insulated from pain by her potion. By the light of the few torches that had been relit, she could make out that most of the warriors had left the hall and as she rose to her feet, surrounded by the whirlwind, the few who remained backed away and fled.

"Hold!" came a deep voice, and she turned to see Arl Svafnir in the doorway leading to his private chamber. He was leaning on the wall for support and dried blood stained his shirt. His face was pale, but he had a sword in his hand and his eyes were steel. He gathered himself, pushed away from the wall, and took a step towards her.

Anike drew herself up, standing in the middle of the vortex, dark hair billowing in a cloud around her head. She met his gaze. "Not this time, my lord," she said defiantly.

Svafnir took another step towards her, his blade held steady in front of him, advancing by sheer force of will.

"I have no wish to hurt anyone else," she warned him. "I just want to be free to live my life."

"So did the people you killed."

Anike flinched at that truth. "I cannot bring them back to life but I can atone for their deaths by my future deeds."

"That is not your choice to make. I decide how you pay for the crimes you have committed here." Svafnir took another step forward.

"No," said Anike firmly. "I am the only one who knows enough to render a fair verdict and I condemn myself to live with my guilt, and charge myself to prevent such catastrophes from happening in the future. That is my judgment, Arl Svafnir." She raised her cloak, echoing her action before the bear on Vanir Heights, and read the flight pattern. "*Prana*," she said, her voice ringing with assurance.

Svafnir halted, his eyes watchful for the effect of the spell, sword raised in guard. Suddenly there was the sound of running feet. "Father!" shouted Bjord from the entrance and he loosed an arrow at Anike. The wind tossed it aside as she lifted into the smoke. Had she still been in any doubt, her defiance of Arl Svafnir had ended her life in Trollgard.

Now she just had to get her father away. To cast the spell on him, she needed both to see the pattern and know exactly where he was. She lifted through the opening in the roof and listened from within the cloud of smoke. Confusion and clamour reigned in the yard below as warriors milled about trying to find her but through the tumult, she could hear Siv calling for ladders. There was no time to waste. Her questing fingers found the vellum stuffed into the top of her bag. Rising until she cleared the smoke and could read again, she unfolded the scroll. "Get to the top of the chimney and put out your arm," she called to her father and reached into the cloud for his hand.

"I can't find you," he said, his voice coming from well out of her reach.

"Never mind," she said. His voice had located him precisely enough for her to target the spell. "Just do not panic this time. *Prana*." She levitated him out of the smoke and grasped his hand. "Hold on tight." She flew upwards as fast as she could with her father trailing behind her, then headed out of the stone town. Shouts rang out as the warriors guarding the wall spotted them in the moonlight and a bowstring thrummed, sending an arrow into the night. Anike flew in the direction of the forest, hoping to convince Bjord that she was escaping that way, before dropping low to change course and head towards the sea.

She landed briefly to renew the flight spells. "Where are we going?" Darek asked. "Why are we not heading back into the town?"

"I am sorry, Father, but we cannot stay in Trollgard. I am going to leave, and you will have to come with me now. Bjord was going to put you on trial as a witch if I did not give myself up. If you stay, he will try that again."

"He can't do that, girl."

"It's a misuse of his power but I think he will, just to get back at me."

"Arl Svafnir would never allow it."

"Did you see the Arl?" asked Anike. Darek shook his head.

"I did. He is barely able to walk. Bjord rules for now and he is desperate to catch me. I think he will do almost anything."

Darek was silent.

"We have to go away, Father."

"I see. You are probably right, Anike. Bjord treated me badly, and this will be an uncomfortable place to live if he is in charge. I wish I could collect some things from home though."

"The important thing for now is to get away. Olaf should have your boat ready for us." She lifted them into the air again.

Torches were lighting up along the east wall of the stone town but there was no sign of activity on the north side facing the beach. Any hunt would probably wait for dawn and it should be some hours before someone thought to search for them at sea. As they flew closer, Anike saw that her father's fishing boat had been drawn down to the edge of the water and made out Olaf standing beside it, waiting. She headed towards him and landed a few paces away.

"You have thought of everything, haven't you?" Darek said.

Anike smiled faintly. "I have tried," she said. "I wish it was not necessary."

Her father took her arm, squeezing gently. "You would have made your mother proud." He coughed, a little nervously. "I am proud of you too, Anike. I do not need to treat you like a child – I see that now.

THE DEMON AND THE WITCH | - 273 -

You have grown into a strong woman. I was worried that the burden of witchcraft would have broken you but you have proved me wrong."

Anike felt herself flush in the darkness. She put her arms around him. "I love you," she said simply.

Olaf coughed, and she broke away. "I see you managed to stir the atlberg up, but I am glad you made it out safely, both of you," he said. "The boat is ready, as you can see." He looked at Anike. "Did you have to hurt anyone?"

"Perhaps some bruises when they tripped over each other in the darkness, and someone skewered my father with a war dart."

"Anike's potion dealt with that soon enough, though," Darek said with a hint of pride.

"Where will you go now?" asked Olaf.

"Along the coast to start with, and then south. We will find somewhere a long way away and set up a new home. We can fish, and I can find herbs, study the runes and deepen my understanding of witchcraft."

"Perhaps you should forget the witchcraft and just concentrate on improving your herb lore?"

"Olaf, witchcraft will always be part of me. I cannot ignore it so I have to master it. I think I can do more good in the world by trying to understand and harness it than I will be able to with my herbs. Ultimately, I may even learn about its origins." Enthusiasm rang through her voice as she continued. "I might even be able to find other witches and teach them how to control their power. Eventually, witches could be accepted and live in peace among their family and friends."

Olaf's face was in shadow as he looked at her. He reached into a pocket and brought out an earthenware flask. "Drink this. It will give you strength for a few hours, at least enough for you to get the boat round the next headland."

Anike took the elixir. "Thank you, Olaf, that's a good thought, but Father needs it more than I do." She passed it to Darek.

"My thanks, Olaf," said Darek. He drained it in a single long draught and handed the flask back to Olaf.

"You had a good future before all of this, Anike," said Olaf regretfully. "It's a shame this has been your fate."

"We must all do our best and work with what happens, good or bad," said Anike. "My path leads elsewhere now. Farewell, Olaf."

She started to push the boat the last few paces into the sea. Darek went to the other side to help but as he placed his hand on the boat, he swayed. "Anike, I don't feel too good," he managed, then keeled face-first into the sand.

"Father!" cried Anike, running round the boat towards him, suspecting a hidden wound. She knelt next to him, turning his head so that she could look into his eyes.

"Don't worry, Anike," said Olaf, softly. "He will be fine." Something in his voice, a note of regret perhaps, made her look up at him just in time to see the flask in his hand smash into the side of her head. Light exploded behind her eyes, then she fell into darkness.

- 24 -

The Ashes of Childhood

Anike fought her way back to consciousness through a sea of pain shot through with orange flames and the electric blue of lightning. Something sticky was holding her eyelids shut and when she tried to raise her hand to wipe it away, she found that her arms were bound behind her back. She managed to open her eyes a crack, but the daylight seared in and sent waves of agony through her mind. Deeper down, the demon followed her consciousness up through the currents of anger, pain and fear, like a shark rising from the depths. Closing her eyes again, she embraced the image of the sea, then froze it around the demon to confine it once more. She did not need any further complications. She was in enough trouble.

Her eyes opened fully at the second attempt and the pain slowly faded from brilliant agony to a dull throb. The blinding light resolved into shapes and patterns and she realised she was lying on the cold stone floor of the Arl's hall. Sunlight poured in through the unshuttered windows and the hole she had made in the roof. She felt the hard stone under her side, the sting of the tight bonds around her wrists and ankles and the rough taste of a gag in her mouth.

A male voice behind her called out, "My lord, she wakes!" Several blurred figures levelled spears at her as she shifted on the ground. She turned her head and Olaf came into focus, sitting on a bench at the nearer end of one of the large tables that dominated the centre of the hall. Her cloak and her bag lay in front of his feet together with rune-covered pieces of cloth, torn from her tunic and sleeves. As she stirred, he turned to look at her with haunted eyes.

Heavy footsteps sent shivers through the floor and into her body as they drew closer, then her chin was pulled up sharply and Bjord was glaring into her eyes. "I was worried you would sleep through your own hanging, witch," he hissed. "You will be tried at midday, so you only have a little time to beg forgiveness from the gods. Tavic is setting up the scaffold for you now. This time there will be no escape, Anike, no second chance. I will have justice for myself and all those you sent to Hel's realm before their time." He shoved her chin back hard, and her head hit the floor. Lights flashed behind her eyes, but she raised her face and stared defiantly at him.

She felt a hand on her shoulder. Olaf was beside her, looking up at Bjord. "There was no need for that," he said, a hint of controlled anger in his voice. "Cruelty, my lord, does not become someone who embodies justice in the eyes of the people." Bjord snorted and stalked away, and Olaf resumed his seat on the bench.

Through her pain, Anike struggled to reconcile Olaf's support with his betrayal of the night before. Slowly she drew in her legs and rolled to a sitting position, half expecting one of the men to send her sprawling once more. Perhaps the warriors were also shamed by Olaf's admonishment because no blow came and she was able to look about her. Olaf appeared deep in thought, a haunted expression on his face. Slad was sitting on a stool behind her with a large cudgel in his hands and near him stood three men with spears. Throughout the hall, warriors and thralls were busying themselves, speaking in muted tones and casting swift and fearful glances in her direction. Darek sat on the floor under guard near the throne, with a rope binding his wrist to his ankles.

Svafnir emerged from his private chamber, one arm over Siv's shoulder for support. He looked much as he had done the night before, save for being dressed in a clean tunic. With Siv's help, he hobbled past the throne and the table. Siv halted a few paces away and Svafnir took the final steps towards Anike unaided. He regarded her silently for a moment.

"You were in error last night. Consider the chaos if everyone asserted the right to judge themselves or choose what laws applied to them. I could not allow that even if you were not a witch. I think you understand this, not that it matters now. There will be a trial in public and it will be my judgment, not yours, that determines your fate."

He turned away, put his arm around Siv's shoulders again, and they slowly crossed to his throne. She helped him sit, then lifted Darek to his feet. At Svafnir's nod, she cut the thongs binding him.

Bjord went up to the Arl. Anike did not hear what he said, but Svafnir's response was clear. "He is to be set free."

"But he might be a witch too," Bjord protested.

"Don't be ridiculous, Bjord," said Svafnir sharply. "We have Anike now. You do not need Darek as a hostage."

"He flew, Father. Tell him, Siv."

"Do you truly think he would have called out for help if that was his own doing?"

"It could have been a ruse."

Svafnir just looked at his son. Bjord was not ready to give up. "He knew about her, though. How can you live with a witch and not know it? Only a witch would hide another witch."

"Darek is not the only one who has known Anike for years, spent time in her company and suspected nothing, is he?" Svafnir's reply was scathing and Bjord flushed. "That would be a dangerous rod to make for your own back. Suppose, when you are Arl, someone aggrieved by your decisions accuses you of being a witch because you too knew Anike intimately?" He flicked his fingers dismissively. "By acting out of convenience and without evidence you have gone too far. We rule by law, not by whim."

Bjord bridled. "At least my plan worked."

"Only by chance, and by the quick thinking of another." He glanced briefly at Olaf, who bowed his head. "Darek, come here." Anike saw her father shuffle forward, flexing his arm to restore the blood to it. "You are free to go. You have my apology for Bjord's actions towards you. He is, I fear, young and too hasty."

"Thank you, my lord." Darek bowed. "But my daughter? She has never meant any harm, I swear. She has always tried to help people."

"It is natural you should ask that," the Arl told him, his expression neutral. "I do not hold it against you, but I will not release her. You may speak at her trial if you wish. There must be a trial, Darek." Svafnir let his eyes close for a moment. When he opened them again, Darek started to speak but Svafnir cut him off. "No. Enough. Go now, I am tired."

Siv took Darek's arm firmly and led him to the door. As they passed by Anike, Darek tried to pull away but Siv held him back. "You may not speak to her, Darek." Darek struggled and shouted, "Save yourself, Anike. Get away! Don't worry about me!" before Siv dragged him out.

Bjord sullenly watched him leave and then hurled a wooden cup across the room. It struck the wall and Anike could hear it rolling across the floor in the sudden silence.

"That is enough, Bjord," said Svafnir sharply. Bjord stomped to the ale barrel, defiantly took another cup and drew himself a long draught. The Arl pulled himself to his feet, walked unsteadily back to his chamber and shut the door behind him.

Olaf leaned down to Anike and whispered, almost as if they were discussing a patient, "Svafnir thinks that Bjord should have let you run. Holding Darek was not only unlawful but it put a lot of people at risk." He knelt beside her and wiped the blood from her face with a wet cloth. "I really am sorry, Anike," he murmured. As Anike jerked her head away from his touch, he looked at her and bit his lip. "I owe you an explanation, and for you to understand I need to tell you a story." He looked over her head. "Give us a little privacy, Slad."

Slad hesitated.

"A few paces is plenty. What, do you think I will let her go when I was the one who captured her?"

Anike did not turn her head but she heard Slad move away, grumbling under his breath.

Olaf spoke softly, his voice only reaching Anike's ears. "It is important for me to explain myself. You won't forgive me, but perhaps you will understand."

Anike stared up at his face, curiosity battling with fear and hurt.

"You may not care why I betrayed you, but I want you to know I didn't do it out of malice or hatred. Will you at least listen to me?"

Anike saw Olaf needed to justify himself. This man, her mentor, master and friend for many years, had turned on her just as she thought she was safe. The betrayal was a knot of hurt inside but curiosity was stronger than spite, and she wanted to know why he had done it. Whether his explanation made the hurt worse or better, she wanted that knot unpicked. Carefully, she nodded.

Olaf relaxed a little and his face creased in thought for a moment. "Anike, my life has been dedicated to healing, and I have learned cures for many ailments and saved many lives, but fifteen years ago I was unable to save my wife, Selma and my son." His gaze rested on her face. "What very few know is that they were killed by a witch, and I was there."

Anike drew in a sharp breath.

"Your father told you my family was killed in a Larten raid. The witch was part of that raid. The same man who killed Svafnir's wife, Elin." Olaf paused, and then the story he had kept locked inside for so many years seemed to burst forth. "It was a large raid – four ships. I had set up in the hall to treat the wounded and my family was sheltering here as I worked. Some of the raiders got over the wall. My son, little Woden, was seven and he picked up a knife and slipped out to go and fight them." Tears welled in his eyes as the memory played out in his mind. "We went after him, Elin, Selma and I, but he ran into the stables in pursuit of a couple of raiders, and we followed. Elin killed one of them and the other ran. We were just about to take Woden back to the hall when another man came into the stables and cut us off."

Anike could see the pain in his eyes, raw even after all this time. She leaned forward a little to listen, for Olaf seemed to be talking to himself now, lost in his past. "He had a great sword with runes engraved on it and all around his body was a shimmer, like crystal, and he was so very strong. Woden froze in terror and Selma went to pick him up. Elin and I attacked the man, but he just brushed me aside and I fell behind a hay bale. I think that is what saved me. Elin was good with her blade and held him off for a moment but then he spoke a rune and froze her in place next to Selma and Woden. Only her eyes moved. When he spoke the rune again, all colour and life seemed to drain out of all three of them. I saw them die in front of me, first Woden and Elin, and then my Selma." He closed his eyes and Anike too could almost see the horror of the scene as he relived it.

Olaf drew a breath and went on hoarsely. "The witch turned back to me and raised his sword, but Svafnir was suddenly there and drove him outside into the melee. I crawled to my son and tried to get him to drink a potion, but he was gone. It was too late for Elin and Selma as well." Olaf shuddered. "So I have seen what witchcraft can do firsthand. It took my family from me and you must forgive me if I find it hard to believe in a good witch. I tried to accept you, Anike. I knew you and when you told me you wanted to get rid of the power, I thought that I might be able to, but when you returned it was still within you. I believe you regretted the killings but I could see you were holding a storm in a flask and you would eventually release it."

Despite the betrayal, Anike felt a stir of admiration and respect for her old master. It took a wise man to accept he had prejudices and a brave one to try to challenge them.

Olaf was continuing. "You have a terrible strength inside you and despite your good heart, you came back from your journey changed. You were confident and beginning to accept your power and use it to achieve what you wanted. You challenged the harrowling, partly to save the town, but partly to demonstrate your own mastery. You came to rescue your father, not in humility, but with arrogance and you were starting to use witchcraft to bend the world to your will."

Anike thought of her confrontation with Svafnir the night before, denying him the right to judge her. Olaf was not entirely wrong.

"I gave you the benefit of the doubt, though, and you managed to get your father out without hurting anyone and so I nearly let you go, even then, telling myself you would be different." He closed his eyes for a moment. "I so wanted you to say you would give up your power and walk away from the temptation, but you gave me the wrong answer. You still wanted to use witchcraft, to explore it further. I feared what you would become, not when you lost control but when you thought you were justified. You had turned down a dark path without realising it. It would take you to a place where you would use the power for your own ends, to dominate those who disagreed with you, and you would rationalise every step on the way. You would have ended up like the man who killed my wife and son. I could not bear to see you become that."

He stood. "I am sorry, Anike, I don't hate you, but in the end, you would have been corrupted and I could not let you loose on the world to become a tyrant. I admire you for trying to turn the power to good ends, but no one is strong enough to resist that temptation."

Anike stared up at him. This was a stark, rational explanation, a cutting out of flesh at the first sign of infection but she could hear the conflict in Olaf's voice. Like Bjord, he was rooted in a desire to help people but while Bjord was certain in his actions, Olaf's worries that he was wrong were eating him inside. He knew his choice would end her life and deny her the opportunity to turn from the path he predicted. He had made the agonising decision to save many lives by sacrificing one closer to him, a decision made with his head even if his heart rebelled against it.

She did not envy him the choice and could understand how he had reached that difficult conclusion, but for all his experience he did not know everything. While she accepted that there was a general tendency for power to corrupt, it was impossible to be certain how each individual would act. His certainty was as arrogant as hers. However, the truth was that she had not wanted the power, and if she could have rid herself of the demon she would have, despite the measure of control she now had. Since that was not possible, she could only choose not to be a victim, to use and seek to understand witchcraft. The demon, with its unwavering urge for chaos and destruction, was a constant reminder of the harm she could do, making her only too aware that terrible acts were only a slip of her will away. Olaf did not know that. She had not told him, and now it was too late.

Olaf and Bjord had both done what they thought was right, but they had not understood who she really was. She was the woman who had pushed Bjord out of the way of the ball of fire, taking the consequences on herself, and who had recognised and defeated the demon. She had realised she could use runes to control it, but was still humbled by the knowledge that her power was only borrowed. That truth confirmed her humanity and grounded her in a way Olaf could not understand. Hilda had taught her that the runes could only describe the present and that the future was not yet written. There was no unchangeable fate and her destiny was hers to decide, not to be taken from her by the fears of others.

She still had a choice, and she chose to live.

The gag in her mouth prevented her speaking and without the spell patterns she had written down there was little she could do, even if she could talk. Her clothes and her bag were well out of reach. There was only one course left to her, and even now she shied away from it. She thought about what she had to do, and what it meant. She had always wanted to live in Trollgard, to be welcomed and respected, and until that moment she had not wholly accepted in her heart that the town's rejection was final. Even when she was forced to flee after the battle with the harrowling, she had harboured a spark of hope that she could find a way back, but she had to let that go. She had to accept without reservation that her life in Trollgard was finished, to move on acknowledging the potential for Olaf's dark vision of her future, and rely on her strength and determination to avoid it.

She needed to speak. Olaf was still looking at her, eyes searching her face. He wanted her forgiveness, or at least her understanding. He wanted absolution for his betrayal, and that gave her a chance. She tried to talk through the gag but was unable to form words. She swallowed and looked at Olaf, pleading with her eyes. Olaf hesitated, then his desire to hear her overcame his caution, and he leaned forward and pulled her gag away.

Anike paused, knowing this was her last chance to decide between execution and risking lives to gain her freedom. Everyone around her had made their choice and now it was her turn. Her future was hers to decide.

"I understand, Olaf," she whispered as he leant forward to hear her. "You did what you thought was right and that is all any man can do. I forgive you." She caught his gaze and held it. "Now, run!"

Olaf's expression turned from relief to apprehension, then outright fear. He backed away and started for the door. Inside her mind, Anike smashed the chest of ice. She dropped every barrier, every bond she had used to hold the demon back, and her mind rang with the desire to destroy.

"Fire!" said the demon through Anike's mouth.

- 25 -

The Eye of
the Storm

Flames roared out from Anike's body, incinerating her bonds and flinging Slad and the others away in an explosion of fire and sound. Men screamed as heat washed over them, igniting clothes and hair, and fear followed in its wake.

She felt like a passenger as the demon made her body stand, watching and listening from behind a veil. Having deliberately ceded control, there could be no illusion that these actions were her own. She felt the pain in her wrists and ankles where the ropes had burned away, but the demon did not seem to notice her body's discomfort.

At the sides of the hall, beyond the reach of the burst of fire that had freed her, some people were cowering or trying to flee but others were turning to their weapons. Bjord held a war dart and was drawing back his arm to cast it.

The demon painted the hall with images of runes. "Fire!" it said again, and smoke filled the chamber, pale grey near the windows and roof but dark where men on the ground were trying to orient themselves. Around her were sounds of coughing but Bjord's annoyingly well-aimed dart flew out of the murk and grazed her side. She could feel the pain sapping her own will, but the demon ignored the injury and gathered energy for its next attack.

Through the pain, Anike struggled to regain control over her body. The demon had broken her free from her bonds, something she could not have done herself. No-one had suffered fatal injury yet, but she had to bind it again before that changed. To her horror, the demon resisted her attempts to confine it. It seemed stronger, or perhaps she was weaker.

A rune pattern formed in her mind as it selected an assault that it could use without seeing its targets, but now she was actively struggling to displace the demon, Anike heard the word "*Vata*," when it used her lips to speak. The hall was filled with a howling gale, with crosswinds so savage that they cut like knives, bringing cries of pain and fear that could be heard even over the rushing wind. The clamour was accompanied by the sound of shattering pots and rending fabric. The demon had used this spell on the hunters by the river but with men trapped inside the hall and blinded by smoke, it was even more devastating. Terror filled the room.

The blade of a great axe cut through the grey cloud a handspan from her face. Siv, who had never shown fear in Anike's memory, had aimed blind at the sound of her voice.

The demon might not heed her pain but it did need her alive, so it dropped to one knee and let the backswing of the axe pass over her. "*Prana*," it said, and she sensed a wave of force pulse out from her, followed by a crunch and shouts of pain as several people were flung against a wall she could not see.

All around her, she heard moaning from the floor as people tried to shield themselves from the wind. She felt the demon's satisfaction as it drew in power to strike again. Mustering her will, she tried to create another prison but the demon shattered the image before it was fully formed. She had correctly foreseen that the demon would free her body and then sow chaos before moving on to killing. While she wanted to escape and had been prepared to let the demon hurt those guarding her, she had not intended to survive at the cost of another's life. Her intention had been to regain control before anyone died and she had not expected it to be this hard. She had not felt so powerless since it had first joined with her. Consciously or subconsciously, she had always been fighting the demon but when she deliberately released it she had abandoned all of her barriers and had underestimated how much she had relied on them. Unless she found another way to master it, the injured and terrified people in the hall would soon be dead. Olaf's fear that her confidence would turn to arrogance had come true more quickly than he would have believed possible.

The smoke suddenly evaporated and she found herself looking at a scene of devastation. Men and women lay on the floor or cowered beneath tables. Most were groaning, but some lay very still. Anike saw Siv crumpled against the wall, her axe lying beside her twitching fingers. Bjord was hunched with his arms over his head. Olaf, fortunately, was nowhere to be seen. The wind died and everywhere frightened faces looked up, praying the ordeal was over.

The demon allowed them a moment before shattering their hopes. "*Agni*!" it said, and simultaneously every wooden object in the hall caught fire, from the benches and tables to cups and bowls and the wooden hafts of weapons, even carved symbols of the gods held in imploring hands. The flames roared towards the ceiling, forcing those still conscious to shield their faces from the heat.

As the demon focused its attention and power on the destruction it was wreaking, Anike gathered her will again, spurred on by the sight of the desperate people in the hall. With her inner eye, she saw tendrils of smoke and fire from the demon winding through her, wrapping around her innermost self and isolating her from her body. She concentrated on the landscape within her mind and imagined ice around that core of her true identity, letting the clarity of cold radiate out. On each coil of flame, she formed the rune of ice. The tendrils, shot through with fire and lightning, froze, and then shattered as she struck them with images of stones.

She took a deep breath, then turned all her attention to the internal conflict, letting the sights and sounds of the hall fade. The demon, a shifting mass of energy, seemed to turn to face her and glow more brightly, ready to do battle once more. It rushed at her like a comet, burning her and trying to push her back. Fragments of the demon's thoughts and intent flickered around her and she knew that in releasing it deliberately, she had allowed it to spread its influence into the depths of her mind. It was manipulating her subconscious with images, turning it against her. She sensed a void behind her, a yawning pit in her mind, and realised that the demon was trying to thrust her will and sense of self into it. It meant to bury her there, deep within her own subconscious, so it could use her body as it willed. If she ever managed to free herself, it would be far too late to help the people of Trollgard. Energy flared around her, staggering her as the demon tried to drive her towards the void.

She fought back, visualising the rune of stasis and expanding it around her to create a zone of calm and stability against which the demon's fury rebounded in rainbow shards of energy. It redoubled its assault, fire and lightning lashing all about her, but the energy was reflected away as she rallied and started to push back.

The demon reached past her with arms of smoke. Unable to force her to retreat, it pulled on the edge of the void, dragging it towards her. She could feel the emptiness looming behind her.

She had to purge the demon's influence and wrest back control of the fabric of her subconscious. At the distant limits of what she could conceive, she formed an image of water, the white foam of a wave breaking as it thundered towards her battleground with the demon. It surged in from the edges of her mind, building in force and power as it approached, until it broke over them. The jagged patterns of energy that the demon had used to infiltrate her essence were swept away as the wave tore through her mind and poured into the void the demon had formed, filling and then sealing it. Anike let the power of the ocean surround and support her.

The demon drew in upon itself as the wave covered it then burst outwards, ringed by an aura that vaporised the sea on contact, but its mastery over her subconscious, the domain of their conflict, was gone.

Still the demon fought. It rushed her again, its aura of energy annihilating the water as it came. It surrounded her with fire and smoke while it lashed her with lightning and invisible talons of disruption. It was trying to tear her apart but, for all its fury, this was a pattern of attack she had defeated before.

She sensed its desperation and froze the border of water, turning the boundary between it and the sphere of energy that surrounded the demon into ice. The white surface of the inside of the sphere reflected the demon's outpourings of energy back on themselves in a cascade of colour. Drawing on everything she had left, she contracted the ice sphere with the demon at its centre.

The demon drew in on itself, brightening to the incandescence of a star, then exploded outward, throwing itself against the ice and sending cracks through the imprisoning shell, but Anike focused her will and the fissures closed. She forced the sphere smaller and smaller.

The demon seemed to scream as the walls shrunk around it, then it subsided, its final effort spent. Anike held its prison like a pearl in the palm of her hand, and she closed her fist around it.

Her senses flooded back into her body, bringing with them the pain from her burns and other injuries but she pushed it aside and opened her eyes. Little time seemed to have passed in the burning hall. Men and women lay unconscious or were groaning, curled into balls trying to make themselves as small a target as possible. A few were helping others towards exits to escape the fire. Out of the corner of her eye, she could see Rogar on his hands and knees, coughing.

Bjord was just pushing himself upright. Charred and bleeding from numerous small cuts, he forced himself to his feet, defiance radiating from him. His eyes met hers and he took an unsteady step towards her. Flickering orange light cast dark shadows over his face, emphasising the determined set of his features. His courage and resolve were palpable as he advanced, pulling his sword from its sheath. Even the demon's display of power had failed to cow him. Anike saw that driven by his pride and a fierce desire to protect his people, and despite his fear of witchcraft, Bjord the warrior would not run from this fight. She flung back her head and drew herself up, waiting for him. He raised his sword to strike.

Anike punched him in the face.

Caught completely by surprise, Bjord fell backwards, the sword spinning from his grasp. He landed heavily on his back, blood pouring from his nose. Blinking back tears of pain, he tried to rise, hand groping for his blade.

"*Prana*," said Anike, carefully releasing a thread of power into a simple pattern of runes in her mind before confining the demon again without doubt or hesitation. Bjord's sword rose from the floor and came smoothly to her hand. She pressed the point against his throat and he froze.

"I am leaving now, Bjord." She gestured at the burning room. "This is not something I desired. We did not need to fight, but you chose confrontation. All this could have been avoided if you had simply let me leave."

"This was your doing! Only yours!" Bjord spat. He tried to rise but stopped when the sword point drew a drop of blood.

"I accept responsibility for my part in all of this. I hope you are wise enough to do the same." She looked about her. "No one has died. When I have gone, just think about what would have happened if I had not pushed you aside on the mountain and it was you who had been struck by the lightning and become the witch." Bjord's mouth dropped open, and she pressed a little harder. "Say nothing. I am talking now. Next time you find something new, try to understand it before you decide to destroy it. Your actions have consequences, and fear is no way to rule or lead. It will likely end with prejudice and persecution, making enemies when you could have friends. But I am not your enemy."

She bent down, picked her tunic sleeve off the floor and read the pattern on it. "*Agni*." Every fire in the room went out.

"I am leaving for good, Bjord. You have taken away from me everything I have here, even my father, who will never be safe from you if I remain."

"Kill me now, or I will hunt you down, witch," Bjord said, wiping the blood from his face.

"No, you will not," said Anike quietly. "I know you too well. You will not leave your domain to go on a wild and foolish journey with little hope of finding me. I am no threat to Trollgard once I am gone and you will not abandon your father and your people. You are a prisoner of your duties and the expectations that surround you. But I am free."

Anike let the sword fall to the ground and walked away. No one tried to stop her.

- 26 -

The Journey

Anike stood at the edge of the forest by the road leading east from Trollgard and watched the waves rolling onto the beach, washing away her childhood. She bade it farewell, then turned to set her feet firmly on the path to her new life.

She had picked up her bag as she walked from the hall but had left her potions behind for those who might need them after the demon's assault. This might have added to Bjord's humiliation at his defeat and while he would be tempted to take rash action, she doubted that Svafnir would allow him to pursue her. Everyone in the hall had heard her say she was leaving for good and having left them defeated but alive, she doubted that many would be eager to face her again.

Her father was safe from Bjord. Svafnir had made his position clear and with her gone, it would be petty to persecute her father. She suspected that Svafnir would pointedly comment that small-mindedness did not become an honourable warrior. In any case, after today Svafnir would take care not to let Bjord risk her revenge.

She did regret that she had pushed Olaf to actions that had destroyed his long friendship with both her and her father. He and Darek would probably never speak again. Olaf would feel vindicated in his decision by her attack in the hall. He had been balanced on a knife's edge over his choice to betray her, and she had selfishly exploited his doubts. As a result, she had nearly become what he had feared. She would bear that warning in mind when temptation struck again.

At least her father would remain in the community he had always known. If some townsfolk shunned him, his knowledge that she was safe would more than compensate for that. He had finally realised that she was capable of living her own life, had seen that becoming a witch had not broken her and had let go of his overwhelming need, born from her mother's death, to protect her at all costs.

For her own part, she had dispelled the illusion that she needed Trollgard and that her only place was in the embrace of its familiarity. The demon had forced her to confront her limitations, and in doing so she had found the confidence to start a new life wherever she chose.

The thought of the demon reminded her of her inextricable companion. Its will pulsed within her, imprisoned by her images but still struggling against its bonds. She was its warder now. She had seen what happened when she released it. In that choice lay the potential for the dark future Olaf had feared, but that very knowledge had also deepened her resolve never to take that path. While she had to remain alert, her guard was more than up to the task. If she avoided overconfidence, she was more than a match for the demon.

She walked on, listening to the forest birds and the distant cries of the seagulls, feeling the sun on her back, and she savoured the lightness within that came from leaving problems behind. Free from her childhood and her recent turbulent past she could go where she wished, live the life she chose and seek answers to all the questions that recent events had raised. She could delve into the origin of the demon, and the quest to understand that would lead to deeper secrets.

Setting her bag more firmly on her shoulder, she smiled and walked on. The sun was high and the wind was at her back.

The End

GLOSSARY

Runes

Chaos Forms
Agni – Fire
Eneki – Lightning
Folor – Luck
Izik – Chaos
Prana – Movement
Vata – Wind
Osc – Veil

Law Forms
Ranak – Frost/Ice
Unda – Water
Barak – Strength
Log – Law
Ert – Stasis
Kappa – Earth
Ilun – Seeming

Other Forms
Vit – Life

Rune – a character representing an aspect of reality
Form Rune – a rune symbolising an elemental part of reality, such as fire
Aspect – a more complex concept based on modification of a form, such as light or smoke
Effect Rune – a description of how a Form acts, such as flight

Mythology

Draugr – a mythical creature, a dead lord or warrior who rises from the grave to seek vengeance

Fenris – a giant wolf, one of the sons of the god **Loki**, reputed to have killed **Odin** at **Ragnarok**. Also the name of Olaf's dog

Freya – goddess of love and war

Frigga – goddess of motherhood and women, wife of **Odin**

Gods – most of the gods died during **Ragnarok**, but they are believed to live on as spirits

Heimdall – a god, who once travelled through **Midgard** and ordained the three castes of humanity, **jarls**, **karls** and **thalls**. Loki and **Heimdall** killed each other at **Ragnarok**

Hel – goddess of the dead

Loki – a god, who turned against the other gods and fought against them at **Ragnarok**. **Loki** and **Heimdall** killed each other at **Ragnarok**

Midgard – the human world

Mimir's Well – a legendary well whose waters gave mystical knowledge

Muspelheim – the fire world ruled by **Surtur**

Niflheim – realm of the dead who did not die in battle, ruled by **Hel**

Nokken – a mythical creature that takes the form of a beautiful man, woman or horse to unwary into the water to drown them

Odin – ruler of the gods, reputedly died at **Ragnarok**, killed by **Fenris**

Ragnarok – a climactic battle just over a thousand years ago, in which almost all the gods and giants were killed fighting each other. The gods that died are believed to live on as spirits.

Surtur – the chief fire giant, ruler of **Muspelheim**

Thor – god of thunder; died at Ragnarok

Valhalla – the afterlife for heroes who die in battle

Vanir – godlike beings, allies of the gods

Yggdrasil – the World Tree, which holds all the worlds in its branches

Culture

Archipelago – islands that make up the known world
Arl – the ruler of a town and the surrounding area
Arlberg – a walled compound containing the Arl's Hall and supporting buildings
Elixir – a potion, salve or oil made from herbs with very potent properties
Got – a resident of **Gotlund**
Gotlund – island and kingdom in the southeast of the archipelago
Jarl – highest status caste, made up of warriors and rulers
Karl – middle caste of craftsmen, farmers and traders
Larten – a resident of **Lartenland**
Lartenland – island and kingdom north of **Gotlund**
Seer – a wise man or woman who casts runes to reveal information
Thrall – lowest caste of bonded servants and slaves
Trollgard – a town on the north coast of **Gotlund**
Ulsvater – a town on the north coast of **Gotlund**, west of **Trollgard**
Witch – a human who uses supernatural powers to bring death and destruction
Witch weather – a sudden storm, usually appearing out of a clear sky, considered to be an omen of disaster

Acknowledgements

Thank you to everyone who contributed to this book, both consciously and in less direct ways.

My parents, both published authors, gave their constant support and much-needed criticism throughout, but even before I set pen to paper I had the help of the gamers for whom I originally created the world of the Saga of the Witch. My thanks to them, for their enthusiasm and ideas which helped make this world a better place. I also have to thank my writing group for their constant help, suggestions and encouragement.

My gratitude to all my beta readers who made the story a great deal better, and to the very dear friend who gave me the name of my protagonist, albeit unwittingly.

Finally, I must thank my child for being my inspiration.

About the Author

Rohan Davies lives in Norfolk, in the United Kingdom, near the sea.

He has read and enjoyed fantasy books his entire life, and has spent most of it designing and playing role-playing games. The world for the Saga of the Witch was originally created for a role-playing game.

Rohan worked as a lawyer before starting to write and design games full-time.

Look out for

THE GIANT

AND

THE WITCH

Book Two of the Saga of the Witch

Printed in Great Britain
by Amazon